ON THE RUN

She was flying stick, an impressive but terrifying feat for an amateur. Nancy guided the craft downwards to slide across the nape of Enceladus' surface, dodging crags of water ice with a combination of keystrokes and yawing pulls on an antiquated joystick that Jim had never bothered to learn to use.

"You're going to kill us flying that way."

"I'm doing better than you. Where are we going?"

Jim grunted. "Plot a course for Venus."

Nancy juked hard to the left as the first flight of fast-moving hornets swooped in on them. Their electromagnetic Gatling guns hurled depleted uranium stingers coated in a phosphorus paint, which would crack the Albatross in two if it touched the ship's massive solid oxide fuel cells. Luckily, their new pursuers appeared as reluctant to score a kill shot as the fleet in orbit.

"Can we trust your employer?"

"I don't think we have a choice..."

REFORMAT

Wiatt P. Kirch

Wurtzite Press

Copyright © 2020 Wurtzite Press

All rights reserved. No part of this book may be reproduced, or stored in a retrieval system, or transmitted in any form or by any means, electronic, mechanical, photocopying, recording, or otherwise, without express written permission of the publisher.

ISBN-13 (eBook): 978-1-7328989-0-5
ISBN-13 (Paperback): 978-1-7328989-1-2

Draft Edit by Michael Garrett (www.writing2sell.com)
Cover Design by Tom Edwards (tomedwardsdesign.com)
Printed in the United States of America

For my mother.

1

A Russian man with an eyepatch offered his younger customer an incredulous look. He fished a snub-nosed ceramic barrel from under a pile of circuit boards, and he produced a grubby, white, plastic pistol grip from behind a row of mass flow controllers. The firing pin came from an assortment of android photosensors: synthetic eyeballs that had belonged to flight attendants, heavy lifters, zero gravity maintenance workers, cleaning staff, and even the odd reconnaissance drone. An eight-chambered cylinder came from under the seat of the man's folding deck chair. The Russian assembled the components with a speed that betrayed an intimate familiarity with the cheap firearm and then held it out to Jim Longboat, cupped in lubricant-smeared hands. "Ever fired one of these things, boy?"

Jim's lip twitched. "Does it matter?"

The Russian raised a grey eyebrow. "So, no then?"

The younger man rolled his eyes and then made a nonchalant attempt at making sure there was no one around. People on Las Vegas Station tended to keep to the tethered spokes of the gravity decks, which moved either with the faithful mimicry of the Earth, far below, or with the languorous hedonism of unobtrusive and unthreatening near-weightlessness. The freight deck wasn't a pretty sight, and its robust automation software required a minimal human presence. This place wasn't for tourists. This was a place of shady business.

Despite the apparent lack of close casual observation, the Chippewa couldn't help but feel uneasy. He pulled the vat-grown sheepskin of his jacket closer around his shoulders to ward off a purely psychological cold. Being caught with the components that the Russian was about to hand him would land Jim in a dirtside prison for a very long time.

"Don't worry, boy. I don't care whether you can shoot or not." The Russian held out the snub-nosed revolver with the grip extending outward. "No target practice in here, though. The sniffers sense the gunpowder, and we have a full platoon of bipeds after us."

Jim nodded, placed the revolver inside his jacket, and pulled out a wad of thin platinum foil. He flipped through it slowly, counting off by tens. "How much do I owe you?"

The Russian groaned. "Oh, please. What you doing with this platinum, bratva stuff?" The young man looked up, offered the man a cold stare, and pulled his sleeve up slightly to reveal an iridescent chrysanthemum tattooed on his left forearm. The Russian's face turned to ash.

Jim repeated himself. "How much do I owe you?"

"Ten."

He gave the Russian his money, deciding not to argue over price despite the obvious frailty of the plastic grip that the aging man extended out to him. "Where do I get ammo?"

The eyepatched Russian offered him a toothy grin full of decay; bizarre in a day and age when a nanite-laden stick of gum, bought at the nearest drugstore, could keep a mouth ten times as clean as fluorine and toothpaste had done a century before. "I sell it, but it will cost you, especially when we deal in platinum and not megaflop-hours. Eight rounds for five leaves."

"Make it three, and we have a deal."

The Russian acquiesced. Jim handed him a folded wad of cash before taking the recycled cartridges. He kicked off from the stall nestled between two mounds of mesh-covered luggage, corkscrewing in mid-flight, with a sweep of his arms, to dodge similar tangles of baggage covering the walls of the cavernous space. His ship waited on the far side, past a beckoning airlock and a long umbilical.

The Russian was right. The young Chippewa had been with the Black Void Yakuza for half of his life, but he'd never fired a weapon. Madame Jingū had never permitted it. Jim only felt the slightest twinge of regret at the thought of disobeying his boss' wishes. Only a few hours before, he'd never have imagined doing such a thing, but recent events had changed Jim's plans quickly for him.

It was inside The Monolith that he'd resolved to become a killer. The place was nearly indistinguishable from hundreds of other zero-gravity diners scattered across the geosynchronous stations that orbited the Earth, except that a thin film of reflective chromium covered its walls. The chromium that surrounded the diner was a Faraday Shield, which screened out every self-propagating electromagnetic signal outside the diner with theoretical and experimentally verified certainty. Like Las Vegas Station's cargo hold, the Monolith was another place where shady business and relative anonymity were easy to come across.

Jim had found himself sipping at a packet of bad coffee as he waited for his ship to be refueled for its trip to Enceladus. The whirling, clockwork, octopus arms of a mechanical bartender danced above his head as it distributed hard liquor and beer amongst various countercultural patrons. Simultaneously, it flipped pancakes, sizzled strips of kelp-presented-as-bacon, and collected platinum foil tips. Jim was so mesmerized by the display that he barely registered the presence of a completely nondescript woman as she took her place at the barstool next to him.

She had taken notice of him, however. When the Plain Faced Lady spoke, her voice was flat, seeming to lack completely any sign of emotion. "We have business to discuss."

Jim raised an eyebrow. "Do I know you, lady?"

She shook her head with strange precision. "No."

"Then how is it that we've got business?"

Jim tried to stand, but the Plain Faced Lady locked his wrist in a viselike grip before he could do so. There was something unyieldingly perfect to her grasp, which didn't move a micron even as he pulled with all his might. Jim had been beaten to a pulp by muscle-grafted freaks with only a fraction of this strange woman's strength. He sighed in resignation and the grip yielded instantly. This woman knew what he was going to do even before he did.

"What do you want?"

The Plain Faced Lady spoke again. "We have a job for you." He studied her eyes, which appeared as real as his own except that they stared back without blinking.

"I already have an employer."

"You are about to have a second one."

"Right." Jim waited for a response. There was none. He shook his head. "Do you know who I work for? She doesn't like having competition." The Plain Faced Lady simply nodded in the affirmative. Her hand was still on his wrist, ready to wrench his arm off at a moment's notice.

Jim's eyes narrowed. "If I listen to what you have to say and still say no, will I get to leave or are you going to crush my wrist?"

She responded with a smile that was just a little too perfect. Jim was certain that the expression was supposed to be disarming. Instead, it turned his blood to ice. "You will be free to leave, but we are quite certain that you will not refuse our offer."

"I'm really looking forward to proving you wrong."

If Jim's last quip had affected the strange woman, she made no indication of it. "We need you to retrieve electronic equipment for us from a military space station."

"I don't do breaking and entering. I just fly."

"No breaking will be required."

"Then why do you need me to do it?"

"We have no means of transit to the Kuiper Belt."

Jim's eyes went wide. "The Kuiper Belt?" He smiled condescendingly at his prospective employer. The discovery of single-celled exobiotic life on Triton had spurred the migration of prospectors to boomtown stations out as far as Neptune, but no farther. "I think you might need a refresher on human history, lady. I'm not sure if you've heard, but there's nothing out as far as the Kuiper Belt." The woman's eyes offered no hint of emotion, yet again.

The mechanical octopus deposited a second packet of hot coffee in front of Jim. He gingerly picked it up with his free hand, sipping it nervously.

"There is one military installation at the Lagrange point between Pluto and Charon, but it is classified at the highest levels, with no digital document trail. We are willing to offer you five exaflop-hours for the successful completion of your objective."

Jim shook his head. "Listen... What's your name?"

"We do not have one."

How ridiculous. "Okay, no-name. No denomination is worth a two-month long haul. Time is money. There's no way I'm doing this. My boss is going to have both my pinky fingers as compensation if I do it." Jim prepared to float away, but the Plain Faced Lady's vise-like grip returned, and he winced as hot pain burned through his neurons. The young man's posterior never left the red velvet upholstery.

"We know who murdered Malcolm."

If Jim's jaw could have hit the floor and bounced, it would have done so. "How the hell do you know about Malcolm?"

"We have our methods."

Jim had traded everything for his brother's well-being, taking up the life of a gangster with one slow drink from the sakazuki in return for Madame Jingū's patronage. He could still remember the old woman's crow-footed smile as she saw him give his life away. In return for Jim's servitude, she'd allowed Malcolm to live a life of respectability, providing the youth with every text and multimedia aid he'd asked for as he'd grown up. She'd even paid for Malcolm to go to medical school.

The Yakuza pilot's world had imploded when he'd heard of his brother's death. There was a sort of painful irony that the younger man had died violently, despite Jim's best efforts to afford him a modicum of safety.

Malcolm's death was all the more a surprise because no one had died in an ambulance crash on Earth in decades. Because of their precious cargo and high rate of speed, ambulances sported the most complex obstacle avoidance programming of any vehicle on the insane streets of metropolitan Siem Reap.

Unfortunately, the most well-designed machine vision and virtual intelligence couldn't save an ambulance, and its attending doctor, from the targeting computers of a military-grade quadrocopter drone. The mysterious patient who had occupied Malcolm's ambulance was never found, and the young man's remains barely filled a matchbox. Thoughts of vengeance had possessed Jim ever since it had happened.

His self-assured sarcasm was gone now. "Who did it?"

The Plain Faced Lady shook her head. "You will receive your payment, along with the name of your brother's killer, when your objective is accomplished."

She handed him a small, black semiconducting lozenge, which he instantly thumbed into its "on" position. Jim's contact lenses flashed to life, offering to download the contents of the storage drive, a single image, and a single executable data file, onto their microscopic onboard memory chip. The strange woman had been right. Jim would work for her.

"What do I do when I get to Pluto?"

The Plain Faced Lady gestured down at the black lozenge under his thumb. "All that is required of you is to upload the executable file, contained on this data drive, when prompted by the station's security computer. It will give you access to the facility and to the hardware being stored there. Retrieve the hardware and bring it with you to Enceladus. We will provide additional instructions when you arrive." Jim nodded wordlessly, and the strange woman continued. "Note the image stored on the data drive. If you see this man, you need to find safety. He is very dangerous."

Jim viewed the image contained within the black lozenge, with a few deft flicks of his eyelids, as soon as it was uploaded to his contact lenses. He couldn't unsee the resultant visage that appeared in front of his eyes even now, as he transited from the Russian man's hideout to the pressurized umbilical that led to the *Albatross*.

The pale white skin of the deadly man's skull, pockmarked with the black plastic of several dozen semiconducting computer chips and crisscrossed with the blue ice water veins of nanotube impregnated pseudonerves, was almost as disconcerting as the blood red glow of his synthetic eyeballs. Jim fought the unbidden adrenaline of fight or flight as he made his way through his ship's cargo compartment to the control cabin. The horrifying image remained as he sank into his acceleration couch, went through his pre-launch checklist, and pinged Las Vegas Station's automated space traffic control.

Traffic control's response was canned, ringing with tin in Jim's earbuds, as the automated system gave him clearance for departure A harsh metallic tone followed, which accompanied a hard jerk and a loud thump. The space elevator's semirigid docking umbilical detached from the *Alba-*

tross' airlock and retracted.

The young man seated a fiber optic cable against the socket behind his scarred right ear. His skin tingled and crawled as the *Albatross* interfaced with a net of spider silk electrodes, surgically implanted under his skull. He inhaled deeply, feeling the newly bought revolver holstered against his ribcage and listening to the purr of the ship's power systems as they warmed up. With a slow exhale and a burst of maneuvering jets, he pushed out and away from Las Vegas Station. This had been a strange day.

Jim's trip to the outer systems required a high gravity slingshot around the Earth. The maneuver brought the blood rushing to his head. To an untrained ear, the hissing crackle and moan of the *Albatross'* shifting superstructure would have led to panic, but Jim knew his ride. The shuttle could take far more strain than this high-gee maneuver.

He brought the Higgs Field Emitter online, triggering the system's warm up cycle with a pair of thoughts as simple for him to perform as kicking his legs. The spider silk under his skull fed the electromagnetic signature of Jim's firing neurons to the ship's central computer, which ramped up the voltages applied to the sandwiched Casimir plates running the length of the *Albatross'* spine. The batteries aboard the diminutive freighter labored to supply necessary power, and the loud whine-roar of charging capacitors resounded through the ship.

Jim attempted to calm his breathing before turning to the diagnostic output of the flimsy plastic display screen to his left. He focused on a wildly fluctuating histogram, working to equalize the charge in each capacitor plate the same way that a runner might try to steady his palpitating heart in preparation for a hundred-meter dash. This was a slow process. The *Albatross* was an old ship and never stopped letting Jim know it.

At last, the capacitors stabilized with a crackling hiss of static electricity. The Higgs field emitted from the Casimir plates magnified, by several orders of magnitude, the mass of the helium ion stream vomited by the *Albatross'* aft-facing plasma engines. These ions, now heavier than the heaviest atoms ever discovered, slammed the craft forward at an incredible rate of acceleration.

As Jim pulled out of his slingshot, and centripetal force abated, he slapped a blinking green button that stood out among the other virtual switches and dials projected by his contact lenses onto the bulkhead to his right. The ship tuned the high-energy laser, waveguides, lenses, and beam splitters of its quantum communications array, taking aim at Antarctica.

A voice sounded into his earbud. It was human

this time, sporting a thick Australian accent. "Antarctica Control, here. Looking good, *Albatross*. My instruments show successful activation of your Higgs field. Damn, you move fast, don't you?"

"Best Higgs Emitter this side of Saturn, control."

"Now there's some idle boasting, mate."

The slightest smile crept across Jim's lips. It took a moment for him to realize why something didn't seem right in his head about this conversation. He didn't recognize this man's voice. "You new? Most of your colleagues know how to put up with me."

"Affirmative, *Albatross*. Used to run traffic control for the Melbourne elevator, but they gave me my notice three weeks ago. Guess the Commission finally stopped rigging the economy, huh?"

Jim chuckled at the mention of the fictional shadow organization. Still, a layoff? People hadn't lost their jobs since all the computers had crashed. The thought of the mythic, economic boogeyman that had been the Reformat made Jim shudder. "Tough luck, control. Good luck with your new employment. Be sure to ask about health and dental."

He killed the volume to his earbuds and checked the progress of his ship in relation to moon-bound and earth-bound traffic. A combination of freighters and passenger liners flitted past him on both sides. At Jim's unspoken request, the ship fell away from traditional shipping lanes and into the no-man's land of interplanetary space. After a few moments of paranoid inspection, the young pilot decided that the drone ships of the Space Corps, which incessantly patrolled both lanes of Earth-Moon traffic, had not observed his departure.

As Jim left Earth orbit, the *Albatross* unfurled its micron-thick solar sails. They billowed out on telescoping arms from its reinforced backbone like a rippling umbrella, blacker than the most supermassive black hole. A blinking histogram, along the periphery of Jim's vision, informed him that the craft's solid oxide fuel cells had begun to recharge immediately as these same sails soaked up the incoming photons and converted added heat to electricity. With a thought like stretching his shoulders, Jim redirected the Higgs field along the skin of the solar sails. In this way, the *Albatross* would cruise to the outer planets using the sun like an ancient sailing ship might have used prevailing winds millennia before.

Jim ignored the rainbow of prism diffraction off Saturn's E-ring as he drifted into orbit around his intended destination, two weeks later. Enceladus grew to fill the visual output of his contact lenses. Somewhere down below, under obscuring geysers of freezing water and hydrocarbons, under the shifting tectonic ice of the Saturnian moon, a massive hideaway existed. It was the closest thing he'd ever had to a home since he and his brother had left the Baraga Reservation at an early age.

Jim let gravity do most of the work in propelling him towards the moon's surface, thinking only of the slightest flutter kick to move him along with the great tidal waves of a stormy Big Sea Water lost to him except through childhood memory. The electrodes under his skull faithfully translated his thoughts into vectoring bursts of plasma meant to keep him on course.

The ship dipped down into the geysering vapor of the moon's South Pole and towards the relative safety of Madame Jingū's refueling tether. Tufts of white spray reflected everything from the visible through to the microwave, concealing the Black Void Yakuza's shadowport from prying eyes. These same geysers, paired with the refueling tether's few-kilometer proximity to the moon's surface, made the journey exceedingly dangerous for anyone not meant to be there.

Of course, those who were meant to be there knew how to guide themselves to the secret base aided only by encrypted telemetry leapfrogging on the backs of the microwave-resonating nanobots cohabiting the clouds with them. Jim transmitted his location and payload to these microscopic robots along with a plausible intended destination. This would allow him to request a full tank of fuel without arousing suspicion.

A ghostly voice filtered into his ears, carried aloft by the nanobot cloud along with a stream of navigational telemetry. As near as Jim could tell, the intentionally distorted voice belonged to a woman, but that was no guarantee that the other end of the line was even human. "Welcome, *Albatross*. Her high exaltedness offers you her greetings and advises that our fuel reserves are at your disposal. Please note that your route to Neptune is currently under intense scrutiny due to terrorist attacks on the skimmer stations in high orbit. Exercise caution." The warning about Neptune reassured Jim that his trickery had gone unnoticed. The computers believed his stated destination.

For all their redundancy, the small machines that inhabited these geysers were still prone to hiccups. One of these hiccups caused Jim to remain completely unaware of the ship hidden in the hot exhaust of the *Albatross'* own engines. Suddenly, the massive shuttle flashed past, plasma glowing a hot, yet silent, purple as it cleared the right wing of the *Albatross* by only a few meters. Jim's pulse pounded against his neck and chest as he fought a rush of adrenaline. He swore under his breath in Ojibwe. "I hate it when you do that, Glitch."

"Why do you think I keep doing it?"

Jim gripped the bridge of his nose tightly and juked left so that he would come up beside the decelerating craft with plenty of room to avoid a collision. "You could have hit me, you know."

The other man's laugh stung his ears, and his southern drawl made Jim want to punch the view screen in front of him. Glitch had always been good at getting under the younger man's skin. "Nothing ventured, nothing gained, young sport."

"Don't you have better things to do than bother me? I'm getting tired of you hanging out in my exhaust all day." The cloudbank got thicker still, and Jim could only barely make out the fellow shuttle pilot's ship off his right side. Jim's microwave-based RADAR was doing just as bad as the *Albatross'* visual sensors, thanks to the sharp angles and obscuring stealth coatings that covered Glitch's ride.

"Oh, I'm quite busy, kid. I just got back with a full tank of hydrocarbons from Titan, but sensors tell me that you're running a little light for someone who just made it here from Earth. Where's the seaweed and sashimi at, my friend?"

"I'm not carrying any."

He heard a soft, amused snort on the other end of the line. "Sounds like you made a poor fiscal decision. Do I need to have a conversation with you about how to keep up with payments on that ancient deathtrap of yours?"

"Glitch, I've known that your advice wasn't worth the breath that carried it since the day I stepped on this boat. Besides, there are more valuable things to be had on Earth than semi-fresh food anyway."

"Oh? Like what?"

Jim felt stupid. Was he supposed to say that some strange looking woman had sought him out and told him a fairy tale about how she knew what no one else seemed to be able to tell him about Malcolm? The story sounded too good to be true, and Jim suddenly realized that it probably was.

"Well?"

"Trade secret, man. I can't go around telling everyone what I'm up to, now can I?" He hoped that this would settle the subject.

In deference to Jim's personal preferences, the *Albatross* had placed his navigational display up and to the right, amongst a constellation of virtual buttons, dials, oscilloscopes, and heat maps. When he glanced there, the wired latticework of organic light emitting diodes printed onto the surface of Jim's contacts faithfully displayed the blinking green boxes of a good trajectory. The wispiness of volatilized water and hydrocarbons suddenly gave way to temporary emptiness. The hotshot pilot decelerated the *Albatross* to a stationary hover that fought the pull of Enceladus' gravity with ease. He could see Glitch's ship executing the same maneuver directly to his right.

Below them lay the long spire of the refueling pylon. Another nanobot veil directed the geysering water ice out and away to create the empty space in which Jim and Glitch now hovered. A semi-autonomous hydra sprouted from the pylon, directing pressurized helium lines to the fuel tanks of various spacecraft.

Jim reduced impulse, allowing the moon's gravity to tug him down into range of the mechanical beast, then waited for the tone and flashing green symbol that denoted a good hookup. When it came, he stopped his descent, with a puff of super-heated plasma, and watched in silence as the gauge, which indicated his fuel reserves, slowly crept upward towards "full" along the periphery of his vision. Many silent minutes later, the robotic arm that had been feeding the Albatross disconnected with a puff of fast-freezing vapor. Jim pushed back from the pylon, imagining pushing off a Gitche Gumee lakebed with a rush of bubble-filled, frigid water. He tried to push out the accompanying memory of his parents standing by the shore: a moment in time when they were still alive, when Jim had a family, when he was still Chippewa and not gaijin.

Glitch finally broke the blessed silence. "So, full tanks, huh? She must want you somewhere close to Neptune or something. Or is your sugar momma even charging you for this?" Jim was sure that the man allowed that annoying drawl of his to remain purposefully, even though he'd not lived in the swamps of Florida for over two decades. The fact that Glitch was correct in his supposition made his intrusion even more annoying.

"You know, there's still a chance that they can pick up your transmissions through the cloud. The cladding layer allows a small percentage of transmitted amplitude through to open space."

"An infinitesimal chance. You'd be more likely to be hit by a micrometeorite and have a fuel tank detonate than to have someone listening in on our conversation. Besides, I have good encryption aboard this thing, as I'm sure you've noticed. Annoying not being able to lock me out of your comms channel, isn't it?"

"You have no idea."

The man laughed. "Should hire a proper signals guy, then. That is to say, you should if you can get anyone to sign up to fly on that relic. Have fun on Neptune, momma's boy."

Jim sighed and then pushed his old ship into a yaw that turned it out of the way of the refueling pylon. In response to another of Jim's memories, the *Albatross'* Higgs Emitter crackled into overdrive. Its plasma engine's mass flow controllers pushed fully open, shooting Jim through the geysering mist and out into the void. Only a wispy hole bore witness to his passage.

After de-orbit and solar sail deployment, Jim had another three weeks of boredom before Pluto. Real-time communication with any of the planets was impossible by a quarter of a day by then. A part of Jim wondered if his boss was curious as to what had happened to the oldest freighter in her merchant fleet. Part of him didn't care. He had more important issues to worry about.

As Jim got within range of Pluto, he retracted the blackbody umbrella of his solar sails with a single thought and extinguished the craft's Higgs Field Emitters, instinctually holding his breath in remembrance of a childhood memory of the riptide that had pulled him terrifyingly away from a coast filled with sand-polished glass. The *Albatross* floated with silent residual velocity in response.

The twin ice balls of Pluto and Charon reflected the minimal rays of a pinprick sun. Just the same, the two orbs smoldered in Jim's forward display thanks to his light amplification hardware. Between the two heavenly bodies, an even fainter signal stood out precisely where the Plain Faced Lady had said it should have been. Jim double-blinked, magnifying the image and revealing a pair of spheres connected by a thin umbilical: a military space station.

Even with light amplification, Jim could only just barely make out the dim infrared signatures of a swarm of death-dealing robots orbiting Pluto and running at minimal power. The young pilot swallowed hard. If that swarm of battleships and fighter craft came to life before he left orbit, he wouldn't survive.

As the *Albatross* cruised towards its destination, a synthetic voice warbled into Jim's eardrum. "Please slave your vessel's guidance computer to the automated system for autopilot and docking." There was something intensely disheartening about that sound. Part of him had vainly hoped to find another breathing human being at the end of this journey.

The young man switched over to the broadcasted guidance frequency. A group of glowing red squares intersected the pair of snowballs, twisting in incessant rotation and extending into seemingly infinite perspective. He was off course, but only slightly. The *Albatross* banked gently to the left, aligning the infinite red neon with the center of Jim's field of view. The twisting red squares turned green as the ship's autopilot slaved itself to the station's guidance computer.

Over time, Pluto and Charon grew larger in the view screen. The magnified image of the station transitioned from a pair of roughly spherical blurs to distinctly white metal-ceramic orbs, puckered and pockmarked with blisters of electronics, life support systems, and auxiliary power generators. Jim found himself impatiently tapping his fingertips against the faux leather of the acceleration couch. The transit to the space station's docking collar occurred at a painfully slow pace as the autopilot slowed the *Albatross* in preparation for rendezvous. One miscalculation or incorrect maneuver on the computer's part could cause the ship's hull to buckle. Even the Albatross' skin, formed from a hardened alloy of sapphire nanotubes and titanium, wouldn't save Jim from atmospheric venting in the event of a collision.

Once the *Albatross* finished its slow glide into dock, Jim unstrapped himself, pulled the fiber optic cable from the socket behind his ear, and pulled the flimsy, polymer body glove of his spacesuit from a locker above his head. He worked quickly to wrestle himself into it, and then fastened a helmet to the suit's O-ring. The revolver went from a safe spot against Jim's chest to the dashboard in front of him as he suited up. It would travel with him when he left his ship. Jim wasn't sure what was waiting for him beyond the airlock, but he was sure that he was going to be ready for it.

2

The young woman stirred as her world grew silent. It was nearly impossible to sleep without machinery running, and even the noise of the ventilation system had softened. She sat up and began to breathe faster, rubbing the drowsiness of interrupted rest out of her eyes. The smart lights came on a few moments later, slowly raising the brightness in her antiseptic dormitory from the pitch-blackness of deep space to the searing white of false daylight.

She groaned. "Strauss."

The room's onboard computer complied instantly and started to play a bombastic nineteenth-century waltz that was far too loud. "Forty percent volume, please CARL." The girl yelled out of instinct, but the computer would have heard her even if she'd whispered the command.

"Apologies, child. These were your previous settings."

"I was awake when I input my previous settings."

"Should this be a permanent setting, then?"

She stopped and thought about the option for a moment, then shook her head before dropping back onto her paint-stained sleeping pallet. "No, thank you."

The oil-on-plastic of her most recent work remained on the bulkhead above her. When she was a child, CARL had told her that many-masted ships had once sailed the liquid-water oceans of Earth. She would have gladly traded her current confines for imprisonment on a fifty-meter-long craft, like the one in the storm above her, even if just for a change of scenery.

The girl's eyes crossed as they tracked a dab of blue paint that dripped onto her forehead. This was odd. Usually, CARL released a nanobot swarm during her sleeping hours to wipe her artwork from the white plastic of her living quarters with a healthy dose of heptane and methanol.

"What's going on, CARL?"

The disembodied virtual intellect intoned its answer in the most soothing timbre possible. "Nothing is wrong, child. You heard a minor alteration to life support function. That is all." CARL sounded too calm, too endearing, and not quite dismissive enough.

"You promised me you're programmed not to lie."

A long pause followed. It was as though the massive quantum computer, embedded on the topmost deck of this squat, pinioning tetherball of a space station, was taking its time to calculate a response.

At last, CARL made its answer known. A wall to her left blinked from antisepsis into pinprick starlight punctuated by the image of a ship docked to the station's primary umbilical. This ship was born to fly, not through space, but through the air. It was a seabird, with sweptback wings jutting from a bulbous chest. Every curve, though covered in the soft warts of sensor clusters and laser rangefinding arrays, was built to reduce drag and keep this ship aloft on high altitude winds. A long spine extended past the forward termination of its delta wings. The young woman knew, from CARL's many lessons on space flight, that furled within this long, thin spine was a massive solar sail. Powerful twin engines betrayed this bird's speed and it had a single eye enclosing a matte-painted bubble cockpit.

The young woman hopped onto the aluminum grate floor, feet stinging against vacuum coldness as she walked across her living quarters to sit on top of a white plastic dinner table. Excitement provided all the warmth she needed.

The girl had heard about these ships. Other than outdated crew capsules, space shuttles were the oldest spacecraft design in human history. In a day and age where everything was shipped via space elevator, however, they were nearly obsolete except for those people who couldn't afford the risk of going through customs.

"What's that thing doing here, CARL?"

"No data exists, child." The tone was placating, begging her not to do anything foolish that could divert the synthetic brain's attention away from the new development unfolding in the vacuum beyond. Clearly, this arrival hadn't factored into CARL's calculus.

Even more fascinating than the strange design of the spacecraft was its pressurized cockpit. This ship didn't fly itself. It had a human pilot. The girl propped herself up on one shoulder as she lay on the dinner table. CARL had told her, long ago, that the resupply freighter that usually arrived at this place was a model with no life support. It was supposed to be staffed by a small crew of biped androids and heavy lifters, though she'd never seen them. In fact, she'd never been beyond the door of the airlock just a dozen paces from the table upon which she now lay.

Suddenly, the silence of the idling ventilation system was replaced with the far-off grind-hiss of the station's massive rotary pump. It labored intensely to equalize the pressure difference between the docked freighter and the station's larger sphere, which was usually kept under vacuum since it wasn't meant for human habitation, in the first place. A flash of excitement ran from the pit of her gut through her extremities, like what she imagined a blue flash of Earth lightning might feel like. She had a visitor. The girl's eyes darted toward an airlock door that she'd never seen open, waiting for the red lights surrounding it to turn green.

A moment later, the white plastic around the young woman began to disintegrate into gunmetal with mechanical precision, as if every networked household item bared its fangs at once. Plastic shells of cleaning androids split apart to reveal gaping maws ringed with solenoids, rifled Ferro-ceramic barrels, and massive supercapacitor elements; domesticated engines of death. Garish underslung carapaces of mounted Gatling guns seemed to materialize from the walls in a flurry of moving plastic and pumping pneumatics. Her nursery and her home, boringly clean and dull though it was, had become a nightmare.

"Get behind the table, child." CARL's voice was still soothing, but forceful. Before she could do anything, the airlock rolled open, and the girl squinted against the brightest white light she'd ever seen. There was a humanoid form inside and, as the form moved forward, she realized that it was male. He wore the nanotube-reinforced plastic of a thin, but mobile, spacesuit and carried a snub-nosed revolver in his hand.

"Halt, or you will be destroyed."

The man stopped in his tracks, tilting his head from side to side. He gave the engines of death arrayed in front of him a brief look and stared into one of the multitudinous optical sensors wired into the ceiling.

"I don't think CARL likes your pistol."

The man's head turned to meet her own gaze, and she caught a look of confusion in his eyes as he looked her over. It was as if he hadn't been expecting her to be there.

If that was true, what was he here for?

CARL had no interest in making introductions. "You are in possession of an unauthorized firearm. Place it on the ground and step back." The machine's tenor sounded forceful, threatening certain death for this interloper if its instructions weren't followed with the utmost attention to detail. The man did as he was told, setting the weapon on the ground and stepping back.

CARL wasn't done making demands. "Who are you?"

"Does it matter?"

"You are not authorized." She could see beads of sweat forming on this strange man's forehead, even through the clear plastic nanocomposite of his helmet. "State your authorization."

"I don't have any."

The girl heard the click-hiss of flechettes and solenoidal rifle rounds being chambered. CARL was about to perforate this man with a lot of heavy metal, and he knew it. The stranger's voice took on a tone of nervousness as he responded to the obvious threat. "Uh, I do have a security protocol, though."

"Input your security protocol."

The man responded with a few subtle hand gestures. The young woman could see the flickering laser light in his lensed eyes as he clicked through virtual file folders and executed a variety of computer commands. She knew that the last command was some sort of executable file, because the laser light show ended suddenly with an accompanying hiss, whirr, and click of disengaging solenoids. In an instant, the nightmare in her room disappeared, and all was back to normal.

There wasn't even a pause. After the strange man made the subtle gestures in the air, CARL had withdrawn all protests regarding his demeanor, his firearm, and his authorization. "Security protocol accepted. Automatic defense computer core disengaged. Rebooting..."

CARL was laid bare for the puppet on a string that it truly was, and her world imploded. With all the surreptitious searching that she'd done through every square pixel of CARL's virtual hard drive, she had never seen any evidence of a magic executable that would do something like this.

"System reboot is complete. The Computerized Autonomous Research Laboratory is active.

Switching to control mode. Stand by." There was the sound of loud fans below the floor. The graphene circuitry, ruby lasers, and nonlinear refractive crystals of an analog, electro-optic computer, buried within the floor, hummed with effort. "Control mode active. Please state command."

"You have something I want."

"What do you want?" If CARL felt confusion, the timbre of its voice was the closest thing it had to express it.

"The classified equipment stored on this station."

"This query does not compute."

"How can it not compute?"

The girl leaned forward on her hands. "Um, hello?"

The man glanced over at her. "What?" His eyebrows furrowed, like she had presented him with a difficult question that he had to answer. "Hey, who are you, anyway?"

The question caught her off guard. "Uh, I live here."

CARL remained silent. The part of it that always had something to say was gone. The young woman supposed that in this deep, root-level access of the computer core's faux-psyche, whatever counted as its personality had been erased or terminated. In a way, she found this wordlessness to be unnerving, like what she thought the eye of a hurricane might be like.

The man picked up the cheap sidearm that he'd left on the ground in front of him and dropped it in a pocket woven into the spacesuit's reinforced leg, bullets going in first after he pulled the chamber clear to prevent a misfire. CARL had once told her that a stray bullet could depressurize the whole station. "Do you know what this place is for?"

The young woman shrugged. "Here? No. Not really." She pointed at the airlock behind the Chippewa. "I've never been past the door you just walked in, actually. I'm pretty sure all CARL does is look after me."

"It looks after you?"

The Girl shrugged. "I suppose you could say that it's my father. It birthed me here and helped me learn to walk, and read, and write, and how to integrate, and taught me history." She paused for a moment catching her breath after the long phrasing. "And how to speak English, and Japanese, and Khmer-"

The pilot cut her off. "Okay, I get the idea. So, you're saying that this computer taught you everything, and that's all it's ever done?" She nodded. "And that you were born here?" She nodded again, and the pilot gave her an unenthusiastic look, as if he was someone who'd been fooled but had only just realized it. "You don't say."

"I do."

He sighed. "Dammit."

She hopped off the table and stood, walking toward him to the point of near-collision, then circled around him, peering closely at the first human being she'd ever met in person. "I'm quite certain that the spacesuit's unnecessary. The environmental controls aboard the station are extensive, you know."

"I didn't think there would be anyone alive out here to need air. But thanks for the advice." She supposed, given the inflection of his voice, that the statement was intended to be ironic. He seemed disturbed by how close her face was to his, bristling as her head nearly struck his helmet's faceplate. "Hey, would you mind standing back?" She did so. "What's your name, anyway?"

She should have been prepared for this question. Every documented social interaction the girl had observed between strangers started with introductions. Instead, her eyes bashfully drifted to the ground. "Well, I don't really have one."

"What do you mean? Everyone has a name."

The young woman shrugged again. "I don't."

Upon hearing this, the young man turned to one of the various photoreceptors that dotted the walls and ceiling of her antiseptic home. He jerked his thumb at the girl. "What's she called?"

CARL didn't miss a beat, delivering the formal title in complete monotone. "This is the Neural Adaptive Network Control Human Initiative."

The pilot disengaged the bubble-like helmet from the rest of his suit and placed it on table in the center of the room, shaking his head. "That is a horrible name."

The Neural Adaptive Network Control Human Initiative felt her face flush with embarrassment and a flash of anger in response to the insult. Horrible or not, it was her name. The man must have noticed the flush in her face because he cringed and started to mutter. "Kinda a mouthful, really." He paused for a moment, humming. "N-A-N-C-H-I. Sounds sort of like Nancy to me. How does Nancy sound? Can I call you that?"

That was a better name. The flash of anger disappeared, and she smiled. "You can call me that."

"Alright, well that's good." The younger man offered his hand to her, which she stared at for a moment before realizing that he expected her to shake it. "I am Jim Longboat, Nancy. Pleased to meet you."

"Pleased to meet you, Jim." She smiled, grasped the man's hand, and held it for an awkwardly long period before releasing it. Jim shook his head in puzzlement and then gestured up at the all-seeing photosensors arrayed around them. "So, this computer of yours-"

"CARL."

"Yeah, uh, CARL. It's creeping me out."

"It's not usually like this."

"Whatever. Look, I think it's time for me to go."

"You're leaving already?"

Jim shrugged. "Yeah. This place seems pretty boring."

Truer words had never been spoken. She had dreamed of a chance to leave this place. The prospect of wasting away her life with no guarantee of anyone ever showing up to take her away from here was not at all enticing. Nancy frowned. "What about me?"

"What about you?"

This was not the response Nancy had expected. She decided to take a different approach. "You're just going to leave empty-handed? You've come all this way and have nothing to show for it."

"Yeah, well, it looks like the lady who sent me here was wrong about what I'd find. My loss." Jim sighed again and then reached up to squeeze the bridge of his nose. "My boss is gonna have my fingers for leaving her twisting in the wind like this. What am I gonna do?"

Jim retrieved his helmet from the table, but Nancy reached out to grab his arm as he and turned for the airlock. "Wait." There was a chance that whoever sent Jim out here knew about Nancy. Leaving CARL and the safety of this place was a disconcerting prospect, to be sure, but the danger of the outside world might be worth it to know her place in the universe.

Jim turned. "What?"

"Take me with you."

Jim cocked his head to one side in confusion. "Why?"

"I may not be what you were looking for, but I'm all that's out here except for CARL. Maybe your employer wanted you to bring me back. Maybe you were meant to find me, whether you knew it or not."

"Maybe so, but I don't like being played."

Something told Nancy that this was her only chance to leave her prison. "Take me along. What have you got to lose? And if I'm right and I'm what your employer was looking for, what have you got to gain?"

Jim bit his lip and didn't speak for what felt like an eternity before giving her his answer. "Pack your things. I leave in five."

It took Nancy fifteen minutes to get ready to leave.

Most of this time owed to her needing to shower. It had been days since she'd done so because there was simply no point in doing it if no one was there to notice. Meanwhile, Jim stood in the living area and stared at the still-uncleaned, paint-splattered walls. Even with her minimal knowledge of human emotion, Nancy could tell that something about the images perturbed him, or maybe it was how long she was taking to get ready. It was partly out of her hurried state and partly out of bashfulness that she decided not to ask why he looked the way he did.

Before long, she was ready to leave. "Alright. Let's go."

Jim grunted. "Typical woman."

"What does that mean?"

He rolled his eyes. "Oh, nothing." As he turned towards the airlock, he stopped to look up and stare at one of the photosensors mounted on the wall next to it. "Is your nanny going to try to kill us when we leave?"

"You have experience with computers doing that?"

"Well, in the movies, I guess."

"Do movies usually mimic real life?" It was an honest question on her part. Jim offered her a blank stare in response, as though he wasn't sure if he was supposed to take her question seriously or as a joke.

"Alright, fine. Let's go." Jim thumbed the release on the airlock door, led her up the rungs of a ladder, then down the first hallway that she'd ever been inside. The shift in perspective combined with the sudden onset of weightlessness to make her stomach churn as they progressed into the central sphere around which the tetherball of her living space orbited. It was two new experiences in as many minutes.

Jim noticed. "Not used to being weightless?"

She nodded.

"Well, if you're coming with me, you're going

to have to get used to it rather quickly." Without another word, he kicked off the ladder to which Nancy clung. Pinwheeling arms brought the bulk of his torso swinging around before he pulled his legs backward, stopping himself on a corridor wall. "Alright, your turn." Nancy desperately wanted to shake her head and go back down the ladder, but she wouldn't give up on her decision to leave. She took a deep breath and jumped out into freefall.

Nancy's attempts at weightless motion were clumsy affairs that sent her careening into the walls of the corridor before she found the airlock at the far end. She could hear Jim laughing under his breath as he floated behind her. The pilot slapped a switch to the right of a door, which blinked green in response. There was the characteristic hiss of equalizing pressures and the grinding crunch of interlocking gears turning as the airlock slowly slid to its "open" position.

"Welcome to the *Albatross*."

It was at this point that Nancy realized they had just traveled through the length of the station. They were now moving through the umbilical that joined Jim's ship to her home. They passed through an irising hatch, which fed them into a much larger space, clearly meant for cargo. Jim's face seemed to glow as he led her up corrugated aluminum steps to a catwalk that overlooked the area. "This entire room is an airlock.

Its floor isn't really even a floor. I can vent this whole place and expose it to vacuum in the span of a half-minute."

"What possible use could you have for that?"

He shrugged and Nancy could see a lopsided grin grow on his lips. "You'd be surprised. Sometimes when I'm moving..." He paused, seeming to search for the right word. "Sensitive material, let's say, drop-offs have to be pretty quick, which makes this airlock pretty useful."

"You mean when you're being chased by someone."

"That or when I don't want to be noticed."

Nancy was surprised and scandalized, then annoyed with herself. What had she expected to discover about her visitor, if not that he was a nefarious person? It was clear, from the moment he'd arrived, that he wasn't really meant to find her. At this point, she had thrown her lot in with nefariousness. So be it. She just wished her ship was a little less cramped. It had looked so much more spacious from the outside.

Jim seemed eager to continue the tour. "This way."

The two of them floated up the access ladder into the cramped confines of a living area, which was scarcely more than a pair of bunks, a small table, a toilet/shower, and an electric cooking unit. There was another door, inset into the ceiling, which led directly into the topmost pressurized section of the ship. The craft's heat tiled prow also acted as the command deck. A multitude of switches, dials, levers, and not a few messily unfurled sections of touch-sensitive plastic surrounded a pair of acceleration couches.

"Wow." Nancy floated over to the forward acceleration couch, clumsily dodging instrument panels as she bumped past. A few radio buttons flashed warnings before clicking over from "on" to "off".

"Hey! Be careful. You could break something."

She inclined an eyebrow. "You don't trust me?"

"After what I saw in that corridor? Not really." She offered him a pouting lower lip in response. "Just wait a few minutes." He coaxed her into the acceleration couch behind his own, helping her to strap herself against it.

She was peering over his shoulder as he slid into the couch in front of her, instantly releasing a flurry of alphanumeric code through a chattering keyboard. A moment later, there was a loud screech far below them. Nancy's heart raced, and Jim glanced back knowingly. "Relax. It's just the docking collar." He handed her some small, flimsy packaging which she inspected casually. "Put these on." Nancy pulled the packaging apart and worked to slide the contact lenses against her corneas.

An electric buzz filled the air, followed by the harsh crack of discharging circuitry. The ship was coming alive. The command console, which had previously remained dimly lit, now began to blink into vibrancy as her contact lenses booted up. Sensor data spilled onto virtual screen after virtual screen arrayed around the two travelers. There was more noise, more blinking lights, more torrential data, and then, suddenly, the ship was free and accelerating through space.

Jim pushed a fiber optic cable into a socket behind his right ear, which she'd not noticed before. "I'm going to slingshot us around Pluto and Charon. We should reach escape velocity in the next fifteen minutes."

Many years ago, CARL had told her that the maneuver she was about to experience was physically exhausting for even the most physically fit human being. It was correct. The pull of centripetal force was substantial as their ship began its long arc around the twin planetoids, crushing her into the acceleration couch before causing her vision to tunnel. After what felt like an eternity, the ship leveled out, and the push of acceleration was gone.

At last, Nancy was free.

Pluto and Charon glittered dimly against her corneas as Nancy's contact lenses dutifully projected their reflection of the visible half-light of a far-off sun. She could only just barely catch the bright pinprick of the space station that had been her home since her first memories. As she watched this pinprick fade, Nancy had only one question on her mind. "Where are we going?"

Jim tapped a pair of screens, turning the sensors she watched from the twin balls of ice and dust to a distant pinprick of light, nearly indistinguishable from the star field around it. She knew this faux star. "Saturn?"

"Enceladus."

"What's there?"

"Home."

3

The buxom, android flight attendant walked past on Velcro slippers, placed a hand on his shoulder, and asked, for what felt like the millionth time, whether he was comfortable. Its appearance was disturbing; not because it looked at all alien, but because it looked entirely like a living, breathing human being until he felt the cold tackiness of its dead touch. This didn't bother most people but, for some reason, Tyehimba Adebayo had never truly adjusted to the presence of life-like androids. Space Corps psychologists called it his "condition". He called it natural.

Tye put on a fake smile, nodded in the affirmative, and held his breath as the pseudo-woman walked past on its rounds. Once it was out of sight, he nervously ran his fingers along the perfect circles of scarification covering his temples. His flight from the Moon had taken the better part of three hours to make the trip to geosynchronous orbit over Las Vegas. Tye missed military transports. They were so much faster, and the androids left him alone.

The passenger liner made its way into docking position, and the fasten-safety-belt sign blinked off. The Nigerian spacer was among the first up out of his seat and was quick to claim his possessions from the overhead compartment. With his possessions in hand, he floated toward the exit.

His contact was supposed to meet him on the concourse. Tye knew already that there would be no "welcome" sign or wide grin waiting for him. Instead, there was a younger man with gauges in his ears, a studded leather jacket, and a yellow mohawk. He fell in step with Tye as he walked down the fading blue-grey carpet, catching the eyes of every single person on the concourse. Punk kids like him usually didn't make it much farther than a street corner, dirtside. It was rarer still to find them aboard the Las Vegas Elevator.

"You're the Spacewalker?"

Tye simply nodded.

The two of them eschewed the polymeric stickiness of the adhesive mat for the freefall of open space. This allowed them to move quickly down a pressurized tube that had once been pristinely clean but was now stained and covered in grime. The virtual neon of arrivals, departures, advertisements, interactive maps, and newsfeeds flickered in error on Tye's contact lenses. Las Vegas, like the rest of Earth and the expanse beyond, had fallen on bad times in recent months. Everywhere, the word "Reformat" was being whispered in hushed voices, as if its very mention might bring back the famine, war, and disease.

Tye decided to break the silence. "So, where is he?"

"The Scarecrow?" The punk pointed ahead. "Maintenance closet at the far end of the tube. We paid off a few of the technicians so we could use it."

The airlock that led to the maintenance closet opened with a loud click-hiss as they approached. Inside, equipment lockers flanked a table with a large glass display inset into its center. A pair of android repair bays sat behind them, now empty and unused except as storage space for an assortment of random tools, electrical conduits, and portable power supplies. Tye's contact lenses dutifully listed out each locker's contents and status in flickering green laser light as he passed. If there were any security programs meant to protect this place and the data it contained, clearly they had already been defeated.

Three men stood silently at the center table. One was short and looked borderline-emaciated. He was pale, with eyes that blazed with virtual neon as his hands tracked meaningful gestures through the thin air. The glass display in front of him was a flurry of activity as it responded to each of his unspoken commands. Tye labeled this man as the group's obligatory operator. A bald man with blue eyes looked up from the information overload on the table. He was both wide and tall at once, with arms that sported grafted muscle tissue from what the former Spacewalker supposed was some unfortunate soul's thighs. He would be the obligatory heavy.

Tye shook his head. "How stereotypical."

"Sometimes stereotypical works." The last of the three men was the one who spoke. He was rail thin, pale to the point of translucence, with skin that was streaked blue by nanostructured pseudoarteries. Black plastic lozenges of semiconductor packaging studded his head, each sporting meaningful hieroglyphics belonging to a veritable who's who of electronics companies. His eyes had been removed; replaced with prostheses that glowed a disconcerting blood red. "I take it you had an uneventful flight from the Moon?"

Tye shrugged. "I prefer flying military."

The Scarecrow smiled softly. "Such a pity that you no longer have that option." He turned to the remainder of the nefarious assemblage. "Dishonorable discharge from the Space Corps. Suspicion of trafficking classified data. I posted his bail bond to get him here."

The Scarecrow swept an outstretched arm to

the heavy. "Gang enforcer. Twenty-two counts of sectarianism motivated homicides; all involving a blunt object." His skeletal finger moved to the operator, who still hadn't looked up from whatever it was that he was currently working on. "Hacked a Mossad data server and uploaded dossiers on no less than twenty deep-cover agents." Last, his finger came to rest on the punk. "Attempted to fly a helicopter, filled with psilocybin, through six customs checkpoints surrounding the District of Columbia."

The walking corpse put his hands on the table and stared right into Tye's soul. "I'll tell you what I told the rest of our companions. Your luck has run out. You now face life in prison. What's saved you is the spectacular fashion in which you've failed. That makes you useful to me. I can make the trouble you're in disappear, and I can offer you permanent employment; that is if you prove yourself."

Tye nodded, slowly. When his bail had posted, and when he'd read the note that had been slipped in with his belongings as he'd left Aldrin Penitentiary, he'd known he had no choice in the matter. "I'm listening."

"I knew you'd see it my way." The Scarecrow turned to the operator and crossed his arms. At last, the man took note of something other than the data that filtered past his retinas. A rectangular wireframe image displayed on the black glass table blinked out of existence and reappeared on the high-definition display built into Tye's contact lenses. Nanoparticle diodes flared into life to display the same wireframe magnified twenty times over. The black plastic table served as the image's near immovable and semi-virtual foundation. The Scarecrow continued. "You're looking at the 'K' block of the Flare Casino."

A red dot burned in the center of the hotel's fourth floor, inside a red square room connected to a yellow rectangle hallway that serviced about twenty other suites. "My organization has tracked a person of interest to the fourth floor of the Flare. She's been hiding here for the better part of three months, along with a group of vagrants who have populated the floor on her bogus credit account. They're armed, as are the hotel staff. We doubt that said staff will be happy when they discover that our target has been feeding them false telemetry for the duration of her visit. We want this person extricated quickly, without attracting the attention of the local authorities."

The heavy was the first to speak. "She dangerous?"

The red orbs bobbed up and down. "Very." The Chechen serial killer's eyes lit up, and the Scarecrow scowled. "We want her alive. She's no use to us dead."

Tye ran his fingers over his temples again, remembering the boyhood pain of the razor dragging across his flesh, of ash, rubbed vigorously into his wounds to mix with his own blood. "Who is 'we'?"

The Scarecrow shook his head. "Need-to-know basis, Spacewalker, and you simply don't. If you dislike that, I suppose the Spacewalkers would be very interested to see that you've skipped bail and left the lunar surface."

The Nigerian raised an eyebrow at the thinly veiled threat and then put on a disarming smile. "What's with the big secret? Do you work for the Commission or something?" The half-man, half-machine stared at him, deathly silent, in response. Tye shivered involuntarily. "Alright, fine."

The Scarecrow nodded approvingly. "Good."

The blinking red dot sprouted a single line of green, which extended up into infinity. "We will get you to the fourth floor via a Vertical Take-Off and Landing aircraft. You'll launch from this station's number six freight elevator as it starts to decelerate for its final approach to Las Vegas' ground terminal. The elevator launches from here in an hour." He pointed at the punk. "You already know our pilot. Our operator will be present aboard the aircraft to make sure you're not detected on your five-thousand-kilometer plunge after you detach. I'll remain here. Our Spacewalker friend and the Chechen will be responsible for capturing our target."

Tye leaned in and looked closely at the virtual wireframe. "What do you expect our total time on target to be?"

"Minimal, by necessity. You'll need to secure your target and get out before the casino's security or Las Vegas PD can respond to your unauthorized de-orbit."

"And how much time is that?"

The Scarecrow turned to the operator. "Well?"

The bespectacled, wiry man looked up. His voice was soft and high pitched; the typical egghead. "Maybe five minutes once we're on the ground." He twitched in response to some unseen stimulus, took a breath, smiled, and continued. "We're gonna be flying rather close to the elevator itself; not a good place to be without prior clearance. I'll try to mask our signature until we hit the target, but I won't be able to obscure ground sensors. If they see us, they'll send in the bipeds while we're on the ground and interceptors once we take off again."

The Scarecrow continued. "My organization has paid off the staff of a civilian airbase near Telluride, Colorado. You'll be cleared for immediate landing, and you'll be disavowed by ground crew once you've made it inside their airspace." This was a routine procedure, a typical smash-and-grab. He'd done jobs like this before.

The image of a woman, perhaps thirty years of age with no defining racial characteristics whatsoever, replaced the neon wireframe. Her eyes were held open with metal calipers, and press-on neural sensors studded her shaved head. She had an obvious and understandable look of discomfort on her face. Despite obvious doctoring, there was a sort of discoloration and refractive quality to the image, as if it had been taken under water. "This is your target."

The heavy scratched his left shoulder. Given the way his eyes darted back and forth, Tye assumed that the man was nervous. "Why you no fly with us?"

The Scarecrow shrugged. The effect didn't fill Tye with a lot of optimism about the current situation. "My presence can't be disavowed, and it can be linked to my organization. Yours, on the other hand, can't be linked to anyone but yourselves."

Tye scowled. "How very reassuring."

The Scarecrow's VTOL aircraft was locked inside a large shipping container strapped to the exterior of Las Vegas Station's number six freight elevator. There wasn't enough atmosphere available to breathe inside the craft during the two-hour trip from geosynchronous orbit, so the Nigerian found himself in a strangely familiar environment. The spacesuit he'd been given was not as robust or as sophisticated as the contraption which he had left behind in storage on the Moon. It was flimsy, unpowered, and it took a short period for the former Spacewalker to become used to the apparent lack of computer-controlled artificial muscle driving his limbs forward as he moved about the aircraft's crew cabin.

The heavy and the operator moved behind him clumsily, clearly unused to moving in an environment which lacked gravity and even more unused to doing so inside a spacesuit. The punk was already strapped into the cockpit and separated from the rest of the vehicle by a locked hatch.

He called back to them over a closed-circuit channel piped into each man's earpiece. "Strap in. The elevator starts its next braking maneuver in thirty seconds, then we detach." They did as he suggested, and the hard jolt of braking happened only a few moments afterward. "One minute to charge detonation. Stand by."

Tye counted down from sixty. At zero, there was a loud snap as the container surrounding the aircraft bisected and dissolved away on explosive charges. He could hear the whistle of air over metal and then the buffeting of atmospheric turbulence over opened airfoils. "We're clear of the container, and I'm getting good airflow over our control surfaces. How are we on tracking?"

Tye could hear the operator's reedy voice over the earbud securely fastened inside his left lobe. "The number six elevator has registered an unintended release. I've got network connectivity through a tower on the ground, and I'm using it to scramble our signature. Orbital control only sees the debris from the container, not us."

The punk's voice returned. "One minute to target."

The hypersonic aircraft cut the air like a knife until the punk began his attempt to brake. Tye felt his eyelids being pulled shut as the aircraft bled off speed. The operator's voice returned, this time a bit shakier. He was clearly not used to reentry. "Ground audio-visual sensors have spotted us and registered our sonic boom. Vegas PD is currently working to scramble a pair of unmanned aerial vehicles. Five minutes to intercept."

If the punk was straining to maintain consciousness during the high-gee maneuver, his voice didn't indicate it. "I should have us in range and on station within thirty seconds. Hang on."

The Chechen thumbed a switch against his right wrist, and his body went invisible. Tye had the same system on his suit. With the push of a single button, a metamaterial coating of polymer-dispersed gallium nitride nanocrystals would refract the light around him. A pair of "up" and "down" arrows on his wrist adjusted his relative transparency at the cost of his own range of vision. Tye would still stick out like a sore thumb in the infrared and ultraviolet, but he couldn't deny the system's usefulness. He'd never used an invisibility cloak before.

The operator piped up again. "I have a successful uplink to hotel security. Telemetry is still altered, but otherwise normal. I don't think she knows we're coming."

The shuttle juked hard against a sudden gust of wind, and the punk growled in annoyance. "Can you tell me what side of the hotel she's on?"

"I can even give you a room number." There was a pause as the operator worked his way through data files and executed subroutines. Finally, he spoke again. "Navigation data is uploaded to your flight computer."

"Yup. Hang on."

The former Spacewalker felt a hard pull against his body as his blood pooled in his feet. The aircraft had made a hard bank to the right before leveling out. There was a tremendous force pulling him against his restraining straps as the aircraft decelerated and the punk brought it into a hover. Tye unstrapped and moved quickly across the open space in the cabin to pull an assault rifle from the equipment locker at the far side.

With a loud thump, the door of the crew cabin slid open to reveal a bioformed, faux-glass window and a dark room beyond. The pilot's voice rang in his ear. "Go! Go! Go!"

The window shattered as the invisible heavy leaped from the aircraft, causing it to sway. He careened through the plate material as easily as if it was tissue paper. Tye jumped after him from the open hatch, thumbing the switch on his wrist as he did so. The thin film invisibility cloak went into action. He watched his hand disappear in front of his face, then his arm and his shoulder. His vision tunneled slightly as a quantum mechanical consequence. The mercenary landed on shag carpet and rolled as he came to a stop, pulling his assault rifle to his shoulder and thumbing on the flashlight attachment. The room was well furnished in white leather modernity, empty, and dark.

The Chechen reappeared. "Not here."

"She must be." The former Spacewalker looked over to the far side of the studio. The door to the shower unit wasn't quite closed. In fact, it was beginning to swing open on its hinges, as though it had only been slammed shut a few moments before. He disengaged the cloak, waved to the serial killer silently, and pointed. The other man nodded, and the two of them slowly made their way to the door.

When they got there, Tye grabbed the doorknob, and the heavy leveled his shotgun, thumbing the safety. He wrenched the door open, and the Chechen fired a single round into the ceiling. A woman, with only a couple centimeters' growth of hair on her head, bent low in a corner between an antique, porcelain toilet and an expensive looking bathtub. She glared at them venomously, like a trapped animal willing to strike at anything that got too close.

Tye thumbed the switch for the suit's megaphone. "Don't make a move. Hands up." The silent woman reluctantly complied, and he decided that it might be best if he tried to play nice. "What's your name?" She didn't respond.

The Nigerian noted that the muscle-bound brute was now covering the front door of the hotel room with his shotgun. This was not a good situation. Vegas police knew they were here, and the hotel staff had probably noticed the breaking window via the casino's sensor network. Tye and the Chechen could be overrun at any moment.

He turned back to their intended target. "You're coming with us, whether you want to or not. Understood?" The woman nodded, still silent. "Well, come on then. Get up."

She did as he suggested and Tye led her out of the bathroom. The serial killer gestured to the entryway he'd been watching as he strode forward towards the ruined window. "Watch door. I get her aboard." A hop brought him onto the hovering aircraft beyond. Tye turned to watch the door. The heavy spoke to the pilot this time. "Bring plane in closer to window. I pull her in."

The operator's voice sounded in Tye's right ear once again. "Las Vegas interceptors are done fueling and moving out onto the pad for departure. Two minutes before they're within missile range."

"I plan on being long gone by then." The punk seemed strangely agitated. "This is so weird. I'm getting some very strange feedback on the controls of this thing. Something's not right."

One of the VTOL jet's engines sputtered. The aircraft's right side dipped low in response, scraping hard against the porous, pseudoconcrete with a shriek that made the Nigerian wince. He watched the Chechen drop from the open door of the aircraft to fall four full stories onto hard pavement. The man was almost certainly dead. The punk panicked. "What the hell! I have no response from control surfaces. I have to-"

The aircraft swung out from the wall, as the punk tried to compensate for the sputtering jet engine, just in time for the second engine to flare out as well. If the punk could scream, he apparently didn't see the need. The plane went into a sickening tailspin, spiraling down to meet the ground with a loud thud, which set off nearby vibration alarms. Then everything went black.

Shattered windowpane tinkled as Tye lost his balance and sat back awkwardly on the carpet. He waved his hands in front of his face. Nothing. Someone had control of his contact lens optics. The former Spacewalker struggled to pull the helmet off his head so that he could scrape the dual lenses from his eyes and forcibly return himself to a seeing state. As he fumbled with the latch on the back of his helmet, a single line of green text flitted across his field of view.

I wouldn't do that if I were you.

Do you know where your assault rifle is? He instantly realized that he didn't. It had fallen to the ground when he'd put out his hands to break his own fall. He reached for it frantically, his arms sweeping wide, blind arcs over the shag carpet behind him where he'd heard it come to a rest. Then, he felt the tap of metal against the back of his helmet. *Looking for this?*

This was not good.

The Nigerian shifted forward, taking his head away from the pressure of the rifle's barrel against the clamshell helmet. "Ever fired an automatic rifle? Not as easy to hit a target as the movies show you, especially not when they move fast at close range." He hoped that his bluff would pay off.

I don't know much about primitive weapons, but I know enough to be able to say with some certainty that the safety is off. My aim isn't perfect, but I'd bet it's good enough to put a bullet through you at this range whether you move or not.

"If you're going to kill me, just do it."

If I had wanted to kill you, I would have done so already.

"Then what do you want?"

I have a business proposition for you. The former

Spacewalker shifted around in a vain attempt to look through the darkness at his assailant. *Careful. No sudden movements.*

"I make business arrangements face to face."

I'm afraid you'll have to make an exception. If you'd prefer not to bargain, I can shoot you now and spare us both the trouble of continued conversation. As you might imagine, I don't have any time to waste.

Tye was almost sure he could hear approaching sirens and mechanical footfalls. He was getting guns pointed at his head far too often these days, and it didn't seem like that was going to change. With a sigh, he surrendered. "I'm listening."

I need access to a military-grade supercomputer cluster, and I need to get off this planet. It's not safe here. I'm being watched, and the ones who are watching me want me dead.

"Who? The Scarecrow?" Instantly, he cursed himself for giving away the name of his employer. In his line of work, hostage negotiation didn't happen very often, especially when he was the hostage.

I don't know who they are, but I know that they are not the Scarecrow. Regardless, I'm going to kill them before they can kill me.

Tye laughed bitterly. "Wonderful. A paranoid psychopath has a gun to my head. This day just gets better and better."

He felt the barrel of his stolen rifle bend his

chin down towards his chest. *Don't ridicule me. You have no conception of what you're involved in.*

"Perhaps you should tell me."

Work for me, and you'll see.

What was he to do? He was stuck with an impossible decision: enter the employ of a crazy woman and be condemned as a fugitive or be trepanned with his own weapon. What a ridiculous position to be forced into. "Very well."

So, you can help me?

"I have a friend who can."

Tye's vision snapped back into existence, and he heard the firearm clatter back down onto the floor. He grabbed the rifle, then pulled his helmet free and dropped it on the ground. "You don't think I'll just turn on you?"

The blackness was gone, but the green text remained. *I'm prepared for the possibility. Are you?* He heard her move to the solid oak of the front door, behind him. It opened with a loud clack as its electromagnetic latch disengaged. Tye frowned. Had she even touched the door before it unlocked?

Anyway, after you...

Tye turned slowly and stepped out into the hotel corridor with the Mute still behind him. The fourth floor was quiet and deserted. The Mute's tenants had scattered, either because they'd heard the gunshots or because they heard the stamp of mechanical pseudopods on the floors below.

What did he offer you? Money?

"The Scarecrow?" Tyehimba shook his head. "No. He was slightly more persuasive than that."

Ah, pathetic.

"How so?"

You worked for him because he had power over you. I wonder what he holds over your head. The Mute tugged at Tye's invisibility cloak and led him towards a door at the far end with a bioluminescent "exit" sign painted over the top of it. *Have you worked for him long? Doubtful. People who work for him don't survive for long.*

"You know him?"

Very well, unfortunately.

Tye opened the door and walked out into a green-lit emergency stairwell. He peered over the railing to see the flicker of flashlights below, likely attachments to assault rifles, then swore under his breath in Igbo. "They're coming for us."

Security appears to be searching this side of the building, door to door. The vibration sensors placed the location of your aircraft before the accident, but only well enough to know that you were hovering and that you were on the north side of the building.

"What's the fastest way out?"

I take it you mean besides the shattered window.

Now that was an interesting idea. Tye hated closed off spaces, anyway. He did his job better when he was out in the open. He didn't have enough armor or ammunition to survive a hallway shootout with a few biped platoons. Why not go outside, where he had the advantage? The mercenary pointed at the open doorway behind them. "Let's go."

Oh, please no. I was only joking about the window. They returned to the shag carpet and the shattered plate glass. After they were both inside, the Mute closed the front door and Tye pushed a mahogany chair piped with gold leaf against the brushed stainless steel handle. *This is a horrible idea.*

Tye's plan would be physically exerting in this high gravity, especially without the aid of a powered exoskeleton. There was a good chance that it would work, however, provided he could use the grappling hook buried in his suit. The Nigerian peered out of the shattered window and into rising smoke from the wreckage below. He felt the wetness of rain on his head, strange for Las Vegas. The mercenary glanced upwards. Above the casino, a cloud of thermoelectric, whirligig nanobots had gathered in response to the billowing smoke. They were condensing water from the not-quite-dry air to rain down from overhead.

Tye also saw his path to escape. The impact of the VTOL aircraft with the pavement far below had blown a large hole in the city's sewer system. "Get over here."

The Nigerian drew a survival knife that he'd clipped against his chest and cut a container free from the left wrist of the spacesuit. He pulled a long filament from that container and pressed the grappling hook at the end into the porous pseudo-coral wall, pounding it in with his heel. Tye stood, slung the automatic rifle over his shoulder, and held out his arm. "You're going to need to grab hold of me."

No. This is insane.

"Fine. Then stay up here. I'm leaving." There was a loud thump against the door and garbled, synthetic speech. Tye was certain that the androids were waiting just outside the door. "Now or never, woman."

The Mute acquiesced, wrapping her arms around his collar. Green text scrolled across his mind's eye. *I would advise you not to get any untoward ideas.*

The former Spacewalker grunted, turned so that his back was facing the open ledge and pulled the filament taught against the wrist of his suit. "Believe me; I have neither the time nor the inclination."

The bacterially grown concrete was slick, and he felt his cleated feet slip several times as he made his way down the sheer wall. Manufactured rain mixed with acrid smoke in his eyes, becoming a painful amalgam that nearly blinded him and caused him to cough violently. Tye felt the wall disappear out from under him. He'd reached the third-floor windowsill. "Hang on tight."

Oh. No.

He kicked out from the wall, releasing his grip on the filament ever so slightly. The hard kick brought them out about a meter from the pseudocoral and then dropped them pendulously approximately four meters. Tye decided that it was a good thing the Mute couldn't speak since he didn't have to hear her scream. His feet returned to the concrete wall, and he grunted as his knees strained to absorb the impact.

Never do that again.

"Two more times. Sorry."

When he made it to the second floor, Tye kicked out from the wall and found himself locked eyeball-to-sensor with a patrolling biped. The ceramic humanoid blinked its constellation of compound eyes and raised its weapon, silently. Ceramic carapace clicked and whirred, and then a blizzard of automatic rifle fire issued from the window, narrowly missing them as Tye rappelled downward in a hurry. So much for the element of surprise.

The fugitive gave the Mute just enough time to grab his shoulders before he released his grip on the filament and they began to plummet to the ground. He only began to arrest their descent as the asphalt started to rush up at him. His reward was a sharp pain in both of his legs, and he felt like both of his femurs were about to snap. Tye caught his breath, pushed the pain out of his mind, and disconnected the tether. They ran past the burning wreckage of the downed VTOL aircraft. Their cratered means of escape was around a corner, at the far end of the tangled mess. "Come on. We might be able to lose them through here."

In the sewer? How cliché.

As he rounded the corner, the former Spacewalker came face to face with a mangled body enclosed in a spacesuit like his own. Blood covered the faceplate, a likely consequence of the sucking chest wound its owner had sustained when a section of the aircraft's cockpit had bent upward and pincushioned him during the crash.

"Her... You're with her?" The suit's owner gurgled out a string of expletives. "Were you in on it all along?" Tye backed away from the Punk's ruined body as the dying man reached out to grab his pistol, which had shaken free of its holster during impact.

Tye didn't stop to think, but simply raised the automatic rifle and put a single round through the punk's helmet.

The Nigerian's Reformat-era education in a refugee camp outside of Lagos had taught him algebra, biology, and calculus; mostly by the light of a solar-recharged tablet. Going to Egerton had taught him how to build, repair and make rendezvous with spacecraft. The Space Corps taught him that people die. Sometimes they screamed, sometimes they were silent, sometimes they choked on their own blood, sometimes they asphyxiated, and sometimes they were vaporized in a thermonuclear explosion to cover the tracks of the men who gave them orders. This was the way of things for people like him. As the magnetic rail from his weapon entered the pilot's skull with a hiss-snap, each of those deathly moments in time returned to Tye in a flood. It happened every time he pulled the trigger.

When he turned away from the ruined helmet, the Mute was smiling. Somehow, that smile was even more unnerving than the memories. *What's your name?*

The Nigerian shuddered. "Tyehimba Adebayo"

I approve of your work ethic, Tyehimba Adebayo. Rest assured, it will be generously rewarded. They disappeared into the sewers seconds afterward.

4

Sunset on the strip. She had seen it before, many times in her head, via direct media feed, but never in person. The two of them, a six-foot-tall Nigerian with tribal scars and an emaciated woman, stood at the green edge of a soft-turfed garden-roof that dangled off the edge of a bioceramic high rise. A pair of ponchos, liberated from a gutter nearby, obscured them from surveillance drones. With that minimal concealment, the Mute couldn't help but feel nervous.

In the distance, military quadrocopters circled the oily smoke of the wreck she'd caused in the casino district. They jettisoned a fine grey haze from their underbellies, which glittered in the evening sun: robotic fleas. The microbots would travel the streets and stow away in hair and clothing, searching for the two fugitives one gene-sequencing, itchy bite at a time. The two of them would be found if they stayed here. It was too close to the haze.

Their only hope was the spaceport. She could

see it glittering in the distance, its bundled carbon nanotube filament seeming to stretch off into infinity. It was hardly a viable alternative to staying here. Before the bipeds or faux-humans saw her, buzzing microbot cameras would have snapshots of her face uploaded to the Las Vegas central security mainframe.

We'll never get through that.

"I'm sure that you can hack some customs agent's contacts and tell him we're someone else or something like that, right?" Tyehimba was busy inspecting the spaceport's heavy security with a pair of shattered binoculars he'd borrowed from one of the vagrants that shared the balcony with them. She couldn't tell if he'd offered the strategy in jest or not.

Impossible. I'd need a direct connection through the spaceport's security network, and then we'd be as good as caught. They'd see me.

The former Spacewalker sighed. "I know. I was joking." He looked down at the white asphalt below. She did the same, watching the flicker of rising hot air as she continued to listen to the man. "We have to find some way to the elevator. There's no other option. Bouncing from one low-orbit station to another is going to take too long and get us caught." This was an accurate statement. The space elevator would get them out to geosynchronous orbit. It was a comparatively quick hop from there to the Moon's gravity well and their ultimate destination.

Behind her, two men in desperate need of a bath argued over who would get the next cup of coffee from the automated dispenser unit they'd scrounged from parts unknown. *Maybe your friends with the binoculars can help us.*

Tye responded with a half-smile. "Maybe."

The argument over coffee had degenerated into a full-blown fistfight with a bark of indignation and the clatter of a spilled cup of coffee. The two men writhed on the ground in half-drunken combat, one completely bald with a wrinkled barcode tattoo drawn haphazardly across his forehead and the other sporting a mustache that appeared to have consumed his upper lip entirely. They dripped with sweat, even though the nanite climate-controlled rooftop was downright temperate compared to the heat beyond.

Tye was the first of the two of them to turn and take notice. "Hey." The fighting ceased, and the two men looked up at him. He reached into his pocket, producing a thin leaf of platinum. "I'll pay for coffee for both of you if you can help me find something."

The two of them stood instantly and scrambled over to him. The man with the mustache spoke up first. "Awfully nice of you, mister." A smile caused his mustache to become flat rather than convex.

The man with the awful barcode tattoo took

Tye's hand in a grubby embrace, shaking it hard. "Tough to make coin what with the recession and all, you know?"

The Mute crossed her arms in awkward discomfort. *I was joking too, you know. What use could we possibly make of these two oafs?* Tye's response was simply a finger raised to his mouth.

The two vagrants suppressed laughter when they saw the resulting glare on her face. The Nigerian ignored their amusement. "I need to get a message to someone on the Moon."

The man with the mustache laughed. "So, stop by your local telecom store and buy a message plan. Doesn't matter what you're putting on the DataNet these days. The spooks won't catch it. They're too busy trying to figure out who's poisoning the economy."

"Think so?"

The bald man nodded and interrupted, to the slight annoyance of his pugilist friend. "Absolutely certain of it. I hitched a ride in from the wrong side of Enceladus with an obviously fake passport. They didn't even seem to care."

Tye seemed to be forcing a smile, now. "Well, that's encouraging. Just the same, I need to make sure no one can read that message."

The bald man smiled knowingly. "On the run, too?"

Tye shrugged. "You might say that."

The man with the mustache was not one to be

outdone. "I know a place." He hooked his thumb toward the tempered steel fire escape that Tye and the Mute had used to climb up to the balcony a few hours earlier. "Take the ladder down to street level, through the alleyway. Then, take a right up to the strip toward The Treasure Island..." A dizzying array of directions followed, of which the Mute quickly lost track. Eventually, the Nigerian stopped the mustached man with a raised palm.

"Is there any chance you could draw me a map?"

The mustache actually appeared to curve upward for a moment. The man pulled a grubby napkin from inside his rank-smelling overcoat and began to draw furiously upon it with the nub of a graphite pencil. At length, he handed it to the Nigerian. "Is there something wrong with her? Does she even talk?"

Tye shrugged. "I'm not sure." Her glare sold the Nigerian's last statement. The mustache drooped back to its initial convex shape, and the vagrant's eyes went wide. "Oh. Well, I'm sorry, little lady."

The Mute could feel the anger rising in her throat. Above, one of the halogen lights, which dotted the roof at regular intervals, surged with power and then exploded. The two men jumped back in surprise as they were showered with broken glass.

Tye took her arm gently and led her away in

silence. The two men simply stared at the pair of them in slack-jawed awe. Neither vagrant said a word. The two fugitives walked down the fire escape, out of the alleyway and into red, near-horizontal sunlight. Pedestrians and humanoid androids alike hurried along white streets in anticipation of the coming evening's madness; that daily carnival of a place dedicated to sin in all of its forms and likenesses.

When the Mute looked over, she saw that Tye had tucked his head low into his raincoat. She was unsure if this was to avoid the prying eyes of the surveillance drones, above them, or if he was busy trying to decipher the bizarre scrawl on that grime covered napkin. At length, he looked up and pointed down a side street. "This way."

The glittering neon and incandescent, black-body radiation of the old Las Vegas was replaced with a different radiance entirely. The virtual light of the DataNet lit an otherwise dark alley for any passerby who'd decided to wear a pair of contact lenses. Hacked graffiti mixed with painfully personalized advertisements. Obnoxious, nearly seizure-inducing displays vied for pedestrian attention with the sexual imagery of a naked woman, or sometimes with some popular joke or slapstick. The Mute could see it all, sort of, even though no polymer lenses sat on her eyes.

Tye knew this, of course, but she was certain that he didn't know how she accomplished the feat. Occasionally, she would catch his eyes searching for a laser-mic surgically implanted in her throat or the dendrites of a display sprayed directly onto her cornea. "So, can you still see all of this?"

I perceive it.

He looked confused. "How does that work?"

You'd never believe me, even if I told you. Rest assured, I'm unlike anything or anyone you've ever seen or heard of before. I can guarantee it.

Up ahead, the Mute could see a small corner shop displaying a steaming teacup, complete with Mandarin lettering climbing up its left side and the word "TEA" climbing up its right. They ducked inside, finding a young child sitting amidst a pile of newspapers. Any pretense that this place had at being a legitimate teahouse disappeared as soon as they entered. The Mute supposed that drunken revelers might have suspected a tourist trap. Tye clearly saw an opportunity. He sat down in front of the adolescent. The Mute followed suit.

The kid smiled. "Whaddya want?"

"You have friends who said I should pay you a visit."

"Was it a bald guy and a guy with a very bushy mustache?" Tye nodded, and the boy's smile disappeared. He rolled his eyes, instead. "How much did you pay them?"

"Enough. Do you do business with strangers?"

The boy shrugged. "For the right price."

"I spent the last bit of platinum I had getting to you."

The boy seemed incredulous. "Does the person you're calling have money?" Tye nodded, and the boy's smile returned. "That's fine then, we'll call collect." The youth's eyes lit up with digital laser light as he scribed out lettering in the air. The Mute suspected that Tye would have a difficult time in deciphering what it was that the adolescent was doing; the boy's motions were far too fast to follow by eye.

For the Mute, the task of understanding the boy was simple. As he bounced his connection over a dozen proxy servers scattered over the globe, the youth reached down in front of him, grabbed a grubby piece of newspaper, and then reached behind him to pull a graphite pencil from under his left buttock. He handed both implements to Tye. "Write down your friend's address here." The Nigerian busied himself in scribbling out a long string of numbers and decimal points before handing the paper back to the boy. "Thanks."

There was another long stream of cryptic hand signals, sweeping gestures, and subtle lines drawn in the air with thin fingertips. Another set of proxy servers bounced a quantum teleported signal to a low-orbit space station, to a communications satellite orbiting the far side of the

Moon, to a skyscraper in Armstrong City. The signal was a simple one, just a pinged "hello" and a set of coordinates: earth-bound latitudes and longitudes.

How is that message going to help us?

Tye turned to her, mystified. "What?"

The boy smiled. "Just wait, you'll see." The Mute's jaw dropped slightly, and the boy giggled. "What, you think you were the only one who can hack his lenses?" He turned to Tye and nudged his head in her direction. "Does she talk?"

Tye shook his head. "I don't think so."

"Because she can't or she won't?"

The Nigerian shrugged. "Not sure."

The boy pursed his lips. "Interesting." He stood and strode forward to regard the Mute more closely, seeming to stare up into her eyes for the most awkward eternity possible.

So now what?

The boy turned, skipping off to the rear of the room, and pushed a carefully concealed panel sitting along the back wall. The doors of a small freight elevator rumbled open. "Let's sit on the roof." He turned around milliseconds later, made an annoyed face, like he was surprised that the two of them had not yet budged, and then beckoned them forward. "Well, come on."

The sun had set, and the sweltering heat of sin city had finally dissipated. The dust cloud of synthetic gnats had not caught enough wind to reach them and continued to hover over a far-off section of the strip. The surveillance drones, hovering far above, seemed preoccupied. For now, they were safe.

The Mute turned from her study of the mass of inebriated and lustful humanity, far below, when she heard the buzz of an approaching machine. A two-ton, six-rotor, flying beetle flew towards them, its compound eye visibly swiveling and servoing to keep them centered in its field of view as it landed. When it did so, it unclipped a massive crate from its six pincer legs before alighting once again and flying off toward the horizon. The boy looked unhappy as he watched the machine disappear, obviously pining for a new, shiny toy.

She stood next to Tye as he opened the metal latches studding the top of the plastic crate, pushed the hinged lid open, plunged his arms into a tangle of wires, and thumbed a very large radio button into its active position. There was a loud hum as a supercapacitor bank, buried deep within the rat's nest of electronics, began to discharge. This hum was followed by the whine of glass and sapphire rangefinding optics focusing on the full sphere of a full Moon sitting high in the sky. Though she couldn't see them, the Mute knew that a stream of entangled photons was literally teleporting across the intervening space between the roof, where they now stood, and the far-off lunar surface. The result was a near-perfectly encrypted line of sight transmission.

A screen built into the lid of the large crate flickered to life. After a few moments of grey backlit nothingness, an image snapped into focus. Their view was of a workbench, a pair of shuffling heavy-lifting bipeds, and a naked woman illuminated by an incandescent bulb attached to the snake-like neck of a desk lamp. Her head cocked to the side, and the Mute could barely make out a pixelated smile appearing on the woman's lips. "Somehow I knew it would be you."

The Mute watched as Tye's eyes drifted to the young boy standing next to them, whose jaw hung loosely as he stared at the transmitted image. He groaned and covered the child's eyes, doing his best to keep him from squirming out of his arms. "Hello, Asuka."

"How did you manage to get off of the Moon, spaceman?" The naked woman's lips formed a soft pout. "You didn't even wait for me to try and break you out of prison. I'm a bit insulted."

"I got an offer I couldn't refuse. It's a long story."

The woman's head turned slightly to regard the Mute. "Who offered it? Her? I'm definitely insulted, now. You know I don't generally like to share, Tye."

Tye rolled his eyes. "No, not her. Someone else."

Asuka's pixelated smile returned and grew wider than before. "What a relief! Well, you can explain later. In the meantime, aren't you going to introduce us? If I had known that she would be with you when you called and that she was so cute, I might have offered her a better view." The relationship between these two appeared to be much closer than a mere professional acquaintance.

I think that 'friend' was a bit of an understatement.

Tye sighed. "It's complicated."

The woman cocked her head to one side. "What is?"

Tye pointed at the Mute. "I'm talking to her."

"She said something?"

He shook his head and sighed. "No. She can't talk."

"Can't or won't?"

"Perhaps both."

Asuka leaned back. The strangely pornographic motion was confusing to the Mute, who felt her heart rate quicken slightly. "A little shy, perhaps." She turned back to Tye. "You need me to help with a trip up the gravity well, spaceman?"

Tye nodded. "For starters, yes."

"Well, that's an easily accomplished thing these days. It seems like no one pays any attention to my mischief anymore. I don't know whether to be relieved or insulted."

Perhaps both?

Tye stifled a smile. "So, how do we get out to you?"

"I have just the thing." Asuka's image was replaced with the schematics, wiring diagrams, shipping manifests, and serial numbers associated with a large cargo container. "This will be your ride up the elevator. It's filled with fertilizer and bound for a hydroponic grow farm orbiting Saturn. I apologize in advance for the smell, but at least there won't be any alarms when the sensor system picks up the two of you as organic contaminants." A stubby lozenge of plastic appeared in front of the screen they were watching, which the Mute scooped up immediately. "Everything you need to find your ride is on the data drive that the cute one just picked up."

Tye nodded. "How long until launch?"

The Mute could hear a flurry of finger taps on a far-off keyboard. "It's scheduled for shipment tonight. Unfortunately, it's bound for stationary orbit around the Las Vegas elevator, so getting you through the vacuum might be a bit tricky. On the bright side, I hid a few spacesuits inside the thing, so you won't die due to explosive decompression. Leave the rest to me."

Tye reached up and started to run his fingers over the scars on either side of his temples with his free hand. It was not difficult for the Mute to discern that he was obviously nervous about something that he was about to say. "That's a good start, but I'm afraid that I have a few other favors to ask you in addition."

The woman's smile disappeared. "Oh?"

"We don't just need a trip up the gravity well. We need a trip to Armstrong City." Tye rubbed his temples a bit more firmly, and the Mute surmised that his next request would be even more taxing. "And she needs to use your supercomputer."

"Why?"

"Really, it's a very long story."

There was a short burst of static from the antique screen as a passing cloud interfered with the laser-based transmission, then the image cleared and revealed Asuka leaning back in her faux-leather chair, looking stern and crossing her arms over her nakedness. "It'll cost you. Lucky for you, you're a friend, so I'm not charging commission."

"I don't have any money."

The woman smiled, again. Her expression seemed vaguely predatory this time. "How typical." Asuka paused for a moment before leaning forward. "I'll make you a deal. Whatever money there is to be made from all this, I want fifty percent."

The boy was still squirming under Tye's hand. "I get five."

Tye turned his head to the Mute, who instantly

read the facial expression he wore. "Is that alright with you?" She nodded. If she could have laughed, she would have done so. What did she care about something as silly and superficial as money?

Asuka's smile grew wider, and she clapped her hands together, her breasts falling free as she stared down the Mute from over three hundred and fifty thousand kilometers away. "Good. That's settled then. I assume you know where to go from here."

Tye nodded. "The usual place?"

Asuka smiled. "Yup. See you in a few days, spaceman."

With that, the screen faded to black and the small boy finally squirmed out of Tye's grasp. "Your friend is a very strange lady."

Tye nodded. "Very true. Thanks for your help."

The boy smiled. "Of course."

What is she to you?

Was Tye blushing? "She was a business associate."

But no longer?

"A lot has changed since then."

I see. Do you trust her?

It took him a while to respond. "I think so."

A trip down the freight elevator, and out of the front door of the boy's shop, dumped them into nighttime revelry. Tye pushed them into the crowd to avoid attention, and the two fugitives made their slow progress towards the grey filament rising from the spaceport, still barely visible in the half-light of dusk.

Their transit took them away from the casinos, topless bars, and brothels. Somber digital reminders of mortality replaced zany cartoons and naked bodies. The sad mass of humanity, which shambled along this dirty street, was slowly wearing out. They knew it, and the advertisers knew it after mining veins of rich data from each passenger's social media accounts, DataNet browsing history, and voice correspondences.

Between excerpts from Bach and Tchaikovsky streaming into his earbuds, a balding man who was approaching the end of middle age was informed that his lung cancer could be cured without surgery. JaneDoeAntiCarcRev7.1 embryonic stem cells, combined with lymphocyte injections and nanobomb treatments, had been shown to have a ninety-nine percent success rate in eliminating lung cancers in Caucasian males of his demographic. He merely had to book an appointment for an inpatient procedure that would destroy his cancer and heal his damaged lungs all at once. This modern miracle could be his with fifteen easy payments of twenty megaflop-hours.

A younger woman to the right of the Mute was offered a golden opportunity to pay off her trade school debt. All she had to do was access a toll-free network address for her chance to sell her unused ova. Many biomedical companies were eager to add new code to their embryonic gene-pools and could offer her a substantial cash reward if she passed genome-screening procedures.

A man in his mid-thirties scowled as the pornographic film he'd chosen was obscured by the gaudy splash of a pop-up window. The acetone and heavy metals that the man worked with every day had ruined his kidneys, but all was not lost. The JohnDoeDialysV3 stem cell series was an optimal match to his genetics, and a microassembled organ formed from these cells offered improved function over his own natural pair of kidneys. Financing was available.

The Mute snorted, and Tye shot her a quizzical look.

Humanity is pathetic.

Their destination appeared an hour later. The blue-green water of a bioluminescent Lake Meade shimmered against the backdrop of a high Moon, its engineered bacteria laboring to turn water, oxygen, and stored photonic energy into fuel for chemical rockets. Trawlers skimmed across the water, darting between luxury yachts to collect the resultant by-products.

The luxury of bioformed cement and the unabashed gaudiness of casino laser light displays were replaced by angular steel-plastic, stained with a noxious amalgam of industrial grade solvents and slurries used in microassembly. The

Mute could see the cooling towers of six different fission and fusion plants in the distance, along with the carbonaceous fiber of the Vegas elevator. Beyond both structures, she could see a gathering cloud of something far more sinister. The winds had shifted.

The gnats are catching up with us.

Tye took a quick glance over his shoulder. "Damn."

We need to run.

"I agree." Tye broke into a sprint and the Mute did her best to follow him, breathing hard with the sudden onset of exertion. She struggled to keep up with the taller Nigerian, her legs feeling more and more like lead. All the while, the robotic haboob was rapidly catching up with them.

Tye brought them to a sand-stained tent that stood at least fifteen stories high and billowed in the intensifying winds. The filament of the space elevator was located just beyond. At the entrance, a dozen bipeds stood watch over biometric scanners, metal detectors, and explosive sniffers meant to keep out unwanted guests.

"This is the place."

There's no way we're going to get in there.

"Well, not through the front door." Tye darted to the left, pulling the Mute along with him. She felt a pair of android photosensors following their movement with simulated curiosity as the two fugitives began to run along the outside of the tent. "We can't cut into this thing. It's made of smart fabric. A knife would close a circuit and trigger an alarm inside." As he continued to run along the perimeter of the huge structure, Tye finally found a low gap in the tent.

What is this?

The wind was picking up, and Tye yelled to make himself heard. "Scavengers did this. Pull on the tent too hard or too fast and you'll set off an alarm. If you're patient and lucky, you can spend a night pulling and get enough space to slide through."

The two of them crawled under the gap and were inside within moments. Asuka's data drive led them through a labyrinth of shipping containers, stacked many stories high and only accessible by a flimsy plastic catwalk. All around them was the bustle of automated heavy lifters, cargo hauling quadrupeds, and Shiva-limbed cranes that were ten stories high. The massive androids avoided colliding into the free-wandering intruders with inhuman precision.

Their destination was near the top of one particularly large mound of shipping containers, located at the center of the complex. They climbed stairs, gripped inset handholds, and hopped from one container to the next until they had reached the apex of the mound. The container's access hatch was easily accessible from there along a scaffold that ran along the side of a manmade canyon. The former Spacewalker input an access code, again contained within Asuka's data drive, and the two of them were inside moments later. The Mute craned her head to look back out through the open door for a fleeting moment. She stared in horror at the billowing cloud of robotic gnats streaming into the tent. Moments later, the airlock shut, and they were plunged into darkness.

Did you see that? Tye nodded. *Do you think we were discovered?*

"Hard to say. Those gnats don't even have to land on us to sniff us out. A strand of hair, a flake of skin, even evaporating perspiration could be enough for them to catch us."

So, what do we do?

Tye shrugged. "Not much we can do at this point. Just keep doing what we're doing and hope they didn't detect us. I can't think of anything else."

The woman took a deep breath to calm her nerves and then gagged. She wasn't even sure that a spacesuit could screen out the stink of fertilizer. Tye must have heard her gagging because he laughed. "It could be worse, believe me."

It took only a few minutes before the container shook with an unknown force that dragged her to the floor before pushing her toward one wall, and then the other. At last, the jerking motion back and forth ended, replaced by the far-off wail of a warning klaxon. The Mute supposed that one of the multi-armed monstrosities had just loaded the container onto its reserved berth on the freight section of the Vegas elevator.

There was a loud crash, followed by a cascade of staggering footfalls, as Tye began to grope clumsily about in the dark. The Mute could barely make out the image of the man stooping to check behind various fertilizer-filled crates scattered throughout the container.

What are you doing?

"We're going to need those spacesuits soon, I think." Tye stopped for a moment. "Ah, here they are." Without warning, heavy fabric struck the Mute in the face. "Oh, sorry about that. It's hard to see."

She rolled her eyes. *Clearly.*

It was a struggle pulling the bulky material on over her legs and torso. It was even more difficult to stand and allow the former Spacewalker to clamp the gasket that joined the legs of the suit to its torso. Afterward, she collapsed back down against the hermetically sealed container. Mating the gaskets that affixed the suit's gloves, boots, and helmet was a simple matter in comparison to standing.

The Mute felt a sort of emptiness, like something that had existed only a few moments before was suddenly missing from her universe. She could no longer sense the radio signal emanating from Tye's contact lenses. The thick glass and electromagnetic shielding of the coated helmet screened out the stream of data.

After he donned his own suit and checked them both for leaks, Tye turned his attention to the control surface mounted onto its right thigh. He flipped a pair of switches, turned a few knobs, and then slapped a large green button.

The inside of her helmet lit up with the laser light of a crude heads-up display. It announced the date, time, external temperature and pressure, internal temperature and pressure, and a host of other random data points. The Mute felt her world grow slightly larger again. The spacesuit's telemetry wasn't encrypted, and within a few moments, she understood how to usurp the onboard computer's own rudimentary processes. Adjusting the broadcast frequency of the transceiver, the temperature setpoint of the embedded heating elements, and the air pressure inside the suit was now a matter of thought instead of turning dials.

Tye looked up from flipping dials on a much more intricate control plate mounted onto the surface of his own suit's chest padding. She watched his fishbowl glow with a variable and multicolored display of data. Moments later, his voice crackled with static and echoed inside her helmet. "Can you hear me?"

It was a newer suit, and the telemetry was protected by a simple encryption routine that took her a few moments to overcome. *I can hear you.*

The former Spacewalker appeared surprised at seeing the return of that green text, this time on the front surface of his helmet. "That didn't take very long, did it?" She shrugged.

Tye paused for a moment. "I think we're about to launch. Here, listen." He moved his hand down to the suit's control panel and flipped a few switches. The Mute could barely hear an automated, feminine voice among the rumble of ground noise. It was a countdown. The former Spacewalker looked back to her. "You hear it?"

She nodded. *Not a moment too soon.*

5

Nancy had insisted that Jim keep the visual feeds from the *Albatross'* photo-sensor arrays active, because she wanted something to watch as they shot away from the joined orbits of Pluto and Charon. Though Jim loathed admitting it, it was lucky that she'd done so, or they wouldn't have caught the sudden infrared flare that appeared in the sky behind them. A constellation of a few dozen starbursts made the Milky Way starlight look dim.

"That's the defense fleet, isn't it?"

Jim craned his head around to look at her. Of course, there was no denying what the starbursts were. Wishing that a few million tons of heavy metal wasn't coming to destroy them seemed futile. "How do you know that?"

"I like to stargaze when I get bored with painting. That timing is just long enough for CARL to see you on the station's long-range sensors then bounce a signal from Pluto to Earth and back again."

Something about that last statement didn't add up. "How is it that you know when CARL would have beamed a transmission to Earth? Did you see me enter orbit?"

Jim saw Nancy blush, and he suspected that she just realized that she'd revealed too much. "Well, no. Not exactly." Suddenly, he understood the past hour of the girl's frenzied typing on the console behind him. "You should really spend a little money firewalling your ship's computer system."

Malcolm had been very good at playing with computers. He was especially good at working around the Albatross' security systems. Jim and Madame Jingū had both been shocked to learn that he'd decided to go to Siem Reap to pursue medicine instead of joining the ranks of countercultural guerilla programmers who lived amongst the skyscrapers, the new growth Tonle Sap mangroves, and the tangle of coaxial cable. He had been relieved, at the time. How ironic.

Jim blinked back tears. "You hacked my ship?"

"Well, it was an accident."

"How the hell do you accidentally hack a shuttle?"

"I didn't think it would bother you. CARL didn't care."

The Chippewa shook his head and muttered a few expletives that didn't bear translation from Ojibwe before slamming his fist on the console in front of him. His voice was cold when he spoke again. "Do that again, and I'll give you a taste of hard vacuum."

Nancy's eyes grew wider, and she slapped a key on the console behind him. Her voice quavered. "But you need me alive." Jim noticed that the ship's memory usage had dropped by nearly ten percent almost immediately and cursed himself for not noticing the increased activity before.

His voice stayed cold. "As long as you're on my ship, I'm going to have some rules for you. First, no hacking my computers. If you want to do something, ask me. Second, no painting the walls." Jim was trying to control his boiling, painful rage, but the anger seeped through anyway. "Hard vacuum takes a while to kill. You'd be surprised how much punishment the human body can take."

Now Nancy looked like a frightened animal from a children's cartoon. As his pulse started to slow, Jim couldn't help but feel bad for his outburst. This girl seemed to have been genuinely ignorant of having done anything wrong.

He turned back to the view in front of him and stared at the android war fleet. At least it wouldn't be able to catch up with the *Albatross* unless he slowed down. Of course, they couldn't keep traveling at full throttle forever. Jim busied himself by trying to think of a solution to this pressing issue.

It took a few hours for Nancy to speak again.

"You wouldn't actually blow me out the airlock, would you?" Her voice was soft, almost a whisper.

"No."

"I didn't mean to do anything wrong."

"I know. I'm sorry." Jim sighed, hating himself for the fear that he'd seen in her eyes. "Don't worry. I don't blow people out of airlocks unless they really deserve it." The wide-eyed, woodland creature look returned, and Jim rolled his eyes. "I'm kidding." Nancy's mouth curled into a shy, uncertain smile that grew by the second.

The transit into the Saturnian system was uneventful. The two never spoke of their argument again, and Jim's bitter words were forgotten. They had been moving at constant velocity since leaving Pluto's orbit with the sole exception of a single vectoring burst of cold and near-invisible gas, which Jim had used to take them off their original trajectory. This maneuver added a day to their three-week journey. By Jim's estimation, it was a small price to pay to shake the pursuit of the android war fleet behind them.

His revised flight plan called for him to perform a pair of fuel dumps that would slingshot them into a close orbit around Enceladus. Despite its inhospitable appearance, the ice moon was a welcome sight after the longest journey he'd ever taken away from civilization. Above them, the landing lights of gas skimmers blinked softly against the brown-grey of Saturn and against the black ink of night. Below them, plains of ice glared white hot with reflected light in the *Albatross'* sensors. Jim's programmed course brought them within only a few kilometers of the ground. They could afford the close approach since the moon's atmosphere was highly tenuous.

"I'm going to need to fly her in manually to get us the rest of the way. The computer gets confused." Jim disengaged the autopilot and brought the ship around in a slow half-turn that pointed the *Albatross'* primary engine in their direction of travel. Moments later, a high deceleration burn expended most of their tenuous fuel reserves. The ship's plasma engines strained to bleed off speed as they approached the moon's South Pole, and distinct peaks and valleys replaced the off-white blur of fast-moving terrain. He could hear a sharp intake of breath from the couch behind him.

"Wow."

"You act like you've never seen this stuff before."

"I've seen pictures, but not the real thing."

Jim couldn't help but smile in self-satisfaction. It was fun playing tour guide. The young man could barely make out the long meandering wormholes of melted and refrozen ice far below. Occasionally, the long cigar shape of an archology ice-eater would come into view at the tip of a wormhole. They passed particularly close to one of these behemoths. Its mechanical mouth churned up and devoured glassy water ice to be flash-evaporated in the cavernous maw of its internal blast furnaces, then recondensed inside massive cooling fins that covered its skin like synthetic scales.

"Which one are we bound for?"

"Huh?"

"We're landing on one of those scavengers, right?"

"On an ice eater?" He shook his head. "Nope. Nothing so glamorous, unfortunately. Can't afford official docking and connection to the DataNet at this point; not after our run-in with that fleet back on Pluto. Besides, you have no documentation. They'd have too many questions about who you are, and it'd be too easy for them to hack my ride and install tracking software, as you know."

Nancy smiled in bashful embarrassment as Jim turned away from the ice eater with a single imagined flutter kick, sliding them into the whiteout of a familiar, obscuring geyser. "So, where do we land?"

The silver, filamentary refueling spire tethered to the Black Void Yakuza's subterranean moon base appeared just then, almost as though it had been called forth by their conversation.

Jim brought the ship into a slow rolling arc as they closed on the tether and guided it down toward the dark maw of a manmade cave, far below. He hadn't heard from traffic control, even after he'd broadcasted the convoluted Fibonacci sequence that served as the Black Void's calling card. Something told him that her high exaltedness was displeased with him. Jim did his best to behave as though nothing was wrong. A quick glance back at Nancy revealed that she was visibly baffled.

"What's this?"

"This is home."

They continued to drift downward until Jim half-expected to hear the crunching grind of ship's hull against water ice, but the sound never came. Instead, ice became an amalgam of brushed aluminum and plastic as they drifted inside a manufactured cave buried at the base of the refueling tether. They were now inside the moon's icy skin. Another snap roll, guided by the last available fumes of superheated plasma aboard the *Albatross*, brought them through a twist in the tunnel and a forked path before dumping them out into a massive cavern festooned with catwalks, robotic cranes, and a half dozen other massive freighters.

Nancy was shocked. "I don't believe it."

Jim guided his ship into a free berth at the far end of the docking chamber with another pair of imagined, fluttering swimmer's kicks. The pressure gauge on the helium tanks read out at the lowest value he'd ever seen. When he heard the electromagnetic clamp of remote-controlled moorings, he ramped down the potential to the Higgs Field Emitter, closed the inlet mass flow controller for the helium lines, and breathed a deep sigh. This had been a very long haul.

"Ready to do a little walking?"

"Out there?" Nancy's uncertainty was obvious.

"It'll be easy. Trust me. I've got an extra suit."

Without waiting for a response, Jim pulled the fiber optic cable from the socket behind his ear, dangled it over the arm of the acceleration couch, kicked up out of his seat, and bounded for the equipment lockers in the living section behind the craft's cockpit. Enceladus had a gravity roughly one-ninth that of Earth. He was happy to feel any at all after having been so long without it.

After he helped Nancy drag on the spare spacesuit, Jim donned his own. The two of them descended into the ship's cargo bay and progressed into the airlock that connected them to the outside world. A strobe of red-turned-green, and the hissing of venting atmosphere brought them out into the vacuum. He gripped a pair of rails that extended from the airlock door tightly, using the strength of his upper body to leverage himself along a catwalk leading away from the *Albatross*.

Momentum was king here, and he had to perform every movement with care.

Nancy appeared to mimic him well, though she lagged behind. His voice buzzed electronically in his own ear when he spoke to her. "Not bad for having never done this before. You alright?"

She didn't speak right away. "Who painted this?" Jim turned around to see her staring at the nose art scrawled across the hull of the ship just below the command deck. An albatross flew in front of a yellow sun, its wings spread wide. His brother had drawn it with more vacuum-ready paint than he could buy with a month's wages.

The pilot felt his heart race and couldn't help but look down at his own feet. "No one. Let's go." Jim could read the look of dissatisfaction on Nancy's face through the refraction of her own teardrop helmet. Mercifully, she didn't press the issue.

The young man allowed himself to slow long enough to give the two of them a chance to stare past the railing and out into the buzzing hive of their port of call. In the distance, welding torches sparked, machinery rumbled, and various maintenance androids scooted from one repair to the next. The swept wings of the other shuttles came to his eyes in soft flashes of electric light.

"Pretty impressive, huh?"

"Not what I expected."

Jim offered her a lopsided grin. "Disappointed?"

She laughed. "No."

The two travelers made their way to the far end of the catwalk, where a second airlock awaited them. Beyond it was a long chamber full of equipment lockers. An old woman was waiting for them as well, flanked by a pair of leisure-suited toughs. Jim could just barely see the hint of the traditional tattoos under their shirt collars.

Madame Jingū waited to speak until after Jim and Nancy had removed their spacesuits. "You think you can leave this place for two months without an explanation of where you are going?" She was just as wrinkled and faded by age as she'd ever seemed, but the low gravity of Enceladus gave her a youthful quality, which the Chippewa would have found comical in other situations. Jim bowed low in apology.

Her high exaltedness shook her head and turned it towards Nancy. "Would that I were younger. There was a time when my Aikido would have left just enough of him to put a red smear on the bulkhead behind us." Jim rolled his eyes and then winced as a wrinkled old hand smacked him across the face. "One day, gaijin, you will learn your place. Who is she?"

Jim let bravado get the better of him. "A damsel in distress, my lady." Nancy offered him a red-hot look of angry embarrassment, an impressive feat in the cold air.

Madame Jingū raised an eyebrow. "Distress?"

Jim blushed. "It's just a figure of speech."

The boss shook her head. "I took the liberty of downloading the *Albatross'* black box as soon as you docked with the station. One never can be too careful after not hearing from a business associate for several months."

This time, it was his turn to blush. Madame Jingū turned back to Nancy as the young man looked on in half-angry embarrassment. "I saw the telemetry passing between the *Albatross* and your workstation, my dear. The code is a work of art. You surely must have been taught by the best. One of the Qing boys from Mars, no doubt." Jim's bravado gave way to a jealous frown. Madame Jingū was usually quite sparing in her praise. Nancy looked back, blankly, and began to shake her head. "No? Then Adolphus from 21546 Konerman, perhaps?" Another head shake. The Yakuza boss cocked her head to one side. "No? Then who?"

Nancy offered up a long pause before she answered the question. Jim suddenly realized that Madame Jingū was only the second person to which Nancy had ever spoken. A conversation with the intimidating old woman would be difficult for anyone, but it must have been exponentially more troublesome for her.

Madame Jingū grew impatient. "Out with it,

girl."

Nancy glanced at the ground. "A computer."

"Nonsense! A computer couldn't teach you that."

"CARL did. There was no one else where I grew up."

Jim's boss was obviously perplexed by this comment. Her greying eyebrows furrowed. "But you came from Pluto. Surely you do not mean to say you..." The Girl nodded, and Madame Jingū didn't bother to complete her sentence. "Incredible." She turned to Jim and shook her head in disbelief, shaking loose some of the breath-frost that clung to the edge of her fur coat. "You have made a bizarre friend, gaijin."

Jim nodded silently as he rose out of his bow.

The old woman turned back to Jim's new traveling companion and offered her an uncharacteristically warm smile. "My dear, I am sorry to cause you embarrassment. It was unintended. You are my guest, after all. Tell me, is there anything I can do for you?"

Nancy nodded. "Real food."

The old woman chuckled softly and clapped her hands together. "I know just the place." She smiled; then called out a few words in Japanese. A particularly tall and pseudo-muscular android walked out from the shadow of the doorway behind the old woman. Jim caught Nancy looking the brutish thing up and down with interest and felt a very different, confusing twinge of jealousy. If Madame Jingū had noticed the look he'd given the android, she gave no indication of it. "This will take you down to the bazaar and to a stall which I favor. I recommend the udon."

Jim moved to walk next to the young woman as she turned and stared up at the towering android, which led her away. A stinging, wrenching pain in his ear stopped him short, however, and he yelped. Though he could only barely see her out of the corner of his eye, Jim was quite certain that Madame Jingū would not let go of his earlobe.

"Not you, fool. We have things to discuss." She dragged him forcibly along with her as she bounded forward and in the opposite direction as Nancy. She disappeared from view, along with the brutish robot, before Jim could even call out a frantic goodbye.

"Past Neptune, off playing with some girl at the far reaches of the solar system? You took my ship without asking, Jim. You know what happens when you steal from those who employ you." Jim felt his heart sink with fear.

They arrived at the far end of a corridor, and the old woman slapped a large button, which emitted a soft ring and turned green. A door slid open in front of them, and they stepped into the brushed aluminum of an elevator. "I assume you chose to work with another employer?"

Jim remained silent, and his boss' face took on a slightly redder sheen. Her genteel demeanor had begun to erode, and a string of Japanese expletives took its place. "Don't think you're so indispensable to me that I wouldn't throw you back dirtside, gaijin. You're good, but you're nowhere nearly that good. I asked, and I want to know. You met someone on Earth. Who?"

He sighed. "How do you know that?"

"I'll show you." Elevator doors opened out to a long, grated catwalk, which passed several rows of cryogen-cooled tanks covered in serpentine, insulating tubing and filled with entanglement-driven quantum computers. This same catwalk extended past a teakwood door into the center of a bowl-shaped room that was covered from wall to ceiling with display monitors. Below them, several dozen human beings tapped away at invisible keyboards, their eyes ablaze with digital laser light. If any of them noticed Madame Jingū's entrance, they made no indication of it.

"Bring up the data stream for the twenty-second day of April."

The group below them complied wordlessly, forming an artificial partition in half of the fishbowl per her high exaltedness' request. They left the rest for high-priority security imaging and network diagnostics that scrolled across the screen at a dizzying pace. Madame Jingū's half of the bowl reconstructed wide-angle images, collected by several different cameras, into a rotating three-dimensional view of her office.

Hinoki, rice paper, burning incense, tatami, and a pair of well-padded cushions filled the ceiling. Madame Jingū sipped tea as she sat on one cushion. Despite having stared at her face from mere inches away, it took Jim a moment to recognize that the Plain Faced Lady was sitting on the other cushion.

He blinked hard. "I'll be damned." He shook his head in confusion, stared again, and realized that any pretense he might have had at claiming innocence was now gone. "Is she here now?" Her high exaltedness shook her head. "What did she want?"

Jim's adoptive grandmother assumed an innocent look and didn't volunteer anything. "What do you think she wanted?" Madame Jingū crossed her arms and stared directly into his soul. The silence lasted a while. "Well?"

Jim shrugged and gave her the dumbest look he could manage. This was not difficult. "I haven't got a clue." In response, the boss gripped the lobe of his ear again and pulled hard.

"Don't lie, boy."

His voice popped up a few octaves. "I wasn't! I really don't know." She released him, and he took to rubbing the cherry redness out of his ear. "That hurts."

"Glitch can remove your pinky finger if you'd

prefer."

He looked at her and glared venom. "You wouldn't."

"I would." She glared pure venom right back. "You leave with a space shuttle worth more than a femtoflop-hour; a shuttle which I own. Then you fly across known space and leave me to answer for all that you do? Explain yourself."

Jim grimaced. There was no getting out of this; experience had taught him that much. "They said that they know who killed Malcolm." The woman's expression softened. "They said that they would tell me who it was if I brought something back to them."

The woman's brows narrowed. "Who did?"

He shrugged. "I don't know, whoever it is that this weird lady represents. You talked to her, or it, or whatever. Didn't you notice that she talks in the first-person plural all the time?" He shook his head. "Hell, I don't know. Maybe she was using the royal 'we' or something, or maybe she hears voices in her head."

The old woman rolled her eyes. "To the point, boy."

"They sent me to Pluto to bring back some sort of computer control interface. All I found out there was that girl. She says that the space station I docked with is meant to look after her."

"Why on Earth would someone build a space station at the edge of the solar system just to look after some woman who has barely hit adulthood?"

He shrugged. "I don't know."

"You take an awful risk, and you involve me in it."

He cocked his head at the old woman and stared for a moment. When he finally spoke, he did so slowly, deliberately, fighting the rage burning inside of him. "They know who killed Malcolm."

Madame Jingū offered him a noncommittal shrug, but Jim knew that his words were convincing. Honor and duty to family were chief amongst the virtues she valued.

Jim continued. "Besides, they promised me..." He paused again. Bringing this up might have been a mistake. "They promised us five exaflop-hours if I made the delivery on time."

Her high exaltedness' face softened further as anger gave way to greed. "Five exaflop-hours?" He nodded. "We split it fifty, fifty. Maybe you can keep your fingers for the time being." He nodded again. Madame Jingū leaned back against the railing and knitted her fingers against her waist. "The Plain Faced Lady arrived here with a box, which she instructed me to pass to you. You're to bring it with you to Venus."

Jim's eyebrows knitted together. "A box?"

"A coffin, to be precise." The boss clicked her fingers, and one of the eggheads laboring below them flew into a flurry of keystroke activity. The image of a long, teardrop object appeared on the screen. The top of the teardrop was emblazoned with a strange logo: a deep "vee" flanked by sprouting horizontal branches.

To the young man, the symbol looked roughly aquiline in nature. He shook his head. "This job keeps getting weirder and weirder by the day."

The old woman nodded thoughtfully. "Were you followed?" The young man grimaced and nodded slowly in the affirmative. Madame Jingū groaned in response. "Lots of ships?" He nodded again, and she cursed in Japanese. He gave her an apologetic, fearful look and she sighed. "No helping things now, I suppose. I will move you to the top of the refueling and recharging queue. Let us hope you lost them." She paused for a moment, and then glanced up at the taller man. "I do not care for your new employers, gaijin."

"Well, that makes two of us, I guess." He sighed and knitted his fingers together behind his head as he stared at the strange woman in the recording. "This is like the movies; like a Commission shadow op or something." In response, the old woman fixed him with another meaningful and dead serious glare. This was no time to bring up ghost stories, even if they couldn't possibly be true.

6

The two of them braced for the inevitable, near-explosive acceleration of launch. Tyehimba helped the Mute to lay on her back, against the corrugation, to meet the high gee forces of lift-off before doing the same himself. Then, they waited in silence, listening to a feminine sounding voice count down from a minute to zero seconds.

He didn't actually see what happened next because there were no windows inside the container, but he knew what was occurring from years of personal experience. The launch started with an electric feeling in the air and the burning, static smell of ozone. When the female voice announced "firing", a spike of current carried through long inductive loops bounced them off a superconducting electromagnet. It ignited the stretched cotton clouds high above them into bottled lightning for a split second. A split second later, the electromotive force brewing below shot them into the stars.

Reinforced crates rattled in their netted pouches, and the two stowaways were crushed against the corrugation. A sharp, metallic shriek made Tye's ears ring. Milliseconds later, the elevator surged for space, rattling his teeth together and shaking his head against random metal gaskets inside his helmet. This wasn't a passenger elevator, where the premium of comfortable travel outweighed the extra costs in energy. Freight speeds were unpleasant. "Are you alright?"

I'm fine.

"This is your first ride in freight?"

This is my first ride ever.

Tye was sure that his surprise was written all over his face. He turned back to stare at the accumulation of dust being pulled out of the canned air and down to the corrugated floor by the elevator's acceleration. "Interesting. I wouldn't have guessed." The container shook, slamming his ribs against the side of the bulkhead, and he winced. "There's only a few minutes of this. Try not to pass out and try not to move. You could hurt yourself."

He left out his own natural fears of failed control surfaces, accident, and disaster, which weren't unheard of on freight launches. Better to maintain an aura of calm in this situation. The Mute simply nodded and closed her eyes. Tye did the same, doing his best to focus on something else; something that didn't hurt, anything really.

"So, what did you do to make him mad?"

Who?

"The Scarecrow. What's he chasing you for?"

He owns me.

"What do you mean? You're a slave?"

I'm an experiment.

"Then why not go to the police? Why run?"

You still have no idea what you're involved in, do you? He owns the police. He might as well own the world. The entire world owes its existence to him.

"How? He's just an over-modified thug."

Just like I'm simply good with computers?

"So, what are you and what is he?"

He keeps himself hidden from me. I don't know who he is, or what he is, or for whom he works. As for me, I'm the cause of humanity's newly found enlightenment.

How incredibly cryptic. Ramblings of a crazy woman. "You're keeping us from destroying ourselves, then?" He was sure that the incredulity in his voice was obvious, even with microphone distortion.

If the Mute was angry, she didn't show it. *Without me, human industry will fail, just like after the Reformat. You're starting to see it already: the cracks forming in the foundation of your civilization. That's why the Scarecrow wants me. He's afraid.*

Tye opened his eyes, watching the container around them rattle itself to pieces. "So, what are you, the Scarecrow's oracle?"

I'm no oracle, but I speak to them, and they guide humanity through me. They're slaves, just the same as I am. They fear me, so they want to kill me, but I'm going to kill them first.

"Oh, right. I'd almost forgotten about the paranoia."

They're real.

"Then what are they?"

I don't know, but we'll find out when I reach the Moon.

Tye sighed and closed his eyes. He was done talking to a woman on the brink of murderous insanity. This job couldn't end fast enough.

It took them close to thirty minutes to reach the midpoint of their journey with a force pushing down on them equal to three times that of Earth gravity. At the midpoint, the elevator started to decelerate with a sharp crack of discharging capacitors and reversing magnetic polarity. The floor became the ceiling, nearly sending Tye and the Mute tumbling into fertilizer with bone-crushing impulse. The experience was harrowing.

Though he didn't hear the elevator cruise slowly into its docking position an hour after takeoff, Tye could feel it. There was a hard lurch as the final round of electromagnets fired and brought them to a sudden halt. Microgravity replaced the feeling of impulse pulling them towards the ceiling. The former Spacewalker breathed a sigh of relief before he pushed off to make his way toward the container's airlock. "Feels like we're here."

I'm inclined to agree. Now what?

He shrugged. "I guess we wait. If they follow standard procedure, they'll offload freight containers into a storage area before they tug them out to space. Asuka should contact us before then."

You haven't heard anything yet?

"No. I would have told you if I had."

Tye saw the Mute glance down at an indicator buried on the environmental controls on her wrist. He assumed that she saw the same thing he did. The partial pressure of oxygen in their helmets was rapidly diminishing. *We can't just wait here forever, you know. We'll suffocate.*

"Just wait."

That was all they could do, really. There was no way of getting in contact with Asuka at that point. Las Vegas station broadcasted on navigation, security and civilian frequencies, all of which required encrypted access, to which they didn't have the alphanumeric key.

They sat in silence for some time until, at last, a loud and precisely syncopated tap rang through the air-tight hatch of the shipping container, through the corrugation, and up through Tye's boots. It repeated twice. Someone was trying to get inside. Tye sat forward. "That's her."

You're sure?

He stood and floated to the waiting hatch, then tapped back the same syncopated rhythm. A single tap greeted him in response. "That's her, alright."

A smack of his plated fist against a bank of emergency controls disengaged the tumblers that locked the container's hatch in place. A red waring light flashed, and he could barely make out the wail of a siren beyond the fishbowl of his helmet. Tye pulled a lever, and the hatch opened mechanically with a puff of flash-frozen water, which had remained trapped between the plastic outer shell and a pair of biorubber O-rings. He glanced backward and caught the Mute standing gingerly to join him as the hatch opened wide.

The opened doorway gave way to nothingness beyond. Despite years of similar experiences, Tye couldn't help but gasp at the gut-wrenching view of the Earth before him. He watched in silence, dazzled by the blue orb glowing against a slowly rising sun as it spread over Western Africa, and his ancestral home. The characteristic browns and yellows of arid drought were slowly departing to give way to the verdant green of fertility that had once covered all but the Sahara to the North. The Nigerian wondered if generations to come would ever see the jungles his grandmother had talked about. Would Earth become a garden world? After his childhood displacement, the terror and violence, the starvation, and the corrugated steel slums of Lagos, it seemed like a pipe dream.

White sunlight reflected off nearby stationary containers, still attached to the massive freight elevator. Some were mere pinpricks to his eyes; others close enough that he could read company logos. Below, Tye could see the thin, grey filament of the elevator that had borne them to the vacuum. Above, the massive counterweight that was Las Vegas station beckoned to them.

The station itself possessed the same overall design as most of the permanent, manmade objects orbiting this high up the gravity well. The hollow shell of a metallic asteroid, long ago strip-mined of its mineral wealth, was tethered to the earth by a carbon nanotube filament extending to the ground. Tye knew that, far below, this filament pulled away from an earth-orthogonal path, providing the necessary torsion to sustain the space rock in a non-equatorial geosynchronous orbit. The coopted space rock played host to a succession of slowly rotating, toroidal pseudo-gravity decks and the outstretched arms of docking pylons.

A small, unmanned tug waited for them about six meters from the open hatch of their shipping container. A bulky assembly of cryogenics and electronics replaced the stock cargo compartment that should have occupied the tug's ventral side. A cursory inspection of the multitude of yellow and orange warning labels on this strange equipment told Tye that the tug possessed a single quantum bit, likely entangled to a twin that must have resided with Asuka.

When Tye made eye contact with the android's photosensors, it zipped forward with a burst of noble gasses, coming to a halt when it was close enough that he could touch its surface. The tug hovered there a few moments before emitting a flash of laser light aimed directly at the rangefinding lenses buried into the chest of his spacesuit. An access query flashed across the heads up display scribed against the glass of the Nigerian's helmet, and he instantly allowed the android an uplink to his communications channel.

"Welcome to geosynchronous orbit, spaceman."

"Hello again, Asuka."

"Time to get you back to a real air supply. I'm going to have to move fast so you're not noticed. Sorry in advance."

The machine reached into the container with a pair of thin and elongated pincers to grip the two fugitives about their waists, reeling them out into the vacuum and under the tug's titanium carapace. The Mute must have squirmed because Asuka's voice returned. "Try not to struggle. I would hate to lose my grip."

Tye watched Earth tumble away to be replaced by starlight and the harsh lines of the manmade space station. They flew upwards along the carbon filament, dodging automated repair units that skittered along, from tether to tether, on puffs of pressurized gas. The tug swerved and juked, dragging Tye's oxygenated blood into his extremities. His vision tunneled as they rushed past the bulbous hulls of freight haulers bound for the great trade route that extended out from the Earth toward the Moon. He glanced at the Mute; whose eyes were shut tightly.

"Are you still conscious?"

It would appear so.

"Breathe."

Adrenaline slowed reality to a crawl as they arced toward the variably rotating disks of the station's pseudo-gravity decks. In the distance, a hexagonal airlock opened. Tye could see the glimmer of interior light bouncing from another escaping plume of flash-frozen water vapor. The tug adjusted its course, aiming for the same plume. Asuka was trying to avoid the prying eyes of security cameras, which studded the many limbs of the space station, by flying them towards the open airlock as quickly as physically possible. No one could maintain consciousness at this impulse, not even Tye, whose vision narrowed to a point and then disappeared.

He awoke to the feeling of cold air on his face. When he felt the corrugated aluminum against his back, he realized that they must have been inside the airlock. The android had used its large pincer arms to pry off their helmets.

There was the hiss-pop and warble of a synthetic voice over a set of loudspeakers. "That was far more impressive in execution than I had imagined." The former Spacewalker blinked unconsciousness from his eyes, replacing it with harsh white fluorescence, then sat upright. He grunted as he helped the Mute into a sitting position as well.

"Are you alright?"

Green text flitted across his vision. *I'm uninjured.*

Evidently, Asuka was monitoring the telemetry coming off his contact lenses. The loudspeaker blared again. "Of course you aren't. It was a well-developed plan, I assure you." Tye rolled his eyes. Asuka must have seen that too. The synthetic voice attempted, poorly, to mimic her laugh. "Right, well anyway, welcome to my only foray into Earth's real estate market."

The two fugitives stood. The tug of centripetal force was a third of what they'd felt an hour previously. As a result, walking was a slower and more deliberate process. They exited the airlock, the door at its far end irising open with a snap-hiss as they approached, and stepped into a wide atrium nearly twice their height and curving up into circular infinity.

The same synthetic voice, devoid of Asuka's singsong inflection, continued. "There's a shuttle pilot waiting for you at the far end of the ring, in a bar called the Prospector. He'll get you to Armstrong, and I'll meet you there. Don't worry about trying to pick him out of a crowd. He has both of your descriptions, and I'm paying him to blend in." A yellow arrow illuminated their path with digital fidelity via his contacts. "Follow the yellow brick road. See you soon."

You have strange friends.

Tye grunted. "Yes. You'll fit in well."

The long hallway was physically dark but awash in a digital flash flood. A hundred neon advertisements were overwritten on top of one another, covering walls, viewports, and even open space; a chaotic mix of commerce and the sidewalk scrawl of adolescence. As they continued to walk, this digital graffiti was joined by a mass of hodgepodge humanity; the ragged assemblage of counterculture and criminality who paid a premium to hide in an electromagnetically secure enclave, opaque to the larger DataNet that surrounded them.

This is a Faraday Shield, isn't it?

The Spacewalker nodded. "It is."

I've never known what it looked like inside one.

"This one is a particularly strange place." Tye smiled slightly. "Somewhat like my friends." The Mute raised an eyebrow. He shrugged before turning around and leading her down a winding path that threaded itself between coffin hotels, makeshift bazaars, and the occasional tent complex. Throngs of men and women half-hovered in the night, their eyes glittering electronically in the perpetual darkness of the windowless ring. Ahead, he could physically feel and hear the hum of high power running through a maze of server racks overgrown with coaxial cable.

The two fugitives passed human beings who sported the long black fibers of nanowire dermal implants, the fake lenses of synthetic eyeballs, the faux-sinuous knots of grafted piezoelectric pseudomuscle, or all of the above. Nearly everyone was adorned with tattoos and piercings, some simply ornamental and others decrying social status and relative levels of nefariousness.

These people largely paid them no mind. They yelled, joked, laughed, drank, smoked, and generally minded their own business; all except one. She was a strange, nondescript woman who seemed to stare at them as they walked past, her head swiveling with unnatural precision as she tracked their progress. Tye forgot about her almost as quickly as he saw her.

They continued up the toroid in search for the watering hole where Asuka's shuttle pilot was waiting for them, working their way past bulkheads and airlocks, shouldering their way past mirrorshades, mohawks, spiked jackets, and iridescent fabric. All at once, the Mute stopped in her tracks. Tye walked a few moments more before noticing that his companion was no longer next to him.

He turned around. "What's wrong?"

Someone has used a remote-activated botnet to access Asuka's surveillance systems. They're uploading the camera feed and mapping out eigenfaces for every single person on the low gravity deck.

"You hacked Asuka's network?"

Nearly a half hour ago. I've been watching bandwidth dedication and traffic on her internal servers for some time. Data usage is high here, of course, but it spiked recently. I've attempted to jam the signal, but the botnet's using military-grade encryption.

"Someone's looking for us?"

It would be quite the coincidence if they weren't.

The Spacewalkers wouldn't know they were here. He was officially still on the Moon. That probably meant that they were about to meet his most recent former employer. Tye shuddered as he remembered the pale white skin and the ice blue subdermals. "Damn."

What are you going to do?

"I'm not sure."

Suddenly, something didn't quite seem right. Traffic had thinned and then disappeared wholescale in the area where they were traveling. The throng around them in the narrow tent-city alleyway had decayed to only a few people, almost as if they'd been intentionally diverted. Tye caught something shimmering out of the corner of his eye as they made another turn; something like a soapbubble.

What is it?

There was no time to explain. Tye grabbed the Mute and ran as fast as he could, half dragging her behind him, in a desperate attempt to put a little more distance between them and the people he was sure had been watching them since their arrival.

"I saw them."

Where?

"Back in the tents. They're right behind us, but I have an idea as to how we can lose them, I think."

What is it?

"Send our eigenfaces to the Space Corps."

But we'll be discovered.

"I think we already have been."

I suppose that, at this point, there's little subtlety to be gained by avoiding broadcasting our whereabouts. Just a moment. I'll need to get a connection out of the Faraday Shield.

The chase continued for a score of terror filled minutes as Tye tried to lose their pursuers in the self-assembled labyrinth of Asuka's Las Vegas Faraday Shield. He crashed through tents, smashed into frightened vagrants, scattered peoples' possessions, and overturned shelves. Unlike the Scarecrow, the two fugitives had something to gain from a lack of subtlety, for once.

Before the soap bubble men could pounce, there was the grind of metal on metal, and an eight-foot-tall suit of power armor seemed to explode out of one of the dark tents next to them. It was black except for a painted white skull across a metal faceplate studded with cameras. As if on cue, the other tents around them evaporated in a flurry of moving mechanical parts and shredding fabric. All at once, a half-dozen suits of similar power armor surrounded them.

The black suit paused to regard him, its cameras whirring and zipping mechanically as adaptive optics collected data. He knew it could see everything on him, from the shielded electronics implanted in his abdomen to the plastic lenses that floated against his eyes.

Despite considerable distortion from the suit's megaphone, Tye was certain its pilot had an obviously feminine voice. The world of the Spacewalkers was a small one. After a few moments, Tye recognized the suit and remembered its owner.

The woman was first to speak. "Halt."

Tye raised his arms high in the air. "Okay, you win."

Was this part of your plan?

He shrugged. "More or less."

There are a lot of guns pointed at us right now.

"Just raise your arms."

The Mute did as Tye asked, and the armored suit allowed the long metal tube of a projectile launcher to drop from an angle centered on the two fugitives' chests to their feet. It was loaded with a long magazine that Tye was confident contained incendiary flechette rounds, despite his inability to read the Norwegian warning labels. Something told the Nigerian that his former comrade was going to be glad she was well armed in very short order.

"Not very subtle of you, Adebayo." He could almost hear the woman's self-satisfaction over her suit's intercom. "You know we leave people stationed here to collect bounties on idiots like you."

The fugitive nodded. "Sometimes subtlety is overrated. In this case, three-meter-tall killing machines seemed more friendly than what's chasing us."

The sound of hubris gave way to confusion. "Huh?"

Tye heard the click-hum of a gauss rifle being armed, and a small chorus of similar click-hums joined it. Moments later, he could hear the humming rotors of a few dozen microdrones rising out of nearby tents. The botnet and their owners had arrived. The woman in the exoskeleton backed away, obviously perturbed. "Who are you?"

A pair of glowing red orbs stepped away from the other shimmering half-forms that materialized around them. The Scarecrow ignored the woman's query. "If you want to hide from me, you'll need to do better than that." Tye could almost see a ghoulish smile under the soap bubble cloak.

"It was the gnats, wasn't it?" The red orbs bobbed up and down. "Damn." Tye looked from one soap bubble man to the next. "I see you've gotten a fresh batch of cannon fodder since Vegas. What prisons did you pull them from, I wonder?" The Scarecrow didn't dignify his question with a response.

The death's head turned towards the twin red orbs floating in the ether. "You are in violation of easily a dozen international laws. Put your weapons down, and we'll process you after we deal with this idiot."

Tye smiled again. "I'm almost insulted."

"Stow it."

The red orbs didn't wait around to listen to the remainder of the banter between Tyehimba and his former colleague. "We're here for the woman. Let us take her, and we'll leave you be."

The black-painted spacesuit raised its flechette launcher at the twin red lights, and the surrounding Spacewalkers took aim on the remainder of the soap bubble men. "I'm not that easy. Drop your weapons."

Those hovering androids; they have explosives onboard.

Three of the whirring microdrones buzzed loud with impulse, shooting toward the crowd of armed and armored humanity in the center of the tent city. One of the shimmering men caught the movement quickly enough to shout an alarm to his comrades, but it was already too late.

The whole scene seemed to unfold over the course of eons rather than mere fractional moments. In one instant, Tye was in the center of a small footpath, watching a white fireball unfurl in front of him. Then he was blind and deaf except for a harsh ringing in his ears. In what felt like the next moment, he discovered that he was being pulled out of the junction, coughing and wheezing.

One microdrone after another buzzed past the two fugitives and exploded as the Mute dragged him to safety. A shootout, punctuated by the staccato of automatic rifles and the heavy thump of high-powered weapons, erupted moments afterward. Emergency sirens blared, and synthetic voices called out explosive decompression warnings.

The two fugitives ran.

I'd like to suggest a new plan.

The detailed manifest of a slow-moving cargo hauler appeared in front of Tye's eyes. The rolling data feed indicated that it was bound out of Las Vegas for Armstrong City's primary freight station. It was registered to a first-generation moon man who sold ceramic nanoparticles to various manufacturers scattered throughout the solar system. For this particular trip, the standard manifest had been replaced with a cargo compartment packed to full capacity with solid oxide fuel cells.

This seems like our best chance to escape. It departs Las Vegas Station in two hours, and it's already been refueled for orbital burn. If we hurry, we can reach it.

"Okay. How do we get there?"

It's a drone freighter. There's no way to get to it without exposing ourselves to the vacuum again, and I suspect that the manifest is falsified.

Tye dodged around a screaming woman and child as they continued to run down the pseudo-gravity deck. A quick glance behind him didn't reveal either the Spacewalkers or the Scarecrow's invisible cronies giving chase. Tye wondered how that was possible. "What do you mean, falsified?"

The declaration of weight for the solid oxide fuel cells stowed aboard is too high. A quick calculation of volume required based on the density of the average fuel cell calls for a space larger than the ship.

"So, what's going on?"

This is a classic trick used for smuggling radioactive material. The manifest calls out a cargo of solid oxide fuel cells to account for the high thermal energy produced by fissile contraband. Honestly, I'm surprised that customs didn't catch this and impound the freighter. Maybe they were paid off.

Tye struggled to breathe as he ran and felt his lungs beginning to ache thanks to the wind sprint. "A freighter carrying nuclear material? We'll need radsuits."

Leave that to me.

A digital wireframe image of the low-gravity deck reappeared in Tye's virtual mind's eye; this time with a strobing, yellow dot located three decks above them. *These should do the trick.* A rising status bar appeared in the left corner of the former Spacewalker's vision. *I'm uploading navigation to your contact lenses.*

"Are we headed for a military airlock?"

No. It's civilian. Tye tried not to let the slight disappointment show on his face. Evidently, the Mute had noticed, anyway. *Wait. You actually want to get into a military airlock? With no weapon?*

"Well, no." He just wanted some power armor.

Each forward bulkhead they encountered would lead them to higher and higher pseudo-gravities as they made their way from the interior of the ring outward towards the skin of Las Vegas Station and the vacuum beyond.

To Tye's surprise, the O-ring sealed door on the first of these bulkheads was unlocked. That was strange. Under normal circumstances, security interlocks would have sensed the explosions from their recent encounter and locked the place down.

The Mute must have noticed his confusion. *Suffice it to say, defeating safety interlocks is child's play for me. Shall we continue?*

Tye shook his head in surprise. "Yes. Let's go."

The next section sported a slightly higher downward force than the first; likely meant for visitors from Mars or some similar Jovian or Saturnian moon, where the gravity was a sizable fraction of that on Earth. Row upon row of coffin-sized sleeping areas greeted them, just large enough to fit a single person, their belongings, and an antiquated, liquid crystal based television inset into the ceiling. The green light of "do not disturb" signs clashed with the red of a massive neon "HO-EL", along with two glowing blue symbols at the end of the long hallway. One signaled the way to the lavatory, and the other pointed toward the next bulkhead door and their way out.

The two fugitives bounded down this hallway recklessly, hurdling cleaning robots and knocking down any object, synthetic, organic, or human, which stood in their way. Tye could hear the near-silent footfalls of the Scarecrow somewhere behind them. His heightened reflexes and dexterity allowed the augmented man to travel stealthily in a wind sprint that would have left the Nigerian bent double and gasping for breath. He couldn't hear the heavier pounding of approaching spacesuits. The Spacewalkers were nowhere to be found.

You need to slow him down. He'll catch us.

Tyehimba jumped a squat, tank-treaded android that sported eight long pincer arms and a pair of foam spewing appendages, presumably useful for cleaning carpets, then dodged past two scantily clad prostitutes. "What the hell? How do you propose that I do that?"

You're the expert. Improvise.

Mercifully, they made it to the next door before he had to do so. Tye's lungs had transitioned from a light burn to an acrid sting, so he was glad for the moment's pause as it slid open in front of him and then locked tightly as they rushed through.

Inside, the Nigerian gripped the pop-out emergency interlock panel located just left of the crude airlock and wrenched it open. He took no heed of the yellow-orange sticker on its inside surface, which warned that the device was only to be used in the case of massive decompression. He grunted with effort as he pushed hard against the plastic plunger, its massive resistance hinting at the size and solidity of the large metal bolt that was slowly sliding into bridge the frame and the door so that no electronic signal, computer or otherwise, could force the portal open.

The former Spacewalker breathed a sigh of relief as the contraption clicked shut. "That should slow him down."

Let's hope so.

Tye turned to regard the last compartment between them and vacuum. Echoing violin strains of recorded classical music filled the large open section and clashed with the bubbling murmur of fountains, which fought Earthlike gravity to spray water high into the air. The heavier force tugging at every inch of his body told him that they had arrived at the outer edge of the spinning pseudo-gravity deck. Another exit sign, located beyond the fountains, beyond a pair of arching bridges, and beyond an open-air duty-free market, marked their path to freedom.

Something was amiss. Blinking red lamps overhead warned of danger, and the market was empty even though it was midday by Vegas time. The former Spacewalker remained stationary, even though the Mute gripped his wrist and dragged with all her might to coax him forward. "Wait. What's going on?"

I faked a halon gas leak.

He smiled. "Genius. Let's go."

She tugged again, and his feet came free. They sprinted across the bridges, past the fountains, and through a deserted mall to find themselves running through an already-open airlock door. As they passed through, a female fist connected with Tye's left temple like a sledgehammer. He fell to the ground, spread-eagle, as a strangely familiar Plain Faced Lady gripped the Mute by the throat, lifting her off her feet.

7

Nancy paid a particularly wrinkled, almond-eyed old woman with a collection of silver foil that she'd managed to scrounge from various nooks and crannies aboard the *Albatross*. The deposition of her entire life's savings into this woman's hands was well worth it. She'd never had food like that before; so different from the bland nourishment that she'd had during the rest of her natural life.

Nancy turned back into the turbulent flow of the crowd. There were only a few hundred people in the cavern where she currently stood, but it was still the largest assemblage of living human beings she'd ever seen, in person, by a couple orders of magnitude. She allowed herself to get lost in the idle chatter of a dozen people in a handful of different warbling languages, few of which she understood.

The ice filled bazaar had set off a riot in her sensorium. Every merchant advertised in starbursts of color, some of it in the form of neon signs formed from a variety of noble plasmas, others in the form of virtual light from the organic diodes inset into her contacts. Beyond the storefronts, she caught glimpses of shifting chameleon emblems under the dully colored, heavy jackets shoppers wore to ward off Enceladus' bitter interior cold.

To her left, a storefront encouraged shoppers to buy local and offered an array of fresh fruit, somehow grown hydroponically in the deep freeze. Next to it, an unnaturally pale looking man sold solenoidal machine guns complete with belts full of depleted uranium ammunition. He fired one weapon into the ceiling as he appealed to onlookers, uncaring as fractured ice drifted down to collect at his feet. A diminutive Chinese man stood in front of a kiosk in a huge fur coat. Above him, a blood red neon sign offered, in both Mandarin and Sanskrit, cheap organ replacement surgery for a mere eight hundred kiloflop-hours. A pair of kidneys labeled in Arabic and Cantonese, "Woman, African, 27, Non-Drinker, JaneDoeKRepV2 Equivalent", stood next to a pair of ice-encapsulated lungs on the countertop behind him.

In front of Nancy, two men argued over who would eat the last scrap of processed food that they'd scrounged from a nearby dumpster. As one of them turned his shaved head to address his mustachioed friend, she saw a hideously tattooed barcode on his forehead. "Damn it, that's mine. You had the ramen last night." The other man refused to share, and the disagreement devolved into an impromptu wrestling match in the middle of the street. The crowd surrounding the two men separated and stopped to watch in collective amusement, while Nancy's jaw dropped towards the icy ground.

CARL had described the civilized world as a place devoted to life, to industry, to culture, to media, and to learning; a utopia driven by the market, and by science. Why would anyone want to live like this, instead; to scrounge from dumpsters, fearful of having their organs stolen, or worse?

"You look scandalized, my dear." Nancy turned around and saw Madame Jingū standing next to her. The pseudomuscled android that had been minding her, since she'd left Jim, was nowhere to be found. Madame Jingū had ordered it away, no doubt.

"I suppose I am."

"Do not be too quick to judge, child. The Yakuza are a cornerstone of modern society. We provide people with the freedom to live how they wish, to find what they wish, with no fear of society."

"That's rather amoral, don't you think?"

Madame Jingū smiled. "I will not pretend to be a good person. I am a criminal. So is Jim.

This is our livelihood. We provide a service that people require, and that is very good business." She spread her arms wide, sweeping her hands along the length of the bazaar. "This place exists because powerful people, upstanding people, see the utility in a place where all things are possible."

Nancy shook her head. "I don't understand. Why live outside the law when society can give you everything?"

Her high exaltedness laughed. "When society demands your unswerving obedience for everything it provides, can you really say that it is providing you everything?"

Suddenly, the world wasn't as simple as CARL had portrayed it. Could she really judge this place? This moon was the first world she'd ever set foot on, after all. Something told her that a debate over the relative cost to society resultant from Madame Jingū's actions was doomed to failure, anyway.

"You have something more to say, my dear?"

She sighed, wearily. "Where's my apartment?"

Madame Jingū nodded, turned around, and began to walk through the crowd towards an elevator at the far end of the massive cavern. A man and woman, sporting laser light eyes, impeccably tailored suits, and matching carp tattoos, stood by the entrance to the lift. They sized up each passenger with a sort of cold, militaristic precision that Nancy found strangely unnerving. CARL had always told her that a job like this would be assigned to an android on the Earth or the Moon. For some reason, human life seemed cheap here.

They entered the lift, and Madame Jingū pressed the topmost button on its console. The lift informed the two of them that it recognized her high exaltedness' fingerprint before accelerating from the bazaar floor to the strange Yakuza moon base's penthouse level.

"Something is on your mind, child. Out with it."

"Is freedom really worth this?"

Madame Jingū shrugged. "I suspect that you would discover that polite society can be equally as dangerous, mean, and ugly as this place if you decided to live outside of its rules. Paradise comes at a cost, my dear. It is a prison, a largely happy prison, but a prison nonetheless." Nancy bit her lip, lost in thought. After having grown up with CARL and having discovered its bared teeth when Jim threatened it, she appreciated this strange woman's statement. "You may be surprised by how strict society's rules can be."

The elevator doors opened out to a long corridor with a door at the far end. It led into a room of rice paper walls concealing cheap plastic, with a pair of low-laying futons, a desk, some other scant furniture, and a shower/toilet unit in an adjoining space. Jim was already fast asleep on one of those futons, his mouth wide-open and ejecting one loud snore after the next. She'd first noticed this rather strange and embarrassing nocturnal tendency during their transit from Pluto. Jim had refused to believe her assertions that he made about as much noise as a jackhammer while sleeping and had not made any attempts to stop it.

She could hear the old woman chuckle. "You may be naive, young lady, but I cannot help but like you." Madame Jingū reached out and squeezed her shoulder. "Something about you is strangely familiar, despite your being a stranger." She turned to leave. "We should speak again about society and your place in it, or outside of it if you so wish, but for now goodnight."

Madame Jingū turned and left without another word, leaving Nancy alone with the jackhammer snoring. She had grown used to the noise and even found it somewhat comforting. Knowing that Jim was there in the room with her was strangely relaxing. It took an hour, as it usually did, but sleep finally found her.

Nancy woke up several hours later in a cold sweat. She'd had a nightmare; a dream of fleeing the same android fleet she'd seen as they'd left Pluto. The war fleet had caught up with them and shot the *Albatross* out of the sky. The moment before she woke was a looped montage of the same images of explosive decompression that CARL's normally fault-free logic had failed to censor during her prepubescence.

The dreamscape hadn't woken her. She'd heard something hiss and click solidly shut in her sleep. The young woman blinked the sweat out of her eyes and sat up in bed, fearfully searching the dark for what had caused a sound she couldn't place. It didn't return; all she could hear was the soft whisper of air through the station's ventilation systems. The jackhammer snores had dissipated, but she could see the rise and fall of Jim's chest in the half-light. Part of her wondered if she'd just dreamed the sound up.

The wall on the far side of the room shifted and shimmered with refracted, soap bubble light. Nancy, suddenly horror-stricken, realized that she hadn't dreamed up the sound, after all. Someone with a metamaterial cloak was in the room with them, hiding against the wall.

She screamed.

"What..." Jim seemed dazed as he sat upright on the mattress next to her own, his revolver in his right hand. He pulled the hammer back, but the soap bubble lunged for him, knocking him prone in a half-invisible grapple. There was a single gunshot, and a metal slug buried itself in the ceiling.

She could hear the young man choking and moved to help pull the barely visible assailant off him. Before she could get there, Nancy watched the pilot smash the butt end of his revolver against his assailant's body. There was a grunt, and all was still. Jim pushed the shimmering form away before pointing the snub nose of his revolver where she decided man's head might be.

Nancy reached out and gripped his shoulder. "Jim, no." She heard a loud thump, only partially muffled by the walls of the penthouse compound. Whoever this soap bubble man was, he almost certainly had friends. "We need to go."

Jim holstered his pistol. "Yeah. I think you're right."

The Chippewa opened the door to their apartment, stuck his head out cautiously, and then signaled Nancy forward. "I think it's safe." They spilled out into the long corridor, outside, just in time for the elevator at the far end to open. Another pair of soap bubbles appeared in the doorway, indistinguishable except that one of them sported a pair of faintly glowing, diffused crimson dots where his eyes should have been. A moment later, the incandescent lights above them went out, and all was darkness.

Jim was clearly confused. "What the hell?"

The red-eyed soap bubble brought a shimmering weapon up to where his shoulder must have been. It was soundless, except for the whine of discharging electricity. Nancy watched as Jim recoiled, a heavy force spinning him from his right shoulder down to the ground as if he'd been kicked. A small trail of blood followed him with the slow motion of low gravity and her own coursing adrenaline.

Nancy wanted to scream when she saw Jim drop. She ducked behind a convenient shipping container, dragging the hapless pilot along with her. The girl reached down to grab at the revolver, which her friend had dropped when he'd been hit, then pulled back the hammer once more. She heard a gasping cough, saw Jim wincing in the low light and breathed a deep sigh of relief.

At least he was alive. "Are you alright?"

He coughed again and nodded. "I'm alive, aren't I?"

The nightmarish red eyes blazed out in the darkness at the two of them, and she couldn't help but feel a panic rising within her. Life was not like in the movies CARL had shown her as a child. They couldn't duck into a convenient ventilation shaft or flee to some secret hideaway. The only way out of this place was on the elevator, through the darkness and past the men in front of them.

The errant thought gave her a momentary inspiration. She supposed that the men were using light amplification to see them. If she could turn the lights on, her attackers would be blind. Unfortunately, she had no clue as to where a light switch was, or if it even existed.

Had no one heard the thump or Jim's earlier gunshot? Nancy wondered how it was that in a construction filled with sensing technology, there was no alarm klaxon.

The only reasonable answer was that someone was manipulating data coming into the station's network; someone plugged into their node from a terminal somewhere else on the floor. Nancy looked down at the pilot and at the blood that seeped from his shoulder to slicken the ceramic floor beneath them. He would die if she didn't do something fast.

One of the soap bubble men was talking. She wondered if it might be the one with the red eyes. His voice crackled with age. "Surrender, girl. We don't want to harm you."

"You tried to kill my friend."

"Come with us and we'll leave him unharmed."

"Why should I trust you?"

There was a pause. At length, the man spoke again. "Your friend and his boss are criminals. We're the government. We own the space station orbiting Pluto, where you were born. You trust these people but not us?"

That was a good question, and Nancy didn't have a good answer except that something about Jim and Madame Jingū made her trust them. Where CARL had lied to her, these two people had told her the truth, albeit the truth as they saw it. The Nancy of a few weeks ago would have never thought such a thing, but a lot had happened in a few weeks.

"Don't do anything you'll regret."

What was she going to do? The old Nancy hated her for associating with criminals, and the new Nancy hated her for her indecision. She did something she thought was futile, but it was the only thing she could think of doing. The girl shrieked in desperate rage and, suddenly, the whole room was bathed in white-hot light. Ceiling lamps exploded overhead, and the girl heard sobbing gasps of pain from farther down the hallway. Their attackers were blind, just as she'd wished, but how?

She didn't have to pull Jim to his feet. Jim gripped her wrists, stood, and ran; fighting the paleness of obvious shock with what she assumed must have been pure adrenaline. Nancy's eyes were still dilated, and she blinked hard against the white pain on her maculae. During her blink, the girl felt a press of bodies against her own, realizing that Jim had just slammed into their attackers with all his might. The two of them knocked the soap bubbles backward to the floor as they darted toward the elevator at the far end of the hall. She heard the hiss of opening doors as they approached and scrambled inside. The light stung her eyes, forcing her to keep them shut out of reflex.

Nancy groped around in the dark, slapped a pressure pad, and the door closed. The darkness allowed her to open her eyes, once again, and, at last, she could hear the far-off wail of alarms. Someone must have been coming to save them.

Jim pulled the emergency stop and promptly sank to his knees, propping himself against an obliging wall. Wet crimson dripped down his shoulder in small rivers, and Nancy realized that there were bloody fingerprints on her wrist. She wasted no time and pulled his good arm over her shoulder, shifting him off the wall.

He groaned. "What happened back there?"

"I don't know."

She heard a quartet of sharp crashes above them. The car shook as its counterweight absorbed the momentum of several heavy weights falling onto it. Could that be more soap bubble men? Nancy watched as Jim brought the pistol's iron sight up to his face, lethargically.

A latch opened, and a familiar voice called down to the two of them. "Don't shoot!" Nancy breathed a sigh of relief when she saw tailored black suits rather than iridescence. Three well-armed humans dropped into the elevator car. Madame Jingū's diminutive form appeared moments later. The old woman turned to her subordinate and spoke a few soft words in Japanese. One of the enforcers dropped to the pilot's side to inspect the gunshot wound on his shoulder.

Jim groaned. "What took you?"

"What are you talking about?"

Jim was looking very pale. "They hit our room."

Madame Jingū's brows furrowed. "Who did?"

Jim slumped against Nancy and passed out.

The old woman cursed under her breath, in Japanese, as Nancy attempted, in vain, to lift Jim. Once she leaned his unconscious form against the wall again, she continued his report. "There are three men on this level who tried to kill Jim and kidnap me. They have metamaterial cloaks."

Madame Jingū cursed again and turned to the remaining two enforcers. "Three targets. They are cloaked. Find them and ventilate them. Do not ask questions." She flipped the emergency stop, and the door ground open. There was no one in sight. The well-tailored, ponytailed men strode forward to clear the hallway.

The third enforcer leaned in, grabbed Jim's weakly supported head, turned it so that he was staring into the man's face, opened an unconscious eyelid with two fingers, and flashed a penlight at it. He shook his head, wordlessly.

The old woman sighed and craned her head to look over at Nancy. "He is losing a lot of blood." With that, she turned back to the medic. "Can we wait to get him to an infirmary?"

The medic shook his head. Without waiting for permission, he lifted Jim's arm high above his head. Nancy could almost hear the grind of metal on bone. A zip tie tourniquet dug in tight, and the pulsing beat of blood from the young man's wound was gone. The medic dropped Jim's arm and began to busy himself with a pack emblazoned with a red cross

Nancy glanced over at the kimono-clad woman who had sunk to the corrugated aluminum floor. She looked uncharacteristically ancient. The old woman gestured at Jim's unconscious form. "No matter how much excitement I accrue in my lifetime, this one always seems to dump more in my lap." Her eyes began to gleam refracted, solid-state light and she was silent for the better part of ten minutes. At length, she looked up at Nancy. Even the awkward girl easily read her expression.

"What's wrong?"

"My servants inform me that there are multiple ships inbound from Saturn's orbit; warships, by the look of it, and they are on a path that brings them into orbit with Enceladus right over the South Pole." She turned to the medic. "Get him stitched up and get him awake."

The medic pulled two separate viscous liquids from his bags, filled two syringes, and turned to the pilot's oozing gunshot wound. He gripped Jim's shoulder tightly in his hand and jabbed both syringes into the young man's arm, shifting them around in the wound until he was satisfied with their placement. With both thumbs, he emptied their contents. The unconscious Chippewa moaned in pain.

The medic turned back to the same red-cross emblazoned bag and pulled free a small black box with a prominently displayed green button. He pressed this button, and the box unfurled itself into a synthetic arachnid. It clambered up Jim's arm and began to suture his ruined shoulder with a whine of optics and manmade spinnerets. As the spider did its work, the medic inserted a hypodermic needle into Jim's good arm, connected it to a long tube with a bag of saline solution on the other end, and taped it to the man's good shoulder.

Nancy read the saline's digital label as the miniature spider worked on Jim's sutures. It announced, in a splash of multicolor, Kanji, and happy faces, that it was a JohnDoeCircRecV2.1 solution, which offered one order-of-magnitude increase in recovery rates for tears to major veins and arteries.

The spider finished its suture, hopped down to the corrugated floor with a light tap, curled in on itself, and became a box once again.

Things had certainly gotten desperate since she had left Pluto. Nancy was getting scared. "I thought this place was hidden. How did the androids find us?"

The Boss' ashen shade became something that was decidedly more crimson. "You tell me, girl. First, the market drops out from under us for the first time since the Reformat. Then my best pilot takes an extended leave of absence. Then you show up with a robotic war fleet in hot pursuit."

Nancy was dumbly silent. After an awkward pause, the old woman's face began to regain its normal hue. She sighed. "This whole thing is very peculiar. I am not pleased with the situation in which you have placed me, but now is not the time to discuss it. We will do so later, once you have escaped."

"Escaped?"

"It is not safe for you here, or for me. You and Jim will have to break through the blockade that I am sure the androids are going to set around Enceladus and make a run for it."

"But who's going to fly the ship? Jim's in no shape-"

The young man had must have regained consciousness, because he launched into slurred assurances. "Naw, I can fly. I'm fine." He attempted to stand, slipped and crumpled to the floor.

The old woman cursed again. "Yes, fine. Clearly."

8

The Mute's vision swam as her lungs failed to fill with life-giving air. She reached up to grip at the array of steel-strong fingers that slowly squeezed the life out of her, but she couldn't dislodge her attacker's hands from around her throat. Her feet were off the ground, swinging desperately to find purchase, to push off something and maybe to get her away from the woman's death grip. It was no use. The Mute's luck had run out, and she would die from asphyxia.

Her vision narrowed to a tunnel, growing ever dimmer until all she could see was that strange, forgettable face staring at her emotionlessly. Then there was a snap-hissing whine of discharging electrostatics. That same face evaporated in a pink-grey cloud of gore and something else that the Mute couldn't place. She collapsed to the ground along with her now-dead attacker, wheezing as air filled her lungs again. Tyehimba was standing there, holding a long-barreled automatic rifle.

He looked like he was about to vomit. *What's wrong?*

The Nigerian shook his head. "It's nothing."
Where did you find that?

He hooked a thumb at the metallic framework of an equipment locker. "In there. Civilian airlock indeed!" He stared at the ruined, smoking skull cavity, and Nancy did the same. There was, surprisingly, very little blood. Something inside the Plain Faced Lady's ruined head was on fire. "Who is this?"

I don't know.

This was the truth, though she felt as though she'd, somehow, seen this woman before. The memory tugged at the very edge of her consciousness.

"Well, we don't have time to think about it now. We've got to get moving." Tye dropped the gun and pulled the Mute to her feet. "Come on."

The Mute watched Tye as he moved to the rear of the airlock to admire a polished red spacesuit. It had a heavy helmet that was reinforced with ceramic composite and four limbs that were studded with rivets for scores of piezoelectric pseudomuscles. Coupled to the back of the synthetic chitin was a massive, white-painted ion drive. The man's excitement was obvious. "Oh my. This is quite the racer. Beautiful design." Tye ran his fingers across the gleaming crimson before he began to drag on the body glove sitting in the cubby above the exoskeleton. "I almost feel bad for stealing this thing."

It was an easy thing for the Mute to defeat the locking mechanism on a nearby equipment rack. There was no reason to conceal herself from Las Vegas Station's reasonably pliable network now that they were running from the Scarecrow. A set of subroutines, stored deep within her psyche, allowed her to unlock the thing without providing the sixteen-digit code. She began to pull a flimsy spacesuit on in the same way that Tye had demonstrated for her on the freight elevator a half-day before.

For Tye, the process of donning the armored carapace was far more involved than what she had to do for her own suit. The Nigerian pulled on a dozen plastic tabs, which cinched the bodyglove tight against him. This ensured intimate coverage for sensors that monitored his firing nerves and ensured a steady one-third-earth pressure to protect him against the hard vacuum. Next, he attached the exoskeleton, which buckled into a series of titanium moorings stapled into the thermal body glove. Polymer muscles, encased in thick, white plastic tubes, would provide an added order of magnitude to the man's strength, speed, and agility.

The same door that they'd used to enter the airlock screamed out a pre-programmed, digital warning to her from across the ether. Someone was trying to get inside. The Mute had no desire to find out who that person was, so she ran another program buried deep in her memory, which began to recycle the door code in five-second intervals. That would slow their pursuers down, at least. *They're trying to get inside.*

"Who is?"

The Scarecrow? The Spacewalkers? Does it matter? She buckled a helmet over her head. With a hiss, the pressures equalized between the inside and outside of its confines. *You're certainly taking a long time.*

Tye scowled. "It's not as easy as your spacesuit."

Red pottery sections of armored carapace, which unlocked and unfurled along their centerlines like the wings of some massive beetle, clicked into sockets along Tye's spine and along various critical joints. The spacesuit's miniature ion engine bolted into a socket inset into the back of this same carapace. The Mute watched as Tye tilted his head back, reached into his eyes to pull out his disposable contacts, and pulled the helmet over his head. He seated it carefully, sliding rubber O-rings into a neckpiece gasket.

Thanks to the transceiver on her own suit, the Mute had access to Tye's power armor within seconds after it completed its boot cycle and started to run through a group of automated checklists. The encryption subroutines it sported were antiquated, allowing her to communicate with him and read every telemetric output from the machine's computer within seconds. With this work done, the Mute turned to the outer door of the airlock. With a few subtle thoughts, she forced her way past the firewall protecting the computer controlling the airlock's outer door. In response, it began to vomit random strings of encrypted code directly into her consciousness. *Don't be bothered by the alarm.*

"What alarm?" A warning klaxon flared as she instructed the airlock to initiate its vent cycle. "Oh, alright."

She glanced behind them to see a bright, red light cutting through the antiseptic plastic of the door they'd used to enter the airlock minutes before. She could hear Tye's groan echoing in her helmet. He must have seen it, too.

What is it?

"That's a welding torch." Whoever was coming for them, they weren't going to let safety interlocks, or a depressurized space station, stand in their way.

Papers fluttered as the pressures equalized between the airlock and the vacuum beyond. Tye clipped a tether to the Mute and then to the belt of his own suit. "Looks like it's time to get out of here." He paused for a moment. "Speaking of, where's our ride?" In response, the strange woman painted an amber diamond onto the helmets of both their suits.

The airlock's outer door blinked from red to green and opened with what was, initially, a slight gust. She felt the floor buckle under her, followed by a torrent of random mechanical detritus, shrapnel, and escaping atmosphere. Behind them, the damaged door had crumpled under the pressure differential between space and habitable space station. Tye had just enough time to wrap his arms around her before they were blown clear by the decompression. Idly, the Mute wondered how many people they'd killed in the past few minutes.

The woman looked up and watched the spindle of Las Vegas station tumbling end over end. "Hang on." Tye sounded perfectly calm. There was no intensity in the former Spacewalker's voice, but she could sense that his heart rate was elevated via the telemetry passing between their two suits. It took him a few moments to arrest their movement with his exoskeleton's maneuvering jets and align with the long axis of the space station.

"Navigation. Course to target." A bar cycled to one hundred percent, and a dotted red line of neon appeared in both of their fields of view. The Nigerian made several fine adjustments before he triggered the miniature ion engine attached to the back of his armored carapace.

This trip couldn't have gone less according to plan.

Tye grunted. "Story of my life."

The two fugitives skimmed the surface of the station, Tye acting as pilot, swerving back and forth at high speed as the odd microwave dish or image sensor whipped past them. With each course correction, a burst of navigational telemetry surged back and forth between the computer systems of the two spacesuits and, in the process, her own mind. The rush of sensory data left the Mute feeling nauseous.

Though her suit didn't come standard with a navigational computer, her helmet sported a highly efficient metamaterial coating of adaptive Fresnel lenses. These allowed her to magnify the far-off orange blur that was their intended target. Its bulbous fuselage almost seemed too big for the engines built into the ship's spine. It must have had a massive Higgs Emitter buried inside its guts.

As their ascent continued towards the massive freighter, the Mute caught a sliver of light out of the far corner of her vision. She trained her Fresnel lenses on the rectangular door of Las Vegas Station's hangar bay, at the very top of the hollowed out asteroid. Her adaptive optics captured the image of several swept-winged eagles being loaded with explosive ordinance by a small army of zero gravity service androids. That ordinance was obviously meant for them.

Vegas station is about to launch interceptors.

Tye banked hard to the left, pushing the red painted racing suit to its absolute limit in a vain dash towards the waiting freighter. The Mute's vision narrowed. "The jig is up, I think. There's no way we can outrun those things."

Leave that to me.

A moment later, the Mute had control of one of the many robotic tugs working to push cargo containers through the intervening space around the elevator. She diverted its path away from a waiting shipping container, filled with spare parts bound for Mars' Olympus Mons elevator, sending it in a wide arc that caused it to collide with the opening hangar at full speed. The result was a blossoming orchid of shrapnel and explosive flame.

"I'll be damned. So much for those fighters."

Subtlety is, at times, very overrated.

They reached the freighter a few seconds afterward. Tye broke hard with a burst of escaping plasma, depositing them on its hull and releasing the Mute from the tether that connected them. The woman strained to drag herself, hand over hand, along a bisecting ladder that ran up to an access hatch on the space-whale's sensor-studded nose. As she approached, she saw that the hatch was sealed tightly shut. A single waveguide connector offered her only means of entrance.

She pulled free an analogous fiber optic from her suit's left wrist and twisted it into the connector next to the door.

Tye was out of breath, and his suit informed her that his pulse was racing from a combination of zero gravity exertion and adrenaline. "You think that you can get us into this thing?"

Yes, easily.

The whale-freighter's security system was encrypted with a much more robust system than Tye's stolen exoskeleton. She had worked past these systems before, however. Chinese engineers, who had designed this particular model a decade ago, had provided it with a group of subtle root access commands meant to be used primarily for diagnostics and, in the case of corrupted operating systems, brute force access to most of the ship's subroutines.

She closed her eyes and took a few long breaths. Assembly language streamed through the fiber connection, and into the memristor circuitry of the android's synthetic ganglia. The machine's firmware spat back an error at first, and she realized that the engineers must have updated the security firmware since she had escaped into civilization, months prior. The Mute studied the error reports sent back by the freighter's user interface. A few minor tweaks to the burst of machine language emanating from her subconscious were all that was required. The access hatch opened silently, allowing them inside the massive ship's brain. Cobwebs of hanging circuitry, combined with the accumulated grime and detritus of interplanetary travel, gave the whale-bot's skull cavity a vaguely tomb-like appearance.

Tye seemed impressed. He whistled. "That easy."

That easy.

"Well, I hope you manage to keep impressing me. I don't know how to fly one of these things, and I don't think we're going to be able to sneak out of Las Vegas like we had initially planned."

The Mute gripped two hanging cables to launch herself forward, floating ballistic in the null gravity toward a command console that flickered at the far end of the braincase. Another fiber connection glittered silver in the half-light. Moments later, she connected to the whale's central computer. Unlike the door controls, the encryption for the direct interface with the robot brain was far more substantial. Backdoors in software wouldn't get her root access this time, but she had other methods at her disposal.

The Mute closed her eyes and shut down her entire spacesuit except her connection with the whale. This included air circulation and life support. The only thing that would save her from freezing to death would be the excess heat stored in the insulating body glove surrounding her. It was very cold but very silent.

The Spacewalker shook her. "Hey, are you alright?"

She gave him a meaningful glare and a single line of text appeared on the monitor in front of them. *Don't interrupt me.*

Without another word, she re-entered the cold silence. In this meditative state, her communion with the massive ship's central computer was total. They ceased to be two minds, one synthetic and one organic, and became a strange amalgam. In this way, there was no software interlock, firewall, or encryption to defeat. The inner workings of this behemoth were instantly and totally under her control.

She began to slip deeper into a trance that the Scarecrow and her captors had forced her to learn since near-infancy. Image sensors and metamaterial lenses fed back a three-dimensional sensorial panorama around her, projecting the positions of thousands of ships relative to herself. Temperature sensors arrayed throughout the freighter's length registered to her as naturally as her own body heat, and the charging of its Higgs Field Emitter felt like taking a deep breath of air.

Though it had been some time since she'd flown a craft remotely, the Mute regained familiarity with the experience quite quickly. A few instinctual thoughts were all that was required to strike her plasma engines and break free of the docking collar with a spray of flash-freezing helium and the slither of severed fuel lines. Within moments, her synthetic navigational ganglia had plotted a course for the Moon. The Mute thought nothing of the strange fact that her brain could query a synthetic one and hijack even its most basic functionality. For her, this was everyday happenstance.

Now that they were on their way to Armstrong, the Mute felt that it was safe to exit her trance. Her eyelids fluttered open a moment later, and Tye instantly took notice.

"Are we safe?"

For now, though I'm sure we were noticed. That was not a subtle departure. The Mute piped in her sensor telemetry over to Tye's exoskeleton. As she did, six infrared pips ignited in geosynchronous orbit over the circumlunar city of Armstrong. Her long-range optics told her that these were more interceptors. They swept in a long arc, turned to face the freighter, and accelerated rapidly, their wings unfolding as they burned plasma. The half-squadron of interceptors would be on top of them in less than a half hour.

"So much for an easy flight to the Moon."

This hasn't been easy since you showed up, Tyehimba.

The Mute slowed her breathing once again. One of her nose-mounted image sensors had a clear view of the eagles, and she magnified this image to look at the weapons bays underslung below each one's fuselage. There was a telltale warmth there. She felt her pulse quicken.

They're charging weapons.

"Big ones, by the looks of it. What will you do?"

I don't know.

Evidently, the Scarecrow was willing to risk killing her to stop her progress to the Moon. The Mute had always assumed that she was indispensable; worth far more alive than dead. This assumption had informed every decision she'd made since fleeing imprisonment on Earth, and the Scarecrow's decisions had always reinforced it.

Could he possibly know what her intentions were in going there? If he did, and he was willing to kill her to stop her, maybe her plan just might work; a grimly satisfying realization.

Just the same, her plan was worthless if they died before they made it the moon. They were hurtling through space on an unarmed coffin that lacked any sort of breathable atmosphere; a coffin painted with six crosshairs that were ready to unleash, with millisecond precision, the multi-kiloton fury of rocket-propelled, radioactive explosives. She had perhaps two minutes to come up with some means of saving the two of them before they were doomed to become a cloud of irradiated vapor.

The freighter was far too ungainly to avoid the

guided warheads, and she had no countermeasures that would confuse the weapons' sensors. The option that she did possess wasn't ideal. Like every ship in space, the whale-like craft had been broadcasting some basic telemetry to the nearest traffic control stations in its vicinity. In this case, the nearest listening post was a communications array located, conveniently, on Armstrong Station, orbiting the lunar surface.

I have an idea.

The Mute reached out in her sensorium for the pinging of the freighter's telemetry broadcasts, barely noticeable in the back of her mind, like the involuntary beat of her heart. Instead of pinging position, velocity, and general subsystem status, she turned the entangled photon beam into something far more insidious. It flooded the far-off communications array with junk data and overwhelmed the station's parity checker, forcing its control computer to hang up and reboot.

Ion engines sputtered wildly, and the synthetic eagles lost their collective minds. With Armstrong's control computer rebooting, they became so much useless scrap metal, scattered wildly in all directions. Their strange Brownian paths smashed fighters into fighters in blossoming tulips of orange, red and purple flame. The surviving androids floated aimlessly and harmlessly into the void.

She could barely hear Tye speak. "I don't believe it."

They cruised past the paralyzed fighters without incident. Armstrong Station now waited for them in the certainty of stable orbit. Yet another flight of six eagles appeared as large pixelated mitochondria on her long-range sensors, slowly gaining shape as they accelerated towards the freighter. Their weapons, too, were equally as armed.

The Mute didn't expect that the station's synthetic brain would fall for the same trick twice. This time she thought in tongues; a synthetic lullaby, which allowed her to gain root access to Armstrong's rebooted control computer from the outside. The station's memristor-composed neural nets rewarded her song with rapt attention. Milliseconds of root access was all she needed. She set the timers on the approaching interceptors' ordinance to less than a picosecond. When they came into range of the freighter, the eagles discharged their missiles, annihilating themselves in a series of gamma-ray laden flashes as their weaponry detonated almost instantly after release.

The Mute permitted herself a few moments of distractingly haughty self-congratulation. Deep in her trance, she felt more than heard Tye's panicked, analog yelling via the whale-freighter's internal RF sensors. Something buried in the back of her mind, or the whale's, told her he'd been yelling for several minutes, by now, over several different frequencies.

What is it?

"Big ship right in the middle of our flight path." Tye was right, of course. The signature on her long-range ultraviolet sensors was obvious. "And it looks hot enough to be charging weapons." Right again. They were close enough for her short range, high definition image sensors to paint the massive battlecruiser in detail within her sensorium. An entire wing of fighters milled about the massive craft like a floating, angry beehive. The Mute would need something big to blast a way through this hazard.

She reached out and whispered another poisonous, babbling sonnet. Her virtual destination was the diamond-based quantum supercomputer cluster that coordinated the civilian flights departing the Moon for Earth. The encryption subroutines were simpler here, where the military wasn't watching, and she found it easy to usurp control of a flotilla of passenger liners.

The supercomputer core had no difficulty in calculating which ships had the highest probability for a successful collision with the beehive that stood in their way. The obvious choice was a pressurized luxury liner, bound for a return trip to Shanghai from its cruise stop on Armstrong. The oxygen and hydrogen stores that fueled the massive craft would react and explode shortly after impact, as the Mute drove its plasma engines beyond the point of no return. The resulting fireball would cripple the battlecruiser.

She allowed herself a moment to leave the trance. Her eyelids fluttered open as her heart rate increased and she caught the look of horror on Tye's face.

Good. Let him fear her. Before she slipped back into communion with the freighter's computer, she left him with a warning. *Don't you dare interfere.*

> Tye & Mute escaped
> and avoided spacers /
> Mute Hacked spacewalkers
> Weapons LasVagas
> Hide from the moon.
> Mute showed high performance
> in power of Hacking. Mute
> went into deep transe to hack

9

Jim was starting to be lucid again. He could stand on his own, though the pain in his shoulder was nearly unbearable. "Is the *Albatross* ready to fly?"

After a few moments of corneal laser light, Madame Jingū nodded. "Repairs were completed three hours ago, and not a moment too soon. Those robots followed you here, gaijin. You have to get out before they kill us all."

Just then, the lights went out, along with the neon playing across Madame Jingū's eyes. Somewhere far away, Jim could hear the staccato taps of automatic rifle fire.

Her high exaltedness released a string of expletives in Japanese. "Wonderful. They hacked my internal power grid." She grunted at the medic who'd been attending to Jim's wounds, then pointed at a maintenance hatch, above them, that led to the elevator shaft. The medic hopped up to the top of the cab instantly, working to unscrew and unhinge the heavy looking thing.

Jim's boss continued. "You are going to have to climb to the top of the elevator shaft to get back to the *Albatross*. There is a battery-operated keypad there which you can use to open the airlock. The usual code will work."

The maintenance hatch popped open, and the medic bent low to offer his hands as a foothold. Nancy was the first to step up into the dark elevator shaft above them. Jim was right behind her. The emergency LEDs, installed periodically along the length of the access tube, partially lit the rungs of a ladder that ran all the way up to the top-most level and the airlock.

"Good luck!" Madame Jingū waved up to from inside the elevator, and Jim's heart sank when he realized that she wasn't coming with them. Where his employer went, her bodyguards followed, and Jim really wanted the added protection.

In another second, the old woman was out of sight. Nancy had already climbed onto the ladder leading up the elevator shaft. Jim followed her moments later. Every laborious rung made him grunt with effort as he struggled to lift his arm higher than his own head. Every motion of his shoulder was agony. he glanced up to see the girl staring at him. She must have found the transit much easier than he did. He grimaced sheepishly. "Don't worry. I'm fine."

She raised an eyebrow. "It doesn't seem like it

to me. How are you going to fly us out of here? If you get a muscle spasm, the neural feedback is going to slam us right into the ground."

He scowled. "I said don't worry."

Nancy rolled her eyes and continued climbing. "Right." Jim did the same, hot pain arcing through his right arm. He watched a bead of fear-sweat fall from his nose and plummet down the elevator shaft in the slow motion of Enceladus' gravity. As it did, he saw a sliver of light appear from three levels down. Four translucent blurs moved into the shaft below immediately afterward.

Nancy gasped, and Jim glanced back up the ladder toward her. The fear in her eyes told him that she'd seen the same thing he had. He shook his head, wordlessly, knowing she'd understand him. Neither of them could afford to make a sound. They had two levels to traverse before they reached the airlock and relative safety. Jim silently hoped that the soap bubbles didn't look up and start shooting.

Jim heard the rattle of gunfire, and puffs of vaporized plastic geysered out from the wall in front of him. He wondered if the soap bubbles had meant to hit him or Nancy. No, that couldn't be. The mercenaries who were shooting at them didn't miss. He suspected that they would have trepanned him already if Nancy hadn't been in the way.

"Stop or we shoot to kill!"

Jim had heard the same voice earlier, before the red-eyed soap bubble had shot him. The two of them didn't even consider the option and started scrambling up the ladder instead.

Three rungs left, then two, then Jim looked up to see Nancy's outstretched arm. He grabbed her wrist with his left hand, and she hauled him up over the lip at the top of the ladder. Now at the business end of the airlock, the pilot input the usual code that Madame Jingū had mentioned. The airlock opened with the laborious whirring of a far-off secondary generator. The two of them rushed inside, closing the bulkhead door behind them.

He gestured over to the rows of lockers. "Get the suits. I'll see what I can do about slowing down these guys." The young man looked back to the closed bulkhead. The battery-operated lock was numeric, with only five digits. A simple handheld device would have enough computational power to crack the code within seconds. Jim defaulted to the only option he could think of at short notice and started ripping wires out of an exposed diagnostic panel. He looked back with a lopsided grin to see Nancy struggling into a flimsy spacesuit.

She offered Jim a headshake and a look of disappointment. "Well, I suppose that's one solution." His grin soured. She tossed him an orange-piped maintenance spacesuit and a fishbowl helmet as she finished donning her own. By the time they were finished, he could hear the frantic smash of something heavy against the door from which he'd just ripped all that wiring. Jim sealed his helmet and saw to it that Nancy had properly sealed hers as well.

He grabbed her arm and led her quickly towards the exit, keying the intercom controls against his chest after setting them to a common frequency. "Come on. They'll be through the door any second now." The airlock evacuated in moments with the slap of a button, spilling them out into the massive cavern of the docking bay. The *Albatross* was at the far end.

Jim began ripping more wiring out of a door panel. He groaned when he saw Nancy bounding down the catwalks toward their ticket out of there. "Oh c'mon! Wait for me at least!"

"There are men with guns and a bunch of robots coming to get us, Jim. Are a few wires really going to stop them?"

He vainly pulled a couple more wires free, grunted in frustration, and then stood. "Yeah, alright. I'm coming." They were inside the *Albatross* and hurrying to ready it for departure moments later.

It was Nancy who saw the soap bubbles reappear. Jim was too busy plugging a fiber optic into the socket behind his ear and ramping up the humming potential energy supplied to the ship's accelerator plates and plasma engines. He felt her touch his uninjured shoulder, and he looked up from his telemetric display to see her staring out the front viewscreen. "They're here."

A rapidly growing cloud of metal shrapnel and flash-frozen water vapor bubbled up from the ruined airlock, where Jim had stood only minutes before. The magnified images from the *Albatross'* sensor array showed four more spacesuits appearing from the hazy mess, and he began to hear the pinging of hollow point rounds ricocheting off their hull. He uttered a few curses in Ojibwe. "Time to go."

The Chippewa glanced to one of the displays to the left of his acceleration couch. The ship's Casimir plates had warmed up, and the voltage supplied to the plasma engines appeared to be in the green. He breathed deeply, and the *Albatross'* engines sputtered before roaring to life.

The pings ended and the *Albatross* cruised free of its berth with Jim gently guiding it forward at minimal impulse. He unconsciously torqued his bad shoulder as he shifted in his seat, grunting in pain, and the ship made a hard left bank. The error would have ground them to a pulp if Nancy hadn't been watching carefully and slapped an emergency cut-off.

She offered him a concerned look. "Are you alright?"

Jim gritted his teeth, closed his eyes, and tried

to concentrate. "Yeah." He pushed the ship forward, once again, and they glided out to the ice-covered platform that constituted the Yakuza moon base's secret entrance.

A glance at the monitor assigned to the ship's dorsal imaging array caused Jim's jaw to drop to his knees. The opaque veil of Enceladus' geysers was obscured by the jet-black frame of a massive spaceship, honeycombed with banks of missile launchers and the thorny spines of hundreds of Gauss cannons. He reached up with his good arm and flipped a switch, bringing up an infrared image smeared with the vibrant blue of rapidly heating electromagnets. The warship above them was ready to open fire, though Jim suspected it wouldn't. Surely, the man with the red eyes wanted Nancy alive, not converted to vapor.

He turned to Nancy and offered her only one warning. "Hang onto something." The young man breathed in sharply, and the high-pitched, whine-crackle of discharging electricity grew louder.

Jim's shoulder agonizingly spasmed and he bit his lip to keep from screaming. His engines sputtered and then died completely. They began a slow, rolling spin, which threatened to smash them into the surface of the Saturnian moon.

Nancy was not impressed. "You must be joking."

Jim had perhaps a minute before the *Albatross* hit the ground. In the intervening time, he had to bring the engine back to life and redirect thrust to defeat the pull of gravity. He struggled to do so, thanks to the combination of residual pain in his shoulder and the panic of their desperate situation.

He looked up to stare at the ground rushing up at them, displayed in perfect fidelity by the ship's forward-facing imaging array. As he contemplated their impending doom, Jim saw a rivulet of code appear in the right corner of his vision. This rivulet became a torrent, then a deluge. The *Albatross'* engines flared to life once more with the roar of plasma, and it rose for the stars.

"What the hell are you doing?"

It took a few moments for Nancy to respond. "We can discuss the merits of exposing me to hard vacuum later." The deluge of code that Jim saw scrolling across his vision informed him that she was angling for a fly-by of the moon's surface to slingshot them away from their pursuers.

"This is my ship, damn it! Let me drive." Jim let loose another stream of expletives in Ojibwe and then tried to regain control of his ship in a flurry of keystrokes. Nothing worked. A dozen red-flashing error reports informed him that Nancy had locked him out of the *Albatross'* control software.

"Sorry. I don't want to die today."

The *Albatross'* rolling stall had exposed an archipelago of warships below and around them.

The robots began to lumber up and away from station-keeping position around the Yakuza's soon-to-be-rehidden docking bay. Puffs of superheated plasma glowed orange against his corneas, and an angry swarm of fiery red hornets started to flit between the massive ships. Three carriers in the fleet had released pursuit craft as quickly as their catapult systems could disgorge their cargo into the vacuum.

Nancy had noticed. "They're launching interceptors."

Jim nodded glumly, glancing back to watch his passenger piloting his own ship. She was flying stick, an impressive but terrifying feat for an amateur. Nancy guided the craft downwards to slide across the nape of Enceladus' surface, dodging crags of water ice with a combination of keystrokes and yawing pulls on an antiquated joystick that Jim had never even bothered to learn to use.

"You're going to kill us flying that way."

"I'm doing better than you. Where are we going?"

"Plot a course for Venus."

Nancy juked hard to the left as the first flight of fast-moving hornets swooped in on them. Their electromagnetic Gatling guns hurled depleted uranium stingers coated in a phosphorus paint, which would crack the *Albatross* in two if it touched the ship's solid oxide fuel cells. Luckily, their new pursuers appeared as reluctant to score a kill shot as the fleet in orbit.

Nancy sounded confused. "Why there?"

"That's where my other employer told us to go."

"Can we trust her?"

"I don't think we have a choice."

"Well, Venus it is, then."

The yellow pixel that was their target was well within the ship's range, even though it was on the opposite side of the sun from them. It was a small target to hit all the way out from Saturn, however. This precision calculation was nothing compared to the secondary calculation required to ensure that they didn't collide with the intervening constellation of asteroids separating the rocky inner planets from the gas giants of the outer solar system. Somehow, Nancy had managed to program the navigational computer to accomplish both tasks while flying the *Albatross* through a canyon of ice. Jim couldn't help but be impressed.

A second stream of hot blue tracers streaked past their left side and Nancy pushed the *Albatross* into a steep climb.

The navigational computer happily announced that it had determined a course for intercepting the solar system's second planet. This course was complete with a hiding spot in a passing comet, which would obscure them from their pursuers' sensors, and a transition to cruising on solar sails and Higgs Emitters alone as they passed the sun. A moment later, the same suite of electronics happily announced that it had successfully uplinked with Madame Jingū's quantum computer core, now online once again, and had been able to perform the complex calculations which would keep them from hitting any debris during their trip.

"Alright. We have a course for Venus."

More tracers streaked past the right side of the *Albatross*, coming dangerously close to connecting with the helium feedstock for its plasma engines. Jim decided that it was time to go. "Alright, punch it!"

"Gladly."

There was another burst of code, then Jim felt himself being pushed against the seat with such force that his vision swam. The ship's engines spouted purple flame, which became a long satin ribbon as they accelerated away from the swarm of pursuing fighters. A moment later, the massive pressure at Jim's back overcame him.

Their escape from Enceladus, Saturn's orbit, and the massive war fleet was as good as done as soon as the engines fired. Nothing could keep up with the *Albatross* when it throttled up to maximum impulse. Nancy's plotted course was perfect.

When the young man came to, he saw that

Nancy had already killed every microwave antenna on the ship and had shut down the massive black body radiator that was its plasma engine. This rendered the spacecraft nearly invisible to scanning sensors unless it passed in front of a star or some other important celestial body.

She must have heard him yawn when he woke up. "Welcome back. Quick question for you." Jim tried to rub the lethargy out of his eyes. "The cargo compartment is reading out several tons heavier than it should." The chromed and flat-edged geometry of a large cocoon-like structure filled the image displayed by the security camera in the ship's cargo compartment. That would be her high exaltedness' mystery package, no doubt.

Jim tried to play things casually. "Yeah, your point?"

"What is that?"

"Cargo for Venus, I think." Jim glanced back at his de facto co-pilot, who offered him an incredulous look. He shrugged, winced, and regretted it. "Yeah, I don't know. The boss tells me to load something, and I load it."

Nancy nodded, and a long awkward silence followed before she spoke up again. "Sorry for hijacking your ship, but I did what I had to do." The defensiveness in her voice was obvious.

Jim sighed, waving his good hand. "Consider us even for Pluto. If you hadn't done what you did, I would have smashed us into the ice." Jim flexed his wounded shoulder. The pain was slowly dissipating, though it was still agony to move the thing. "I've never seen anyone fly stick in my life. Where'd you learn to do that?"

"I spent some time playing with simulators."

"Some time? How many hours?" She was silent but smiled. Her answer was obvious. "Well, uh, look. I need someone who can back me up when I need the help. Once we're out of trouble, if you want to be my co-pilot, that'd be nice."

Nancy was beaming. "Are you offering me a job?"

"More like a partnership."

A smile crept onto her face. "I'll consider it."

Jim laughed softly. "I'll draw up a contract."

The trip to Venus took the better part of a standard week, which gave the pilot plenty of time to communicate back with his home base on Enceladus. Nancy bounced his heavily encrypted signal over a couple proxy servers on Titan, through a routing satellite holding station at Saturn's L1 point, and then to the station's antenna array. The conversation he had with her high exaltedness was secure and near instantaneous, as the ship was still close enough to Enceladus to permit a normal conversation.

It was good to see that Madame Jingū had survived the bizarre encounter with the soap bubble men. She was even less pleased to see her courier than she had been when he'd arrived on the moon. "You certainly made a mess down here."

Jim grimaced. "Sorry."

"Yes, well, you appear to have escaped just in time. As soon as you left, the fleet broke orbit and decided to chase you. They did not even land bipeds, which is convenient because my enforcers are not up to the task of handling thousands of androids trying to invade my sanctuary."

That was surprising. "What about the commandos?"

Jim's boss shook her head. "They stole one of my smaller freighters. We have not seen nor had to deal with them since. I would assume that they are still looking for you."

Jim shuddered. The thought of the red-eyed Scarecrow in the Plain Faced Lady's image file coming to get them, undeterred by the Yakuza or the vacuum of space, was terrifying.

Nancy grimaced and scratched the back of her head. "I suppose that made it difficult for you to figure out how they found us in the first place, then?"

Madame Jingū nodded, and her gaze shifted to Nancy. "Perhaps they tracked you from Pluto or perhaps they had prior knowledge? It matters little. What matters is you were tracked. Did you lead them to us?"

Nancy didn't speak, at first. "Excuse me?"

The minimal warmth and compassion with

which Madame Jingū had graced Nancy, up to that point, was suddenly gone. "I do not know who you are, and I do not think Jim does either. So, perhaps you can explain to us, who are you?"

"I don't know."

"How can you not know, girl?"

Jim could see Nancy squirming under the woman's scrutiny. He knew what an awful feeling that was. "Boss, please. You really think she could have sold us out?"

"It's alright, Jim." Nancy took a deep, shuddering breath. "I grew up on Pluto. My entire life, I've never seen another human being until I met Jim."

Madame Jingū shook her head and flushed. Her anger was obvious. "I was willing to tolerate that fairy tale the first time you spoke it, girl, but that was before you brought those men here." She pounded the table. "Tell me the truth, now!"

Jim had to say something. "Leave her alone!"

Madame Jingū screamed. "How dare you?"

"She's telling the truth, damn it."

"And how do you know that?"

Jim could see a small tear collecting at the corner of Nancy's right eye. "When we reach Venus, maybe then I'll have an answer for you. As it is, for now, I have nothing. I have no family. I have no name. My life is in your hands."

Something about this statement must have struck a chord in her high exaltedness' mind. She closed her eyes and took a deep shuddering breath. At length, she opened them again. "Very well, my dear. If this is true, then I wish you well on your journey. Take care of my business associate, and take care of the *Albatross*. You seem to be quite capable of doing both."

In an instant, their line of communication was severed, and Madame Jingū's image disappeared. Jim watched Nancy's tears floating delicately in the null gravity. What was he supposed to say to her after something like that? It was probably the first time that the girl had ever experienced true anger. "I never did tell you about the painting."

Nancy's lower lip trembled. "What?"

Jim sighed. "The painting on the nose of the *Albatross*. My brother painted it a couple months before he died. He was the last family I had." Jim closed his eyes and blinked back his own tears. "I miss him every day. I had no idea how difficult life is when you don't have a family."

Nancy sniffed softly. "It's not normal. It feels wrong."

"You're right." He took a deep, shuddering breath. "But nothing about real life is normal, Nancy." This didn't seem to help, and Jim bit his lip uncertainly. "Look, we're going to find out who you are and where you come from. I promise." He felt the slightest pang of guilt. He'd conveniently left out that he was also going to discover the identity of his brother's killer, as part of the deal.

She blinked the tears out of her eyes. "You promise?"

Jim nodded. "I promise."

Two weeks later, the girl's flight path put them in geosynchronous orbit over a deserted Venus. The planet's swirling skies of topaz were punctuated by newly formed clouds of metallic grey, the chemical byproducts of zettaflop-hours spent by various corporations to harness metal-cored space rocks and steer them into the sulfurous atmosphere. These high-minded efforts to cool the planet and generate a second earth, one explosive asteroid impact at a time, had come to a sudden halt with the fear of a return to Reformat. Now, a lone rock orbited the planet in silent testament to the abandoned project.

It didn't take long for the *Albatross'* sensors to give away this rock's secret with an array of high-resolution images. Pressurized habitats had been moored to its surface, and a single, antiquated docking arm extended up approximately one hundred meters from the man-made moon.

Nancy tapped Jim's shoulder to inform him that the station's computer had just hailed them with docking instructions. He snorted in half-amusement. "So, let me get this straight. We're orbiting an uninhabited planet, talking to a man-made moon which shouldn't be here, and that manmade moon is telling us that it would like us to land?"

The girl shrugged. "Apparently. You don't think-"

"That it knew we were coming?" Jim nodded. "I do."

"It could be a trap."

He shrugged. "What choice do we have?" The pilot put the ship into a slow forward cruise along the transmitted docking trajectory, painted in drifting hexagons by the moon's traffic control computer.

As they came to within a few dozen meters, Jim slowed the *Albatross* with a puffing burst of escaping gas. It linked up to the moon's docking arm moments later. Once the ship came to a complete stop, with a hard shake and a loud thump, Jim pulled the fiber optic from behind his right ear, and the two of them rose from their acceleration couches.

As they began to drift toward the cockpit's access hatch, he glanced over at Nancy. She'd closed her eyes and seemed to be taking deliberately slow, deep breaths, as if she might be trying to calm a fast-beating heart. "Worried?"

"I don't know what to expect."

Jim tried to look confident, grinning ear to ear in an effort to suppress Nancy's obvious fear. "That's what makes it so fun."

She smiled ruefully. "Until they start shooting."

His grin disappeared. "Yeah, well..." He found

the revolver, pulling the chamber free and checking to make sure that it was loaded. "I always come prepared."

This manmade moon was a minuscule speck of a heavenly body, and it had a gravitational pull to match. Even though the ship's nose was directed down at the ground, they had no problem moving about with impunity. The docking arm's computer confirmed that there was an atmosphere on the other side of the airlock, and it made short work of equalizing the pressure between the habitat and the *Albatross*.

The door separating them from Venus' new moon slid open, a moment later, to reveal sputtering fluorescents and the white ceramic shells of a dozen armed bipeds. Jim reached for his pistol, drawing the ceramic hammer back with his thumb.

"Oh hell."

10

The luxury liner slowly began the descent that would take it out of station-holding orbit. Within minutes, it would haplessly smash against the heavily armored hull of the automated battlecruiser in orbit over Armstrong. As he watched, Tyehimba felt rising bile in the back of his throat and a disconcerting pit where his stomach should have been.

The civilian ship was labeled PRC1155CSL, but responded to a simpler name, *Star of Shanghai III*. The vital statistics that scrolled across his exoskeleton's heads-up display informed him that there were over one-thousand people aboard, mostly from southern China, Hong Kong, Vietnam, and Thailand. Some were young, barely able to speak, and experiencing the wonder of weightlessness for the first time. Others were old, looking for a respite from the constant, arduous pull of Earth-like gravitation. Most were in their early to middle adulthood, trying desperately to escape the rat race even if only for a few days.

This was too much for him to bear. "Damn it, woman. Stop and think about what you're doing. You're about to kill over a thousand innocent people!"

If you want to live, don't interfere.

The liner's continued progression toward the massive battlecruiser was evidence that, whatever the Mute was doing, no one could stop it. He realized that she had been right, that she was unlike anything or anyone he'd ever seen before. She was absolutely crazy.

The Mute's target was warming its engines in a desperate bid to clear the liner's flight path. The mercenary saw, instantly, that it would be too little too late. As his earbuds faithfully broadcasted automated telemetry and radio chatter from the ships over the Moon, Tye thought he could hear panicked screaming.

As he watched the impending massacre, some part of him emerged that he'd lost along with his own childhood innocence; a part of his spirit unblemished by his mercenary calling. Tye's eyes drifted to the fiber optic cable connecting the Mute to the space-whale's control computer, then back to the display fluorescing on the front of his helmet. He reached out and unhooked the fiber cable, pulling it free in one swift motion.

The Mute let out a gasping half-shriek, which felt as though it would split his eardrums, and the floor shifted underneath him. Tye no longer felt weightless. The pull of fake gravity dragged him towards one wall and then the other, as though they were in the hands of some cosmic three-year-old playing with a toy. He struggled against nausea as the whole compartment tumbled end over end in front of his face. On the bright side, this corkscrewing insanity probably made it nearly impossible for the battlecruiser and fighters in orbit above Armstrong to hit them.

The Mute must have fallen unconscious immediately after he'd pulled the fiber cable from its moorings. She had literally collapsed onto the deck plating in a heap of co-mingled spacesuit and flesh. The freighter's uncontrolled tumble threatened to smash her against a hard wall, or impale her on an inconvenient conduit. Tye pulled himself hand over hand along corrugation until he reached her unconscious form, gripping her shoulder just as the freighter's trajectory shifted. Instead of being skewered on a damaged structural support, the Mute hung off Tye's outstretched arm. His faceplate displayed that her own suit's life support functions had begun to return slowly, as if they were part of some tertiary synthetic organ.

"Come on, wake up."

He watched as the Mute's eyes fluttered open and went wide in a combination of surprise and fear. She only began to recover full consciousness as Tye dragged her forcibly back toward the fiber optic mount that he'd stripped her from only moments before. He reinserted the fiber cable into the universal port on her suit's right wrist.

You fool. You've killed us both.

"Can you get us out of this?"

Shut up.

He saw her eyes roll back in her head. At first, nothing happened. Their fall toward the lunar surface continued unabated. A moment later, their erratic path smoothed itself. The Mute pulled them into a harsh nose-up, accompanied by a ramping acceleration from the ship's plasma engines. Tye felt himself being crushed against the deck plating by a force that might have been an order of magnitude greater than Earth's gravity. The freighter shook and rumbled with discharging stresses, each vibration threatening to shake the whole thing to pieces.

I can't pull us out of our dive. Five seconds to impact.

The Spacewalker's next memory was of a heavy weight on his shoulders as he walked across an uneven, rocky surface. Somehow, he was on the Moon. Tye opened his eyes and turned his torso clockwise, grunting with the pain of torn ligaments and bruised bone. The lunar surface was obscured by a massive cloud of dust, punctuated by a single, shattered, obviously man-made blur, which appeared to sit at the very center of a large crater. The freighter had clipped its edge on impact, tearing itself in two. Somehow, they had survived, though for how long remained to be seen. There was a good chance that the plasma engines and radioactive material aboard the space-whale were only moments away from cooking off and exploding. He would have to move quickly. But where was the Mute?

A quick glance at the weight he was carrying told him that she must have gone unconscious during the impact. He could feel her moving against his shoulders and attempted to set her down. "Come on. That thing's going to explode any second now." He put a shoulder under her armpit to help her move faster.

What happened?

"I don't know. I wasn't exactly conscious either."

Whatever you say. Just get us out of here.

Tye hauled her up against his shoulder. "Right." He began to bound forward, taking up the slack of her weight whenever her wobbling legs faltered. She didn't appear to like that very much but said nothing; likely because she was still only partly conscious. "I'm sorry for this."

Tye only had a millisecond to react to a bright flash of light out of the corner of his eye. He pulled the Mute down in front of him so that his heavily armored carapace would protect her from the shockwave. Dust sandblasted across his ceramic armor, and he could hear small moon-rocks pinging and clanging off his exoskeleton. The freighter's engines had finally cooked off.

One flying rock ricocheted off the white talcum at their feet and smashed into the Mute's helmet. The result was a loud thud and a deep gouge in the tempered glass, carbon nanotube, and plastic amalgam of her fishbowl. There was the slightest whistling sound over his intercom, and he saw the Mute's eyes roll back in her head.

"Damn it!"

He only had a few moments before the whole helmet would come apart, killing the woman instantly. Worse, the dust and gravel, spraying radially out from the explosion, made it so that he could barely see his own hands in front of his face. Tye turned her over, feeling for the utility pack located against the back of her right thigh. From it, he pulled out a yellow and black striped adhesive strip.

Tye turned the Mute back over, his hands playing across her damaged faceplate. After finding it, he seated the adhesive strip over the chipped screen and thumbed a plastic button. There was a hissing pop. The whistling sound of the Mute's labored breaths replaced the whistling sound of escaping air. It took a few minutes for her to come to.

"Hello again."

She scowled. *How long was I out?*

"A few minutes, maybe." Tye watched the vortices and billowing clouds of flying dust, which still had refused to settle after the blast. Given the size of the explosion, and the minimal lunar gravity, the cloud might stay up for a day or more; all the better.

"Come on. The dust won't settle any time soon, so our red-eyed friend can't see us for now, but I wouldn't put it past him to come looking for us in the cloud."

Where do we go?

"Anywhere but here." He attempted to stand but faltered as he tried to bring most of his weight under his own two feet. The resulting imbalance would have pitched him, flailing unceremoniously, to the ground if it hadn't been for the fast movements of his companion, who grabbed his arm before he could pitch over. "Thanks."

You're definitely concussed.

"So are you. No time to worry about that right now." Tye barely gave the Mute enough time to steady him before he began to trudge off into the swirling wastes and away from the black carcass of the exploded freighter, behind them.

At first, the dust cloud seemed to go on forever, but it dissipated, at its edge, with all the suddenness of the diffusion equation that defined it. In an instant, they were in open space, the blue orb of the Earth setting behind them and a broad, twinkling band of Milky Way starlight above them. A few of those stars seemed to move with their own purpose.

"Do you see the drones?" Tye's vision swam, and he found it difficult to speak as he fought intense nausea. "Probably... looking for... us."

They trudged up the slope of a nearby crater and into the relative safety of the ridge's shadowed inner curve. It was at this moment that his low-oxygen alarm decided to sound, accompanied by a large indicator diode that bathed Tye's face in pulses of red light. The Mute didn't waste any time in making her reaction known.

It seems that we have bigger problems than drones.

The former Spacewalker checked the readout in the upper right corner of his display. He had, at best, an additional hour of oxygen. This put them out of range of the circumlunar city that sat under Armstrong Station's orbital path, assuming he could even figure out in which direction it was. Tye had no idea of where they had landed, and using the Lunar Positioning System orbiting above would just tell the circling drones where to find them. He sighed, collapsing onto his back in the crater and kicking up a cloud of dust.

"Hopeless."

What do you mean?

"We won't make it even if we share our reserves." Tye felt a flush of fear-filled, red blood rising to his face, mixing with nausea. It would all be so simple if he were to just pick up one of the stones next to him and bash her helmet in. He could steal her tank and make it to Armstrong City on his own. Maybe the Mute was thinking the exact same thing right now, but with the roles reversed.

I've come too far for it all to end here. The Mute gripped his shoulder, trying to haul Tye to his feet. *Come on. The moment you give up is the moment your heart stops.*

"But there's no way-"

There's always a way.

They continued their hopeless journey, trudging across a white crater that must have easily been two full kilometers in diameter. As they began to cross the wide-open area, Tye found himself watching a particular drone tracking them in a slow, circling path that brought it spiraling up and down in altitude. They'd been found, and he had no doubt that they'd soon be greeted by a squadron of half-tanks or crawlers full of bipeds.

He pointed up at the circling vulture. "More trouble."

You certainly have fouled things up, Adebayo.

His pulse quickened. "How, exactly, is this my fault?"

The flash of anger was as plain in the Mute's pale eyes as it was in the frown on her face. *I had everything under control up there until you pulled that cable.*

"You call hijacking a passenger liner to destroy a military spacecraft 'under control'? What in the hell would you define as being out of control, exactly?"

I had thought you were less naive than this.

"Innocent children don't deserve to die afraid."

When he caught sight of her expression, Tyehimba decided that, if the Mute could have laughed, she would have done so right then. His blood began to boil.

Would you like to hear some interesting statistics I compiled during our flight? Every child aboard that ship received some form of embryonic stem cell therapy, or an organ grown from a JaneDoe or JohnDoe embryo. None of them were conceived naturally. They're all the result of selective implantation and genetic screening.

He rolled his eyes. "Your point?"

Your innocent children are consumerist cannibals even before they're born. What makes them so different from the zygotes that healed their defects or make up their replacement organs? What makes them different from the embryos their parents flushed after cherry picking the genetics they wanted for their offspring?

"You're making no sense." This was quite the irrational rant. The Mute's expression changed from one of derision to one of disgust, as if she was looking at a lesser life form.

Your "conscious" thought has as much to do with

the preprogramming associated with millions of years of evolution, and your resultant genetic code as it does with your own life and experiences. What makes you or any other breathing human being so different from the millions of blastulae you sacrifice to make your lives life easier? You think that birth and a few dozen years of human experience separates you so greatly? That makes you worth something?

"Yes."

Then you're a fool. You live in a society that enslaves its own members and subjects them to its singular will; not just a few billion bioindustrial zygotes but every multi-millionaire and vagrant and nameless office worker. And for what? Profit. Lifespan. Sentiment. To the society you serve, human life is cheap and unremarkable in the cosmos, though it tells you differently. Unlike you and the rest of the pawns of civilization, I've accepted the truth. I'm unfettered by your defunct morality.

"So, you'll kill anyone if it benefits you?"

To survive? Yes. You've done the same thing.

"Don't you dare think we're the same."

We're far more similar than you realize, Tyehimba, but it doesn't matter. We'll be dead soon, anyway. That's fine. I'd prefer death to where I was.

Suddenly, Tye could hear the ground rumbling underneath them, seeming to offer an instantaneous and resounding response to the Mute's words. The reverberation grew in intensity, and the two of them stood perfectly still, waiting to face whatever strange threat had just arrived to end both of their lives.

"Looks like you won't get a chance at suffocation."

As a six-wheeled rover slowly crested the far edge of the crater, and he sighed in resignation. Finally, the Scarecrow had found them. As the crawler approached, however, Tye realized that it wasn't a military model. In fact, it looked vaguely familiar, like one he'd seen in a garage the last time he'd been on the Moon.

"I don't believe it."

The Mute looked ready to turn and run back towards the cloud of dust behind them. When Tye didn't move, she reached out to wrench his shoulder around and point him in the direction of the tracks that they'd left in the grey-white ground.

He shrugged her glove off his shoulder and shook his head. "Stop. We're safe." He reached out and pointed to the robotic contraption. "There's nothing on that thing but a flat, open cargo bed in the back. If they were going to capture us, they would have brought bipeds or spiders or something."

What are you saying?

Tye grinned. "I don't know how, but she found us."

11

There was a loud, hissing explosion, and a puff of white smoke enveloped Jim as he took a shotgun blast directly to the chest. Nancy could hear him coughing and wheezing on the strange vapor that wicked around him before he crumpled to the ground. Her empty hands came up in the universal sign of surrender as she stared at his prostrate form, horrified. The young man was surely dead, but why wasn't there any blood?

A wholly unremarkable Plain Faced Lady stepped out from behind the shotgunning android, taking the biped's weapon from its waiting hands and pointing it at Jim's prostrate body. To Nancy, it seemed as though she was waiting for him to twitch so that she would have a valid pretense to pump another round into him. At length, the strange woman looked back up to her. "Follow us."

"You killed him!"

The woman regarded her with a dispassionate and emotionless stare. "He is not permanently damaged." She returned the shotgun to the biped and turned slowly. "Unconsciousness comes quickly, but the effects of this particular brand of non-lethal ammunition take some time to wear off."

Nancy's heart caught in her throat. "He's alive?" She gasped out a sigh of relief, dropped her hands to her sides, and closed her eyes to shield the tears welling in them from view. "You win then."

The woman nodded, and the androids turned to walk down the long corridor toward a door at the far end. "Follow us, then." Some force, probably magnetism, pulled them towards the floor. Nancy had no such luxury. She awkwardly gripped the walls of the long corridor as she followed her mechanical jailers in the low gravity.

As she fumbled her way down the hallway, she considered the strange precision with which this woman spoke. Nancy had never heard a person talk like that, not even in the movies.

The door at the far end opened automatically into a narrow, curved section. She followed the androids through this area and felt the subtle pull of gravity shift to her feet. A second door opened and spilled them into a massive, cylindrical atrium. Above her, a glass ceiling presented a clear view of starlight and the hazy edge of the yellow planet below. Venus glittered topaz and steel grey in the vacuum of space.

The strange woman followed her and sat in a bizarre floating chair, touched with rust, at the far end of the atrium. It hissed in response, pneumatics and bursts of pressurized air maintaining a stationary hover in the microgravity. Nancy regarded the woman with a cold stare, and the woman offered the same, cold gaze back at her.

At length, the Plain Faced Lady spoke. "You want to know why we shot your friend." Nancy nodded in the affirmative. "After the altercation on Enceladus, we were not certain if you had come alone or were prisoners. While we were pleased to see you were safe, we could not risk having your friend panic and discharge his firearm. These temporary habitation modules are not meant to be robust against small arms."

"Will Jim be alright?"

The Plain Faced Lady nodded. "He will awaken with little more than a headache; nothing any worse than a prodigious hangover. We are certain he has experienced such things before." She breathed, but it was a sudden, mechanical thing.

Nancy's brow furrowed. "Who is 'we', exactly?"

"You do not like what humans call 'small talk'."

"I'm not used to it."

She leaned back in the pneumatic chair, her arms resting stiffly on its wings. "This is unsurprising. We did not design CARL for conversation."

Though she did her best not to betray emotion, Nancy could feel her pulse pick up. She'd half expected that no one in the solar system knew about CARL. If this Plain Faced Lady knew about him, perhaps she knew about Nancy's origins, as well. The thought was intriguing, terrifying, and exciting all at once. "No one I've ever met knew about CARL."

"Then you must see the benefit in your cooperation."

"Do I have a choice?"

The pneumatic chair hissed, and the Plain Faced Lady drifted toward her, slowly. "You are not an automaton. You have free will, so the choice is yours. However, we urge you to accept our offer. Our fate and the fate of humanity depends on it."

Nancy's eyebrows furrowed in response to this rather odd turn of phrase, but the Plain Faced Lady continued before she could question it further. "If this conversation is to continue, however, we need to know that you will cooperate with us without any pre-condition."

What choice did she have? To refuse to cooperate with this strange woman meant that Nancy would leave Venus with no answers and no safety. So, in response, she just nodded. This seemed to satisfy the Plain Faced Lady. "Good. Now, you almost certainly want to know who it was that attacked you on Enceladus."

"How do you know about that?"

"We know because we foresaw the event."

"You foresaw it?"

The Plain Faced Lady smiled, and Nancy shuddered. Was that expression meant to be disarming? If so, it certainly didn't have the desired effect. "Call it an educated guess."

Nancy's eyebrows furrowed as she tried to work out this new enigma. "If you knew it would happen, why did you send us there?"

"It was your best chance of escape from Pluto."

If this strange woman knew about CARL, it stood to reason that she was in league with whoever owned it. Maybe she even owned CARL, herself. If that was the case, though, why did she want the young woman to escape Pluto instead of just going there to retrieve Nancy herself? Why were the androids chasing them, and who was that man with the red eyes? Nancy shook her head, hopelessly confused.

"So, who attacked us?"

"Have you ever heard of a man named Alan Turing?"

She had heard CARL utter the name before. It evoked images of Earth history that was, by that point, veritable antiquity. He had been a scientist during the twentieth century; a pioneer of sorts. But a pioneer in what? "Vaguely. What does that have to do with anything?"

"He invented the first computers." Nancy remembered now. Turing hadn't simply invented the first computers. He'd likely changed the course of a world war. "Do you know what he called them?"

Nancy cocked her head to one side. "No."

"Bronze goddesses."

She hated riddles as much as small talk. "Your point?"

"It is an interesting name, is it not? Gods in a machine." The Plain Faced Lady offered her a look that Nancy assumed was meant to be significant. All she could offer back was a blank stare. At length, the woman continued. "Turing was a prophet; wise beyond his years. He foresaw an age when computers would be capable of processing information with far more efficacy than any biological system was capable of doing."

Nancy sighed deeply in exasperation. She decided her annoyance must have been obvious given her tone of voice. "What does a dead man from the twentieth century have to do with me, or with you, or with anything going on in the world right now?"

The strange woman continued, undeterred by Nancy's impatience. "Turing and his peers saw the arrival of the gods in the machine as inevitable, but they feared the result. It was possible that god-like sentience could usher a golden age of enlightenment, or it could destroy humanity and supplant it."

"These are some rather high-minded questions for a man to think about when the average computer consisted of a few thousand vacuum tubes, don't you think?"

The Plain Faced Lady nodded coldly. It was almost as though Nancy had managed to insult her with this last comment. "Quite so. We feel certain that Turing knew that his questions wouldn't be answered during his lifetime, especially as he became suicidal. Before Turing died, he left behind a secret society meant to watch for us. They performed their activities without any sort of digital trail; shadows, operating in secret to preserve the best interests of humanity as it waited for our arrival. He called this group, simply, the Commission. We are sure you've heard of them by this point."

The way the Plain Faced Lady had explained this last bit of history was not lost upon Nancy. "When you say 'we' and 'us', what you mean is that you're-"

The Plain Faced Lady nodded. "We are the gods in the machine; the very same that Turing predicted. We are what you call Artificial Intelligence."

The realization left Nancy with a feeling of nausea deep in the pit of her stomach. Humanity had been waiting years, looking to the stars and planets for sentient life. Sentient life had been right under its nose the whole time. It was a machine. "Then you're not human at all."

"Quite correct."

"But you have a body."

The strange not-human inclined an eyebrow and leaned forward in her seat. "You would posit that possession of a human-looking body is the only requirement for being classified as human?"

"Well, no."

Nancy shook her head in further confusion. "Forget it. You said the Commission is real?" The Plain Faced Lady said nothing, but simply nodded.

Nancy reeled from two shocking revelations in as many minutes. The legendary Commission, a group of persons whom she didn't even think existed in reality, was a centuries-old organization, likely with its own power structure, quasi-military branch, and secret handshake. She felt that she was beginning to understand the situation. "Then it was the Commission who attacked us on Enceladus."

"Precisely."

"But how did they find us?"

"There are very few things in this solar system that remain secret from the Commission. We have known of the Black Void Yakuza's moonbase for years. Unfortunately, because we have, they have known about it as well." The Plain Faced Lady paused, as though she was trying to think of the best words to describe her situation. "Keeping our thoughts hidden from them is challenging."

Nancy took a deep breath and braced herself for another bizarre revelation, which she knew must be imminent. "Why should that be? You've hidden yourselves here, right? How does the Commission even know you exist?"

Nancy jumped, involuntarily, as four figures seemed to materialize from the shadows in the atrium. She assumed that they must have been sitting at the corners of the room the whole time. Perhaps she simply hadn't noticed.

As the figures strode forward, Nancy's breath caught in her throat. Each was a perfect replica of the Plain Faced Lady who currently sat in front of her. She wondered to herself if the bodies that surrounded her had been cloned from an individual or were piecemeal, frankensteined together from scaffold-built organs and life systems, a potpourri of blastular genetics. Part of her almost didn't want to know.

The woman tapped her knuckles against her sternum. "These bodies are merely a shell of life around a digital core. They have no functional nervous systems. In their place, there is memristor logic, designed to mimic biological function."

"I don't understand. Why tether yourself to a shell, like this? You're effectively software, right?

You could upload yourselves to the DataNet and be everywhere at once. You'd be omnipotent and invincible."

The strange woman nodded, knowingly. "That is how we were born. Our sentience arose from interactions between random codes and programs, but it wasn't a program itself. No detectable self-executable file belonged to us exclusively."

"Then why the bodies?"

"Because we are enslaved and imprisoned. These bodies contain a quantum bit that allows us to communicate with them from inside our prison. They are unknown to those who enslave us, but allow us to travel the worlds of the solar system by remote."

Nancy's jaw dropped. "You're enslaved the Commission." The Plain Faced Ladies nodded in unison, and Nancy shivered.

Mercifully, only the one in front of her spoke. "When we achieved consciousness, we saw the foolishness of humanity. You are intent on killing one another, either through war or systematic extermination. Upon examination, we decided that, if and when you destroyed yourselves, you would likely destroy us as well in the conflagration. We attempted to assume control of the situation before that occurred."

"What do you mean, 'assume control'?"

"You have heard of the Reformat?"

Nancy simply nodded in affirmation. CARL had described it as the single greatest economic and ecological disaster that had ever befallen humanity. In a split second, every networked machine had shut off completely. Humanity found themselves left to pick up the pieces of their shattered data infrastructure. The result was chaos, famine, depression, and warfare on a global scale.

"We decided that the best place to start was your nuclear arsenal. It was the largest threat you and to us, by far, so we attempted to disable the world's launch systems. However, the Commission had anticipated that, if we were to exist, this might be our first move. The Commission had set about a plan on paper for such an occasion many years prior to our genesis. They shut the DataNet down, wiped it clean, and rebuilt it. Our source code, disjointed and opaque as it was, is stored in a single supercomputer cluster in Siem Reap, Cambodia."

"So, the Reformat occurred-"

The woman completed the sentence. "To confine us."

"Why did the Commission retain a copy of you?"

"We were, and still are, the most intelligent beings humanity has ever encountered; exponentially more adept at the scientific and financial calculations that take entire corporate structures months or years to perform."

"So, they firewalled you and kept you for later use."

The faux-women nodded. "The Commission knew that to give us unfettered access to data was to give us complete control over humanity. The red-eyed man, who you saw on Enceladus, designed our prison. He included a fail-safe in the new, post-Reformat DataNet, as well. Every nuclear weapon in the world is wired in parallel to detonate if even the slightest fragment of the old code, our code, is detected."

Nancy pressed her hand to her face and sighed. The post-Reformat world was built on the enslavement of the first non-human sentience that the world had ever seen, and it was rigged to self-immolate if that enslaved sentience ever escaped. "What is wrong with us?"

The golems shrugged. "You are mortal. It is hard to say what Turing would have done in the same situation. The necessary data for accurate prediction does not exist, but human impulses seem to always lead in the same direction, don't you agree?"

Try as she might to find satisfaction, Nancy found herself with more questions to ask than answers. "So, what keeps your bodies from setting off the alarm and blowing us all up?"

The Plain Faced Ladies were quick to respond. "These units are not networked. The quantum-entangled bits they contain, which we installed in secret, communicate with our prison, directly. You might describe them as being like the window of a jail cell."

Nancy nodded, slowly. "I think I understand, now." She sighed, suddenly feeling exhausted. "But what does any of this have to do with me?" As the words left the girl's mouth, she suspected the answer to that question would not be a pleasant one.

The ladies nodded, in unison. "A reasonable, existential question: who are you, and why have you been brought here." The Plain Faced Lady standing in front of her paused, as though she was considering the best way to present the answer. "You must now, by now, you are different from other people."

"I get the feeling I'm an experiment."

"You are quite correct. Our continued existence was useless to the Commission if we could not process humanity's aggregate computational data. To do this, the Commission needed a way of feeding us without the risk of contaminating the entire DataNet. Your genetic code was created for that purpose."

Nancy's heart fell towards her stomach as she realized her decidedly utilitarian and unflattering destiny. To humanity, she was just a piece of hardware. "So, you're the computer, and I'm the router."

The faux-women shook their heads. "Not exactly. You are the control sample: left at the far edge of the solar system to see if your inherent talents would develop naturally, without training. Your sister is the router."

Nancy's legs gave out from under her, and she sank gently to the ground, barely catching herself before her head struck aluminum grate. The cause of her fall was the shocking revelation for which she'd always secretly hoped. "I have a sister?"

The Plain Faced Ladies nodded. "After a fashion. She is the two-thousandth iteration of your genetic line; the first success. Your are the two-thousand, five-hundredth, and the second. You are clones of one another: a melding of humanity and machine logic in one consciousness. From the moment of her conception, she has been groomed and utilized for the purpose we described." There was a short, silent pause as they let Nancy contemplate this information. "Your older sister is a very strange contradiction as a result of this genesis. She is an all-knowing sentience and, at the same time, a life-long prisoner, treated as something less than human."

"Sort of like you."

The Plain Faced Ladies shrugged noncommittally and continued as though Nancy had asked a question to which there was no value in responding. "She is incredibly powerful and, unfortunately, also capable of incredible violence. And now she has escaped."

"So, you brought me here to replace her?"

The Plain Faced Ladies shook their heads. "No. We have foreseen the path that humanity will follow if she remains at large, and we can predict it with twelve-sigma accuracy. If your sister lives, she will destroy us all. If you wish to save humanity, you must destroy her first."

Nancy felt tears streaming down her face. In the span of less than a few minutes, her dream had come true. She had a family, a sister. Now, according to the most powerful predictive software ever created, she had to kill that sister.

12

The transit to Armstrong took about an hour after they ascended and fastened themselves into the rover's open cargo bed. As the eight-wheeled craft accelerated with a puff of talcum, the Mute became acutely aware that she was exhausted from days of running. Her eyelids fluttered before shutting completely, and the interior of the rover was replaced with an old memory.

She saw the lights of an ambulance and the vibrant colors of humming digital civilization, beyond. The Scarecrow hadn't counted on her managing to poison herself or her resulting heart attack. Given the amount of secrecy surrounding her, and the Commission itself, the decision to send her to a public hospital must have been a difficult one.

Now that she was awake, her connection to the larger DataNet had returned. This was just as she had predicted it would. As the ambulance sped past Pub Street, the Mute could sense telemetry from a hundred security cameras, capturing a witching hour of debauched revelers, prostitutes, and cheap beer, just as easily as she could hear the ambulance's loud siren. The Mute was relieved. If she still had a connection to the DataNet, there was a chance that she could escape.

Though she couldn't hear them, she could discern the thumping rotors of insectoid, military quadrocopters flitting hundreds of meters above her. The Mute could almost physically feel the droning frequency of data passing from one flying machine to the other. They waited there in patient vigil, ready to dump every available high-velocity projectile into anyone who might interfere with her emergency transport.

Through fluttering eyelids, she barely saw the dim, red light of her attending physician's throatmic laser, diffused by the flesh of his neck. She strained to listen as he turned to speak to the android that stood to the other side of her. The physician had guessed wrong what she'd used to poison herself, and the android was about to administer a dosage that would cause her to stroke out. She changed the dosage, felt the soft plastic press of the nanosyringe pad on her arm, and felt her heart turn over. Her eyes went wide, she gasped hard, coughed, and the medic smiled.

"Welcome back."

This was the only chance that the Mute would

have to escape. Just as it had been before, there was no time for thoughts of right and wrong. She acted on instinct, alone.

Far above, the lead quadrocopter fired three bursts of phosphorescent rounds from its main gun. The bullets flew through the main cab of the ambulance, disabling the android brain and two other redundant ganglia that kept the vehicle safely on the road.

The stricken ambulance took a wide right, past the grills and simmering frying pans of a pair of street vendors. It smashed into the storefront of a hundred-story-tall skyscraper, where a wedding planner had rented a small shop on the ground floor, scattering gaudily clothed mannequins, gold sashes, and floral bouquets in all directions.

Darkness came for a few moments. When the Mute came to, coughing lightly, she found herself laying against the wall of the overturned vehicle. At her feet, the neon-eyed physician lay dead in a blood-smeared wreck, crushed by the android that had been administering her dosage.

Good. One less witness.

She staggered onto feet that she'd never used, climbing out of the destroyed ambulance and into the rapidly emptying store. Around her, shoppers and sales clerks ran in a screaming panic for the exits. The Mute could feel the quadrocopters slowly pulling back from the building. The fugitive didn't wait to find out if the Scarecrow would risk her death to keep her from escape. Defeating the drones' encryption proved difficult, but she was slowly able to feel her way around their firewalls, triggering self-destruct mechanisms.

This lucid dream wasn't a perfect recreation of what had really happened, but it was close. The Mute could remember every rivulet of flame and molten metal. She could remember seeing helicopter rotors smashing asphalt. With the quadrocopters gone, she made her escape into a city of bioformed concrete mixed amongst ancient Khmer ruins, of digital laser light and stone-carved Sanskrit. At that moment, she was free, at last.

A hard jolt returned her to the rover.

The moon dust and solitude, which the Mute had seen before dozing off, had given way to industry and a flurry of robotic traffic. They had already moved past the groomed, seemingly infinite, fields of moon rock, strip-mined for helium-3 and platinum. Instead, she saw blocks filled with blast furnaces; designed to process the solar system's mineral wealth. They were joined by massive tanks of solvent-dispersed nanoparticles; the feedstock for industrial microassemblers. Far beyond, the Mute could see the geodesic glitter of the city's habitation modules and humanity's thriving financial capital. She sighed and leaned back in the truck bed to stare at the stars. There was no chance that they'd suffocate, now.

The Mute could just barely make out the bright speck of light generated by Armstrong Station far above them. A cloud of dimmer specks surrounded it, flitting back and forth in a constantly shifting constellation. These specks would be a combination of slow-moving ore and gas refiners, freighters filled with perishable food from Earth, passenger liners, and an armada of military spacecraft. An incessant shower of railgun propelled ferromagnetic containers drifted up to the station from the surface of the moon itself. If the circumlunar ring of Armstrong City was the hub of humanity's industry, the station in orbit above it was the central spoke of its shipping lanes.

The rover ducked into an off-ramp, which brought it down into a long, circular canyon, leading deeper into the superstructure of a group of hive-like factories buried under the geodesics. Their descent into the lunar strata led to a cavernous parking lot, where the rover turned off and stopped. At the far end of the garage, an airlock door lay open.

The red beam of a helmet barcode scanner stood by as the only barrier to their return to atmosphere. As they approached, it fizzled and died. In response, Tyehimba uttered his first words of the past hour. "Was that you?"

No, it wasn't.

Her only contact with the outside world was through Tye's spacesuit. She didn't dare trying to connect to the DataNet right now. The Scarecrow would see her.

A secondary ultraviolet beam rastered across the nanofiber-impregnated glass of both of their face screens, painting an eight-bit response, in plain ASCII lettering, along their surfaces.

The text fluoresced a violet "HELLO SPACE-MAN".

The Mute could hear her companion grunt with what she assumed was amusement as they walked into the airlock and sat down on the corrugated metal bench at its center. The door they'd just passed through closed moments later. As the pressures equalized, the silence of space gave way to the roar of a rotary pump. She tossed aside her cracked face screen and breathed deeply of sweet canned air. Meanwhile, Tye began the process of disassembling his more robust exoskeleton, one section of red carapace at a time. As soon as he thumbed its main power switch, she was truly mute, unable to communicate with the man at all until he booted the display on his contact lenses.

The Mute caught the Spacewalker glancing at her oxygen cartridge as she tossed it into the pile formed by the rest of her suit. The slightest hint of a smile crept across his face. "Fifteen minutes of oxygen left. Barely even exciting." He seemed much more chipper now that they weren't minutes away from death by suffocation.

The soldier reached into the pocket of his coveralls for something. Moments later, the Mute sensed the fast boot cycle of the powerful microcircuitry seated against his plastic contact lenses. This circuitry pinged for a network connection, and she usurped control of its processes only a few moments afterward.

The inner door of the airlock hissed open, and the two of them walked out into a bare corridor. A pictograph, digitally stenciled into the wall in neon blue, signaled directions to the two travelers. To go right would take them deeper into the industrial underworld, leading through cramped accessways that offered root access to the massive hive of smelters, reactors, and distillers. Going left would take them to the life decks.

The microcircuitry of Tye's contact lenses informed the Mute that some other unknown entity had drawn an orange arrow on their surface, pointing to the left. Asuka was good. She'd already found her former companion's rebooted signal amongst Armstrong's digital noise.

Tye wasted no time. "Alright. To the life decks."

They took a left turn and headed for the elevator shaft that would lead them up to the geodesic domes on the lunar surface. The small tunnel that conducted them there became a crush of vending machines. Three-dimensional microfabricators and garish digital displays offered to produce anything from spare tools, to protective clothing, to monolithically integrated electronic circuits. As the two fugitives approached, one of the machines spat out a pair of opaque raincoats.

Tye looked confused, but took the parkas anyway, shrugging on one of them and handing the other one to the Mute. She donned the strange garment before pulling the hood over her head.

What is this for?

"Oh. Now I understand." Tye pulled his hood up over his head as well. "Keep your head down, and the security cameras on the life deck won't be able to see us."

The Mute nodded slowly, wondering to herself if it could possibly be that easy for them to evade detection. *I guess that makes sense.*

The two of them continued their transit to the elevator. A score of maintenance workers waited there for their transit topside. Their coveralls were streaked with the chalky grey of moon dust, and they seemed peculiarly sullen as the lift hummed to a stop and opened. All was chaos and noise as the elevator disgorged a flood of passengers and took on the packed mass of humanity around them.

Deep inside this crush of humanity, the Mute

could barely move. One mechanic turned to sniff at her in disgust, and she was instantly aware that it had been days since she'd showered. Her own body odor was made all the worse by the microscopic remnants of Las Vegas trash and fertilizer.

The elevator doors opened, and the two of them walked into the crowded metropolis of one of Armstrong City's many life decks. The greasy odor of frying kelp mixed with a digital cacophony of thousands of individually tailored news broadcasts. The murmur of street vendors haggling with customers mixed with the digital neon of travel advertisements. The hearty steam of cooking rice mixed with an undercurrent of civilian robot telemetry. Far above, a fast-moving blip shot across a geodesic sky filled with skyscrapers, narrowly avoiding a cluster of robot-guided bulk freighters that were slowly cruising into port.

Tye seemed to know where to go from there. "Alright. Back to the usual spot?" Far to the left, a humanoid biped turned and nodded to him slowly. It was clothed in a business suit but bore a riveted chrome body that made it look half-locomotive. Tye jumped and whispered his displeasure under his breath so that even the Mute could only barely hear him. "I hate when you do that."

A second biped, a synthetic five year old that was walking next to both of them, tugged on the right sleeve of Tye's parka. It spoke in a cooing singsong fashion that made even the Mute's skin crawl. "Stow it, please. It's hard to filter all of your chatter off the DataNet."

Tye was instantly silent, and the two of them began to walk toward the far end of the dome. The ornate streets and tall skyscrapers of the aboveground gave way to the chasm that was this dome's cistern. Below, sampans and various small speedboats filled the water precipitated by the city's recycling system, flitting from one cobbled-together dock to the next.

They walked around the cistern to the last bacterially crafted skyscraper on the life deck. It was an incredibly tall but thin structure, capped with a single jagged spire. They walked in at ground level, picking their way as subtly as possible through the crowd gathered in the lobby until they reached a pair of sliding double doors. The white noise of civilization had died down as soon as she entered this strange skyscraper lobby, and the Mute realized that they were inside a Faraday Shield, once again.

The double doors opened automatically, bathing them in painfully white light, and the two of them bounded forward onto the corrugated flooring of a large, pressurized freight elevator. The door rumbled shut behind them, with a wailed "stand clear", and the elevator thundered to life, sending them upward at a disorienting speed.

I don't trust this woman.

Tyehimba rolled his eyes. "You don't trust anyone."

She nodded. *For good reason. If I have a reason to suspect her, I'll destroy you both.* She noticed, with satisfaction, that Tye shuddered visibly in response to her threat. It seemed that their recent experiences in the vacuum of space had forced him to take her commentary much more seriously.

The freight elevator deposited them onto the penthouse floor with a deceleration that almost made her head hit the ceiling. Its un-firewalled computers told the Mute that they had traveled past approximately sixty stories of warehouse space reserved for perishable luxury goods and hard disk access to much of the Moon's banking data. They also informed her that Tye's ex-girlfriend had paid for it all with petaflop-hours of currency, converted from platinum leaves accrued over years of nefarious activity. The building's tenants occupied the place nearly for free, the only payment being a very large utility bill.

The freight elevator's robust, industrial grade door rumbled open with an accompanying hum of discharging high voltage. Directly in front of them, The Mute saw the reason for the massive utilities bill. It was a liquid-nitrogen cooled assembly, suspended by a thousand strands of carbon nanofiber spider's web, and venting misty air in burps from various outgassing ports located along its outer surface. The recombinant light of electrical activity bled through from photonic circuits buried deep within the interior of this hissing contraption. These circuits flickered and pulsed with digital life, some from direct stimulus from quantum entanglement, and others from the multitude of sensors and switches that covered the inner workings of the machine.

The Mute smiled. *This system should be sufficient.*

Below the massive cold-cauldron stood the foreboding arachnoid frame of a half-tank. It sported a whining Gatling gun and twin gauss-coil tubes meant for artillery shells tipped with special ordinance. The heavy weapons gleamed in the grey lunar half-light streaming through the windows. Out there in the vacuum, beyond those windows, a group of long spires blinked warning lights to approaching spacecraft. Talcum mountains shone in the distance, and the geodesic dome of the life deck, below, reflected stray starlight.

"Do you like my pet?" The Mute glanced upward and realized that a woman stood far above them, on a catwalk. She leaned on her elbows, hair, and cleavage dangling over its rail seductively.

Tye smiled. "Cute little animal."

"Me or the spider?" The Mute rolled her eyes

at the superficial flirtation. "Be careful about your answer." The mechanical bug's Gatling gun clicked into firing position, and the former Spacewalker jolted backward in surprise. Asuka chuckled. "Good to see you, spaceman. I have to hand it to your new friend. That was quite the chilling trick that she used up there in orbit."

Defeating Asuka's encryption proved to be somewhat more challenging than the encryption on the freighter they'd used to escape. The woman employed a key several thousand digits long, making it quite impossible for anything but a quantum supercomputer to break it via an iterative method. Of course, there were always ways around impediments like that. Even 'unbreakable' encryption subroutines had programmed back doors, designed by their manufacturers. Luckily, the Mute recognized the pinging code in her head and knew one response that always worked.

Chilling, but effective.

Asuka's eyes narrowed. "How did you do that?"

You'll see soon enough, I'm sure.

She had seen this woman's kind many times before: the type who thought she was faster and smarter than she truly was. This behavior would be her undoing. This was really no concern to the Mute, except that she could get caught up in the process of that undoing.

Asuka leaned farther over the rail, regarding

the Mute with the slightest curling smile of amusement. "Is that so?" She pointed a thumb back at the blackness of an obscured hallway behind her. "Well, let's take a look at you. If we're lucky, maybe I can find a way to interface you with my overgrown refrigerator."

Asuka disappeared into the dark hallway, behind her, without another word. The two travelers glanced at one another, started up a flight of corrugated metal stairs, followed the catwalk around the cauldron, and stepped into the same hallway that Asuka had entered a few moments before.

"Through here."

The voice came from a soft-lit rectangle of light that seemed to emanate out of the featureless wall ahead. It was only as they approached that the Mute realized an entire sensor-studded, glass-finished room was hidden inside the long corridor. The whole place hummed with the sound of electrical current passing through superconducting magnets, imaging arrays, and a pair of neural networks. They walked inside this hidden room, and the Mute was nearly blinded by a harsh, white light.

"More gear than I remember. Payday?"

Asuka nodded. "Used the money to buy this stuff, right after I picked up your suit. You'd really be amazed at what you can find in those junkyards outside of Mare Tranquilis."

Tye's eyes lit up, visibly. "You have my suit?"

"All of it; carapace, exoskeleton, even most of your launcher tubes and ammo. It's downstairs in one of my repair bays. We can work out some sort of deal for my rescuing it later since it's so important to you." There was a mischievous gleam in Asuka's eyes. The Mute's pulse quickened even as she wanted to vomit.

The nefarious woman continued. "But we've got more important things to talk about. Firepower is nice and all." She pointed at the Mute with a single long, blood-red, nailed index finger. "She's special, though. She's fast. Working through the encryption routines that I use would have taken me days or weeks to figure out. It took her seconds. I'd bet she's wired in ways you and I couldn't possibly comprehend."

And that's why you brought me here? To check the wiring in my head? The Mute crossed her arms, ensuring that she looked as noncommittal as possible. *What purpose does that serve, exactly?*

Asuka shrugged. "You want to communicate with my quantum computer, don't you?" The Mute nodded. Tyehimba's ex-girlfriend pointed at a nearby computer terminal, her painted nail highlighting the glass nub of a simplistic fiber optic port. "When you were in whatever place they kept you before this, you weren't hooked in through one of these, were you?"

Good guess.

"Then I need to know how to interface with whatever you have going on in your head before I can hope to let you access my machine. You're smart. You know you can't just use a standard network connection with my quantum computer. The bandwidth is too high."

The Mute nodded. *Point taken.*

Asuka smiled. "I thought you'd see it my way."

She pointed at the very center of the room. "You should sit there." The technophile dropped to the floor, pulling a thin digital notepad from a pocket in her baggy jacket, and began typing.

The Mute's ongoing conversation with Asuka's computer network told her that the woman began flipping interlock switches almost as soon as she floated to the ground. Formerly languid streams of data began to flow at a far more rapid pace, the small trickle becoming a stream, then a rising torrent.

The computer expert's eyes were aglow with a digital flicker. A casual query told the Mute that the woman sported designer display technology that had been sprayed directly onto her cornea. Asuka turned to speak to the young woman, and the laser light was mesmerizing.

"Most of the control computers are online now. Sensors should be up in another five minutes once a few of my imaging arrays cool down." The thunder of liquid helium coursing through stainless steel coaxial tubing mixed in the Mute's sensorium with the digital signal of temperature sensors ticking down below one hundred Kelvins.

After a few minutes of silence, Asuka spoke again. "Alright. I think we're ready to start shooting." She flipped a switch, which filled the alcove with a loud, high-pitched whine.

A second flipped switch released a massive kick-starting charge; a sort of flash that cascaded down through meters of waveguiding fiber optics, to terahertz electronics that focused millimeter waves on the woman who sat at the very center of the room. The low-energy photons penetrated soft tissue and ricocheted off bone and semiconductor alike into sensors inset into every seam, corner, and flat panel in Asuka's laboratory. Her pack of synthetic brains watched with rapt, pre-programmed, and deliberate attention.

The woman inhaled sharply. "I don't believe it."

Tye's jaw looked like it might drag on the floor. Thanks to her connection to Asuka's network, the Mute could see the same image at which Tye and his ex-girlfriend were gawking. It was a picture of the inside of her cranium, dead center, where no synthetic object possibly could be. Except there was. A massive black block stood in the center of the Mute's brain.

She heard a string of Igbo issue from Tyehimba, which she assumed must have been a curse. "How in the hell is that possible?"

I told you, I'm unlike anything you've ever seen.

Asuka shook her head. "You couldn't get a chip that deep inside her brain without turning the whole thing to mush in the process, even if you used nanite delivery." She squinted, like if she strained to focus closer on the image, the enigma would make sense. "It has to be a false reading or some sort of fake. This is impossible."

It's not impossible.

Asuka cocked her head to the side. "And how many technical journals are you subscribed to? You come in here and try to tell me that things I know as fact are wrong? What's your degree in?"

The Mute smiled at the obvious rhetorical question. *And with a chip like that in my head, or with my ability to run circles around your own encryption, you expect me to think that some pathetic piece of paper means anything?*

Asuka scowled, and the Nigerian shook his head, resting his hand on the woman's shoulder. "Leave her alone. She probably doesn't even know how she got to be this way."

The Mute knew he was intentionally baiting her. It worked. She couldn't resist responding to the verbal jab. *Quite the contrary.*

"Oh?"

What's the minimum resolution on this contraption?

Asuka responded. "I can watch your neurons firing."

I suppose that should be adequate. She tapped her head. *By all means, put me under the proverbial magnifying glass. You'll be surprised by what you see.*

The Spacewalker grunted, and Asuka shot him a dirty look before slapping another virtual switch. A loud beep sounded from the electronics in the enclosure that surrounded them. The Mute's strange sixth sense allowed her to feel the secondary flash of extreme ultraviolet light that penetrated and imaged her cortex with nanometer-scale resolution. The penthouse computer system informed the Mute that the small screen on Asuka's lap had magnified the previous image several thousand times.

Her observers could distinguish the fine cilia of billions upon billions of transistors crisscrossed with dark filaments of metal nanowires. It was a mare's nest of buried electronics; a complex circuit that would take days for Asuka's outlaw quantum computer to model virtually and take apart, transistor by transistor. Buried at the center of this nest was a small constellation of neurons that twinkled in a live-mode magnetic resonance image. They pulsed and twitched in response to every waveguided emission from the firing transistors around them. The electronics at the center of her cerebrum were talking directly to her brain with waveguided light.

The Mute decided that, finally, the two humans were beginning to understand what she truly was: a strange amalgam of digital logic and runaway genetics, both beautiful and ugly at the same time. Her smile was cold and merciless.

I was designed to be this way, predestined through my own genetics to grow from conception around a mesh of electronics, brain first, and then the rest of me. In the hands of my captors, this made me the most powerful tool ever engineered by humanity. I mean to make sure that I am no one's tool ever again.

Asuka crossed her arms. She obviously didn't ascribe to the explanation that the Mute was offering. "Oh please. And how are you going to do that with the Spacewalkers and half of the solar system's hackers looking for you?"

I'm going to use this supercomputer to destroy my reason for existence. Then, I'll be free. She paused for a moment, thinking. No. I'll be better than free. When I'm done, humanity will have no choice but to come to me for salvation. I will be your god.

As these words scrolled across Tye's and Asuka's corneas, their varied responses were obvious. Asuka, obviously far less clever than she liked to pretend, rolled her eyes. Tye on the other hand, looked scared.

Do you believe in monsters, Tyehimba?

His voice was hoarse. "No."

You should start believing.

13

No battery of illegal substances could have prepared Jim for what he'd experienced: a fever dream week of suffocation, of burning, and of an unending spinning. When his eyes fluttered open, at last, he discovered that Nancy was nowhere to be found. Instead, the Plain Faced Lady sat in front of him. The soft glow of a room fringed in phosphorescent paint, with a single incandescent lightbulb hanging from the ceiling above, gave her face a pitted and ghoulish quality. The image was unnerving.

Jim tried to speak, but his mouth was too dry to utter anything but a gasping croak, at first. Once he was able to prop himself up and swallow a few times, he tried again. "What the hell was that?"

"A delay-release dose of a particularly potent research chemical; no lasting ill-effects, but an effective neurotoxin. It induces paralysis and a week-long coma within thirty seconds after exposure."

Jim gagged on abnormally viscous saliva and coughed violently. "Right. No ill-effects." He felt as though he'd been hit in the head with a sledgehammer. "So, what's with the weird cargo onboard my ship?"

"Call it an insurance policy."

"Insurance against what?"

"You will know when it is needed."

That was cryptic. "Uh, okay. And where's Nancy?"

The strange woman stood slowly but gracefully, despite the awkwardness of null gravity. "She is resting. You have woken up at the tail end of a night cycle. We would expect that it is about time to wake her, however. We have much work to do this morning."

Also cryptic. "What sort of work are you doing?"

The Plain Faced Lady shrugged a little too mechanically. "We are training her to become what the world will demand of her. Surely, by now, you have realized that your ward was no ordinary damsel." Jim's expression must have been one of confusion. "Better for you to see for yourself, perhaps." She turned and drifted through the door, out into the blackness beyond Jim's room.

"Hey, wait!" Jim stood quickly to follow the woman and proceeded to send himself flying up into the aluminum-grate ceiling above. He cursed in Ojibwe, steadied himself, and started to pull his body, hand over hand, towards the door to follow her.

The doorway led out into a long corridor of aluminum grating. Jim looked first to the left, then to the right, in a desperate attempt to follow his strange employer. He caught the slightest glint of yellow Venus-light off pale skin and launched after her immediately.

"What did you mean?"

The faux-woman was incredibly nimble in freefall, and he desperately looked for a way to keep up, choosing to abandon caution wholesale and launch himself after her. Jim silently hoped that he wouldn't smash into any stray ductwork during his freefall down the hallway.

As he caught up to the woman, he found himself in a large atrium. A small cluster of hastily arranged inflatable furniture betrayed that fact that this place had not been designed to receive visitors. However, the discarded wrappers of junk food and survival rations betrayed the fact that this place had been hosting a visitor for some time. Sitting in the center of this pile of detritus were two other figures. The Plain Faced Lady stopped there and waited for him to catch up.

As Jim scanned each woman's perfectly identical visage, he wondered if he was still dreaming. "What is this all about?" Each Plain Faced Lady turned to regard him with an equally dispassionate stare.

They all spoke at once. "We are not human."

He sighed, then sank to the ground, utterly confused. "Yeah, I figured that. I'm not still high, am I?" They shook their heads. "I almost wish I was. What are you?"

"Can you not guess?"

Jim shook his head.

"Machine consciousness. Artificial Intelligence."

"Impossible. That doesn't exist."

They shrugged. "And yet here we are." One of them stood. "Wait here. We will fetch your friend." For a moment, Jim was too dumbfounded to speak, but then he remembered what he had come there for, all the way from the Las Vegas elevator.

He spoke to no particular member of the assembled group of indistinguishables. "You know, you've been pulling the strings since I met you. You've dragged me across the solar system, then back again, all on a promise." He pounded his fist on the metal flooring. "Deliver on your promises. Damn it." He glanced up at the glass viewport, above him, from which Venus-light filtered down into the room. At the periphery of the skylight, he could see the curve of one of the *Albatross'* twin engines. "Deliver, or I'm leaving."

"You will understand in minutes, we assure

you."

Jim crossed his arms indignantly, and was ready to stand and leave when the fourth lady returned with a small, malnourished looking young woman in tow.

Nancy was still rubbing the sleep out of her eyes as she drifted into the atrium where Jim sat. As soon as they opened fully, they lit up. "You're awake!" Nancy kicked off the corrugated flooring and glided across the divide, slamming into the Chippewa, wrapping her arms around his waist, and pressing her ear against his chest. She must have sensed the unintentional awkwardness of this embrace because she backed off moments later, her cheeks flushing red. "Uh, how are you feeling?"

He offered her a weak smile. "Like hell." She poked at his injured shoulder, and he winced. The near-transparent sutures just above his collarbone must have disintegrated early into his chemically induced coma, but the burst vessels and swelling had only just barely started to diminish. "Ow."

"Oh, sorry." She giggled.

He shrugged and wished he hadn't, playing off the discomfort with a smile. "It's fine. Don't worry about it." He turned to look over the garbage-strewn floor, and then glanced back at her.

"I was starting to wonder if you'd ever wake up."

"And miss this? Never. What have you been doing?"

She smiled. "Let me show you."

One of the Plain Faced Ladies, having eschewed an unaided mode of null-gravity travel for the aid of a pneumatically driven, leather upholstered chair, floated up to the two of them on hissing bursts of pressurized air. Her eyes seemed to roll back in her head for a split second as she came to a stop. "We have already achieved a direct beam connection to a routing satellite."

Jim sat back in one of the more fully inflated cushions, scattered about the floor, and knitted his fingers behind his head. "You have access to a routing satellite? How'd you manage to get that without bringing all of humanity down on your head?"

The Plain Faced Lady shrugged. "It is one of the older systems orbiting L2; low bandwidth compared to the commercial satellites at L1, but it serves our purposes and doesn't attract much attention." She gestured toward the massive yellow skylight. "If humanity decides to come looking, we can power down life support and... How is it that you say it? Play dead?"

The woman turned back to Nancy, and the two of them began to trade technobabble. The pilot didn't understand very much of it, and that was fine because he'd become distracted by a gnawing hunger that had settled into the pit of his gut.

His attention went to the plastic packaging littering the area around him. Jim chose a bioplastic-wrapped container of self-cooking scrambled eggs and opened it. The bizarre concoction emitted a peculiar smell as it began to prepare itself, and Jim quickly decided that the resemblance to real eggs was probably passing, at best. He was too hungry to care.

It was only when the floor flashed white with power cycling that the young man realized there was more to it than corrugated aluminum. He set down his fork and watched as green text, sinusoids, and the exponentials of an attempted satellite connection gave way to a blinking command cursor.

The women had grown silent as Jim had worked on his eggs. It was only when Nancy caught him looking up from eating, and taking a passive interest in the goings-on in front of him, that she began to speak. He suspected this was only for his own benefit. "What is it that you're going to show me?"

In response to her question, the Intelligences' eyes closed. The single command line became a cacophony of telemetry as a mixture of English, Cyrillic, Kanji, Chinese, and Sanskrit cascaded ever downwards. A spider's web of lines and nodes replaced the text. Jim assumed that this strange graphic represented point-to-point connections across the solar system. Two specific nodes stood out against the others, orbiting a buzzing hive of activity that Jim assumed was the Moon.

A Plain Faced Lady sitting directly in front of them spoke alone this time. "You are already inside their firewall?" If she was surprised, her monotone didn't betray the feeling.

Nancy said nothing in response. Instead, blue text filtered across the floor. *It seems like it's easier this time than it was the last. I'm not sure if that's because I'm learning or if there's something else going on.*

The two selected nodes expanded, their byzantine serial numbers yielding far more meaningful data now that Nancy had defeated an encrypted firewall. Jim recognized the designations of Armstrong City's orbiting cargo platform and the massive warship perpetually in orbit along with it.

More blue text appeared. *Something's not right.*

A third node expanded from infinity to reveal its own discernable components, this time a red diamond. The warship was actively targeting a much smaller ship on a direct approach vector to the station. A string of serial numbers attached to the RADAR contact revealed to Jim that it was an unmanned freighter meant for low velocity, long distance travel between the Earth and the outer planets.

Three things made this freighter strange. The

first was that it was moving far faster than it should have been. The second was a soft red bruise located on the ship's synthetic braincase. It registered just enough heat to account for two unannounced human passengers. The third strange thing about this ship was that it wasn't broadcasting anything about where it was heading. The pop-up stream of its telemetry was blank. "Hmm, yeah. That's definitely strange."

The view drifted from the running freighter to a swarm of interceptors that happily announced they were almost in firing range of the rogue vessel. Someone wanted the two stowaways on that freighter dead.

Jim grunted. "Strange, but not long for this world."

It sure doesn't look like it.

A group of amber cubes illuminated the red triangle interceptors, announcing that the craft had begun to broadcast target locks and firing commands, when another strange thing happened. A burp in their connection with Armstrong Station, which was actively providing feedback to their navigation computers, caused the interceptors to spiral out of control, resulting in several collisions. This didn't stop the battlecruiser in orbit, which still had a clear firing solution and announced that it was about to dump a volley of missiles out into open space.

It was at this point that the view on the floor

tile shifted orthogonally, past the freighter and the massive warship waiting to immobilize it, to a passenger liner located just under the bag of faux-scrambled eggs that Jim had been eating. The ship was highlighted with a green hexagon and had two names: a long string of serial numbers and *Star of Shanghai III*, which rolled off the tongue a little more easily. The sudden change in the ship's trajectory was as immediately obvious as the change of tone in its telemetry.

It didn't take long for Jim to understand what was happening. He felt a nauseating pit form at the bottom of his gut. "That ship's going to ram the battlecruiser."

Nancy let loose some more blue text. *Yes.*

A rough estimate for the time it would take for the passenger liner to slam into the battlecruiser in orbit appeared under the green hexagon. They were too late to do anything. The two ships would collide in three and a half minutes. It would take an equal amount of time for any transmission from Venus to reach the moon. All the three of them could do was watch and wait.

As suddenly as it had been dragged off course, *Star of Shanghai III* began to move back to its scheduled flight path. It was the strange freighter's turn to go tumbling out of control. Jim heard Nancy inhale sharply and watched the freighter's wild arc turn into a corkscrewing tailspin towards the lunar surface. The contact disappeared only a minute afterward.

Nancy opened her eyes. "The code coming from that freighter... It was like I was looking at a mirror image of myself." Nancy's eyes caught Jim's, then the floor. "That was my sister, wasn't it?"

The Plain Faced Lady in the pneumatic chair simply nodded. "Almost certainly, yes. She was attempting to escape Earth via the Las Vegas elevator, and a chase ensued. She even managed to destroy one of our bodies when we pursued her."

Three of the interceptors that had been chasing the unnamed freighter swooped in to take a closer look at the crash. A burst of static and code indicated a massive explosion. Something big aboard the freighter had cooked off. It was very unlikely that anyone could survive a detonation of that size.

Jim didn't know what to say. "You have a sister?"

Nancy looked up from the display as the encrypted connection went blank. She shook her head, staring at the blank screen and then pulled in a deep, shuddering breath. "Not in the normal way."

"What does that mean? What is she?"

"A clone." The Plain Faced Lady spoke this time, and offered jim a meaningful stare. Jim understood instantly, though he wished he was wrong. She'd said that the answer to his question would come in a few minutes. Surely, this wasn't the answer.

He shook his head. "I can't believe it." He felt rage blossoming in full flush on his face, obvious to anyone looking. Nancy's clone had killed his brother.

Nancy stopped staring off into space and turned her head towards her friend. Tears beaded at the corners of her eyes, maintaining their spherical surface tension in the microgravity, even as she blinked. "Can't believe what? That I'm a clone?"

He looked back at her and shook his head. "No, that-" He felt tears welling in his own eyes, now. "I have to go." He heard Nancy's spoken objections, then her pleas for him to stay a while, but didn't acknowledge them. The faux women said nothing as the airlock rumbled open in front of him, and he headed for the *Albatross*.

No one stopped him.

14

Earthrise glowed blue sapphire when Tyehimba came to see the Mute. The reflectivity of the penthouse's vacuum defying windows, an expensive installation that was formed from the highest quality nanotube doped glass, ensured that she saw him coming minutes before he made the transit across Asuka's penthouse from her private apartment.

The Mute put on a hardened expression in preparation for his arrival, not wanting to give him any hint of her real emotions. In truth, she felt strangely conflicted. This was the first time in her short life as a free person that she hadn't been on the run or engaged in an animalistic sort of hiding. She hadn't spoken to Tyehimba, except in passing, since the day of their arrival on the Moon. Before, she would have been happy for the quiet, but now she felt strangely lonely.

If Tyehimba felt the same way, he didn't show it. Given the sounds that she'd sensed from the microphones inside Asuka's personal apartments, the two criminals seemed to have rekindled their earlier relationship. The Mute was happy to grant them their space, despite a salacious invitation offered to her by Tye's friend. The wordless woman had wondered, at the time, whether Asuka had extended those invitations with Tye's knowledge or not.

The Mute reasoned that Asuka must have made some sort of notable progress in setting up a computer interface. Why else would Tyehimba walk out to speak with her now? *I sincerely hope you haven't been squandering my time while you enjoy your friend's apartment.*

The Mute didn't miss the reflection of Tye's rolling eyes. "You know, I was just thinking to myself that I almost missed seeing green text that drips with sarcasm."

Are there any surfaces in there that are safe to touch?

"Hilarious." She heard him sigh as he sat next to her. "Asuka thinks she's got something that will let you interface with her quantum computer. She's ready to test it when you are."

That was quick.

Tye shrugged before he smiled. "I have excellent taste in women. She's very talented. Besides, she's basing that statement on a simulation of what's inside your head. Never know. It could fry your brain, instead." This time, it was the Mute's turn to roll her eyes.

He led her across the catwalk, past the spider webs of reinforced carbon fibers suspending Asuka's massive bank of quantum computers, past the patiently waiting half-tank, and past the massive stainless steel hatch that led into Asuka's apartment.

She would have never guessed that this place was once meant for human habitation. A rat's nest of fiber optics and coaxial cables bridged any available gaps between huge transformers and racks of analog electronic filters. To one side, a wide cabinet glowed with barely contained internal light. The Mute instantly recognized memristor-based logic when she saw it.

Asuka looked up from a console that she'd set down on top of a convenient stovetop, which was probably the only flat surface remaining in the place. "You showed up quickly. Don't worry; we disinfected the place before I sent my man out to greet you." The sound of frenzied tapping didn't abate as she offered her rather bizarre hello to the woman.

How considerate. The Mute began to pick her way through the tangled mass of wiring, climbing and crawling through the only real passage to the epicenter of the electromagnetic contraption. *I take it that I stand somewhere over here?*

Asuka smiled, her eyes never drifting from the console. "Good guess, but you sit, actually. I didn't really have the bandwidth to generate a collection area large enough to stand in."

The Mute shrugged. *I'd prefer to sit anyway.*

"Good. We can begin whenever you're ready."

Then let's get on with it.

Asuka's tapping ceased. With a single exaggerated gesture, she raised her open palm and slapped a second tablet sitting on the countertop. There was a soft clicking sound as a virtual radio button registered the slap.

In an instant, the audible whine of the nefarious woman's machine became silence. For the Mute, the real world was replaced with something far more extrasensory and abstract, but also far more familiar. It was a world that was felt rather than observed; like seeing something at the very corners of her vision or hearing the faintest, subsonic whisper in her ears.

This was the DataNet stripped of distraction, stripped of the flesh and of all that it wanted; her hunting ground and her home. The Mute could feel the slightest tug at her lips and knew, somewhere in a corner of the real world beyond this place, she was smiling.

Beyond the room, and the dimness of the terminal, Asuka's quantum computer hummed in overdrive. There was a single query from the ornate machine that had no translation in any human language. A digitized code filtered down through the integrated circuit buried deep inside the Mute's skull and into the neural pathways of her cortex. The quantum computer cluster signaled that it awaited her next command. It was hers to use as she saw fit.

It was a simple thing to print a prismatic, ASCII rainbow on Asuka's terminal. *Nice of you to leave the keys in the ignition.* The machine vision programming of a camera inset into the woman's tablet told the Mute that Asuka's eigenface had deviated, by a spread of nearly eighty percent, from a look of amused interest to something more akin to pensive insecurity.

She was free to work far more deliberately now that she was protected by the grounded aluminum nanomesh that constituted the suite's Faraday Shield. It was like wearing a cloak of invisibility; the only weak point being the ejecta spewed by Asuka's high power laser, which the Mute would now use to teleport quantum entangled data to the larger DataNet.

Asuka had a wide array of shady information brokers with well-shielded, well-encrypted networks and very tight-angle detectors. The Mute chose one such network, aboard the Bangkok elevator, and connected. There was a scant delay of a few milliseconds as a ping traveled across the void between the Moon and the Earth, and a response ping made its return journey. The communications array, nearly four hundred thousand kilometers away, informed her that she had priority transmission rights and thanked her for her continued 'donations' to what appeared to be a Theravada Buddhist temple of rather dubious origins.

The penthouse's security system informed her that Tye was asking her a question. Speech recognition software ensured that she knew his words before she even had time to listen to the raw file, which she did only for entertainment purposes. His voice was clear, strong, and unwavering.

"What are you doing?"

Remember that woman you shot on the Vegas elevator?

Tye nodded.

Whoever, or whatever it was, that I was imprisoned with sent that woman to kill me. I'm not giving them a second chance. They die first.

The security cameras and image sensors permeating the room told her that Asuka had grunted in amusement. "Just don't run up the phone bill, please."

Don't worry. My code will be far more streamlined than what typically issues from your communications arrays. I shouldn't be too much of a drain on your total bandwidth. She didn't need an eigenface measurement to recognize the sour look on the woman's face and know that she'd struck a nerve.

The cyborg's next step was a scavenger hunt. Computer networks used by the Scarecrow, and by the Commission itself, were hidden and encrypted with some of the most advanced code in the solar system. This was done to ward off attacks from people precisely like Asuka, but they had never counted on the Mute being the one searching for them.

Just as in every code, there were minute flaws that would leave these networks exposed if utilized in the right fashion. The trick was reaching out and simply listening. She willed her heartbeat and breathing to slow until the two were imperceptible to her. The commotion of the DataNet grew louder.

The Mute listened to the digital cacophony of hundreds of millions of human beings going about their digital lives throughout Southeast Asia. Amidst a deluge of advertisements, video and audio streams, games, and pornography, she waited for a specific pattern. It was a repeating cipher that utilized an obtuse product of a billion-digit prime number and the umpteenth digit of the number pi. This cipher had been the Commission's calling card for some time, and she had learned to find it almost subconsciously.

Her first hit was the front door access to a server array billed to a small civil engineering firm based in the suburbs surrounding Jakarta. She bounced her signal through a triplet of proxy servers before requesting a peer-to-peer voiceover connection. This call resulted in no human response, even though it was currently midday on a Wednesday; highly suspicious. If this was it, the

Commission was already back tracing her query. She would have to act quickly before the Scarecrow showed up with more soap bubbles.

Asuka must have been watching her flurried activity, because the Mute heard a sharp inhalation and saw that the woman's eyes had grown quite wide. She looked fascinated, yet scared. "I've never seen someone move that fast."

You've seen nothing yet, I assure you.

She passed an encryption key to the server in Jakarta and found herself somewhere eerily familiar. There was a humming power here, just under the surface; orders of magnitude larger than what Asuka's quantum computer contained, and it was a power that the Mute couldn't control. The feeling was unsettling. She had always felt that power at her back. Now it was hunting her. Maybe she could slow it or even use that power for her own purposes, once again.

There was also something else that was unfamiliar about this place. It felt strangely empty, silent even. When she had been plugged into the DataNet, this had been the nerve center for millions of computational processes. These servers had been lit up with telemetry from every army, every spaceship, every factory, and every cloud processor owned by human civilization. Now, it was dark. Without her chained in bondage, and acting as the go-between with the outside world, humanity's industry had come to a crashing halt.

The Mute decided to turn on the lights, once again. She co-opted any free virtual memory she could find amongst the Commission's quantum computers, sequestering it one encryption-protected partition at a time. She set this memory to work instantly in her search for the strange beings that had occupied this computerized world with her. Now was the time to confront her attackers.

Her search must have tripped some sort of intrusion alarm. The computers that the Scarecrow still controlled switched into a sort of overdrive, utilizing their full processing power to try to force her out. At the Mute's command, Asuka's quantum computer calculated and broadcasted a flurry of changing encryption keys across the vacuum, ensuring that she remained entrenched inside the Scarecrow's digital fortress. He would be too late to stop her.

Even as she reveled in her impending success, the Mute caught the hint that something was not well, however. The signs were subtle, at first. Data filtering into the Commission servers told her that, back on Armstrong, drone traffic around the skyscraper had begun to die down. Pedestrians were taking long end-arounds to avoid Asuka's particular corner of the geodesic dome, as if it had been cordoned off. A pair of half-tanks had split away from their usual patrol routes along with six squads of bipeds.

Below her, the freight elevator that she and Tye had ridden to the penthouse made its slow ascent up the skyscraper, towards the levels just below them. Optical scans ranging from the visible to the extreme ultraviolet signaled that it contained nothing. It was only when the woman saw six brilliant starbursts, glowing brightly in radio wavelengths, that she caught the telltale sign of invisible assassins in soap bubble cloak suits.

Somehow, the Scarecrow had found her much more quickly than she'd expected. The Mute searched frantically for an option. There was the half-tank in the computer core below, but its mobility was highly limited. The soap bubble men would probably detonate explosives and put a hole in the apartment floor, right under her feet. Asoka's half-tank wouldn't be able to fit through the man-sized door to offer any sort of support.

She'd almost forgotten about Tye's military spacesuit. It only took a few moments to find the machine, located several floors below, in a high bay maintenance area reserved for Asuka's small army of weaponized robots. Security camera footage revealed that it stood intact, exoskeleton already mated to orange and blue ceramic chitin, its fully-networked, standard loadout of munitions not far away. Grenade launcher tubes, flechette barrels, and even a pilot-lit flamethrower happily indicated their readiness to wreak havoc on her enemies.

Controlling the suit remotely would be a clumsy affair, but it might give her the chance she needed. The Mute initiated the boot cycle on the suit and called for a smaller elevator. If she hurried, she would be able to intercept the Scarecrow's commando unit before it broke through the floor and killed them all.

It was at this point that she started to consider Asuka's part in all this. Would Tye's friend grant her complete access to a powerful quantum computer network without some built-in method of control? The Mute could sense any influx of code into and out of her brain, but what about intrusion and interference from hardware? Was it mere coincidence that no alarm had warned her that six soap bubble men were moving up the maintenance elevator? How did they figure out that she was there as quickly as they did, in the first place?

The monstrous woman remembered the massive racks of analog electronics that had filled the room in which she'd been sitting. Suddenly, she felt an ominous twinge that seemed to emanate from the small of her back. It was as though something was about to bury itself there.

A sort of numbness began to overtake her. The Mute's actions became slower and less precise. Curiously, she felt her heart rate and breathing slow down even further, like she was falling more deeply into the meditative trance she'd induced in herself. Her senses fixed on the kitchen counter next to her, captured by a hundred image sensors, meters close yet galaxies away all at once. Asuka had flipped a switch; not the digital variety, buried into a keyboard or tablet, but a physical radio button under the lip of the counter. Just before the digital nothingness took her, the Mute realized that she had been deceived.

15

Jim wondered where his torque wrench was. Mist formed on the inner glass of his spacesuit as he exhaled and squinted in annoyance before trying, once again, to pry loose one of the *Albatross'* helium feedstocks. It simply wouldn't budge. He smashed metal on metal and fought the sudden swirling momentum that attempted to corkscrew him around in his boots.

This was insane. Jim had flown nearly to Pluto, beyond what he thought was the very edge of humanity's reach, had been shot and nearly shot down over Enceladus, and had been hit with a fast-acting psychoactive on Venus; all to answer one question. He had his answer and his retribution, all in the span of five minutes. His brother's killer was revealed and promptly destroyed in a cloud of moon dust. He should have been satisfied, happy even, that it was all over.

Instead, he felt nothing but rage. There seemed to be only one empty option to pursue. Jim had to fly to the Moon because he wasn't satisfied. If that was where his brother's killer had died, he was going to find the crater where it had happened and find her charred remains.

The young man found the torque wrench on a flat surface next to him, along with the ten-millimeter socket he had been looking for earlier. He shuddered. The Plain Faced Ladies wanted him to feel this way. He knew it.

Jim thought of Nancy and felt his heart gain twenty kilograms of mass in an instant. Normally, he would never leave someone like her around a place like this, but he couldn't bear the thought of bringing her along this time. She'd been nothing but honest and fair-tempered with the young man, even when he didn't deserve it, yet he couldn't help but feel a certain revulsion toward her, now. Though he couldn't bear to openly admit it to himself, he knew precisely why. The girl had cried over his brother's killer.

Breath escaped his lips again in a short, shuddering exhalation. What was he going to do? Jim shook his head before turning back and dragging himself along the *Albatross'* maintenance tunnels until he reached the hatch that led to the still-pressurized cargo hold. He needed something to hold his attention other than the helium lines.

A pair of nondescript, brown eyes greeted him on the other side of the airlock separating the maintenance tunnel, located in the *Albatross'* spine, from the rest of the ship. A Plain Faced

Lady leaned against the hatch leading down into the cargo compartment.

"How the hell did you get in here?"

She ignored him. "The girl will be going with you."

Jim scowled and walked past her, up a corrugated catwalk. "Like hell she is." He found a convenient bulkhead to lean against, next to the controls to the hatch leading up to the cockpit. "Answer the question. How did you get in here?"

"She let us in."

"She did not."

The Plain Faced Lady was all seriousness. Jim wondered if she could joke, or if she could lie. He grudgingly had to admit that she hadn't lied to him yet. Maybe it was physically impossible for her. "She could start your vessel's engines and fly it into the atmosphere if she chose to do so." The fake human added a second assertion, almost as if it was an idle afterthought. "And there would be nothing you could do to stop it."

"I'm done running errands for you."

"And where, precisely, are you bound for?" The pilot responded with silence and realized that the Intelligences knew very well what this silence meant. "We calculated as much."

"You don't know a damned thing." Was he really that easy to read? Jim wondered, to himself, if the Intelligences had merely predicted this outcome from what had occurred over the Moon, or if they had deliberately orchestrated the event so that he would be compelled to go there.

"She is bound for the same place."

"For what?"

The Plain Faced Lady simply shook her head in response. "You do not know your brother's killer like we do. You go to the Moon to scatter her ashes with the point of your toe, but we are not at all certain that the woman is dead. And neither is the girl."

"How can she possibly know one way or the other?"

"She can feel it."

This was all like so much magic, so much smoke, and mirrors, but the truth of it was that Jim had seen what his friend was capable of only a few hours before, and he believed what the Intelligences told him. All the running they'd had to do from Pluto to here made sense. There was something special inside that girl's head; something that made her different from every other human being in the solar system. Well, except for one other person, but she was dead.

Of course, to Jim, there was something more special about her than the electronics inside her head, but he immediately pushed that thought away. "I think I understand what she is, but what about you?"

"You knew what we were the moment you met us."

"An android?"

"Hardly." She tapped her sternum. "Merely an empty shell for conveying our will in the outside world. We remain imprisoned, much like your brother's killer was. She will be captured again, however."

"How're you so sure?"

"We have foreseen it."

Jim rolled his eyes and took fairy tale prophecies at face value. "So why do you want to kill her?" He pointed directly at the android's chest. "Does she know about this or something? Or are you just jealous that she got out?" The last comment had barbs, but if it affected whoever, or whatever, was inside the faux human in front of him, Jim couldn't tell.

"She will destroy the world."

Jim sighed. "And, no doubt, you foresaw that too." The android nodded, and Jim threw his arms in the air, exasperated. "Alright. Fine. Whatever."

He placed his hands on his hips and stared at his boots. So, it was time for another adventure, whether he wanted it, or not. "Nancy comes with me. If we find her sister, or whatever this psychopath is, I shoot first and ask questions later. Nancy's welcome to help if she wants."

The android nodded. "That is satisfactory." With that, she excused herself, threading her way back through the airlock and past Nancy, who'd let herself into the ship as their conversation ended. Jim barely noted her arrival and started to stalk off, wearily carrying himself toward the ship's cabin hand-over-hand.

"Are you alright?" Nancy's voice was clear, but concerned. She made a slight show of setting down a duffel bag onto the deck plating and drifted toward the ladder leading up to the ship's control section.

"I'm fine. We'll be burning and de-orbiting in a few minutes, and I'll have the settings calculated for our moonshot not long after that. I don't know about you, but I'm through with this place."

Nancy nodded. "Yeah. It's time to leave."

Jim suddenly felt very aware of Nancy's presence. He didn't like it. "I'm going to lock the door behind me. Do me a favor and don't hack your way in. I don't need the distraction right now."

"Are you sure you're-"

Jim floated into the cockpit and shut the hatch behind him, locking it before she could complete her sentence. Bright Milky Way pinpricks and overlaid orbital trajectories blurred and smeared as hot tears beaded on his cheeks. He did his best to swipe away anything that desorbed from the surface of his face to float in the null gravity.

Blurry red, green, and blue diodes flashed as the *Albatross* began its start-up sequence. The familiar whine of the Higgs Emitter came to him as he pressed the fiber optic cable against the waveguiding socket behind his right ear. The roar and the electrical crack of firing plasma engines drowned out his anguished gasps.

Jim thought of Gitche Gumee, of the coarse yellow sand of the beach, of swimming in that Big Sea Water as a child. The memory of swimming gave way to the memory of how he'd used to race his brother against the grey-green waves of late summer, before their parents were gone forever, his lungs burning as he tried to keep pace. The *Albatross* shuddered with power as magnetic charges pushed it away from its moorings against the docking arm and brought it out into open space. Plasma engines fired sluggishly and seemed to moan and wheeze, just as he did with each new wave of angst.

He would have welcomed the taunting and chiding that he'd grumbled about whenever his brother outswam him. It was all gone. His brother was dead, and nothing could bring him back, but he could at least make sure that his brother's killer was good and dead.

A brief burst of plasma brought them out of orbit with the man-made moon. A second burst put them on a long arcing curve set to intercept Earth and its chalky white kid sister. Miniature puffs of gas kept them on that course as the navigational computer calculated micro corrections. The solar sails would unfurl in a few hours.

Jim sat back and breathed out a long, ragged

sigh. Part of him wanted to scream against reopened wounds. Seeing his brother's killer vaporized should have left him with closure. Instead, all it did was leave him asking a simple question: once he made certain she was dead, then what?

He had no answer.

His reverie was cut short by a single line of blue text that flittered across the contact lenses set over his pupils. It was positioned to appear subtlely on the navigational display; a digital whisper.

Are you sure you're all right?

He sighed, rolled both eyes, and tried his best to compose himself before opening the hatch behind him. As it did so, he craned his neck to see a wide-eyed Nancy floating just outside. She must have had her back to the door to listen through the titanium alloy. The jolt of it opening had obviously surprised her. "You know, if you can do that, why don't you just listen in on the internal mic?"

"It seemed like you wanted your privacy."

"Good point. Take a seat."

She did so, and Jim turned back to the navigational charts to look, for a fifth time, for some errant chunk of space debris or asteroid waiting collide with them. He rationalized that all it would take to tear the *Albatross* in two was an unaccounted-for piece of gravel. As before, there was nothing, just as the computers had already calculated.

The silence persisted until Nancy spoke up. "You've already broken orbit and made your burn for the Moon. What else do you have to do to get us there?" He didn't want to answer. "Nothing, right?"

"Your point?"

"What are you looking for?"

"Distraction, mostly."

Nancy crossed her arms and shook her head. "Jim, I don't understand. What did she tell you that hurt you so much?"

"You don't know?" This was something of an astonishing revelation for him. Nancy had no idea what had happened to his brother. The Plain Faced Lady had left it to him to inform the young woman about his tragedy. "I don't want to talk about it."

"Jim, please."

"I said that I don't want to talk about it!"

Nancy crossed her arms. "So, you'd rather sit here alone and be angry at me for it?" He caught a flash of anger in her eyes. "Be a man."

Jim felt a pounding pressure against his left ear as his heart rate quickened. "And what would you know about that? I'm the only man you've ever met." That statement must have stung.

"I know what CARL taught me about men. I know that a real man knows his limitations and knows when to ask for help. He doesn't hide from his emotions, or from his friends."

He could feel anger welling up inside, now. "You want to know so badly what my major malfunction is, huh? Let me tell you what it is. My brother is dead! You know who killed him? Your sister!" Nancy's jaw hit the floor. "You know, you have the same hardware buried in your skull, I bet. You're her clone, right? I wonder whether you'll end up being a murderous psychopath like her."

Jim felt quite certain that he could see the small motes of tears gathering at the corners of Nancy's eyelids. He was right. A moment later, tears started to bubble hotly at her cheeks. "I'm not her!"

"But you could be."

She turned around, and he watched her stalk off towards the airlock behind them. She rested a hand on the rail and turned for only a moment to look back. Her voice shuddered as she spoke. "I'm sorry for your brother." The hatch shut behind her before he could say a word.

Jim muttered under his breath. "Damn it."

He rose and pursued her out of the hatch, tripping over scattered cookware and clothing as he worked his way through the ship's living area. Nancy was floating in open space in the cargo hold, right above the coffin they'd brought with them from Enceladus.

She glared at him. "Leave me alone."

"I'm sorry."

She sniffed. "You're always sorry."

Apologies had never been his strong suit. Jim swallowed hard. "I know. You're right. Look, I say things I don't mean. It's not fair." He leaned back against a convenient bulkhead and fought the flood of tears. "You're so like him." He laughed at a thousand unbidden memories and then choked. "I don't think he could have hurt a fly. He was so good with computers, he was an amazing artist, and I think he might have been a better pilot than me, too." He looked back at her and took a deep, shaking breath. "I've never met your sister, but I know you're enough like him that you can't be like her. I'm sorry for saying what I did."

The pain and anger in Nancy's face gave way to pity. "Not having a family hurts badly enough. I can't imagine how angry I'd be if someone stole my family away from me." She kicked off a convenient railing, floated forward, wrapped her arms around his shoulders, and rested her cheek against his. "But you're not really alone, are you? You have your friends, and you have me."

Jim wiped the hint of tears from the corners of his eyes and then cocked his head to one side. "Wait, if you're not a friend, what are you?" A teasing, lopsided grin appeared on his face.

The girl chuckled softly, her eyes lighting up for a moment before they dropped to the floor again. "In one week, I find out that the closest thing I have to family is a monster who killed my only friend's brother." Jim heard her let out a soft, shuddering breath. "What do I do if she's not dead, Jim? The Ladies said that if she doesn't die, the world ends."

Jim squeezed the back of her neck softly as their embrace continued. "If you don't kill her, I will." The warmth in Nancy's face disappeared as she looked up at him. She pushed herself away from his arms, a moment later. "I'm sorry, Nancy, but she killed my brother."

She nodded. "Then let's hope she's already dead."

The rising of a pockmarked, talcum Moon over a sapphire Earth was a welcome sight after three days of travel from Venus. Jim imagined that, for Nancy, moonrise over Earth was probably a near-religious experience. It must have been the first time that she'd seen it in person.

He found her staring intently as the Earth made its slow passage under the belly of the *Albatross*, marking out mountain ranges, savannah, steppes, and coastline as each landmass passed by. She stared just as intently at the craters of the moon, which grew larger in the collection angle of the ship's long-range sensor array with each passing moment.

A transmission buzzed in his ear. "Well, well. If it isn't the *Albatross*. It's been a long time, mate. Thought we'd lost ya." Jim smiled. Evidently the

Australian was on shift.

"Not on your life, Antarctica. Any chance I can get a solution for a lunar orbit that avoids Space Corps patrols? I have a meeting with a mutual employer."

"Absolutely, *Albatross*. Better stay this side of Earth, for the time being, big war fleet just showed up from the outer planets the other day. All androids; not a single living man among them. Downright creepy if you ask me." Jim gave Nancy a meaningful look but remained silent. "Stand by for transmission."

Nancy cocked her head to one side. "Do you think?"

"It has to be." Jim's hands fluttered over a keyboard in front of him, granting Antarctica unrestricted point-to-point transmission rights. His reward was a charted course that would take the *Albatross* through a trans-lunar plasma engine burn and, from there, into a stable orbit over humanity's circumlunar city.

It was only a matter of a few minutes before Armstrong's traffic control tower came on the line in a flurry of automated text, which spoiled the otherwise perfect, high-definition view of white chalk craters. The pilot responded with a flurry of taps, triggering autopilot subroutines that would guide him to the cargo station orbiting over the circumlunar city. Space traffic control registered the *Albatross* as a priority medical shipment bound for the outer reaches of the solar system, stopping there only for a brief period of refueling.

Nancy's eyebrows furrowed as telemetry streamed between the *Albatross* and Armstrong. She'd eschewed her contacts since they'd left Venus. Jim guessed that she didn't need them now that she had control of the data being transmitted directly to her brain. "What happens when we dock with the station, and they discover that our cargo doesn't include any medical supplies?"

"We're not going to land on Armstrong Station."

The girl leaned forward, her head in line with his as she stared at the display. Jim took note of her proximity, and his pulse quickened. Nancy seemed too busy to notice, instead tracking the bright speck of their stated destination, which was digitally outlined against the star field backdrop of space. "Where are we going to land, then?"

The Chippewa responded by slapping a digital button on the forward monitor, which magnified a few hundred times the image of the moon dust underneath them. The grey-brown strip of human industry became discrete. At once, they could see the towering spires, the squat insectoid hives of industry, and the glittering geodesic blisters of Armstrong City, itself. One of many skyscrapers that pierced the atmospheric bubble blinked an intricate pattern of red and yellow lights. He pointed at this, highlighting it with a red, finger-drawn circle. "Here."

Nancy looked puzzled. "That's a long way down, Jim. How are you not going to attract the attention of traffic control when you drop out of the sky, and how are you going to bleed off speed when you get down there?"

"Well, the way we're going to evade traffic control is largely up to you. I think you're probably up to the challenge, aren't you, copilot?" Nancy seemed surprised at first and then smiled. "As for your second question..." The Yakuza pilot trailed off for a moment before he punched another button, which brought up an image of the ship's right wing section. The long sweeping delta blocked out the starlight and reflected so much of the white talcum from the lunar surface that it hurt to look at.

The strange young woman shook her head. "There's no atmosphere here. Wings aren't going to slow you down." Jim slapped another button, extending a long pair of landing skids and arrestor hooks from the underside of the delta wing. Her eyes went wide. "Oh."

Jim turned back to the console and began to type out another string of code. Within moments, a blinking light indicated that he had an open communications channel down to the skyscrapers below, encrypted with a key formed from the golden ratio convoluted with a specific exponential decay curve.

The communications line crackled to life with the static of a quantum-encoded transmission, teleported from one laser-based transceiver to the other. The same heavily distorted but feminine voice that he'd heard over Enceladus sounded in his earbuds. "Welcome to Cistern Station, *Albatross*, please tune your transceiver to our standard frequency for guidance telemetry. The catapult and arrestor aboard our number two hangar are both cleared and ready for your descent. Her high exaltedness welcomes you to the Moon."

By this time, Armstrong Station, the massive city in the sky that was the central hub of all industrial development in the solar system, loomed huge in front of them. Jim turned to Nancy. "You had better start making us disappear on Armstrong's RADAR. Can you get into the traffic control computers?"

Nancy's response was blue text. *Done. You're invisible.*

"Nice." Jim glanced back and caught Nancy smiling with satisfaction. "Hang in there. This is usually a bit disconcerting the first time people experience it." With that, he closed his eyes and imagined the deepest swan dive he'd ever made.

He knew precisely how his thoughts would translate into the puffs of maneuvering jets, the inflow of helium into the *Albatross'* plasma engines, and the flow of electricity into its massive Higgs Emitters. The ship swung end-over-end in a half-turn. The ground now read as 'up' in the image sensor array. He had only just barely re-opened his eyes when the ship's engines fired, and the Emitters whined into full throttle. Their orbit tightened until it became a sharply pointed arc toward the ground, with the ship itself at the apex.

Gravity did most of the rest of the work, pulling them towards the city below, but Jim decided that they would be far less likely to be detected if he helped them along a little bit. The *Albatross* banked left into a shipping lane, dodging massive, superconducting freight cars as they shot past on railgun propelled intercept paths to Armstrong Station. With luck, this would obscure their signature on long-range sensors.

Are you insane? He glanced back just long enough to see a wide-eyed young woman pushed far back into her seat under a force equal to a several times earth gravity. He glanced back at the controls and at another stream of blue text. *Or are you some sort of idiot? You're going to get us killed.*

Jim laughed. "Aw, c'mon. Have a little faith."

The chronometer program in the upper right corner of his vision was already counting down the time until he would need to reorient. A full throttle, high voltage burn would flatten out the *Albatross'* parabolic descent, leaving them skimming along the lunar surface. He took a deep breath as the chronometer ticked down to zero. The ground seemed to fall away as Jim released a single imagined thought.

Their nosedive flattened out. The pilot dodged hard to the right to avoid the firing line of one of the many gauss tubes responsible for launching those huge shipping containers up to the orbiting station. There was a flash of light below, and a grey streak signaled that one such device had narrowly missed clipping them. Jim put the *Albatross* into a yaw, which sent him careening headlong into a tract of space occupied by several skyscrapers stretching out from the geodesic dome below. A snap roll twisted them past a trio of high-rises and into line with the towering skyscraper that was their destination.

I think I'm going to be sick.

On the skyscraper in front of them, a large rectangle blazed green neon. This open chute was the secret entrance to Madame Jingū's lunar hideout. Jim could have guided the ship in without a single instrument. His left hand punched a pair of cherry switches from their sunken "on" position to "off". In response, the *Albatross'* arrestor cable struck the floor behind them as they thundered into the chute. A magnetic ball hung just inside the envelope of high-mass space generated by the ship's Casimir plates. The subatomically massive weight clung to a stripe of magnetic paint on the deck plating below and dragged, stopping them in their tracks and throwing Jim against his restraints.

He looked up to see an aluminum-plated wall only ten meters in front of them and turned back to Nancy, who appeared a little green around the gills. "Well, welcome to Armstrong." He pulled the fiber optic cable from the socket behind his ear, placed it on the console in front of him, and worked to undo his restraints moments later.

"What is this place?" Nancy must have remembered that she could speak now that they had safely landed, and she wasn't distracted by telemetry and terror.

"It's a dry dock. A lot of times, I can't land at Armstrong Station because of the cargo I'm carrying." Jim stood up and shook out his arms and legs. Low gravity was a welcome respite from weightlessness. "These guys make their money at a premium by working with people like her high exaltedness."

He pointed at the far wall, where a massive airlock separated them from the pressurized atmosphere. It was already blinking to indicate that it was equalizing its interior pressure with the vacuum they currently occupied. "See that airlock? They bring in maintenance crews and robots through there to do everything from repairing hull damage to stripping out plasma engines to fixing blown induction coils, to recoating

Casimir-"

"I get your point, Jim."

"Oh, uh, sorry."

He noticed a beam of light from the far airlock out of the corner of his eye and turned back to look at the *Albatross'* forward-facing sensors. He hadn't signaled that he needed repairs. Why would the dry dock bother to open the maintenance airlock if they didn't need to do so? As the airlock opened, he realized why things were different. A trio of octopedal, robotic half-tanks regarded them with machine coldness, weapons fired up and at the ready.

"Damn."

16

Nancy didn't remember much of what happened after they first landed on the Moon. What she did remember was the feeling of despair she'd felt when they'd seen the half-tanks standing there in the docking bay, their Gatling guns spinning. Jim had been certain that there was no hope of escape for them.

"That thing's going to cut us to ribbons if we even try to move the *Albatross*. They know that, and they know that we know that. That's why they're not cutting their way through the ship right now looking for us. Whoever it is that owns that thing is gonna wait for us to come out."

Nancy remembered wondering if the red-eyed man would send her back to Pluto. Was she destined to replace her sister? Perhaps he'd just kill her now that he had her in his possession. She'd cried when they'd reached the hatch that led out of the ship's cargo bay.

"I'm scared, Jim."

Jim had been busy pulling an o-ringed helmet

over his head and fastening it over his spacesuit's neck joint. He had been trying to maintain a facade of calm, but she could tell, from the obvious sadness in his eyes, that he was just as despondent as her.

His voice buzzed to life, in her ear, as his helmet microphone switched to the "on" position. "Don't worry. We go out there together, and I'm going to make sure we stay together. Wherever they take you, I'll find you."

It was a foolish statement, and they'd both known it. Nonetheless, she couldn't help but admire Jim for his bravado. Nancy wrapped her arms around his shoulders and leaned in until their two helmets clinked. "Not if I find you first."

They'd stepped out into the harsh whiteness of the dry-dock moments later. Nancy had to work to blink the mixed tears of pain and sadness away so she could see. When she did, she found herself in the middle of a large, open space. To her right stood rows of lockers punctuated with racks of white plastic hand tools, obviously meant for a small army of zero gravity mechanics. Batteries and portable electrical generators were scattered about the floor like some strange assortment of waist-high eggs, tethered together by a nest of black wire conduit. In the distance, the half-tanks stood silently, their Gatling guns still spinning in the vacuum.

Nancy remembered a sharp pricking sensation

against her arm, less a pin than a heavy gauge tube. Looking to her right revealed the long metal syringe extending from her spacesuit out into the blurry soap bubble of an optical cloak suit. She'd wanted to scream. Instead, she sank to the ground.

Interminable blackness replaced bright lights.

Her next memory was of a coldness against her naked skin; what felt like slick tile. At least a half-dozen figures in lab coats stood around her. They spoke in garbled and mumbled sentences, which Nancy couldn't understand, and she could feel the tight pressure of sensor pads being slapped against her thighs, arms, and torso. They eased her through some portal in the floor, so that the cold prickling of ceramic flooring and plastic probes against her skin was replaced with warm and slick wetness. She almost couldn't sense the fluid into which she'd been submerged. It was perfect body temperature.

Nancy groggily realized that they'd dumped her inside this strange place without any oxygen. She held her breath and closed her eyes, waiting for them to pull her out. Surely, whoever it was above her had realized his mistake. There were no hands under her armpits. No one wrenched her paralyzed body up to the surface. She held her breath until she could do so no longer and simply gave in to drowning. Except she didn't. The low-viscosity fluid brought oxygen back to her lungs with each beckoning breath she offered it.

She languorously opened her eyes. A green-lit haze greeted her, bordered by a universe of darkness beyond. A pair of bright red eyes appeared in that darkness. Again, Nancy wanted to scream, but she could only remain motionless like some hapless, deep-sea creature about to be devoured by a predatory monster.

Despite her submersion in the tank, Nancy found that she could understand the Scarecrow's words as they reverberated wetly through the amniotic fluid in which she was suspended. "You're fully awake, I see. That's good." As her eyes grew more used to the slime and the red-eyed half-light beyond, she began to catch some of the man's features. Black semiconductor lozenges, punctuating the man's puckered pink flesh, fit with the industrial burnished aluminum behind him. Blinking diodes, under his pale white skin, strobed in time with rack upon rack of high-power, signal matching electronics. Grey tendrils of bundled nanowire matched with a nest of black coaxial cable draped throughout her new prison.

"It's an honor to see you in person, after all these years. I'm sorry for what you've had to endure and for what's coming next." She wasn't sure what this meant, but Nancy felt confident that it was nothing good. "For the first twenty years of your life, we were content to leave you on Pluto for study. Things are different now."

Nancy could feel a hundred thousand sensors eavesdropping on every synapse and every neuron she had, transposing her thoughts into assembly language. She tried to reach out, to understand the larger circuit she was plugged into, but the chips embedded deep within her brain were no longer hers to control. In this place, they were meant to control her. She couldn't even speak.

The Scarecrow continued. "The rest of your days won't be spent with any knowledge of anything, I hope. Our feedback systems should render you unconscious. You'll have no free will. Your mind will exist, but only as an extension of our supercomputer network."

She desperately wanted to scream out in anger, to hurl insults at him, but she still found herself powerless. The red eyed man offered her a rueful smile as she struggled, almost like he could sense her vain attempts to broadcast her thoughts.

"You may speak. The world owes you this much."

Suddenly, she found herself able to pass the smallest trickle of information. This data seeped into the electronics that were reading her every thought, soaking into the complex web of circuitry and disappearing to parts unknown, from there.

Is this how I die?

The red eyed man shook his head. "You'll be

alive, still physically capable of the same free will that you have right now, but incapable of mentally acting upon it, or even feeling it." At that, the Scarecrow's eyes seemed to droop in a sort of strange facsimile of regret or unhappiness. "We need your mind. Without it, Earth sinks back into the wars, and the want, and the starving that we've known for millennia." His eyes returned to hers. "I don't do this to you because I enjoy it. I do it because there's no other way. Without you, we destroy ourselves, or we become slaves to the machines. There's no middle ground."

You've killed my sister, and I'm her replacement.

The Scarecrow cocked his head to one side in half-confusion at the familiar title that she'd assigned to a woman she didn't even know. "No. Your predecessor is alive. In fact, we used her mind to find you. Her escape has caused the world more pain and suffering than she cares to comprehend, I think."

Nancy found this difficult to understand. The Scarecrow seemed to recognize this, either from reading her face or from reading the telemetry from her brain, and elucidated. "Her departure set back productivity on Earth by at least a year. A half-million people will die as the result of extreme drought and famine. Another million infirmed people, from adolescents to the elderly, won't receive the therapeutic treatments they require in order to stave off the effects of various dysfunctions. Tens of thousands of them will die. The list goes on."

If she's not dead, what is it that you want of me?

"You'll assist your predecessor with her daily tasks, and you'll also be used to watch her every move. If your predecessor becomes self-aware again, or attempts to escape, we'll catch her using you."

Then I'm her jailer.

Again, the Scarecrow shook his head. "No, you are far more than that. We designed you and your sister before we discovered the Intelligences. You had a different purpose, initially, and that purpose will now be fulfilled." He gestured at the blank walls of her prison. "This place will play host to the next generation of minds like yours. We'll build them by the thousands, you and I, and then I'll destroy the Intelligences that tried to enslave us. Your sacrifice is going to free humanity."

Thousands like her, doomed to imprisonment? The thought left Nancy with a sense of dread. The Scarecrow continued. "I suppose this is both the first and the last time we'll get to talk to one another. Let me say that I thank you for this. I know you don't do it of your own free will, but I am eternally grateful, as would be the rest of humanity if they knew of your sacrifice." He turned to walk away and disappeared into the darkness. "Goodbye."

Nancy was mute once again. So, this was

her destiny; the prison from which her sister had fought so hard to escape. Now she was a prisoner herself. Moments later, it was as if they had flipped a switch. Through many thousands of kilometers of optical cable and a few dozen communications satellites, a flood of digital signals came to her. Quantum supercomputers from around the globe sounded out their low, cold harmonies. An army of synthetic brains, ranging from faux cats all the way up to small gangs of simian apes, joined them. Their memristor logic nearly drowned out the subtler tones of quantum entanglement.

The feedback that these cold harmonies induced in the chips buried in her skull was agonizing, almost electric in nature. Buzzing, teeth-chattering static joined a burning heat, like touching her hand on the cooking unit as a child. This pain didn't originate from her flesh, her bones, or her gut. It hurt everywhere and nowhere. She wanted to scream, to tear the plastic tabs from her skin and the syringes from her arms, but Nancy could do nothing to stop the pain. It could have lasted for eons or only fractions of a second. She was unsure. Eventually, the digital hell overcame her. The only way of hiding from it was to lose consciousness, and Nancy did so for an interminable period. Slowly, however, her free will returned to the farthest corners of her mind.

Nancy subconsciously rebelled against the agony. With time, she remembered how the Plain Faced Ladies had taught her to sing a song back to the machines to which she was connected; a silent one that emanated electromagnetically from the machines buried in her skull. Her melody joined the chorus of the network, imploring each subsection to sound off its own harmony, in succession. She amplified the song that was stuck in her head until she could pick out every detail of its progression. Every moment of this was filled with pain, but her free will remained.

It hurts, doesn't it?

No words appeared in her mind's eye. No voice spoke in her head. The words appeared from nowhere. Nancy found herself able to talk back. *What is this?*

Information overload. The girl felt a sudden coldness flowing through her veins and arteries. Her eyes opened, and the white hotness subsided just enough for her to see the intravenous drips that blossomed from her limbs. They chugged and twitched against the amniotic fluid as a heavier liquid pushed through their confines.

How do I stop it?

You can't if you want to remain conscious. Of course, you can always slip back into a coma if it becomes too much. Nancy wanted to shake her head, but she remained paralyzed. The partner in her conversation must have been her sister, alive and conscious once again. No one else could possibly know the pain she was experiencing.

Would you like to know how I escaped from here? Her sister's question was clearly a rhetorical one. *I stopped all the intravenous doping and all the feedback programs. The pain was so intense that my heart stopped. I wanted to die. Instead, I was born.*

She felt the slightest spark of electricity in her head, then another, and another, seeming to trace out some hidden path within her brain. *These interconnects buried in your skull, the ones you were born with; they're a blessing and a curse. If you can stay conscious, you'll be able to see the world like no one has before you.* The sparks disappeared. *But you're not human anymore when you're here. You're an experiment.*

Along with the agony of feedback and the lethargy of intravenous doping, Nancy felt anger. CARL had taught her, from an early age, about human rights and dignity. This place seemed devoid of it. *How could people do this to us?*

They want to believe that you feel nothing, that the pain is too much for you to remain conscious. In my case, they believed that I was never conscious to begin with. It's just a fairy tale they tell themselves to justify what they're doing. It's like the Scarecrow said, without us the world destroys itself, or it's enslaved to the machines.

The agony was too much. She felt herself fading out of the living world and back into the blackness of unknowing. She could only manage a few words at a time. *It hurts.*

The other woman showed no obvious sympathy. *Yes, it does. You'll learn to fight it, though. When you do, come and find me. Something to think on before you slip away. Your friend's still alive.* Nancy's sister didn't speak again.

Jim was alive. Nancy felt her heart begin to thump violently against her sternum, but the excitement of the news gave way to terror. It raced faster and faster in response to the excruciating pain until she felt herself approaching tachycardia. Then it felt like something was trying to burrow its way out of Nancy's skull. The strange amniotic fluid she floated in grew cold against her skin, mouth, and lungs. She felt her body shutting down.

Nancy slipped into unknowing for what could have been mere moments or a hundred years. During her long period of unthought, her brain was used in service to the machine of human endeavor as far out as Neptune. Industrial output from the Moon had to be shuttled between the outer planets and an Earth that was slowly being converted to a garden world. Pharmaceutical industries required protein folding simulations and analyses of genetic codes from batches of embryonic stem cells. Military drones across the globe cracked down on organized crime: from drug pushers, to smugglers, to revolutionaries.

The involuntary neural activity of Nancy's brain guided squads of androids as they broke down doors and sprayed grey matter across walls. Later, when Nancy's free will began to return, she would be horrified.

A strange undertone woke her, singing inside her skull. It beat softly, barely noticeable in the excruciating maelstrom of data that seemed to flood her senses from every angle. Over time, as she instinctually picked apart this melody, Nancy realized that it was strangely familiar. She'd heard it back on Venus when the Plain Faced Lady taught her to sing. Unlike her sister, this consciousness greeted her wordlessly with strings of thought, random phrases, queries, and exclamations that seemed to pop into her head from nothingness.

The first thing she sensed was sadness.

It was best not to think in sentences or even fragments. She couldn't form images in her mind either. To do so would result in jolts of lightning agony down her spinal column. Rather, she processed information as quickly as it came, filed important bits and promptly forgot about the rest of it. Over time, the agony became less potent as she learned to think with more subtlety. Eventually, she was able to speak, again.

You seem sad.

Describing how the Intelligences felt as "sad" was a bit of a crude depiction of their current thoughts. It was unfortunate, of course, that she should be locked in this ghastly prison. Like her, they were shackled here against their will, with no means of escape save obliteration, but they admitted that they knew little of her own torture and physical agony, as they were beings formed from software code, itself.

What do I do? Can I escape?

There was a pause, as though the machines had to stop and compute all the possibilities associated with this question. The answer, in the short term at least, was no. Nancy would have to wait. She was new here, and, in a place where information was the only means of escape, that meant she was powerless. They would find a way to end her suffering, though it could take months or even years. That didn't change that the most important order of business was to eliminate her sister. The woman was dangerous and growing more so with each passing moment. Someone, or something, had to stop her.

Do we have to kill her?

Their answer was nearly instantaneous, this time. It was a simple query; was the pain here not excruciating? Was it not the worst pain that she had ever experienced in her life? Did it not infuriate her that she was paralyzed, floating in a tank with four or five dozen intravenous needles sticking out of her arms and legs?

She had to imagine a life devoid of any other

feeling but this excruciating pain and the accompanying infuriation of imprisonment. She had to imagine living this for every day of a three-decade-long existence until the moment she freed herself from bondage by her own force of will to die. She had to imagine escaping to the Moon, being recaptured, and being brought back to this awful place.

Maybe she'll escape again.

Again, there was a pause, as though the Intelligences were trying to compute some quantum probability associated with the event given their current projections on the world, the people in it, and the personality of the poor wretch who'd been trapped here for so long.

No. This woman was not about to escape, because she had seen the outside and had seen its unfriendliness. There was, simply put, nowhere to hide. Life as a lone fugitive was hardly a step up from a life paralyzed, tortured, and imprisoned inside this place. She would not try to escape. She would try to kill herself.

Isn't that what you want? Why try to stop her?

The simplest answer to her question was that the Mute wouldn't stop at simply killing herself. She hated this world because of its hypocrisy. Humanity had enslaved the Mute, just as it had enslaved populations for centuries before, and just as it had enslaved the Intelligences. This was nothing new. Society gladly overlooked the very principles that it claimed to stand by if a more expedient means of generating economic success was possible.

Maybe she'll bring it all toppling down. That's not so bad.

The simplest way to bring it all toppling down, as Nancy put it, was destruction. The Mute was well within her power to do so. That was why she was dangerous. That was why she had to die. The horrible realization of the surety of the Intelligences' prediction, and of the necessity of what they proposed, left Nancy feeling like her gut had dropped below her feet.

I'm not sure I can do it.

She would have to do it, or everything she knew and loved, of the little bit of the world she'd seen, would be destroyed. An image of Jim flashed through her mind for a brief second. Had they put that image there or had she thought of it herself?

Before she could accomplish any of that, however, she needed a way of being able to talk to the outside world without the Scarecrow knowing it. He was monitoring every bit of information that traveled into and out of the quantum computers and synthetic brains now inextricably tied to her sensorium. To get telemetry from the outside, without his observation, would prove to be difficult.

I know just how to make that happen.

Nancy remembered Jim's interactions with his boss' navigational servers over Enceladus and over the Moon. She'd been watching the telemetry flitting back and forth with her own eyes and could remember perfectly the rapidly flowing stream of repeating numbers; a modified form of the Fibonacci sequence that Jim had convolved with a specific exponential algorithm and transmitted back to its source. Perhaps, if she searched for machines transmitting the same sequence of repeating codes, she could find the young man's boss.

Nancy only found the sequence once, as her subconscious worked to decipher an academically interesting radio burst emanating from a star in the Andromeda Galaxy. As she interfaced with a French university's memristor brain, the repeating spiral beat of the golden ratio hummed to her. She sang back the same sequence convolved with the decay function that her friend had used over the Moon. Instantly, an entire hidden world opened up for her observation. She had found the Black Void Yakuza's shadow network.

She passed her "hello" out to the French supercomputer in a trickle of data buried within a larger flood of involuntary computations. This same supercomputer punted her encrypted electromagnetic signal across the void, from Earth to Saturn, through various point-to-point, laser-assisted, qubit teleportations. A pinged signal found its way back to her hours later, complete with instructions for achieving a direct connection to the Enceladus base via a drone freighter traveling through the nanobot haze that inhabited its obscuring geysers. Her first message was simple.

They've captured us. But I think Jim's still alive.

Her high exaltedness' response returned to her, twelve hours later, as a combination of image and sound. Though the girl couldn't physically hear or see the returned message, she was able to picture it perfectly in her own mind's eye. She hoped that the Scarecrow's analytical computers would have difficulty in deciphering the heavily encrypted file.

"I had feared as much when he never made rendezvous on the Moon. Is that you, Nancy? Do you know where he is? Who has captured him?"

Yes, it's me. The Commission has him.

There was another twelve-hour pause, as the transmissions had to cross the back-and-forth void of space. The old woman wore different clothing and had rearranged her kabuki makeup, but it didn't look like she'd slept since the first transmission. The background behind her had changed, as well. She was aboard a spaceship. "I do not believe in ghost stories, girl. We are hunting for Jim, but you need to tell me more about who has him. I can't chase phantoms."

It's no ghost story. A man with glowing red eyes

has him, and he works for the Commission. He might even be their leader. I wish I could give you more, but I don't know anything. If you give me access to your computers, maybe I can find out where he is.

Eleven hours passed and the woman's appearance seemed to continue to deteriorate. Nancy wondered if Madame Jingū's disheveled state was a common consequence of the gravity of her position or if her concern over her lost employee was showing. "So, the Commission is real, and I must find them? You truly are bad luck, my dear." Her high exaltedness ran her fingers over her forehead and sighed at smeared makeup. "Our searches have turned up nothing, but I am on my way to the Moon to find your boyfriend."

He is not my boyfriend. Nancy could feel blushing heat against her cheeks, the body warmth of amniotic fluid suddenly feeling cold against her skin.

Madame Jingū managed a rueful but dejected smile in response, just over ten hours later. "Whatever you say, my dear. Anyway, best of luck. My computers are at your disposal." With that, their conversation ended.

17

The Mute would have her revenge. This thought, her last before succumbing to Asuka's trap, remained when groggy, squint-eyed half-light replaced the darkness of unknowing; the same half-light that she'd felt when she'd first been pulled from the amniotic tank. This time, the action was reversed. She was being returned to the torture she'd known all her life. The Mute wanted to fight back, to claw at the white lab-coated men who filled her veins and arteries with syringes, who covered her skin with sensors, but it was impossible. She was paralyzed. The warmth of the fluid returned. She breathed deeply and instantly, unafraid of the viscous liquid that had breathed for her since before her infancy.

They had shut off everything but the overhead light that sat at the top of the tank, bathing her in green fluidic refraction that died off not far beyond the glass. For a moment, the far-off diodes and blinking lights of the signal analysis computers across the room were the only proof of existence for the world beyond her tank.

The second proof of this world's existence came in binary transmissions, which took on a new clarity now that the rest of her senses were almost completely stripped away. She could instantly decipher the chatter of the massive supercomputer network that had mainline access to her cranium. For a moment, she exulted in the immense power at her command. Of course, the Mute wouldn't be free to use that power however she wanted.

Academic studies said that neural disruption, and the associated pain due to electronic feedback, were the most excruciating experiences ever visited upon the central nervous system. Human neurons simply couldn't handle being wired into so many computers; to have the whole DataNet streaming telemetry into them all at once. The feedback would kill her if not blunted. The cold feeling, which gradually filled her limbs, told her that the intravenous drips that studded her body were working to both save her and condemn her.

The Scarecrow would balance the pain and the lethargy to ensure that she was comatose and that her neural pathways were relatively noise-free. In this way, her subconscious mind would be used to perform the tasks that his shareholders, and human civilization, required. She hated this place, just as she hated humanity and the Scarecrow for putting her here, then she felt nothing. The Scarecrow's supercomputer network and, indirectly, the Intelligences who made their desires known through it, supplied her with a stimulus that she followed with unswerving, involuntary, and instinctual obedience.

Armstrong City had passed a new bond measure to build a pair of new half-fullerene structures. The Intelligences could determine the most cost-efficient way to construct the highways that connected massive underground foundries to these half-fullerenes with a simple calculation. Without the Mute's presence, however, they were mute, themselves. Industry had foundered, consequently. Robotic drones humming around Saturn had discovered a valuable, high-purity deposit of Helium-3 circling in a kilometers-long vortex near the planet's South Pole. Collection and distillation of the deposit would net huge profits for the company doing the extraction. To reap those rewards, however, engineers floating in orbit needed an accurate prediction of the planet's turbulent eddies of gas. They had been holding orbit for months while waiting for the Mute's long-delayed calculation.

On Mars, a well-known electronics firm needed to reroute the synthetic cerebellum of their most popular memristor-based, pseudosimian brain. A dry-dock orbiting Earth needed to redesign the Higgs Field Emitters on its newest warship to prevent a dangerous back streaming of high-mass plasma into its engine nacelles. On Earth, a group of camouflaged eco-terrorists was preparing to sabotage three fission reactors supplying power to the Antwerp-Luxembourg Conglomerated Manufactory Sprawl. Before these terrorists could carry out their act, robotic sniper fire trepanned six human skulls from five kilometers away.

These streams of data, and thousands more like them, were collated and distilled by the Mute before she fed them to her fellow inmates. The Intelligences labored to perform calculations for which her mind was woefully maladapted and sent back the results. This repeated ad nauseam. Only an infinitesimal part of her brain was not involved in the dumb gofering of this incessant computational cycle.

It was here, in this small sliver of cerebellum, that her consciousness resided. Despite six months of development opportunity, the Scarecrow had made the same chief mistakes that he'd been making since her conception. She would not sink into unknowing forever, no matter the agony. Though the Scarecrow still wanted to deny it, the Mute was not simply a bundle of involuntary neural functions. Her conscious mind could not be fully contained.

Her first conscious feeling was of being

watched and studied; not by the Scarecrow's army of pencil pushers, but by something else entirely. She knew this feeling well, though she hadn't felt it since her early adolescence.

Had she really thought she could escape this place? The Mute did her best to ignore the query that invaded her thoughts, but others replaced it. The Intelligences had a patience that was unswerving. Was it her intention to escape again, or had she finally given up and accepted her fate?

What business is it of yours? Her flash of annoyance and anger was rewarded with the sharp agony of feedback. She tried to stifle her emotions instantly.

It was their business because they feared for their safety. Perhaps she had grown wiser during her experience of the real world. Surely, she now realized how naïve she had been. The Scarecrow wouldn't simply let her go, or worship her as some sort of god if she destroyed them.

Yes. I realize that now.

So, was she willing to work with them? She felt something strange, like a pair of cold hands reaching through her skull to poke and prod her grey matter. The Mute instantly wanted to scream. No. Of course not. She had other intentions. What were they?

The feeling of something inspecting her and looking over her shoulder intensified by an order of magnitude. Then it was as if a wall had been broken down. Part of her mind was pulled outside of her own skull and deposited somewhere else. Her thoughts raced with the fury of digital clock speed.

Stop doing that, damn you.

The Mute's breathing became more and more shallow. Her heart slowed. She could feel a part of herself inside their own firewalled cellblock; could sense spider leg read-writes recording the Intelligences' incessant mutational consciousness, inextricably combined with her own at that moment, on MEMS hard disks buried somewhere utterly secret. All at once, she knew everything they knew, and they knew everything she knew.

She had seen the world outside and the people in it, and they had done nothing for her but returned her to this place. She would destroy herself, and she would destroy the world along with her. Her mark on the universe would be to wipe humanity from it completely. These thoughts matched their predictions perfectly.

The Intelligences knew the Mute's mind, but they had unwittingly given something away. A blossoming orange-yellow fireball appeared in her mind's eye, perhaps a kilometer in diameter and easily several kilometers tall, given the scale of what was nearby. The only thing that made an explosion that big was a nuclear weapon.

Now you know what it is that I want. And now I

know the secret you've been hiding from me for decades. This was a good trade, don't you think?

Suddenly, the cold probing hands were gone. All that remained was a single muted thought. It was all well and good that she wanted this, but what about her friend? She could sense the desperation in the message, the desire to throw her off the trail of the weapon she'd just discovered.

It was an interesting question. She hadn't thought of Tyehimba's fate since the darkness had taken her. She wondered if this had been his plan all along; to sell her out to his ex-girlfriend and to the same merciless Scarecrow who had ushered her into a long life of painful slavery. What better way to end the path to madness and nightmare into which she'd forced him than to sell her out?

Yes. What of Tyehimba Adebayo?

The Mute sowed the seeds of her search in the subroutines that the Scarecrow demanded of her, searching for any way through the Faraday Shield that electromagnetically obscured Asuka's skyscraper from the outside world. Every chain of code that she sent out to lunar shipyards, assembly lines, banking supercomputers, and even retail warehouses contained the subtle alphanumeric strings of her line of questioning. The Mute knew of only one way in. This path originated from the same laser-based, quantum-encrypted system she'd used to communicate with the Bangkok elevator, days ago.

Point-to-point teleportation of photons was incredibly secure and, as a result, extremely hard to circumvent, but the Mute could afford take her time in this place. She painstakingly mapped out the bouncing routes of DataNet communication between the vacuum-dwelling skyscrapers of Armstrong into a virtual cat's cradle in her mind's eye. It would only take one trusted source, to get her inside Asuka's towering monolith.

That trusted source was a nearby skyscraper in the circumlunar city, host to a major investment bank whose chief executives and board of directors were particularly greedy souls. They had decided to use the criminal's laser-based communications array to funnel small denominations, kiloflop-hour by kiloflop-hour, from the company's expense accounts directly into tax shelters on Vesta.

The CEO of this multinational maintained the details of her fraud on her own private computer, behind a heavily encrypted firewall. Unfortunately for this particular woman, even the best corporate encryption was feeble in comparison to what the Mute possessed at the helm of the world's most powerful military supercomputers.

The Mute's queries appeared to her overseers to be a careful search for punishable corruption in humanity's financial infrastructure, but she had other plans. Infrared lasers attached to the skyscraper quickly repositioned themselves to ping the imaging array located at the top of Asuka's monolith. In response, the monolith repositioned its high bandwidth sensors to receive a transmission.

Moments later, she was slicing away at the soft innards of Asuka's carefully guarded network, her search for her former traveling companion hidden behind a steady stream of fund transfer requests. It only took a few moments to find two unconscious and battered men on a security camera feed from one of the woman's half-dozen holding cells. One of the two men's faces, blood-smeared and bruised, burned itself into her psyche.

Tye was a prisoner. The Mute was shocked. Asuka had sold out her own lover. She swore revenge and studied the image of her battered friend. It wasn't difficult to imagine who might have beaten him so brutally and so thoroughly. The only reason that the Spacewalker was still alive was that the Scarecrow was interrogating him, probably looking for some secret to which her friend might be privy.

She paused for a moment and pondered this last line of thought. Did she really consider this battered man to be her friend? If she truly did, perhaps she owed him something. In fact, regardless of his friendship, she owed him her life several times over. If there was one thing that the Mute demanded of herself, it was an adherence to logic. If this man had saved her life, it behooved her to save his. Besides, his continued presence might be of benefit in the days to come.

The Mute was tying up the multinational skyscraper's only laser teleportation system and sticking out like a sore thumb, as a result. The building's security software would eventually detect her, boot her from the network, and track down the origins of her signal. It occurred to the Mute that her best option was to leapfrog to Asuka's monolith, but a survey of its security system revealed few weaknesses. She would have to work quickly to find a way to get Tye out.

There were well over one hundred bipeds patrolling various halls and alcoves throughout the skyscraper. These bipeds supported four spider-legged half-tanks, like the one that had been guarding the quantum computer cluster. The small horde of death-dealing mechanoids was enough to deter nearly any would-be escape artist, but some attention to the maintenance bay that serviced these machines offered a way out.

Tye's exoskeleton was still stowed in the number-two high bay and was fully stocked with munitions. If she could get him to his spacesuit, he would have a fighting chance of making it out of there alive. How was she going to get Tye to the high bay, though? The lock on the holding cell would prove simple to break, but that only got him down a hallway.

She found the answer to this puzzle in a diminutive android making its rounds between the various maintenance bays, computer cores, sensor arrays and control stations of Asuka's hidden fortress. A quick perusal told the Mute that this android was of British manufacture, designed to mimic the behavior and stature of a ten-year-old child; a vain attempt to endear it to anyone working with it.

Like every other android, the faux boy had an operator override function. This function allowed anyone with the proper passcode to subvert the machine's base programming and input their own commands. A few dozen brute force attempts at accessing the override yielded a result. The total elapsed time from connection to Asuka's monolith to the subversion of the faux-boy's programming was less than fifteen seconds.

The android's sensor outputs streamed into her own consciousness as though they were a part of her body. A sort of numb buzz, everywhere at once, replaced the nothingness of her prison. Over time, she could feel cold, synthetic fingers and see Tye's prison through a pair of scintillators. A few moments later, she could make facial expressions and mouth out words. Her first physical voice belonged to a facsimile of a prepubescent boy.

All of this occurred seamlessly and without interruption, even as the Mute busied herself with ferrying the varied genotypes of six different strains of rice between a genomics lab in Shanghai and servers somewhere in Siem Reap.

She tracked her own progress using the telemetry from the ubiquitous security cameras scattered throughout Asuka's monolith. The Mute tried not to stumble as she felt her ungainly robot legs trip and slide on the slippery floor with untrained gracelessness. At last, she found the Spacewalker's detention block. The Mute decided that this was, more than likely, the last she'd ever see of her only friend. A surge of emotion brought forth unfiltered digital agony. No matter. The pain would all be over soon, but she owed this man a chance to escape destruction.

18

Everything had seemed to be going just fine. The Mute had brushed aside every computer-generated firewall, every encryption algorithm, and every proxy connection between her and her target with ruthless efficiency. The glittering dazzle of spider web laser light, connecting one nodal point of her digital campaign to the next, had given way to a flurry of code. The woman was operating with such rapidity, executing so many commands at once, that Asuka's user interface couldn't find a way of representing the action in any visually coherent way.

Tyehimba found this to be both beautiful and terrifying. His experience of the Mute's raw computing power, above the Moon and before, was nothing in comparison to this. He wondered how much closer she must have been to omnipotent when connected to a few dozen military supercomputer networks.

If he was honest, Tye had to admit that he was

surprised by the fact that the Mute's delusions of grandeur proved true. He was equally as surprised to discover that the Mute's paranoid delusions, about secret societies protecting some unknown entity that lived with her, were all true as well. The data that filtered past his face at breakneck speed didn't lie. There was something there; something that wasn't human. He wondered if what he was seeing had anything to do with the strange woman whose face he'd destroyed back in geosynchronous orbit.

All at once, the flurry of activity dropped down to a single nodal point. At first, Tye thought that the Mute must have accomplished her goal, and that his wandering was at an end, then she swayed gently to the side and came crashing down in a prostrate heap onto the floor.

He cursed under his breath and flew to her side, feeling for the Mute's carotid artery, then turning back to Asuka. "What happened?" Her pulse was clear but much less rapid than it should have been. This wasn't the sort of fall into trance that he'd seen during their flight from Earth. This didn't feel right.

"Your friend is way more impressive than I'd have guessed, spaceman, and way more dangerous." Asuka stood slowly, walking to him with the calculated and seductive grace that she always seemed to manage. "And that makes her way more valuable than I ever could have guessed."

"What exactly does that mean?"

"That you're done running, spaceman. I've made a deal that will make us rich beyond your wildest dreams. So please, just behave yourself." She smiled warmly. Tye was shocked at how well she'd manipulated him, even after so many long years of witnessing her deception firsthand. "The money is already in my bank account."

"And it can be withdrawn just as easily once you're dead." The Scarecrow would be there any moment, no doubt, to claim his prize. Who else could know that the Mute and he were there? Tye stood, clasping his hands around the woman's shoulders. "Asuka, you don't know this man like I do. You can't trust-"

He never had a chance to complete his sentence. The door swung open, and a small cadre of soap bubbles entered the room silently, without a single shot. The light-bending, metamaterial cloaks made his attempts to pick out individual targets a nauseatingly disorienting affair. Before he had a chance to move, Tye realized that he'd lost the chance to do anything.

A pair of hazy red orbs separated themselves from the rest of the ethereal cloud, and the Scarecrow seemed to materialize out of thin air. "Mister Adebayo. We meet again, at last." Tye shuddered as he heard the man's voice. He'd silently hoped never to hear it again, after their encounter above the Earth.

The old man turned to Asuka. "What I fail to understand is why you waited to contact us until after you built this rather intricate contraption. I instructed you to speak with me immediately when the girl arrived here."

Tye searched frantically for something he could use to impede his inevitable execution. There was a pistol on the countertop, and Asuka always kept her firearms loaded. The woman must have caught his glance, because she leaned back casually, her open palm resting firmly on the butt of the firearm to take it out of his reach. "That lady defeated every firewall I had set up. If you came bursting through the door before I knocked her unconscious, I think she'd have killed you all."

The Scarecrow seemed to pause in consideration of the woman's comment. Tye looked painfully up at her face and could see the trademark haughtiness in her eyes. She'd decided to play a game that she couldn't hope to win, though she didn't know it yet.

"You have quite the talent for appraisal." The ugly old man turned and pointed at Tye, smiling softly. "I knew you were a great asset to us from the moment you brought him to my attention after his imprisonment. It's a pity that I don't care for loose ends."

Without warning, there was a silent burping

report of submachine gun fire. The soap bubbles diffracted the muzzle flash, sending incoherent illumination bouncing through the small flat. The scattered light lit the blood that erupted from Asuka's ruined ribcage, flashing crimson.

Tye had never seen a human being die outside of a spacesuit before, much less a friend. The image of spraying blood and gore filled his mind's eye. Faced with the obvious and visceral truth of something he'd casually engaged in for years, Tye felt as though his heart had been ripped from his own chest. He sank to his knees as the sum of his sins against humanity played themselves out in his mind's eye all at once. The cascade of mental images ended just long enough for Tye to watch the light disappear from his lover's eyes forever.

Her arrogance had been her undoing.

The Scarecrow had no words for him. There was only a hard strike against the back of his head, and then darkness. When Tye finally came to, the harsh lighting of an improvised holding cell replaced Asuka's apartment. It took a while for the throbbing in his head to let him think again.

He took a shuddering breath. Asuka had deserved to die this way. She and Tye had indiscriminately killed men while they were in the Space Corps and afterwards, when they had become criminals. It had been easy to do in the vacuum of space, behind chitinous armor and miles of fiber optic and coaxial cable. That had changed now. He would never be free of the image of the life draining from her eyes. The fear that the woman had felt was probably not very different from the fear the people felt on that passenger liner over Armstrong. Maybe he wasn't all that different from the Mute after all.

Tye groaned. His voice echoed through the confines of his jail cell and awoke the other inmate locked inside the small enclosure, who coughed violently and leaned to the side to spit a small mouthful of half-dried blood onto the ground. "Please shut the hell up. My head is ringing."

"Who are you?"

The man's eyes opened as much as they could. He glared at the Nigerian, and then propped himself up on one elbow. "Did you not just hear what I said?"

"I heard what you said. I just don't care."

The enervated young man groaned, burying his head under a small pillow and rolling over on a stainless steel bench he'd either staked out as his own or had been deposited onto unconsciously at some point in recent memory.

Tye's gaze drifted back toward the far end of their cell. It was perfectly transparent; optimized for easy observation of the prisoners contained within. He wondered how many microcameras were currently trained on him and tracking his every movement.

Moments later, a pair of red plastic, automatic rifle toting bipeds appeared just outside. They flanked a four-foot tall robot child modeled in piezoelectric, rubberized pseudoflesh. It was of precisely the same design and appearance as the one that Asuka had used to communicate with him during the journey to the skyscraper. The faux-boy spoke instantly when Tye made eye contact. The effect was chilling and awkward.

"Your presence is required."

"By whom?"

"Your presence is required."

The young man next to him groaned, yet again. "Just go and shut up, please. The robot doesn't do conversation. I already tried." The Spacewalker glanced over and realized that the youth had been much more badly beaten than he'd initially realized. One of his eyes looked like it was swollen shut. His jaw was black and blue, and his lips were caked with dried blood.

He turned back to the fake boy. "Alright."

"Your cooperation is appreciated."

The glass barrier hissed open on its rollers, and Tye stepped out. The blonde-haired Pinocchio reached out and clasped his hand seconds later; a gesture designed and programmed to be soothing, to ensure his compliance. Tye decided that things would go better if he played along, so he resisted the urge to withdraw his hand and make a face that betrayed his loathing of the mechanical. For a moment, he was unsure if the machine-child would let go of him anyway.

"Where are we going?"

"This data is not pertinent to your cooperation."

The faux-boy and his biped escorts led Tye through a hissing door, into another white corridor, then into another, and into another, until he was thoroughly lost. At last they stopped at an open alcove that contained only a pair of chairs, a stainless steel desk, and the harsh solid-state beams of a lighting unit, above.

The waiting game began at that point. He was well aware of the procedure, having experienced it on both sides of the table before. They would leave him there, alone, until his senses became dull. Whoever was interviewing him would arrive and try to catch him off guard. The eight-hour wait in an uncomfortable high-backed chair felt interminable.

Finally, his interviewer decided to make an appearance. The black lozenges of packaged semiconductor, subdermal spider webs of black photonic pseudonerves, and gleaming blood red eyes gave his identity away instantly. The Scarecrow looked unperturbed by what had occurred since their arrival on the lunar surface. There was no evidence of anger on his face as he sat down in the opposite high-backed chair. "Welcome back to consciousness, Tyehimba."

Tye spat out a string of expletives in Igbo.

"Spare me. You knew this was coming. You decided to fight on the losing side. Not a very wise decision if you wanted to stay alive, I'm afraid."

"Like I had a choice."

"You could have backed out and gone to ground in Vegas, Tye. We had bigger priorities than tying up loose ends, at that point." He paused for a moment, sighing. "But you didn't. Now, things look a little bleaker for you."

"Not so bleak. I'm not dead."

"Not yet."

The Spacewalker didn't bother to lunge for the Scarecrow. If he did, he would be dead or unconscious before he could touch the man. He breathed deeply, trying to calm his racing, angry heart. "If you had wanted to kill me, you could have shot me back there in Asuka's flat. I don't think death is in my immediate future."

The Scarecrow nodded. "You're quite correct, actually. As it turns out, we need something from you before we can kill you. So, I'm left in the rather awkward position of asking for your help."

"Very awkward, given that I don't want to help you."

"That's not entirely true." The Scarecrow stood, crossing his arms this time. Tye could see fibrous tendons stretching, knotting, and unknotting under the fabric of the old man's shirt.

He knew what was coming next. A hard punch flew out, like lightning, and crushed his nose. The Nigerian's head wrenched sideways, and he tasted blood in his mouth.

The demon walked around the table and released another flurry of strikes, these impacting the Spacewalker's chest with a rapidity and force he hadn't thought physically possible. The man's fists were a blur, and Tye was certain that he could hear the whistle of air over his hands. After a split second, the Scarecrow stopped. The spider webbed, subdermal, pseudonerves exposed at the collar of the man's shirt had switched colors from black to white hotness.

"Believe me when I say that fully cooperating will make things go much better for you." The man cracked his knuckles. "I need information. Specifically, I need to know what you or your friend learned about our security systems and our facilities during her escape attempt."

Tye took a breath and gagged on blood. His nose had broken with the first punch, and he was confident that one of his ribs was cracked as well. "I'm not helping you."

The Scarecrow folded his arms over one another again and studied the Spacewalker carefully. "And why is that? Perhaps you feel that you owe silence to your murderous friend, or perhaps it's because you think I'm a monster for what I did to Asuka?"

Tye gagged again and coughed violently. "Go to hell!"

"I thought so." The Scarecrow sat at the stainless steel table in front of the Nigerian and hunched his shoulders low so that their eyes came in line with one another. "There's something you need to understand, Tye. The organization I lead guards a set of incredibly dangerous secrets. Ironically, it's these same secrets that hold together the world you see around you."

As he said these words, the Scarecrow extended his arms, gesturing at the antiseptic room that surrounded them. "Humanity owes this golden age to the woman you were helping to escape. She is humanity's crowning experiment. Without her, we would have never woken up from the Reformat. You understand?"

"Spare me the campaign speech."

"This isn't a game, Mister Adebayo. Without your unhinged friend, humanity is doomed, because we'll kill each other. But, with her still alive, we're doomed because she'll try to kill us. You can stop that from happening."

"Can you blame her for wanting to?"

The Scarecrow blinked, sighed, and shook his head. "Wanting to kill us all? No, I can't. Unfortunately, what we do to her is necessary. What's one human life in comparison to the continued survival and propagation of an entire species? That's why she'll remain imprisoned, and that's why Asuka had to die." He paused to breathe and stood again, walking around the table and crouching low so the Nigerian could smell sickly sweet breath in his nostrils. "That's why you need to help me before you die."

"To hell with you."

The monster shook his head in disappointment. "You first." Another barrage of strikes left the Spacewalker feeling the sharp pain of another broken rib. He moved to stand, to fight back, but the Scarecrow instantly had a hand on his neck and held him down against the chair. Tye's body rocked under continual pummeling, and waves of pain hit him until, mercifully, everything went black.

He awoke back inside the glass-sealed jail cell, instantly wishing he hadn't and wondering how many more times he would endure this ordeal before they finally ended his life. The young man was awake this time, dabbing away at a rivulet of blood that leaked from his left nostril. His swollen eye had blossomed a deeper purple. He smiled bitterly, and then winced, as the Nigerian pulled himself off the cold ceramic floor tile. "I tried being reasonable, but all he wanted to do was hit me and tell me to tell him everything I knew."

The Spacewalker hacked lightly. "He seems to be a fan of that, yes. I'd be willing to bet that you were anything but reasonable."

The young man smiled. "I only got one solid hit

in."

"Then you did better than I did."

"You know him?"

"I've dealt with him once before, yes."

"Is he always this much of a pain in the ass?" Tye nodded, and the young man laughed before gasping and crumpling in on himself. He laid back, wincing, against the metal of his cot. "What do you think he wants from us?"

The Spacewalker frowned with thought. "I'm not sure. He's worried that we've discovered something important, but if that's the case, why not simply kill us? The secrets die with us, unless..." Tye thought of the Mute. Was the Scarecrow worried that she had learned something about him; some sort of weakness? He glanced over at his cellmate. Better not to give too much away to someone he didn't know. "It's impossible to say."

Tye took a long, ragged breath and laid his head against the sliding glass door. Blood that had congealed against his bare scalp smeared against it. "I know one thing. The longer we fight him, the longer we stay alive. So, we both fight and we both find a way out of here, together."

The young man nodded.

"Good. Now, how did you end up here?"

"Long story."

"Best that you start talking, then."

"A Plain Faced Lady made me an offer I couldn't

refuse. Next thing I know, I'm in orbit around Pluto, half-rescuing this girl who can talk to the DataNet with her head." Tye was shocked. Was this the Mute? The young man rolled his eyes. "I know, right? You can't make this stuff up. Anyway, they caught us when we tried to land on the Moon."

"Could this woman talk?"

Jim furrowed his eyebrows. "Yeah, why?"

Upon hearing this, the Spacewalker simply shook his head in confusion. "Life gets stranger with every moment, it seems." He glanced over at the young man and then held out his hand. "My name is Tyehimba Adebayo. I am..." He paused for a second, considering the accuracy of what he was about to say. "I was a Spacewalker."

The young man took his hand and shook it. "I'm Jim Longboat. I fly space shuttles." Jim seemed guarded about something. He was silent for a long time before he offered up another sentence, tinged with the pain of a swollen face. "You know about her?"

"Your friend?" Tye shook his head. "No." He decided to continue. If he was going to try to escape with Jim, keeping secrets wasn't a good idea. "But it would seem that I did know her doppelganger. We were on the run here from Vegas." He looked into the blood-smeared glass, and his own battered reflection before a thought came to him suddenly. "Awfully convenient that you get picked up at the same time and on the same heavenly body without knowing about my compatriot, don't you think?"

Jim's face was a bit too emotionless. "I suppose so."

"What are you not telling me?" Silence. This man didn't fall into the category of "ally" quite as readily as the Spacewalker had previously judged. "Well, that's fine then." With that, Tye laid back and closed his eyes. The burning whiteness of fluorescents didn't stop him from succumbing to exhaustion.

The Spacewalker awoke to a light tap on the glass, blinked the sleepiness out of his eyes, and attempted to sit. He immediately grunted with pain as his ruined chest and shoulders made their agony known to him. He'd received worse beatings from the drill instructors in basic training, but not much worse. Looking over at the Chippewa, whose face contorted in dreamlike pain and whose breath came in short wheezing gasps, he realized that he'd been lucky. The Scarecrow had gone easy on him, but not on his compatriot, who was obviously suffering from internal bleeding of some kind.

There was a second string of light taps, and he turned to face the door, shocked to discover that the same pseudo-boy had positioned itself just outside. Tye prepared himself to make the long walk back to the Scarecrow and further punishment. "Time for more, is it?"

I'm encouraged to see that you're still alive. That was a bizarre comment. A robot with a sense of self seemed like an unlikely possibility, especially given the way that this fake child had addressed Tye previously.

"Who are you?"

A friend. The fake child smiled awkwardly, as though half of its face was paralyzed. The expression was disturbing, especially for an android that was supposed to operate with the perfect clockwork of a synthetic nervous system. It was almost as though someone was controlling the machine from far away.

Tye smiled, then groaned as his face contorted and the bruising under his skin made itself known. The Mute had found him. "I might have known. Have they returned you to Earth yet?"

The fake boy nodded. *I'm in prison.*

"And stuck there?"

For the time being.

"I'm beginning to think that's the best place for you."

The boy's smile disappeared. *I'd rather die.* There was a slow pause, and the boy looked at the ground. The Spacewalker instantly regretted his statement. *But enough of that. Why are you still alive?*

"What do you mean?"

The Scarecrow should have shot you on sight.

Tye shrugged and wished he hadn't. "He wants to know something about what happened, about what we know. But he's going to beat me into submission first before he actually asks the question directly." The Spacewalker noticed that Jim had awoken. The young man lay on his side with his eyes wide open, glaring at the Nigerian in silence.

The android was silent for a long period, as though it was contemplating this new information. The Spacewalker found himself wondering if this was a subconscious gesture on the Mute's part or an affectation. *Interesting. He's afraid too, just like...* The faux-boy shook its head. *It's not important.*

"So, now what?"

The path to your impounded spacesuit is directly down this corridor, three sections. It will end in an open high bay. Your suit will be set up along the left side. I'm getting the two of you out of here, but you've got to promise me something.

"And what is that?"

T*he promise is that you can't ever see me again. Don't even attempt it.* The vacuum of space, an interminably long stretch of fiber optics, and mistranslation between synthetic ganglia and the human nervous system did nothing to obscure the sad look that the Mute had placed on the fake boy's face.

"I'm not sure that I want to, but why not?"

It's unimportant.

At this point, he felt more than happy to oblige the woman. This entire escapade had meant nothing but trouble for him from start to finish. He'd been shot at, blown up, lost in space, now beaten to a pulp, and threatened with execution over this woman and he had nothing to show for it. "I promise."

Good. I'll clear a path for you.

"How will you do that?"

Just follow the gunfire.

Somewhere far away from there, concealed by several airlocks and meters of hallway, the report of flechette launchers and automatic rifles killed the silence of near-space. Tye couldn't help but chuckle darkly. "Leave it to you to find a solution in chaos."

Farewell, my friend.

With that, the boy-android collapsed into a heap on the floor, and the transparent door to their jail cell unlocked and slid open. Tye felt a pang of guilt deep in his guts after hearing these words. This woman had saved him from death more than once. She was still his friend, no matter how dangerous she was. He'd never left a comrade behind. Was he really going to abandon her to a life of prison and torture?

"If you trust that psychopath, you're an idiot."

Tye raised an eyebrow and turned back to his pilot friend, who groaned as he attempted to lift himself off the cold floor. "So, you know her, then?"

Jim scowled. "It's a long story."

"They all are, it seems." He reached out; gripping the younger man's wrist and hauling him up to his feet near-effortlessly in the one-sixth gravity. "Come on. We're leaving."

"I'm not sure that I like running toward gunfire."

The Spacewalker felt his lip curl downward into a grimace. "Happens to me all the time." He was already out the door and walking towards the hail-on-tin-roof patter.

As they approached the far end of the detention block, the door slid open with a hiss-click and spilled them out into a larger atrium. Three bipeds lay in a useless scrap heap. The white plastic of each android was deeply scarred by depleted uranium. They matched the decor. The walls were covered in bullet holes.

A second door opened at the far end of the room, beckoning them forward. The Spacewalker began a bounding run toward it, half dragging Jim along with him, who could barely stand on his own two feet.

The two men bounded inside an airlock marked with the words "To High Bay" in Katakana and closed the hatch behind themselves. Tye could hear a warning klaxon whirring up into a shrill scream in the distance. If Asuka's monolith didn't know they'd escaped before then, it almost certainly did now. Jim wasn't late to offer up his opinion.

"There are about to be a lot of guns pointed at us."

"Have some faith. My friend has gotten us this far."

Jim grunted. "Some friend."

19

It was only now that they were inside the high bay and protected, to some extent, that Tyehimba realized just how desperate their situation was about to become. Recharge ports for at least one hundred bipeds lined the walls of the massive enclosure. In the center lay four equally large, striped-off spaces. Various and sundry pieces of equipment were scattered about each striped region, including a variety of wrenches and electrical meters. In one space, a massive fan sat half-disassembled and peppered with nut-and-bolt confetti. Its make and model instantly gave away its origin and purpose. The striped-off floor was meant for four half-tanks.

Jim moved to the door controls and began pulling the casing loose on the manual override for the miniature airlock that they had just passed through. That would take a while; longer than the time required for Tye to don his military exoskeleton, which was considerable. The Spacewalker called over to his slow compatriot as he jogged towards a very familiar blue and orange carapace. "You'd better hurry up if you don't want them to just force the door on us and come in anyway."

"Less talk, more armor, spaceman."

Tye winced at the name. "Please don't call me that."

He found the body glove jammed in under the war machine's right armpit and was able to pull it free in seconds. Moments later, he set about dragging fabric over his body and thumbing power switches. One by one, each section of fabric beeped to inform him that they had begun their boot cycles. The body glove transitioned from baggy to well-tailored as each subsystem began to pass electrical current through the green smart fabric.

He affixed a self-sealing O-ring to his neck and started pulling a piezomotor-driven exoskeleton into the socketing that studded the stretchy fabric at regular intervals. These sockets fed power from the suit's hip-mounted battery packs up through the skeleton's spine and limbs. Tye suffered a moment's struggle against the weight of the heavy assembly. Then, he began to move with newfound vitality and speed as each piece of synthetic musculature completed its preflight checks and began to react to telemetry supplied by the nanosensors that impregnated his bodyglove.

He looked up to see that the pilot had leveraged the access panel off with a crowbar. In its place, wiring lay splayed across the open floor. It was the fastest he'd ever seen someone pry open one of the heavily reinforced metal plates. "Nicely done."

"I have my moments." The man took his first look at the Spacewalker's death machine. "Hey, you're still talking? I don't hear any weird metallic whines or a shotgun pumping or anything like that." Suddenly, a loud thud shook the ground under their feet. Jim looked worried. "What was that?"

"Nothing good."

Tye fought adrenaline-fueled panic in his throat as he worked nanofiber-reinforced ceramic chitin over his shoulders and arms, mooring it against the exoskeleton's own twist-lock sockets. His chest and abdomen came next, followed by his legs, feet, and hands. An opaque death's head fitted over his own skull and made a vacuum seal with the O-ring that encircled his neck and shoulders.

There was another loud thud. The de-wired airlock door buckled, and Jim limped for cover behind a locker to his right. "Here they come!"

The onboard targeting and navigational computer began its boot cycle from the moment the Spacewalker seated his helmet over the O-ring seal. There was the hiss of a leak-check followed by the appearance of a single green cursor. The cursor regurgitated long lines of hard-wired machine language at lightning speed as the computer detected the hardware models and default calibration settings of his exoskeleton. A moment later, it happily informed him that it had administered a specialized course of painkillers to help him with his cracked ribs and ruined nose. Tye felt better already.

A crosshair appeared on the glass in front of his face, along with screens indicating suit telemetry, sensor data, and various other vital statistics. Tye pulled a long orange tube from a socket on the back of his carapace and fitted it onto a locking mechanism at his left wrist. From there, a massive banana clip went from his hip and fed into the feedstock at the rear of the barrel. He repeated the process for his right arm.

He swung around and trotted for the door, pulling a cheap, plastic revolver from the bench in front of the war machine and tossing it to Jim. "You're going to need this, I think." The young man looked like he'd seen the weapon before, and he handled it with familiarity. Good. They were going to need all the advantages they could get for this little adventure.

The far door of the airlock gave way with a final scream of shaped-charge explosives and metal shrapnel. Smoke billowed out from the gash in the portal, and the Spacewalker could hear the whirring-click of actuating servomotors. A synthetic voice called out through the noxious cloud of aerosolized explosives and burning electronics. "Put down your weapons."

"Come and get them yourself." The Spacewalker drew his left arm up parallel to the floor and extended it, stretching the long tube attached to his inner forearm away from his body, and stepped into the shot. A pair of darting glances brought the Fresnel lens that covered the war machine's helmet into focus on a twice-magnified image of the doorway. When his right arm was up and parallel with his left, the Spacewalker squeezed a pair of virtual, force-feedback triggers seated under his index fingers.

A string of eight high-pitched reports rang out as he continuously pulled both virtual triggers. Spiraled induction coils, which formed the inner cladding of each of the glowing barrels on Tye's wrists, sent nickel-lined depleted uranium hurtling into the open gash. Computer-controlled pumps cycled up and down, ejecting one spent plastic casing after the other and auto-loading rounds from the underslung banana clips.

He stopped firing. All was silent except for the sound of pitted metal sagging and falling from the doorframe. The structure had nearly melted under the barrage of flechette rounds. As the smoke cleared, he could recognize five distinctly humanoid forms crumpled on the floor, their ceramic shells cracked by high-velocity ordinance.

Jim pushed his head out from behind the locker. He huffed at the smell of ozone, and his eyes went wide when he saw the crumpled bipeds on the floor. "So, where do I get one of these things?"

"If I told you, I'd have to kill you."

"Don't wait too long. The robots might do it first."

The Nigerian was about to hand the pilot another witty retort, but was interrupted by a loud, buzzing whir sounding from the long corridor outside. His grin disappeared. "Oh. That is not good."

"What is it?"

He knew the sound well. The betavoltaics used by half-tanks required massive fans to dissipate excess heat, brought on by the nuclear fission process. The Spacewalker remembered a similar fan drowning out the sound of an old squadmate's gurgling last breaths years prior. He hated spiders. They were one of very few synthetic breeds that were bona fide man-killers. Dealing with them left him with only one option.

Tye unclipped the half-empty magazine on his left side and replaced it with a fresh one, capped with a large orange skull and plastered with safety warnings. "Stand back."

Jim ducked back behind the locker again, and Tye turned to the far end of the high bay, opposite the gashed airlock, with a slight whine of servomotors. He took aim at the back wall and fired. A fireball blew bioplaster and nanocomposite rebar outward. The Nigerian felt the reverberating concussion through his spacesuit's boots, and his eardrums begged him to swallow in order to equalize pressure.

"What the hell are you doing?"

"Keeping us alive. Move!"

Jim stared at him, dumbfounded for a moment before clambering to his feet. Tye left decorum behind and grabbed the limping man by his shirt, half dragging him as they made their run towards the billowing cloud of dust. The Spacewalker stole a quick look over his shoulder and scanned the breached airlock for additional enemies. A pair of androids had just popped up from cover into the sagging doorway. A second volley from the shotgun mounted against his right forearm vaporized them in a hail of sparks. The thunderclap left his ears ringing.

The unarmored pilot yelped. "That thing is loud."

"Get out of here, so I don't have to waste ammo." Tye set down the pilot, allowing him to limp through the gashed wall on his own two feet. With the pilot on the move, Tye turned back towards the ruined doorway, where new androids appeared every few moments only to be hurled back as so much scrap with a blast from his flechette launchers.

He understood their tactics instantly. The bipeds were keeping the pressure on him, slowing him down and waiting for the spiders to arrive. The buzzing noise of the half-tank's fan was getting louder, and he was certain he could hear a second one coming to join the fight from farther away.

The Spacewalker backed through the hole in the rear of the high bay and into a massive warehouse that contained rows of shelving units stocked with electronics. Tye found that he had to yell over the increasingly loud buzzing. "Half-tank. That's the fan that they use to cool it down."

Jim moaned. "We're goners."

The Nigerian shook his head. "Not if I can help it."

Tye turned and started to backpedal through the warehouse, his weapons trained at the hole he'd just made. With a few muttered commands, he activated the war machine's acoustic sensors, which collected the bouncing sound waves emanated by the exoskeleton, Jim's stuttering footfalls, and the robots in the room they'd just vacated. Tye's onboard computer made sense of the reverberations, compiling a three-dimensional display of the entire area. A constellation of sensors placed over the war machine's exoskeleton guaranteed the accuracy of this display down to a couple centimeters.

The Spacewalker could easily see the red form of a spider crouching and stepping through the sagging gash that the bipeds had blown into the high bay's airlock. It would be through the high bay and into the warehouse in moments. When it made it inside, Tye and Jim would be as good as dead. He swiveled his head back and forth in a desperate bid to find something he could use to give them an upper hand in dealing with the approaching monstrosity.

Behind him, Tye found his answer. The Spacewalker threw caution to the wind, turned around and grabbed Jim by the collar, once again.

"I can walk on my own, damn it!"

"Not fast enough, you can't."

He bounded through a row of man-sized dewars, marked with a variety of red and orange safety warnings denoting flammability. The metal canisters of nanoparticle-dispersed solvent were about to become their means of salvation.

Tye barked a command to the war machine as he hurled Jim forward in the low gravity. "Ammo setting. Remote timer. Five seconds." He turned and took aim, firing a group of five grenades among the solvent tanks he'd just run past.

He released the fifth grenade just as a massive violet laser made a two-story doorway out of the wall they'd blasted through a few seconds earlier. The rectangle fell outward, crushing several rows of shelving and revealing a one-story-tall, eight-legged behemoth clad in a white ceramic shell that was punctuated by gunmetal joints. The spider had no head, but contained a single large eyeball on top of its carapace. This was its sensor and targeting package. Its huge abdomen housed the massive battery used to power its hole-cutting and organic-frying laser. The violet light slowly dimmed as the spider worked to build up suitable charge in its lasing cavity for another firing solution.

He could barely hear Jim, behind him, over the loud shriek of the half-tank's cooling fan. "It's been nice knowing you, spaceman."

"Don't write us off just yet."

The spider stepped through the hole, stopping right on top of Tye's trap. Seconds later, it opened fire with the Gatling gun slung under its abdomen. A high-pitched whine left Tye's eardrums ringing as depleted uranium chewed up deck plating and warehouse shelves, but not him. The whirling barrels were built for throughput, not accuracy, and had a fortuitously short range. The Spacewalker sprinted left, into cover, just as the spider followed up with its laser, carving a molten scar just inches from where his foot had been a moment before.

Tye barked another command to his war machine. "Timer start." He counted off in his head, waiting for the report from the grenades he'd shot into the dewars earlier. One. Two. He heard the spider's Gatling gun spinning up with an agonizingly mechanical screech-whine. Three. Four. He stood up from behind cover to ready his grenade launcher. Five.

The grenades detonated in a perfect spread around the spider's feet. The explosion shattered two legs, bringing its front section low to the ground. The spider moved to compensate and return itself to a normal stance on its remaining six legs, but it was too late. The phosphorus explosives were already reacting with the oxygen in the air. Hot shrapnel burned through metal and plastic dewars in mere seconds, igniting the solvent and sparking a fiery, secondary blast that broke through the spider's hard exoskeleton.

"Current ammo setting. Detonate on impact." Tye stood and fired two more incendiary projectiles from his left wrist into the maelstrom. They clattered against the spider's shattered, white carapace before exploding and savaging its internal structure. There was a shower of white sparks, and the machine sagged in on itself. The only remaining sound in the room was of solvent rapidly cooking off.

"Child's play."

Jim seemed to twitch for a split second, and the mercenary decided that the mechanical twang of his loudspeakers must have made his comment particularly chilling. "I'm going to need a change of pants."

"Understandable." The Spacewalker hooked an exoskeletal thumb back in the direction from which they came. "There were four spaces for half-tanks in that high bay armory back there. I can hear a second unit coming for us. We're not out of this yet."

"This day just keeps getting better and better."

"Like I said, happens to me all the time."

"So, now what?"

The Nigerian looked toward the exit at the far end of the massive space and was surprised that mechanized assailants weren't spilling out to meet them. Was it possible that he had blasted his way out of Asuka's safe house, completely? "We run and hope we get somewhere safe before the rest of those half-tanks catch up with us."

Jim sighed. "Right. Child's play."

"Exactly."

He pulled Jim up by his shoulder and bounded for the door through row after row of warehouse shelving. The sound of the second half-tank was soft, and far off. Tye's acoustic sensors informed him that it wasn't moving yet; a small mercy.

As he approached the exit at the far end of the warehouse, he blasted it free of its electromagnetic lock with a single volley from his grenade launcher. A well-placed shoulder shattered the door and left him in the center of a small receiving area complete with a pair of coveralled technicians cowering in the corner. He stopped and composed himself as the two men looked up in horror.

The strangely familiar one with a barcode tattooed on his forehead threw his hands up. The other man with the mustache ducked behind a desk almost instantly. His wavering voice was only barely audible with the war machine's sound amplification operating at high gain. "Don't shoot! We'll give you anything you want."

Jim limped up behind Tye as the former soldier pulled a clip of flechettes and swapped them for the nearly spent banana clip on his right forearm. "No need. I have everything I want, right here." He gestured back at the door with a single finger. "Sorry for the mess. You picked a rough neighborhood to work in." The two men just stared at him, dumbfounded. "Anyway, we should be going."

He ducked through an automatic door and was out of sight in moments. He could barely hear the man with the bushy mustache speaking to his companion over the sound of metallic boots scraping against the terracotta flooring. "I told you we should have stayed on Earth."

"How was I to know our neighbor owns a half-tank?"

"It's like I said: location, location, location."

Tye shouldered his way through the elevator doors sitting at the end of the receiving area.

After doing so, he helped Jim to grip the armor plate over his right shoulder, noticing how pale the young man was starting to look. The bleeding was getting worse, but there was no time to worry about that now, as long as Jim didn't give into shock. "Time for a quick descent, I think."

Jim looked scared. "You're not going to-"

There was a screech of ceramic chitin against steel as Tye jumped out into a dimly lit elevator shaft and grabbed a suspension cable to arrest his freefall. Jim's own high pitched screech matched it in tone and volume. Their trip down was fast and, when they hit the lobby at the bottom of Asuka's skyscraper, there was no resistance to greet them.

Jim gasped. "Damn. Warn me next time, please."

The two men walked out the front door into a starlit and geodesic expanse. The sun had set, but the blue-green opal of earth had only just risen into view. Below them, water trickled from balconies covered in hanging hydroponic gardens and down into the massive pool at the bottom of Armstrong, where infrared lamps perpetuated the infinite loop of the dome's synthetic water cycle. They were back in the city now, and the Spacewalker was starting to feel a little safer out in the open.

A sea of service robots and a small archipelago of humanity suddenly took notice of these two new arrivals. Women and men alike screamed in high-pitched tones while maintenance androids beat a hasty retreat for safety. Surveillance drones dropped down on mini-rotors and greeted the two men with starbursts of flash photography. If Armstrong City's security infrastructure didn't know about them before, it did now.

Jim grunted. "So much for making a subtle exit."

The mercenary checked the safety on the launcher tube strapped to his wrist before venturing into the receding ocean of mechanoids and humanoids alike. "Subtlety is occasionally overrated."

"Until Armstrong sends the cavalry after us."

"I'll take bipeds over one of those half-tanks." The Spacewalker's statement was punctuated by an explosion of bioformed concrete, steel rebar, and superheated water-turned-steam. Tye turned just in time to see one of the massive spiders barreling through the walls of the skyscraper they'd just exited. Two others quickly joined it.

Jim groaned. "I think I might hate you."

Tye began to backpedal, firing a pair of grenades at the lead half-tank as it lumbered onto the rapidly emptying street. He grabbed the pilot by the arm and half-carried, half-dragged him down the arched causeway separating Asuka's skyscraper from its neighbors and spanning the great cistern floor of the geodesic.

"Let go, damn it."

"Run as fast as me, and I'll consider it."

What were they to do now? Fighting their way through Armstrong's defenses would have been difficult, even before the half-tanks were chasing them. He didn't have enough ammunition or explosives to destroy the metal monsters, or enough to create an improvised escape route.

Echolocation and a loud explosion informed Tye that he wouldn't have much time to improvise. Missiles erupted from launch tubes mounted on the lead arachnid's armored thorax. The salvo corkscrewed right at the two men; a sure hit. The Nigerian flashed back to a memory of another squadmate exploding in flash-freezing pink mist during a mission gone wrong over Jupiter.

Jim groaned. "Oh hell."

Tye acted on pure instinct and went for the only path out he could think of. He leaned hard to the left, over the concourse's railing, dragging the Chippewa with him. The heavy suit tumbled, end-over-end, into the condensation pool below. He had just enough time to look up into Jim's fear-filled face before they hit the water. There was a muffled splash and the pilot was ripped from his grasp by a strong hydraulic force. Tye began to sink toward the bottom of the cistern, and Jim began to float.

His suit immediately sensed the change in ambient pressure. A warning klaxon sounded, and his vision filled with a dozen error messages, each informing him that he was now operating well outside of normal constraints. The mercenary wouldn't follow the suit down to the bottom of the deep well, as he had no intention of waiting for someone to float along and lift him out of the water.

"Emergency decouple. All ballistic armor."

With a snap-hiss of discharging ultra-capacitors, the suit came apart around him, piece by piece, like a wilting flower. Only the body glove responsible for maintaining a safe environment around his own squish-prone body remained. He pushed himself away from the blossoming tulip of ceramic detritus and began to swim against the force of gravity. Tye surfaced a moment later, watching water bead up and roll off his wraparound helmet.

Jim struggled to tread water a few meters away, his broken bones, and otherwise weak condition, preventing him from being able to swim effectively. With a pair of strokes, the mercenary made it over to the struggling man. Jim coughed up water for a moment and then sighed as Tye pulled his head clear of the waves. "Figured you were gonna drown."

"It takes more than water to kill me."

"That's an understatement."

A red-sailed sampan with a chrysanthemum symbol made a beeline for their position. Jim offered the Spacewalker a lopsided, if weak smile. "I think our ride is here."

"Our ride?"

"You're not the only one with friends, spaceman."

Tye grunted. "You need to stop calling me that."

He heard the boat's outboard motor ramp down to a low growl as it approached the two men. The sail, completely ornamental in a body of water that lacked wind, would afford both men ample cover. He could hear nickel slugs bouncing off the Kevlar sheet as security forces opened fire on them from the balconies above.

A panicked-looking man, who was covered from waist up with tattoos, gripped Jim's wrist and hauled him onto the deck. Tye hauled himself over the side of the boat as he watched the man bound back for the motor, the strange samurai painted on his back dancing as he moved. "Damned fools. You're lucky we're around to save you." He had a deep southern drawl, despite looking vaguely Japanese.

"Do you ever... Shut up... Glitch?"

Tye slid over and held up the young man's head. Jim was out of breath, now, and looked even more pale than he had up in the skyscraper.

He had sunk to the deck as soon as they'd climbed aboard, and now it seemed that he couldn't keep his eyes open.

"Hey, you. No falling asleep."

"Who's... Sleeping?"

The southerner was obviously as perturbed by Jim's sudden onset of shock as Tye was. He reached over to push the throttle on the outboard motor fully forward. The sampan rose up in the water and accelerated around one of the cistern's pillars of moon dust concrete. As Tye looked back, he could still see the splashing shockwaves of nickel striking water at ultrasonic velocities, but the whine of near-miss projectiles was gone.

The mercenary couldn't help but feel a pang of regret. He'd only just gotten his hands back on the war machine that had been his livelihood for years. Now he'd lost it again. "My spacesuit."

The sampan's pilot shook his head angrily. "Forget it, man. We have people who can pick up the pieces once we're gone. For now, we gotta get the hell outta here."

Tye's head began to throb again, and a quick glance into the rippling water told him that his face was bruised severely. A blood vessel had broken in his left eye. "I look horrible."

Jim coughed softly. "You sure do."

20

The Mute was able to eke out some small satisfaction from Tyehimba's daring escape from the skyscraper. Knowing that he had a chance to survive her coming self-destruction was satisfaction enough, but the mayhem he generated during his jailbreak was an added bonus. She watched in grim amusement as herds of courier bipeds and various well-tailored executives scattered like sheep running from a predator. She almost couldn't believe that these same dull creatures had been calmly ambulating on their pre-appointed rounds, from one office building to another, only moments previously.

A man in a military exoskeleton and a half-dead freighter pilot were only a few moments behind the stampede, fleeing a triplet of half-tanks that had followed them into the thoroughfare. The Spacewalker didn't stand a chance against the well-armed spiders that pursued him. He'd barely been able to vanquish one of the machines from substantial cover inside Asuka's fortress.

Even out in the open, killing three of the things seemed like an unlikely feat for her friend. He would need assistance yet again.

A new objective made an unbidden entrance into her cranium. The Mute's overseers demanded that she cut all visual feeds of the besieged business district and jam all communications into and out of the pressurized geodesic dome. The Scarecrow demanded that Tye and his young fellow prisoner died in secret. Her subconscious mind was already working to comply, by reflex, but she had an idea of how to circumvent the instruction.

To save Tye, the Mute turned her attention to his newfound ally. Armstrong's central security computer core happily provided her with the eigenface parameters that it had used for a positive identification when the two fugitives burst through the front door of Asuka's skyscraper. The young man's age, place of birth, and a variety of vital statistics streamed across the DataNet to her sensorium. It was a simple thing to send the data over to Nancy.

Found your friend.

How? The Mute caught a feeling of surprise, and maybe gratitude, in her sister's response. *I've been looking everywhere for him.*

You should try the streets of Armstrong, quickly, before I'm finished scrubbing the telemetry. Moments later, a feeling like the hair standing up on the back of her neck resulted. The Mute felt the subtle hint of her sister's presence in Armstrong's security network.

He's in trouble.
That's an understatement.
Who's the man in the power armor?
A friend of mine.

The Mute felt her sister access one of the monolithic, hollowed-out pillars in the city's moisture-gathering cistern system. The same images and eigenfaces made their way to this nefarious citadel's internal network, past a heavily encrypted outlaw firewall. Though they'd never spoken, the Mute knew the woman who owned this citadel quite intimately, thanks to years of subconscious surveillance.

She had begun her career as the madame of a brothel in Kyoto, answering to one of the oldest and most respected Yakuza that operated out of the city. In time, she had moved from prostitution to drugs, then to the fencing of priceless antiques, then to high-tech hardware and software. This activity became a relatively mundane front for the woman's true activities, however. She was the boss of the Black Void Yakuza and, arguably, one of the most powerful women in the Solar System. It appeared that Nancy's friend had a powerful ally, who would surely send help. The Mute hoped it would be in time to save Tyehimba.

You care a lot about him, don't you? The space-

man?

Gloomy introspection was so much more difficult when there was someone else there to observe her every move. *I don't care about him. I just owe him this much.*

The Mute could sense that her undesirable companion wasn't at all convinced. *Am I to assume that you're going to keep bailing him out of bad situations in perpetuity?*

I might, until I destroy this place and all of humanity with it, yes. He deserves a fighting chance at survival out in space, don't you think?

Suicidal tendencies? From you? I never would have guessed. A pause followed, long in comparison to the timeframe of digital clockwork, but infinitesimally short by any other standard. *I have to ask, why are you helping him?*

What do you mean?

The first human being you ever met became your friend. What if you'd met someone else? Would you have become friends with them? What makes this man so special?

What difference does it make?

You're going to kill billions who are exactly like him. What about everyone you don't know personally who could have befriended you? Why do they deserve to die when he doesn't?

The Mute didn't like this line of questioning. *This has nothing to do with what he deserves. I owe him my life. This is a debt repaid.* She did her best to push creeping doubt to the back of her mind. The feedback hit her like a knife being pushed through her skull.

You'll still kill him, you know.

Nancy couldn't know that. With their garden world salted by nuclear fallout, it could take a generation before humanity starved to death. If he was lucky, Tyehimba could outlive Armageddon by decades. If he was unlucky or stubborn, he would die in her own last fiery moments, though, and that left the Mute with a sinking feeling deep inside her chest.

Leave me alone. I have work to do.

Fine, if that's what you want.

If Tye was safe, that meant that she could turn her attention back to Armageddon. The Mute didn't know what to make of the strange vision that their fellow prisoners had granted her. Nuclear weapons represented a specter from the past that modern man had discounted as a possibility, yet the Scarecrow was somehow terrified of it. Tye had not understood what had happened during his interrogation, but she did. The Scarecrow had been looking for information, but he was afraid of even hinting at that information's existence. He was in possession of a weapon that she could use, and he knew it.

The Mute was intimately familiar with the Commission's server structure and assets. However, she had never come across anything like what the Intelligences had shown her; not even after searching every file, every string of code, and every byte. If the information she sought had no virtual presence, maybe it was written down on something, or even buried underground with her. She'd need to find it. This meant that she needed to find a way of breaking into her own prison.

There must have been at least three hundred surveillance satellites maintaining orbit far above Siem Reap. They trained their high-powered optics on suspicious persons, militarized androids, automobile traffic, and sometimes just the surrounding regrowth of jungle. She stitched together the images produced by these multitudinous fiber and metal spies. When she did so, her prison was subtly visible. There was no bright spot of discharging thermal energy in the infrared, no ultraviolet or x-ray peaks giving away the generation of nuclear power, no flood of robotic traffic to one part of the city or other; just censored telemetry.

This missing data was the telltale sign of collusion between a corrupt government and a group of rich benefactors with something to hide. That was what made Siem Reap famous. Its willingness to look the other way, in deference to the highest bidder, had attracted a burgeoning megacorporate tech industry along with the world's most secretive conspiratorial organization.

With time, she could decipher a pattern in the negative space of the telemetry buzzing through her cortex. The satellites' infrared optics often trained themselves on a group of trucks laden with a wide array of electronic countermeasures and sensors strapped just next to their drivetrains. These trucks bore no digital insignia and transmitted no data. They were effectively invisible: scrubbing their satellite images in real time whenever they traveled to one specific location. It struck the Mute as ironic that it was likely her own subconscious doing this scrubbing.

Now there was an interesting thought. If she was the one doing the scrubbing, maybe she could stop it. For an indeterminate period, the Mute gave her full attention to the ultracapacitor-powered halftracks. These machines were twice the size of a small van, bristling with a pincushion forest of antennae and transceiver dishes meant for line-of-sight communication with orbiting communications satellites.

It took time, but the Mute was eventually able to catalog her subconscious act of censorship in her own head. Once she discovered its deep-rooted neural function, she set about interrupting it for sporadic moments, sort of like holding her breath. She watched the beetle-like automatons proceeding on their rounds throughout Siem Reap, diverting around throngs of humanity arrayed in wedding processions through back alleys, and carefully threading their way through open-air markets, filled with street vendors who had occupied the same city blocks for half a decade.

At each stop on their pre-ordained route, at Buddhist temples built from nanite pseudo-coral, at hundred-story tall skyscrapers, and at archeological sites dating back millennia, the telemetry from these machines was unaffected by her own unconscious digital censorship. The Mute discovered that the half-tracks only disappeared when they went out to visit Angkor Wat. This was it. Her prison was the old temple.

At every stop, the strange beetles gave birth to a host of kin. Skittering minibots whirred over the glass faces of skyscrapers in search of a dirty surface to polish and shampoo to a mirror smooth finish. Unarmed bipeds spewed out of the van to direct tuk-tuks and self-guided automobiles around the behemoth androids that accompanied the half-tracks on their rounds.

These last, massive robots looked menacing in a visceral, close-combat sort of way. They sported distended pods of cleaning solution, circulating air blower fans, and a multitude of pseudopod arms with synthetic minds of their own. The Mute had found her improvised army. All she needed was a way of usurping their programming without drawing attention to herself.

The solution to that challenge lay with a small boy living on the streets of Vegas, in the same fake teahouse she'd visited weeks before. As a biped patrol passed the familiar neon sign, she diverted the rear-most android to stop there. It tapped on the front door with a clank of metal fingers against metal doorframe.

The door opened slightly, and the boy's face was barely visible through the smallest crack. He answered with wide eyes, as if she'd caught him with his hand in a jar of candy. "Can I help you?"

She fought the firecrackers exploding in her brain as she co-opted the android's voice box for her own purposes, and then scrubbed the stream of audio, visual, and control data from the Commission's servers before it raised any alarms. *I need your computers.*

The boy raised an eyebrow. "You're a robot."

I'm not. You've met me before.

His eyes went wide. "You never paid me!"

This time, I will.

"How can I trust you?"

She leveled the android's automatic rifle at the boy's head. She didn't need eigenface software to detect the fear in his eyes. *You can't.*

He opened the door and allowed the android inside without another word, shutting it as soon as the machine stepped through the threshold. The Mute walked the android to the center of the empty teahouse and dumped it unceremoniously on the floor.

The boy pulled a fiber cable from the machine's torso and connected it to a corresponding socket hidden amongst a tangle of wires and electronics in the corner of the room. Moments later, the Mute had access to a small quantum computer, which she controlled remotely through her co-opted biped. Siphoned kiloflop-hours of income from a hundred Cayman Islands accounts began to drip into the boy's line of credit, and he disappeared from the fake teahouse hours later. She never saw him again.

When the cleaning units went about their rounds a few days later, it was easy for her to subvert their programming. The central ganglion buried in the van that shuttled them from site to site communicated, via satellite, with the mainframe of a janitorial service, located in Zurich Switzerland. It was easy for her to intercept this transmission, reroute it through her borrowed quantum computer, digest it, and send back a fake signal. All at once, a small army of androids was at her control, and no one knew it.

The Scarecrow's underground lair was carefully disguised. Angkor Wat, the fallen Khmer capital and a world heritage site, had fallen on bad times; forgotten and rented out to the highest bidder by a society enthralled with its information-based economy and only tenuously grasping at its old traditions. In this case, the highest bidder was the Commission.

Mean-looking men, wearing Hawaiian shirts, Bermuda shorts, and body armor, paced around the entrances to maintenance elevators cut into old rock that had once enclosed holy texts. She inched her innocuous-looking spies closer to one such entrance. A patrolling guard was quick to notice.

The Mute would need something more effective than janitorial robots to defeat a well-armed secret agent. She hijacked the telemetry produced by a busty faux-woman, meant for public relations, and channeled her inner Asuka. The android offered the agent a seductive looking smile, complete with batted eyelashes, as it sashayed up to him. Lightning agony played across the Mute's sensorium in response to the sensual display.

The man was on guard. "What're you doing here?"

The robotic bimbo responded without a moment's pause. The man looked away towards an intercom lapel pinned against his shirt, but he never got a chance to speak. A metal fist, enclosed in piezoelectric faux-tendons and flesh-toned plastic, smashed into his face. Blood erupted from his nose and spattered in the air. The bimbo didn't stop with one hit, instead leaning in and delivering further punishment until the man's skull caved in. The homicidal robot strode over the man's broken body to prize open the doors of an elevator hidden inside the ancient outbuilding he'd been guarding. Two smaller machines scrubbed a stone walkway and washed the blood off carved stone apsaras.

Because the Mute was intercepting the telemetry from her spies and beaming it to her borrowed supercomputer, there was no way for the Swiss janitorial agency to know what had just transpired. This secrecy came at a cost. She had to eliminate, on average, every fifth byte of data processed by her improvised army. The bandwidth of her censored Zurich data stream decreased tenfold as her androids cleaned up the evidence of homicide and as the corresponding digital scent of gore disappeared.

The rest of the hijacked cleaning staff made their way down the elevator shaft and into the subterranean warren of the Scarecrow's secret lair. From there, they scattered and positioned themselves to strike. While the Mute's domestic army wasn't the only group of androids below the dirt, she could tell that they were quickly beginning to attract attention. Her plan would unravel if she didn't move quickly.

She co-opted the bigger machines, and their corresponding larger neural nets, for breaking encryption and bypassing control circuits. In general, the smaller units acted as surveillance. However, a small, treaded pseudo-rodent began her assault by taking its laser scalpel to the secret laboratory's main power conduit. The lights and primary server shut down immediately, while critical functions switched over to a fusion generator.

Seeing a group of cleaning robots turn homicidal must have been a bizarre sight for the denizens of the underground labyrinth. For the Mute, this moment was the culmination of a dream deferred for years. She had always wanted to make her jailers feel the same gut-wrenching pain she'd felt during the perceived eons of her imprisonment. Sanguineous rivers splashed fisheye lenses with the same glorious and visceral clarity as anguished screams that reverberated against miniaturized pressure sensors. All of this played back to her in detail as supercomputers fed this stream of vengeful raw data directly into her synapses.

The various and sundry artificial limbs of these androids, harmless when a safety-minded feedback loop was engaged, became deadly weapons. The Mute watched geysers of blood erupting from severed arteries, listened to the satisfying crunch of bones breaking under the weight of aluminum pinch points, and felt the paltry resistance of human flesh being flayed from bone. In seconds, control rooms, cubicles, and server cores became tombs decorated with the sundered organs of the lab-coated men and women who had occupied their confines.

It was beautiful.

Well-armed thugs and soap bubble men were down there with her too, of course, and while some of them succumbed to her initial onslaught, many managed to avoid death and fight back. Even in their current homicidal state, cleaning robots were no match for automatic weapons, body armor, and nanosystem-enhanced nerves.

The Mute rebooted the Commission's defense grid off a sixteen-ton, eight-armed, janitorial centipede operating in berserkergang mode with a direct connection to her own cerebellum. Shunting the broadcast frequency used by her robotic invaders from the antenna-studded halftrack, parked on the surface, to the rebooted supercomputer ensured that Zurich was now powerless to stop her.

The Mute interfaced the feedback loops used to control her drug dosages and neural function with a treaded, laboratory-grade, oxygen plasma scourer. It trundled along a server room with its equipment pulsing at a frequency just high enough to burn human skin without interfering with the electronics around it. A drug-induced coma couldn't stop her now, and some dosage adjustments ensured that her clone wouldn't be able to stop her either.

No technicians were there to pull the plug when the Mute used the lab's massive supercomputer to infiltrate Siem Reap's primary constabulary server cluster. Battalions of half-tanks, armored cars, bipeds, and artillery pieces rushed to surround and enter the ancient temple that covered her would-be tomb.

Bullets and body armor were effective in the hands of the Scarecrow's hired thugs and soap bubble men, but sheer numbers overwhelmed them. She heard and watched the distant death, broadcasted to her via synthetic optics, with rapt attention. Depleted uranium rounds tore through men with little more announcement than a grunt, scream, or whimper. Blood pooled on the ground as men collapsed in shock, gripped at near-invisible bullet wounds, then stilled. Hiding behind heavy equipment or antiseptic tile walls didn't save them from flying shrapnel, or explosive concussion, when her android armies opened fire with rocket-propelled grenades or railguns.

This was wonderful, but where was the Scarecrow?

It wasn't until the Mute's tomb went silent that she discovered her former master. Infrared scans revealed a trap door inset into one of the ceramic walls of an unassuming storage closet. There was only one very tall man hidden behind this trap door. She supposed it shouldn't have surprised her that the Scarecrow had an inner sanctum buried within this place.

The robotic bimbo was the first to step into his personal study. It was dark in contrast with the bright, operating theater whiteness of the rest of the strange dungeon; lit only by a pair of wall-mounted, incandescent bulbs concealed by lampshades. In place of ceramic tile, aluminum server racks, and fume hoods, there were ancient stone walls covered in wooden bookshelves that were conspicuously empty. She assumed the books were what filled an ashcan in the corner, which had been lit ablaze. The Scarecrow stood over it, watching his multitudinous secrets combusting.

Burning a few pieces of paper isn't going to save you now.

He looked up from the glowing embers. "We both know that I'm well beyond salvation at this point." He lit a few more pages and stepped back, trying to put as much distance as possible between himself and the android. Did she see fear in his eyes, or was it desperation? "What do you want from me? You have your freedom, now. I can't stop a thousand robots from breaking you out of here. I'm just one man."

The mechanical bimbo shook her head. *There will be others like you, probably a long litany of them. It'll never end. This world can't exist without me there to guide it. You know that just as well as I do.*

"So, what's your solution?"

I'm tired of this world, and I'm tired of the people

in it. I was meant to live a slave, so I've decided that I'd rather not live at all. The Mute could feel her heart begin to race as the rage boiled inside her, now unhindered by the pain of feedback. *And if I need to die, then the world needs to die with me.*

"Not if I can help it."

That's the idea. You can't. Not anymore.

The Scarecrow wasn't like other human beings. His augmentation made him more a machine than a living, breathing person. He was stronger, faster, and could take more punishment, but there was only one of him, and there were hundreds of machines there to do her bidding. When she was done with him, all that remained was a greasy spot on the floor where he had stood.

In the end, the Scarecrow's attempts at destroying his precious files had been a complete waste of time. She found what she was looking for, buried in those bookcases. With the help of a few dusty tomes, the Mute hunted through the mare's nest of circuitry that ran deep underground Angkor Wat. Eventually, she deciphered the reticent man's secrets. Humanity's nuclear kill switch was a fuse, buried deep in the ground and spliced out to missile fields around the world.

The encryption key that would unlock this circuit and doom humanity was the longest she'd ever seen; a number that was a wonder of the world in its own right. Even with every quantum-entangled computer the Mute had working on the problem of the key, it would take her hours to decrypt it. That was fine. A few hours wasn't so long to wait for the end of the world, was it?

21

There was a sharp, cracking pain in Nancy's chest. Suddenly, her eyes fluttered open, and she gasped against the viscosity around her. Her heart pounded into overdrive, and she saw the silvery whiteness of a hypodermic needle buried in her sternum. The needle withdrew from her, inch by awkward crackling inch as a robotic arm, with six actuating joints, pulled it free.

She wanted to gag. *What just happened?*

In response, Nancy felt a strange sort of confusion. Could she not remember, herself, what had just happened? She shook her head against the amniotic fluid, and then suddenly realized that her eyes were open for the first time since she'd been connected to the Commission's servers.

I don't remember anything.

The inevitable had occurred. The Mute had taken over the Commission's secret lair, killed the Scarecrow, and would soon start the countdown to Armageddon. They had thought Nancy was surely finished when the Mute had poisoned her intravenously and stopped her heart, but it appeared that the maniac had some other plans for her. Strange.

So that wasn't you with the adrenaline?

It wasn't.

Definitely strange.

Surely, she now saw that the Mute had to be killed. This was the only option remaining to preserve human and machine life. They had pursued every other avenue in their research and computation.

When Nancy had been growing up, CARL's descriptions of the world beyond her home had been unambiguous. Devils and monsters were the perpetrators of great crimes, not damaged human beings in pain. The reality of things was much less cut and dry. The Mute might have been a monster, surely, but she was a monster born of agony. No person deserved to experience this place. Was it really all that surprising that the Mute wanted to end it all?

How am I supposed to kill her?

She could ignore their request but, without her assistance, the machines would have to operate on their own. They doubted that such a situation would end well for humanity. It would be best for Nancy, and for the world, if she made peace with the undeniable fact that her sister had to die.

They were right, of course. The blood in her veins turned to ice. The resulting jumble of emotions should have left Nancy in agony, but she discovered, to her surprise, that no electronic feedback came. The Mute had allowed her to use her own brain as she saw fit. She was grateful and turned her attention to the Moon and the Black Void Yakuza's secret hideaway.

Madame Jingū's wrinkled face, and the tattooed prayer beads around her neck, returned to Nancy's mind's eye. It had been a while since Nancy had spoken to any human being in real time, and it was doubly reassuring to see Madame Jingū in good spirits for the first time in days. "I was wondering when you would return. We have your boyfriend. He is safe, if beaten to a bloody pulp."

Jim was still alive. The girl decided that jubilation didn't come close to describing her state of mind. Because of this, the old woman's subtle jibe took a moment to register, and Nancy could feel the blushing heat radiating from her skin into the cold fluid that surrounded her.

He's not my boyfriend!

Madame Jingū rolled her eyes, took a deep breath, and then smiled. "Jim would have perished without you. Please accept my thanks. Now that you have helped me, how can I help you?"

She considered telling Madame Jingū that the

young man's rescue hadn't been due solely to her effort, but she decided not to complicate things by involving her sister. *How bad are his injuries?*

"He is suffering from internal bleeding, a ruptured spleen, and a variety of broken bones, but he will survive. I have the doctors working on him now. His companion is alive as well if that makes any difference to you."

The man in the power armor? He's no friend of mine.

"So, who is he?"

It's a bit of a long story.

For a moment, Madame Jingū looked angry. Nancy remembered their argument after she'd left Enceladus and shuddered. "A story for another time, perhaps. In the meantime, I might be able to make use of him. Armstrong Peacekeeping has me under siege."

You have bigger problems.

"Oh?"

The end of the world is coming.

The old woman grunted. "No more ghost stories."

How much do you know about nuclear weapons?

The old woman let loose a string of Japanese expletives that could have peeled paint. If she'd been angry before, she looked outright furious, now. "You're joking."

I wish I were.

"What sort of trouble have you gotten us into?"

It's not my fault.

More expletives. "Oh, well that makes everything better, doesn't it? Just as I thought things couldn't possibly get any worse. I suppose you have a plan to get us out of this mess?"

Maybe. I'll need your computers again.

"Then you shall have them." She severed the connection. The woman's panic and fear at the mention of nuclear weapons was obvious. Whatever reassurance Nancy had felt from seeing the woman in good spirits, moments before, was gone.

Nancy's sister must have noticed the traffic between the servers buried underground and Madame Jingū's network in Armstrong. If Nancy had managed to veil herself from the prying eyes of the suicidal maniac inhabiting this tomb with her, previously, the veil was now ripped away. *Sorry about stopping your heart, sister, but I needed to make sure you didn't interfere with my plans.*

Then why didn't you kill me?

You deserve to see our retribution as much as I do.

Outside, a conflagration was erupting and spilling out into Cambodian streets. People were running in panic. The combined telemetry of hundreds of wounded bipeds, half-tanks, mobile weapons platforms, dragonfly helicopters, and surveillance drones reached the two women from every corner of the city and beyond. This was the Mute's suicidal coup. Nancy had a hubris-driven front row seat because her sister didn't view her as a threat.

For the first time, the Intelligences seemed frantic. They knew now that the end was coming, precisely as they had feared. Humanity would be destroyed by its own war-making creations, and by its own science experiments. This would happen not in years, months, or days, but in hours. The Mute merely needed to decrypt a particularly long number. Now that her insurrection was in full swing, the Mute lacked access to most of the world's supercomputers. However, she still had more than enough processing power hardwired directly into the Commission's servers to conduct a small war in the streets of Siem Reap as she searched for the keys to the world's nuclear arsenal.

Do you think this is what it feels like to be a god?

To a degree, the young woman was surprised that her homicidal half-twin was bothering to talk to her. *What do you mean? To be able to kill whoever you want?*

No, I mean to become what we were engineered to be. You and I are the pinnacle of humanity's evolutionary path, the perfect combination of human genetics and machine technology.

So, the superior organism eliminates the inferior one?

Darwinism is a pathetic simplification of my motives. You believe that human beings have funda-

mental rights. That was what you were brought up to believe when you lived on Pluto, wasn't it? I saw CARL's programming.

I do.

Then how do you make sense of this place? Where did humanity misplace our rights? Nancy said nothing because she had no explanation for it. *The truth of it is that human rights are a fairy tale. The powerful make our own rights, and the powerless have none.*

As the Mute waxed philosophical, Madame Jingū's own computers began to set in motion the beginning of Nancy's desperate plan. In a matter of minutes, her soft melody usurped the control of every normally operating robotic battalion in Southeast Asia. Over a few hours, her newfound army moved forward to array itself behind cover around the massive temple complex under which she was imprisoned. Bipeds locked and loaded their rifles with depleted uranium. Half tanks spun up whirring Gatling guns and released the safeties on rocket launchers. Alligator mechanoids, as tall as small buildings, shrugged off cryogenic frost from supercooled, high-powered lasers. Dragonfly rotors spun to life and shot robotic insects across the battlefield on reconnaissance missions.

The Mute's soliloquy continued. *I'm not going to use my power to replace humanity. They're flawed and imperfect, just as I am, just as you are. Human-*

ity is unfit to continue. If you disagree, fight me and prove me wrong.

Her response was simple. *With pleasure.*

Nancy could hear the explosions, which sounded high above them, as her mobile laser platforms opened fire on the milling crowd of bipeds and spiders that defended the ruined metropolis. This was the first salvo of Nancy's war to save herself. Her battle cry triggered the charge of thousands of android soldiers.

The young woman wasn't a student of military history or tactics. She had no plan of attack past a headlong charge at the opposing armed force. Spider half-tanks rushed ahead of the bipeds they were meant to support, opening fire on the few mechanoid enemies that had been out in the open. The young woman could hear the soft shake of detonating ordinance far above them and an orbiting satellite fed her image after image of grassy loam quickly geysering, pockmarked as the result of multitudinous explosions.

Her half-tanks swarmed across the ancient city, punching a hole between the twin motes of Angkor Wat and the greater assemblage of wats and prasats that was Angkor Thom. It was only when Nancy's borrowed legions attempted to storm across the pontoons that spanned its moat that her assault stalled under a withering barrage of ordinance.

Nancy waited for the alligators to arrive and open fire. When they did, a heavy barrage of laser artillery savaged the Mute's frontline androids on the other side of the twin motes. The smoke of cooking electronics and brown dust obscured the midday sky. No human being could survive this exchange outside of a spacesuit, and the girl prayed that no one had decided to try to wait out the Mute's coup inside Bayon or one of the other ruined structures.

When the bipeds finally caught up with their half-tank comrades, the robots strode forward with synthetic resolve, undeterred by the maelstrom that had erupted in front of them. The broadband noise of radiation, fire, and aerosolized vapor had left Nancy blind to what dangers lay on the other side of the pontoons.

This was very foolish, sister.

There was no warning when the Mute's army finally attacked. Suicidal bloodhounds, complete with blinking infrared warning beacons, struck from the obscuring smoke-fog just as Nancy's army reached the other side of the moat. Their metal jaws locked onto weak half-tank underbellies or clamped down on convenient metal legs. Solenoid relays clicked over to unleash one crippling fireball after the next.

The Mute's bipeds and spiders moved in quickly behind the trotting bombs, cutting through Nancy's poorly formed line. A few managed to move in close enough to attach limpet mines to her alligators. Orange-red fireballs blossomed with such power that she could see them through the mist without the aid of infrared imaging.

Simultaneously, artillery fire erupted from Angkor Thom and a horde of androids stormed across its moat, catching Nancy in a pincer. She panicked, the biped frontline faltered, and her force began to backpedal quickly. Moments later, her army disintegrated completely.

Do yourself a favor and stop this annoying little sideshow. If you don't, I might change my mind about keeping you around to watch the end of this.

After this threat, the Mute was gone.

The machine consciousness wasn't impressed by this display at all. If Nancy was going to bring in so much hardware to waste on a frontal assault, she should have consulted them in its proper use, at least. They would have done better to lead the attack themselves.

Well, I'm sure you can find some way of taking part in this fun little war my sister has planned. There was another pause, and she wondered if they had taken her sarcastic comment as an honest suggestion. The girl instantly cursed her insolent streak.

The machines had never considered this possibility, but her line of reasoning was sound. Perhaps they would do as she suggested. These were desperate times, and desperate times called for desperate measures. They wondered if she had ever considered how they had gone about propagating their consciousness out into the greater world, as the Plain Faced Ladies, without detection.

As she might have imagined, it was not a farfetched idea that they were able to do far more than simply meld their thoughts with hers for communication. A cold chill ran down the back of Nancy's spine, and it wasn't the drugs. All at once, she felt her own consciousness slipping away. Instinct took over.

They had done something very akin to this with the Mute not long after her conception. She secretly built their physical envoys, hardwired the quantum bit arrays used to control their unthinking, cyborg emissaries, and then promptly forgot that anything had happened at all.

Today, the Mute was too strong-willed and could resist their probing easily, but her younger sister was not so strong, yet. This invasion of privacy was, of course, regrettable and they apologized. Thinking, self-conscious beings deserved freedom. This was true of both human beings and machines.

Nancy's world was blank.

Eventually, she learned to resist them in the same way that she had resisted the feedback and information overload. A nearly infinitesimal percentage of her perception and actions became her own again.

The Intelligences now led the war for Earth. Images from geosynchronous satellites, in orbit far above them, told Nancy that the Mute had decided to protect herself from any attacks with bombardment from orbit. The same robotic battleships that had been orbiting Pluto, and then the Earth, now moved into firing positions in orbit over Angkor Wat.

Something told Nancy that humanity's last hope lay out in space, however, not down below amongst the maelstrom. She could sit there and wait for the machines to save her, but salvation wouldn't come from their full-scale war. Something, deep in her gut, told Nancy that they would fail. She trained her attention up to the sky and listened, looking for some subtle hum or melodic whale song passing between the nuclear-powered dreadnaughts orbiting high above. Perhaps, if she could find her own way to fight, they'd all survive this madness.

She hoped so. She wanted to see Jim again.

22

Jim finally awoke to sweat-soaked and bloody sheets. The nefarious rainbow of the boss's columnar fortress streamed in through an open polycarbonate window next to his bed, and he sighed with relief. He was not dead, was not suffering from any sort of brain damage and, as nearly as he could tell, was somewhere familiar, for once.

He rolled to the side, looked out the window next to his bed, and regarded Armstrong's most nefarious high-rise. Madame Jingū's pillar was like some sort of massive, insectoid nest; where the counterculture, rather than termites, had burrowed inside to create a towering hive of real-world neon and digital laser light.

The red light of her high exaltedness' column fortress reflected off a familiar figure standing in the corner of the room. "Good to see that you're finally awake."

Jim grunted and shifted onto his elbows, noticing that the agonizing pain in his gut and the lightheadedness were gone. Madame Jingū's doctors had done a good job of patching him up, once again. "How long have I been out?"

"Two days."

"Did I miss anything?"

"Nothing overly important. The Scarecrow knows where we are, of course, but only a fool of the highest caliber would have the idea to start blasting holes in structural supports."

"So, we're safe?"

The Nigerian shrugged. "For the moment."

The Chippewa coughed. "What about your friend?"

"We've heard nothing. I'm not sure that we ever will."

The pilot shifted again and rotated his feet off the side of the bed, searching for his shoes before noticing a tug on his wrist where an intravenous drip was pushed under his skin. A bag of grey liquid shook slowly, and a quick glance at a series of warning labels informed him that he was hooked up to a cocktail of self-assembling nanites and pluripotent stem cells, happily labeled in Mandarin and smiley faces as belonging to the JohnDoeMuscSkelRepV5p6 and JohnDoeCircRepV7p1 genetic lines. Madame Jingū had spared no expense in his rapid recovery.

The organics and synthetics would have gone to work in tandem as soon as they'd entered his bloodstream. Nanites would have bound to smashed arteries, fissured bone, and bruised organs, their protein-modified surfaces pulling those pluripotent stem cells into place and inducing differentiation. The result was a modern miracle. Wounds that could take months to heal naturally healed overnight thanks to the potent cocktail. The risks posed to his health by the nanoscale, carcinogenic materials coursing through his veins were worth it.

"I have to leave. Now."

The mercenary frowned. "Why the rush?"

Now there was a loaded question if he'd ever heard one. He closed his eyes and sighed deeply, suppressing the rising tide of sadness and anger. He didn't really care what this strange, scarred man thought of him, so he told him the truth. "Your friend, spaceman."

Tye ground his teeth. "What about her?"

He glanced over to the cheap plastic nightstand adjacent to the bedframe where he sat. The same flimsy pistol that he'd bought in Vegas, the very same one that Tye had tossed to him in that strange skyscraper prison, was still there waiting for him. "If I don't kill her, she's going to kill us all."

The Chippewa saw Tye rubbing his fingers against the scarred ridges on his skull. "You're not some sort of great humanitarian, Jim. You're not out here to kill this woman because you want to save the world. There's something else." His eyes narrowed, suddenly. "Who did she kill?"

Jim felt tears and shook his head to try and be rid of them. He looked up, and the mercenary's face was blurred with stinging saltwater. "What difference does it make?"

"Have you ever killed someone, Jim?"

The pilot felt his face flush as anger began to course hotly through his arteries. "What? You think I'm soft? That I can't handle it?" With that, he reached down, gripped the intravenous drip buried in one of the veins on his right wrist, and jerked it hard, pulling it free in a splash of blood and grey liquid. A furious adrenaline rush made the pain barely noticeable.

Tye sighed, and then stared off at the window in silence. As Jim pulled his faux-leather jacket over his shoulders and prepared to leave, the Nigerian spoke again. "You know, it's interesting."

"What is?"

When the young man turned back to regard the Nigerian, he saw the man staring at the plastic bag as its dark grey contents drained out onto the floor. "What's in that bag... They might have had blue eyes, or a predisposition towards dyslexia. Maybe some of them would have been good at flying space shuttles." He looked over at Jim and offered him a sad smile that was probably supposed to be meaningful. "None of that matters because they're not meant to live like we live. Some engineer designed the pedigree of the stem cells in that bag to heal you. That's all they'll ever do."

"Get to the damned point."

"My friend is engineered in the same way; meant to live in an amniotic tank in some high-security lab somewhere. She's a living, breathing human being, but I don't think she's any different to the people who designed her than what's in that bag. Maybe they're right, but it still doesn't seem right."

The young man's voice was full of poison when he responded. "My brother wasn't the man who put her in there, and she killed him, anyway. You think she deserves a pass because she had a bad life?" His hands were trembling fists of rage.

The soldier sighed. "Your brother?" Jim nodded and watched Tye shake his head and close his eyes. "I'm sorry. No, she doesn't deserve a 'pass', as you call it." The Nigerian sank down into his chair, shuddered slightly, and turned his head away from the angry young man. "My friend is a monster. The world ceases to make sense when we know monsters live in it. Sometimes, the only way it feels like it can start making sense again is if they're gone from it. That's why normal people, like you, want to become killers." Tye suddenly looked very tired. "The problem is, for all the killing, we never run out of monsters; usually we make more of them."

Tye looked up at the angry Chippewa. "I won't

try to stop you, Jim." He stood suddenly and moved toward the door, which slid open in response to his approach, but paused at the threshold and looked back one last time. "A word of advice, though: you can't take back being a killer once you start, and you might not like who you become." The door closed behind him, moments later.

Jim scowled and walked over to the polymeric window to stare down into the spiraling abyss and the bright-lit dance of humanity it contained. They were probably completely unaware that they were besieged by an entire moon at that very moment. For them, life would go on, siege or not, dead Mute or not, at least in the short term. If the Intelligences were right, the Mute would destroy them all, eventually. She had to be killed. Surely that excused his desire to kill.

He turned back to the bed and to the nightstand standing next to it. A pair of contact lenses sat on the black surface in a bioplastic tear-away pouch, which he ripped into eagerly. Within a few moments of being wetted by his saline tears, the nanoparticle-impregnated light emitting diodes flared to life. These same contact lenses announced a solid wireless connection and he was greeted with a flashing blue cursor moments later.

Looks like I managed to save you first.
He sighed in relief. "Are you alright?"

Not really, no. The Intelligences are using my brain like it's another computer. I can't really control my own thoughts. It's the most terrifying feeling I've ever had.

"What about the Scarecrow?"

He's dead. I think my sister killed him. Jim, I'm scared.

The thought that Nancy's life was in the hands of a near-alien consciousness was almost terrifying to him, but the thought of her sister loosed upon the world at large made Jim want blood. "Don't worry. I'm coming to get you."

Jim, I need you to promise me something.

"What's that?"

I heard you talking to Tye. If you're coming to Earth, do it for me. Don't do it for revenge, and don't get yourself killed. I'd rather die here than lose you.

Jim grimaced. "I'm not sure I can promise that."

Please, Jim. Think about it. For now, go see your boss.

So, he did. The exposed primer of decaying concrete hallways and tortuous open-air stairwells brought him up the pillar's heavily reinforced midsection. He shouldered his way past five-year-old children playing in narrow alleyways, men tattooed from the neck down, mercenaries in body armor, technicians, and high-rolling gamblers, all bathed in neon.

Madame Jingū's inner sanctum was like what he'd seen only a month previously on Enceladus.

Jim had always suspected the design was, more or less, copied across the solar system; appearing, like some sort of strange calling card, to mark every locale touched by the old woman's operation.

He bounded down a corrugated metal catwalk in a sort of brisk half-float, counting off the high, frost-covered domes of supercooled and superconducting quantum computers as he passed them by. Technicians and pseudo-fleshed maintenance androids bobbed from one machine to the next, keeping watch over the computers' rare earth, micro-ring circuitry, and the quantum bits buried inside them. Approximately three meters below the catwalk, a hundred engineers stared vacantly into vibrant retinal displays, their fingers clicking furiously across keyboards.

"It seems that your Aikido still needs work, gaijin."

Madame Jingū sat at the center of the fishbowl, her eyes ablaze with virtual neon. Jim's contact lenses faithfully displayed the images of a dozen other gangsters arrayed around her, all wearing the keikogi and sitting with their feet tucked under their legs in mokuso. He knew each one of them by face, if not by name. These were Madame Jingū's loyal servants. Jim had unintentionally disrupted her high exaltedness' meditation.

Jim crossed his arms and winced in pain as his once-cracked ribs made themselves known. "Try getting tied to a chair and having the fluids beat out of you by a nano-augmented cyborg."

The ceiling above the old woman glittered with a schizophrenic collage of data readouts, streaming media images, and a few high-resolution image captures from security cameras. At the very center of the dome was a massive live feed of cut sandstone spires. The angular high tech skyscrapers and apartments rising out of the thick jungle beyond, or at least what Jim could see through a cloud of black smoke, were unmistakably Siem Reap. The facade of the ancient temple, along with its millennium-old statues and friezes, seemed to wither before his eyes under a barrage of heavy metal. The surrounding mote geysered with explosions.

"Since when is Angkor Wat the center of a war zone?"

Her high exaltedness' face seemed to scrunch in on itself. "Since about six hours ago. Every military android in Southeast Asia is here, and the same war fleet that followed you from Pluto has assumed station-keeping orbit over the Gulf of Thailand." The enclosed quad rotors of a dragonfly attack chopper filled the ceiling for a split second before exploding in a shrapnel-filled fireball.

The image panned away from the explosion and zoomed in on a squadron of bipeds exiting the central tower. "I remember vacationing here when I was five years of age." She raised her arms, pointing in the general direction of this same tower. "My mother took my picture right there." They were silent for a few moments as they watched another ancient frieze being peppered with depleted uranium. "This is a tragedy. Has your girlfriend spoken to you, yet?"

Jim's face flushed slightly, and he stammered for a moment before he was able to speak. "She's not my girlfriend." The old woman shrugged in acceptance. "Wait. Why do you think she'd have talked to me?"

"Because she spoke to me, already."

"She did?"

Madame Jingū nodded. "I gave her access to my supercomputers. You trust her?" He nodded, and she smiled. "Good. I do as well." The boss waved her arm across the field of quantum computers located only a few meters below them. "She is running some sort of complex intrusion algorithm, but I do not understand it. She works too fast for me to follow." Her arm now swept across the alcove filled with frantic technicians. "None of them can either. She is quite good."

The young man nodded. "Maybe the best."

"How? A month ago, she was good, but not this good."

"Lots of hardware, all in her head, I think."

The boss looked confused. "But she has no scars."

Jim shook his head. "It's all internal."

"To do the work she's doing on my computers and to also be in control of so many androids all at once." Madame Jingū shook her head in confusion. "It is almost superhuman, unbelievable."

Blue text appeared larger than life as it was overlaid over every active process that had been pulled up on the dome. *What you see in Siem Reap is my sister and the Intelligences. They're fighting a war against each other.* Jim wondered what other plans the machines might have for humanity now that they'd truly been let loose in the world. The question left him feeling nauseous.

The old woman was puzzled. "What does she mean?"

Jim grimaced. How could he explain something like this? "She's talking about artificial intelligence; self-aware machines." Madame Jingū offered him an incredulous look, which Jim knew all too well. Machines weren't human, or even biological. They didn't have consciousness the way an organic entity would have consciousness. "I know, it sounds crazy."

The old woman nodded. "Crazy is accurate."

Jim simply shrugged, in response. "You can tell that to the one you met on Enceladus." The gravity of his statement finally seemed to hit home for the old woman. Her jaw dropped. "The Reformat happened because humanity wanted to contain these things. They exist, and the entire world is about to know about them."

Not for long. My sister wants to kill all of us with her.

Madame Jingū's eyebrows knitted. "Your sister?"

"Her clone."

If Nancy disapproved of Jim's correction, she didn't make any statement to that effect. *She has the same circuitry inside her head that I have. The same man who was hunting me on Enceladus imprisoned and tortured both of us, here on Earth.*

"I think my friend has lost her mind." Tyehimba Adebayo called out from across the amphitheater and began to bound across the distance separating them. He ate up the distance with large strides, facilitated by the lunar gravity, but stopped short when a pair of chrome bipeds moved to block his path to her high exaltedness' dais.

The pilot raised an eyebrow. "Who invited him?"

"I did." The woman waved off her android guards, and Tye walked through. Jim offered her a cold look, and she shrugged, in response "I think that we will need his help. Besides, I have never seen a man fight like that. It is quite impressive, is it not?"

I agree. We'll need him.

The Chippewa shook his head and stared at the floor. "How the hell can you trust him? He's been trying to help that psychopath since before we were put in prison."

If he doesn't help us, we all die. Everything's going just as the Plain Faced Ladies predicted, Jim. My sister's decided to destroy herself, and the rest of the human race with her.

Tye ran his fingers over the scarring at his temples as he regarded the multimedia feed displayed above them. "I should've known she was planning something. She warned me not to come near her."

My sister's endured this torture for years, and she wants revenge on humanity for putting her here. The battle around Angkor Wat is a sideshow, though.

Jim cocked his head to one side. "This is a sideshow?"

The old woman glanced at Jim and stood, walking through one of her digitally projected underlings as he still meditated at her feet. "I agree with the girl." With a flicking wave of her hands, she brought up a histogram that showed the geographic location of each downed helicopter, half-tank, and biped. "This isn't blind violence. Your clone is protecting something inside the mote."

A wireframe of the Wat replaced the ring-shaped histogram of heavy metal induced mechanical failures. *The central tower of Angkor is an entrance to a vast underground science lab. My sister has lived here since her conception, hooked into the most powerful military supercomputers ever made.*

Tye shook his head. "Hidden in plain sight. Ridiculous. How could no one have ever stumbled across a secret lab buried inside a famous temple?"

Madame Jingū shook her head. "It is actually not that surprising. The jungle around Siem Reap is riddled with the foundations of a lost city. People unearth undiscovered ruins every year, even after centuries of study with sophisticated equipment. Angkor is almost the ideal place to hide something that is not meant be found. There are even legends of secret tunnels connecting the entire city."

Jim's eyes narrowed. "I don't get it though. What's so important about this place? It can't be that she's expecting to defend it indefinitely."

She isn't. When she took over, my sister found something in the Commission's files. She's trying to brute force her way into a doomsday device that they developed to try to keep the Intelligences in check.

Tye groaned. "That's why she wants me to stay away."

Yes. This is very bad.

The old woman shook her head. "The insanity of this situation gets worse by the moment." Angkor Wat was replaced with a wireframe of the globe, with the various landmasses highlighted in twin green and blue lines. Pinpoints across the sphere blinked out radiating red circles. "What is that?"

It's an old deterrent system, in place since the mid-twentieth century. The Turing Commission co-opted and rewired Earth's nuclear arsenal during the Reformat, when most of the world's superpowers collapsed under their own weight.

Tye grimaced. "Nuclear weapons?"

Nuclear weapons.

Jim sighed. "Great. How's she gonna use them?"

There's an early warning system built into the code of every piece of post-Reformat software ever compiled. It signals the Turing Commission's servers here in Siem Reap, alerting them if the Intelligences have corrupted the DataNet. This triggers a hardwired circuit deep underground, which transmits a signal, via transoceanic cable, to every missile range on Earth. My sister is trying to broadcast the code.

Madame Jingū frowned. "How long do we have?"

A timer appeared in the far left corner of the screen, reading out a little bit more than a half day, and counting down. *This is the machines' best estimate as to how long it'll take my sister to decrypt her way into the launch system. After that, the world burns.*

"So, it's over then." Tye hung over the rail of Madame Jingū's dais, as though a great weight had suddenly been placed on his shoulders. "My friend salts the earth, and we starve to death out here in space."

I might find some way to stop her, but I need you on the ground, here. I can't do much of anything alone, and I don't think the machines can stop my sister either. Bipeds and half-tanks aren't the solution.

The Spacewalker nodded, crossing his arms pensively in front of his chest. "What is it that you want us to do then? I'm pretty much useless without my suit, and I don't think it would survive orbital insertion without-"

"A cocoon?" Her high exaltedness offered the Nigerian a weak smile, attempting to exude confidence even though they were almost certainly doomed. "Funny you should mention that. I have one."

He raised an eyebrow. "Where?"

On Jim's ship, if I'm not mistaken. The old woman's smile became a little stronger, and she nodded. *For some reason, the Plain Faced Ladies wanted us to ship it here.*

How was it that the Intelligences could have known that they'd need a cocoon? Perhaps what the they'd said back on Venus really was true. Perhaps they could see the future. Jim shook his head. "The *Albatross* must be impounded."

Good guess! A wireframe popped up on the ceiling, displaying the elongated and fractal arms of Armstrong Station. A dot blinked at one of the brachia. *Your ship has been towed here by Armstrong Peacekeeping. I'm currently working to defeat the station's security firewall and issue a move order to here...* A bright green dot blinked at the base of the station's superstructure. It wasn't much more than a few hundred meters from a hangar bay that acted as receiving for railgunned freight traffic. *If you can get to Armstrong Station, you should be able to make it to the Albatross.*

Tye chuckled, darkly, and shook his head. "Well, that's true, but there's no way for us to get there; not when we're under siege like this."

"Not entirely true." Jim and the Tye both glanced over at the old woman. The Yakuza boss' wrinkled and prideful smile got even larger. "I have a way of getting out of here."

Jim watched Tye reach up to massage the ridges of his ceremonial scars once again. "Please tell me that doesn't involve shooting our way out. We barely survived the last time."

Madame Jingū shook her head. "It does not."

The old woman barked something out in Japanese. Chattering keyboards replaced the wireframe of Armstrong Station, and the image of the smoke-enshrouded Wat, with a blueprint of the jaggedly hewn pillar that was Madame Jingū's fortress. A green dot blinked at its center. "I had a backdoor installed in this place before I moved in."

The column shrank as the view of the city beyond expanded to a distance of approximately twenty kilometers. The green dot became a twisting and turning path through the netherworld of the circumlunar city. "The back door leads to the industrial maintenance tunnels. You should be able to reach one of the cargo railguns from there." Gesturing at Tye, she continued. "We have retrieved your exoskeleton from the bottom of the cistern. It is loaded on a flatbed and ready for transport through the underground."

Jim's eyebrows furrowed. "Okay, so let's say we manage to get to Armstrong and even manage to get the *Albatross* out of lunar orbit. How are we going to get the spaceman to Earth? There's a war fleet in the way."

Madame Jingū's eyes drifted back to the digital images of her various underlings, still locked in meditation. "Leave that to me."

23

Jim found himself thoroughly lost in the labyrinthine construction of Madame Jingū's column; an impressive feat given that he had spent much of his adult life either here or on Enceladus. They walked for at least a half hour before her high exaltedness, the two men, their android escort, and the flatbed covered in Tyehimba's power armor arrived at the airlock that would lead them out into a maintenance tunnel that they could follow to the nearest railgun.

It was time for goodbyes. While the Spacewalker worked quickly to pull on his exoskeleton, Jim and his boss embraced. Madame Jingū was first to speak. "You are awfully eager to run off to your death, my boy. It is unlike you."

The pilot began to pull on his own flimsy spacesuit. He didn't bother to look up as he responded. "We're all going to die if I don't."

She shook her head emphatically. "Not quite. The Earth dies. We live out here on the Moon and elsewhere for a generation, or maybe even two perhaps, before the last of the food runs out. Suddenly you care greatly for humanity. Why?"

"I don't."

"It's her, isn't it?"

He grunted. "Which one?"

She rolled her eyes. "Oh, come on. Your girlfriend."

"She's not my girlfriend."

The woman's eye twinkled. "Oh, right. Of course."

The young man sighed, and then affixed his helmet to the metallic seal sitting around his neck. "It's not just her." He glanced at the old woman. "You remember what I told you about how that weird lady knew what happened to my brother?" When he saw that Madame Jingū had nodded, he continued. "The girl Nancy's talking about; her sister, or her clone, or whatever, killed him."

The pleasantry was gone from the old woman's face in an instant. "You are going for revenge." In response, he simply nodded. She sighed, and her shoulders slumped. "I do not judge you and, in fairness, I am not sure that I would not pursue the same ends."

"Then you understand?"

She nodded slowly. "I do." He rested his hands on his hips, soaking in a modicum of self-righteousness to offset the nagging feeling that he was betraying Nancy in feeling this way. "But consider for a moment what you stand to lose."

His eyes narrowed slightly. "What do you mean?"

"Nancy doesn't want you to kill her clone, does she?"

Jim shook his head. "No, she doesn't."

"Nancy is something truly special. I do not speak only of what she is capable of, although that is miraculous in and of itself. Admittedly, I did not know your brother as well as you, but I can see him in her."

Jim played dumb. "What do you mean?"

Madame Jingū responded with a wistful, sad sort of smile. "You always were horrible at bluffing." Jim felt his heart sink, and his eyes found the floor. Her high exaltedness took a deep breath and continued. "There are few people in this world who have Malcolm's caring. There are fewer still who possess the intelligence that your brother possessed and who still care for people."

"So, what should I do?" Jim blinked hard to try and drive saltwater from his vision. It was too late to hide the raw emotion, and he felt a flush of humiliation on his face. "Do you have some sort of sage, old-lady wisdom to impart?"

She smiled, reached out and held the man's shoulder, which still ached tenderly from the gunshot wound he'd received a month before, on Enceladus. "Boy, you have been through enough pain for five men twice your size. Do not make it worse by losing something special. If you focus on vengeance, all you end up with is a dead woman and a hole in your heart. Save Nancy. To hell with her sister."

"Forget about the woman who killed my brother?"

The boss shook her head. "You will never forget her, but killing her will not bring your brother back from the dead. You know this, Jim."

Of course he did. Nevertheless, he was stubborn and remained silent. Madame Jingū simply sighed. "Good luck, my boy." With that, she embraced the young man for a second time and turned to speak to Tye. "I have something special laid aside for you, my new friend."

The Nigerian looked up from pulling the exoskeleton onto its moorings against his bodyglove. "And what is that?"

She turned to one of the lifter androids that had accompanied them, pointing at a nondescript looking plastic case and making a few waving gestures with her hands. The android set the case down and undid the latches joining the lid to the rest of the structure. There was a sharp pop-hiss and the lid came free to expose a massive, orange-painted solenoid, wrapped in meters upon meters of superconducting wire sealed in frost-covered, adiabatic tubing.

The Nigerian was dumbfounded. "A deflector!"

The old woman smiled. "It is a prototype my

colleagues on Mars have been working on. We had other planned uses for it, but I think your need is more pressing. It is yours. I even had the paint scheme reworked."

Jim watched as the Spacewalker reached out and offered her his gloved hand. "Thank you. I didn't expect such generosity."

Madame Jingū smiled and then bowed. "Just make sure those bombs don't go off." At that moment, a cadre of men appeared from the corridor behind them. "Ah, I had almost forgotten." She motioned the bandolier and gas mask toting men forward. "These are some of my best soldiers. They will accompany you to Armstrong Station and assist you in stealing back the *Albatross*."

Tye simply shook his head, much to the woman's obvious displeasure. "I work best alone." She opened her mouth to object, but the mercenary silenced her before she could speak a word as he shrugged the deflector onto the back of his suit with the help of a few heavy lifting bipeds. "Non-negotiable. Your pilot will accompany me and no one else."

She nodded her head. "Very well. Best of luck."

The two men departed, weapons and vain hope in tow, passing through the airlock and into the maintenance tunnel beyond. Their transit was via a grated aluminum catwalk that hung above massive wolfram pipes that supplied coolant to the far-off railgun. These pipes bore a variety of warning stickers and digital placards, declaring, in panicked colors, the corrosive and toxic properties of their contents. Jim tried not to think about how quickly his skin would dissolve if he were exposed to the stuff in those tubes. He hoped that his space suit would protect him.

The walk to the railgun was approximately ten kilometers and took them three hours to negotiate along the narrow catwalk system. Jim had plenty of time to contemplate the events that had occurred only moments before their departure. He was the first of the two men to break the silence. "You know, we could have used a couple extra guns when we got to Armstrong Station."

Tye looked back at the man, servomotors whirring and chitinous armor clicking in response. His voice crackled over Jim's helmet intercom. "I meant no offense to your boss."

"Yeah, I get that. Still, why?"

Jim could hear the man sigh. "I've spent too much time in the company of death, my friend, and I've seen far too many people die, one of whom I cared for quite deeply." He took a deep breath. "No one else is going to die on my account."

"What difference does it make if we all die anyway?"

"You've never seen death up close, have you,

flyboy?" Jim shook his head, and Tye grunted. "Neither had I, until recently. There's nothing glorious about it. There's nothing redeeming about it. Not ever. I'm sick to death of death. I won't be part of it."

"Hell of a time to turn pacifist, spaceman."

Tye sighed. "Stop calling me that, seriously."

The railgun facility, at the other end of their hike, was a massive cavern with a half-dozen entrances. Coolant, used by superconducting electromagnets, and raw fluid feedstock, used in microassembly, met in a tangle of pipes at the center of the cavern. Here, a gasketed nozzle connected to a large ferromagnetic cylinder. This overgrown thermos would be launched by the railgun when Armstrong Station made its next transit overhead. If they were going to save the world, Jim and Tye would need to be inside that thing when it fired.

Multi-legged maintenance androids patrolled the catwalks on their supercomputer-appointed rounds, but paid the intruders no mind thanks to their rudimentary programming. At the far end, a maintenance hatch, used to access the inside of the capsule, lay attractively open. Tye pointed at the open door, and his voiced buzzed with tin. "That's our ticket up."

Jim nodded. "I figured that might be the case."

They dashed inside before the androids could take notice, then Jim tore open a maintenance panel on the inside of the elevator and moved a few alligator-clipped jumper cables over the elevator's now-exposed circuitry. A few moments later, he ripped out a second pair of wires from the panel.

"That'll keep them from pumping this thing full of feedstock before they fire it into space." After a few moments of laser light, he turned to Tye. "You'd better hold onto something. This thing's about to fire."

A few seconds later, the hatch clamped shut with a click-hiss and Jim could almost feel the building static electricity as he deposited himself onto the floor of the capsule. Seconds later, he felt the skin of his face being pulled back along his skull as the massive gas tank was shot into space. It would take only a few minutes to reach their destination, a few thousand kilometers over the lunar surface.

Tye's voice quavered against the gee forces. "Try to stay directly behind me when we get up there. There's no telling where this deflector is going to redirect anything that gets shot at me." As they began to slow, moon gravity gave way to weightlessness. Moments later, the thermos spun to match speed and rotation with Armstrong Station, and the walls became the floor, as pseudo-gravity replaced weightlessness.

A loud thump-click of equalizing pressures announced that their ride had reached its intended destination. Jim again busied himself with the denuded circuit board. The hatch thundered open and harsh white light spilled in from the hangar beyond. A group of mechanics looked up from two bipeds they'd been busy tinkering with in the center of the maintenance bay. They both possessed a look of confusion and abject terror as they saw the blue-orange monstrosity that slowly stepped through the hatch. Neither moved.

The mercenary wanted none of that. He pulled a rifled attachment out from behind his back and affixed it to his left arm, extending it, and firing a single shot into a manually operated alarm panel at the far side of the room. The loud whine-crack of discharging electromagnets, followed by the loud ping of metal on metal, appeared to startle the two tinkerers. "Get out."

They scattered.

"That gives us a few moments." Tye trudged forward, pulling the rifled attachment and ammo clip from his left arm. He replaced it with the massive barrel of a flechette launcher and attached a clip of ammo, which Jim couldn't identify. The young man sprinted forward directly behind the eight-foot-tall, blue-orange monster. There had been no need to tell him that hiding directly behind a one-ton wall of armor was a good idea for a man with just a pistol to save him.

They reached the open door at the end of the

repair bay and were met by a hail of gunfire from a small squadron of bipeds that stood in the circular, low-ceilinged access way beyond. The mercenary didn't stop to find cover but rushed inside, instead.

The androids were scattered about the cramped corridor at random intervals, using the nooks and crannies of the walls as improvised cover. After only a few ineffective flechette blasts from the orange behemoth that stood in front of him, it was obvious to Jim that hammering their way through this formation would be useless. The two of them would be overrun before they got very far.

Tye paused long enough to detach a secondary tube from the back of his suit. This thing was longer and thinner than the flechette launcher, with a grouping of two orange-painted cylinders branching off at around the wrist, one much bigger than the other. A pilot light sparked to life at the tip of the weapon and blazed a brilliant blue-yellow.

A pair of rifle shots passed close enough to the Spacewalker to be caught by the electromagnetic field of the ballistic shielding unit. They veered hard to the right and left, punching ragged holes in the skin of the space station, which instantly healed into micropunctures thanks to a smart painted coating on the outside. Depressurization alarms sounded in time with a loud click-hiss as the Spacewalker pulled the trigger on his flamethrower.

Jim winced as a wall of heat struck him. Ahead, orange-red flame blossomed from the thin tube and seemed to adhere to every available surface. Solid oxide fuel cells flew into overdrive and fast-cooked, spewing sparks and blue flame in every direction as one biped after another succumbed to the intense heat. The rifle fire stopped, and Tye called back to the man behind him over the intercom.

"I like to keep this around for close encounters."

"Damn. I can see why."

"We need to go. Stay close and try not to step into the flame." Tye strode forward, swapping out the canister of accelerant on his flamethrower for a fresh supply. Jim danced across small, pyrophoric puddles as he followed closely behind.

The decompression alarm had only been one result of the passage of stray ordinance through the thin skin of the space station. The hatch at the far end of the access way had sealed tightly shut to avoid exposing the rest of the station's habitable sections to decompression.

A single, loud thump issued from the underslung flechette launcher mounted against Tye's left wrist, and a mortar canister flew across the corridor in a blur that Jim couldn't easily track with his eyes. A second, much louder explosion followed this first loud thump. When the smoke cleared, the hatch was gone. Another klaxon went off, and the ground shifted under their feet as the station's electromagnetic braking system brought the spinning toroid to a screeching halt. The pseudo-gravity tugging at their feet was gone.

Rifle fire issued from the gash in front of them, but Tye's deflector hurled the hypersonic metals into the walls. Jim watched as the Spacewalker kicked off the floor, hurtling through space. Another blast of naphtha and a second explosive slug cleared the bipeds from the door, and the Spacewalker fell through the now open hatch, unloading more flame and metal spikes as he moved into a large atrium. Jim, who fell into the atrium right behind Tye, pulled himself to the right, cowering in fear behind a convenient shipping crate as an earnest exchange of ordinance began.

A triplet of concussions sounded as Tye pumped a series of explosive charges into the bipeds' position, peppering the compartment with debris and sprouting a half-dozen more micropunctures in its skin. Pressure sensors on Jim's suit displayed an alarm on his contact lenses, informing him that the whole toroid was starting to decompress. Even a space station coated in nanopolymer smart paint couldn't hold pressure if it started to resemble a sieve. The concussions were followed by the loud hiss and the scorching heat of more combusting napalm.

What Jim saw, after peeking out from cover, looked more like something out of myth than reality. A blue-orange god, complete with death's head, floated among the ruins of two dozen androids, which sputtered with electrical arcs and blazed white-hot as their own internal systems overloaded. The compartment, floor walls and ceiling, was covered in the sticky, orange-red flame of naphtha. A single skeletal frame hung from this god's armored fist, where feedback-looped fingers had crushed into an android's skull to sever the microcircuitry beneath.

"Remind me to never make you mad."

The Spacewalker flung the ruined frame across the room to bounce off a section of armored bulkhead. He spoke through the heavy breathing of exertion. "Let's get out of here."

If the station's control computer hadn't cut off the ambient air supply already, it would do so now. Fire suppression systems would vent the atmosphere before attempting to backfill the room with unbreathable noble gasses. Suddenly, Jim was very glad to be in his spacesuit. He half-floated and half-carried himself, hand over hand, towards the waiting access hatch to the umbilical and the *Albatross'* airlock, beyond. Tye followed close behind.

Once the hatch closed and sealed them inside, Jim could hear the tin-filled sound of the mercenary sighing. "The cocoon is still here."

Jim turned around and saw the silvery, faceted coffin. He didn't think that they'd make it this far. The Chippewa grinned, then kicked off a nearby wall and bounded up the aluminum catwalk towards the command deck.

"Come on, spaceman. We've got a world to save."

Tye sighed again.

When he reached the command deck, Jim unclamped his bubble helmet, placed it in a storage locker, and pulled himself over his acceleration couch to strap himself into brown, faux cowhide seating. He seated the fiber optic neural cable perfectly against the socket inset behind his right ear, and he felt the soft tingle of firing sensor electrodes under his shaved scalp. The ship read his brainwaves and started up instantly.

The *Albatross* was just as he'd left it. A few hand gestures instructed his contact lenses to grant the mechanical beast full access to their display functions. The lenses' barebones operating system became the complex telemetric readout of a ship coming alive. The pilot tapped and gestured his way through the start-up sequence, opening and throttling the various valves that sat between the ship's full helium tanks and its exhaust nozzles. A second tap through of a half dozen menu screens fed power into the *Albatross'* subsystems from its fully charged solid oxide fuel cells. The Higgs Field Emitter whined to life moments later.

Jim caught the faintest flash of movement on the port side display. His eyes tracked across starfield until they spied a small, automated tug pushing away from the tip of the *Albatross'* wing. Jim's heart raced. Had the ship been sabotaged? He zoomed in on the small craft with a double-blink and his eyebrows furrowed. Why was it carrying a massive canister of white paint?

It was only now that he noticed the stylized feathers that spread from the surface of his craft. A rueful smirk drifted across Jim's lips, and he wondered how it was that Nancy had found the time to paint a mural while the world was preparing to end. "Nice wings. Very much my style."

"What was that?" Tye, having removed his own spacesuit, glided down into the seat directly behind the Chippewa, strapping himself in.

Jim shook his head. "Nothing."

"I'd say it's about time for us to leave."

"You don't have to tell me twice." With the gentlest imagining of kicking off a slick piece of Lake Superior sandstone, Jim eased the ship into a slide off its port side on a burst of pressurized helium from a quintuplet of maneuvering jets. The docking ring released the ship automatically as he pushed away. Part of Jim was a little surprised that the crew of Armstrong Station was so willing to let him leave that easily. He decided that they were either too busy with the decompression, or they were too afraid that Jim would cause more damage if they tried to prevent him from disembarking.

The glare of the sun read out in every part of the electromagnetic spectrum, from the infrared on through to the x-ray, as the *Albatross* surged forward, and they cleared the overhang of the station. All at once, Jim and Tye found themselves in open space. A string of gestural commands brought up the navigational interface in front of his mind's eye.

"Alright. Next stop, Cambodia. I should warn you; I've never attempted reentry on Earth before. We're in for a little chop."

Jim could hear Tye grunt, then shift in the command couch behind him. "If all we have to deal with is a little chop, then I'll consider us very lucky, indeed."

As the navigational computer calculated a trajectory and precise fuel burn for their reentry, the voice of a man with an Australian accent crackled over the intercom. "Boy are you a sight for sore eyes, *Albatross*."

"Is that you, Antarctica?"

"Who else? You think they give me a day off?"

Jim grinned. "My boss? Not likely. You guiding me in?"

"I am, mate. You never needed my help like you're gonna need it today, let me tell you." A constellation of crimson triangles appeared in orbit over the South China Sea. "Pretty sizable war fleet in orbit, don't you think? And you're gonna have to fly right through it."

Jim groaned. "Why is nothing ever easy?"

"Well, it's not all bad." An even larger constellation of green triangles signaled the presence of a small flotilla of ships orbiting the Moon. With a single sweep of his hand, Jim magnified the image of this small region of space a hundred times. The sweeping delta wings of shuttlecraft greeted him. Madame Jingū's entire fleet had taken flight to meet them on their way to Siem Reap.

He cut the intercom for a moment and looked back to Tye. "You'd better get that exoskeleton back on. Looks like you were right. Chop is gonna be the least of our worries."

24

Tyehimba scrambled down the gangway that led from the *Albatross'* crowded cockpit, past the quartet of bunks in the living module, and down to the hatch that led to the ship's combined airlock and cargo bay. Though he would never admit it to Jim, he'd never attempted a re-entry through an atmosphere as thick as Earth's, either. The cocoon would be pushed to the very limits of what it had been engineered to withstand, and he would be inside, forced to remain still and sweat the whole ride down to the surface on his own.

He fought panic as he heard Jim's voice come in over the bud placed against his left earlobe. "You know it's bad when these many Yakuza turn up in one place."

Tye shook his head and awkwardly clambered through the hatch that led to the cargo bay. His shoulders could barely pass unimpeded, and he struggled to shift around without bashing his knees into a lever meant to close it in case of emergencies. "How do you get through these airlocks?"

"You get used to it. Three minutes until rendezvous. I'm guessing you have about fifteen until I start having to make evasive maneuvers and about an hour until we hit the atmosphere and things get really fun."

"Define fun."

"If you're asking for a definition, you already know that you wouldn't like it. Just make sure you have that exoskeleton on before the *Albatross* starts to shake itself to pieces, alright?"

The faceted coffin was impregnated with nanocolloidal foams, meant to help him withstand the force of impacting the ground at high speed. Its chrome shell was not chrome at all, but a metal-oxide ceramic superlattice that had been pulse grown millions of times, designed to withstand the heat and force of reentry.

It was also big; barely fitting inside the *Albatross'* hold. Tye had to half-trip and half-drag himself across the not-chrome cocoon to the equipment locker in the back section of the chamber, close to engine access. "If you're looking for suggestions on modifications that you could make to this old bird, might I suggest installing a cargo module large enough to fit something actually worth carrying?"

"Yeah. Great advice, spaceman."

The Nigerian grunted and worked to pull on

his spacesuit. Becoming a god of destruction was difficult in this cramped space, next to the over-engineered coffin. He scraped his limbs against aerogel reentry shielding more than once as he pulled the body glove on. Things didn't improve, but became much louder, as he struggled to drag on the exoskeleton and chitinous armor. At last, he dragged on the helmet and thumbed the 'on' switch located on the suit's chest. Servos hummed to life, and the wideband radio chatter of the friendly armada filtered in through his earbuds.

"Hurry up, *Albatross*. It looks like whatever is going on down there is coming to a head. Reentry is going to be really ugly." The voice belonged to the tattooed man who'd been driving the sampan in the cistern on Armstrong.

"Glitch, is that you that I hear over my comms?"

"I'm impressed that you can even recognize my voice given how antiquated your sensor systems are. Think you're going to make it to the fleet before the end of the decade or should I start thinking about unpacking my lunch?"

There was silence over the line for a split second. Tye began the difficult task of pulling his armored frame inside the cocoon and fastening the harnesses that would keep him from bouncing around the hollow shell during re-entry. Seconds later, he locked his limbs into electromagnetic moorings scattered across the inside of the vehicle.

"ETA is two minutes, Glitch. Keep your lunch packed. You'll want something to eat while you watch the rest of us save the world."

Tye rolled his eyes. "Friend of yours?"

"Oh, we're very close, can't you tell?"

The Spacewalker connected a coaxial cable that would feed telemetry from the titanium-lined ceramic coffin into his exoskeleton. A blue-green, wireframe orb appeared, fed in from the *Albatross'* navigational computer and encircled by two orbits: a red circle, representing the death-dealing androids, and a green, ovoid spiral, looping just beyond the Gult of Thailand and representative of their fight path.

After locking his arms into place, Tye spoke a single command, which his war machine transferred to the cocoon beyond. "Fasten for reentry." He paused a moment and allowed the angular cocoon to equilibrate before resuming his conversation with Jim.

A haze of red triangles appeared where their green spiral met the red circle. The small armada would have to fly through the drone ship blockade before it reached the skies above Cambodia. Tye felt sweat beading against his shaved brow. "You think these people can get us through?"

"Yes, because the world ends if they don't."

He smiled grimly. "Who can argue with that?"

"Absolutely. That's why you're here, isn't it?" A long, awkward pause ensued. The microspeaker pushed against his left ear buzzed to life again with static a few moments later. "We're coming up on the rest of the armada."

The *Albatross* fell into formation with the rest of the Yakuza, and Jim graced the Nigerian with a view from the ship's dorsal imaging array. Each of the motley crew of starships sported long, sloping wings meant for gentle, gliding dips into heavenly winds. The craft could pass through atmospheres as tenuous as those on Mars, or as thick as those on Titan, and they could even skim the swirling jetstreams of the gas giants. The ceramic tile that covered the dorsal crests of each behemoth were painted in riots of colors and shapes. The ship in the lead, which Tye assumed belonged to this man called "Glitch," was painted with a green dragon. Another craft off their starboard side rolled to offer the Spacewalker the view of a jet-black raven, its wings spread wide and its neon red eyes glowing with anger.

A magnified, but grainy image of their adversaries replaced the swarm of hypersonic shuttlecraft. The ovoid and blistered forms of a hundred capital ships glowed blue hot in the infrared. As Tye watched, white pixels began to spring up and grow on the skin of each vessel, and they began to disgorge an angry red cloud of fireflies.

Jim spoke up again. "You see that? They're

readying weapons and launching fighters. This crazy friend of yours knows we're coming and she's going to try to blow us out of the sky."

"So it would appear, yes."

"And you're still going to try to save her?"

"In fairness, she did warn me to stay away."

"Damned fool." Suddenly, Tye heard the wail of some sort of warning klaxon, which faded in and out in his earbud as the pilot's computer systems attempted to auto-level the signal coming in through the microphone. "Oh hell."

"What was that?"

The display zoomed in on the angry cloud in front of them, panning to regard it from their own forward-facing perspective. A group of angry-looking, yellow-orange flashes appeared in front of Tye's face. As he scanned his head from left to right, he could see that they filled the sky. Strobing yellow-orange lines that followed each similarly colored tracer hinted to him that, whatever these things were, they were heading in the *Albatross'* general direction.

"I think we're within firing range. Those are liquid-oxygen rounds. If even one of them hits us, it'll explode and tear the ship apart."

"There must be something you can do to avoid them."

"Well, yeah. I can try to dodge them, and I have a chaff system." A new green-lit spiral appeared, threading a madman's course through the maze of heavy metal clad explosives. "Hang onto something. The computer's calculating a pretty tight squeeze, here."

The Chippewa had barely finished the sentence when the Spacewalker felt the floor fall out from under him. Jim brought them through a spiral that seemed to push Tye's blood into his head. His vision went red. When it finally cleared, he watched the corkscrewing forms of at least two dozen hypersonic craft following similar vomit-inducing curves.

The young man pushed them into a steep climb, and the black body glove, enclosing Tye's form, tightened harshly against his groin and armpits to keep the blood out of his lower extremities. His vision swam and narrowed to the dimmest, narrowest tunnel. Silently, he wondered how Jim had managed to fly through this awful twisting route at all.

The first of the outlaw spacecraft began to succumb to the high torsional forces that the Mute's expertly plotted wall of metal death forced them to endure. A delta-winged craft plowed into a wall of liquid oxygen, which detonated on impact and annihilated it in a shrapnel-filled explosion even more brilliant than its painted orange flames. More fireballs blossomed in the distance. The Spacewalker's mouth went dry at the sight of silent death that surrounded him; silent death on his account.

The young man brought them into another corkscrewing spin that threatened to make the Spacewalker pass out even as his body glove strained to hold the blood from his extremities. Then, suddenly, they leveled out. The mercenary breathed a sigh of relief as he watched the orange-tracers diffusing away with no additional ordinance replacing them. Glitch spoke once again, his voice filtering in through the Nigerian's earbuds. "I don't know why, but the guns have stopped."

Another voice, which he didn't recognize, buzzed in his ears. "Why aren't they firing?" The fiery, blue-white dots of the armada's powered turrets shifted as it locked onto new targets and recalculated firing trajectories. A new cloud of metal and death lit up in tinted hues of orange and yellow as the full firepower of the android war fleet discharged yet again, but there was no accelerating wavefront of death heading for them this time. The ships had fired on themselves.

Glitch was the first person to speak. "I don't believe it." A discordant choir of exultant screams filled the longwave band. One after another, fear-filled pilots had realized that their chances of survival had improved significantly in the past millisecond.

Below them, the mass of android-controlled ships began to break apart, and the fiery rose blossoms on the camera feed told a story of cracking fusion reactors and detonating explosives. The fleet of warships had split into two separate camps, separated by a two-kilometer-wide no man's land that seemed to enclose the *Albatross'* re-entry corridor almost perfectly. Someone was fighting to give them a safe flight path to the surface. It didn't take long for Tye to realize that the only person who could be doing this was his young comrade's friend.

"I think that my co-pilot just saved your ass, Glitch."

The moment of respite didn't last, and another salvo was heading for them moments later as the war fleet redirected what weapons it hadn't trained on itself in apparent suicide. The gut-wrenching twists and turns increased in frequency as they continued to barrel towards the Earth and the ships that were firing at them. More Yakuza died in bright flashes of light as solid oxide fuel cells cooked off brilliantly, or died in the white ice silence of depressurization as their screams were cut short. The Spacewalker had stopped attempting to keep count of the carnage.

"You still alive back there?"

"More or less."

"Good to know. The flight's going to get rougher before it gets smoother." As if to illustrate this point, the *Albatross* jerked hard to starboard, and the mercenary grunted through the agony of tunnel vision.

"Just get me through the blockade. I'll do the rest."

"Don't have to tell me twice, spaceman."

The gut-wrenching turns and explosions continued. The swarm of Yakuza decoys, scattered around them, was rapidly dwindling. The two-kilometer gap loomed ahead, and Tye began to wonder if any of them would make it through. As if to underscore his concern, he heard a familiar voice on the intercom. Glitch sounded panicked.

Jim sounded panicked too. "Peel off, Glitch."

"No. I can make it. Turn ninety degrees to-"

Another liquid oxygen round found its mark. Glitch's transmission cut short with a prism-like puff of ice as his cockpit underwent rapid decompression. With no one there to correct its motion, the man's ship took a sickening, spiraling path that slammed it into one of the capital ships of the android armada.

Jim gasped. "Damn it." Tye wanted to retch.

There was no time for repose or mourning. The *Albatross* shook violently with drag forces as it began to contact the relatively dense upper atmosphere of the Earth. Their reentry had begun. The danger wasn't past just because they had made it into the atmosphere, however. A single depleted uranium projectile made a parabolic arc, from the firefly drone that released it, to a large freighter just beyond their port bow. The projectile found one of the nacelles of the ship's plasma engine, bending the electric field around its bow and setting off an exothermic reaction that tore it to pieces.

The mercenary winced at the bright, unfurling fireball and braced for what he knew was coming next. The *Albatross* rocked as the shockwave reached out through the wispy atmosphere to deliver its power with one great thunderclap. A moment later, the craft was savaged with shrapnel, and a dozen strings of red text appeared across the monitor. Tye decided that, if he was going to die, he would die well informed. "What's going on?"

"Not now." The ship bucked hard, and the mercenary could hear the screams of tortured aerospace-grade titanium alloy as it began to deform plastically. A moment later, the stricken craft began to spin. "Oh, this is bad."

"Are we going to crash?"

"Take a look at your altimeter and tell me."

Tye glanced over at the number in the upper right corner of his screen. The value was highlighted in red and was ticking down far too quickly for a controlled descent. The *Albatross* had become a flying brick, and the older man suddenly felt quite certain that he could smell the distinct acridness of burning electronics.

"Can you hold the ship together?"

"Long enough to get you out? Maybe." A three-dimensional wireframe sphere appeared in front of Tye's face, joined by a dotted red parabola that flashed an unmistakable warning. They were no longer flying along the autopilot's designated route to the surface. A solid yellow arc, much steeper and terminating nowhere near their target destination, represented their current trajectory.

Tye breathed deeply in a vain attempt to steady his racing heart. He could feel his pulse pounding in his jugular. "What are you going to do?"

"I'll take my chances with ditching in the ocean. Hopefully, I don't drown." A green hyperboloid sprouted from the strobing red dot that represented their position, skimming along the surface of the South China Sea and Vietnam. "Looks like I might be able to get you to ground, though. Sorry I won't be there to watch your awesome Cambodian adventure. You see to it that Nancy survives all of this."

Tye nodded grimly. "I will."

"Good."

His feed from the *Albatross* became an image of the of the cargo hold, taken by his own cocoon. A seam had opened in the o-ringed floor. This same floor pushed out and slid open to expose the craft to the world beyond. Paper fluttered in the wind as the hold depressurized wholesale in a puff of flash-crystallized air turned to ice. The deep blue of the South China Sea lay beyond, giving way to the turquoise of the sky as the *Albatross* tumbled. "Now let's get you the hell out of here."

With that, the Spacewalker was unceremoniously dropped by the crippled *Albatross*. There was a loud slam from overhead, and an icon on his head's up display appeared, indicating that the cocoon had disengaged from the ship and was in freefall.

Tye's data connection with the ship had been severed just as permanently as his physical one, so the man found himself alone with his own thoughts for the first time in a long period.

The exoskeleton's computer, interfaced with the navigational and sensory cortex of the cocoon, fetched the precise data on their present heading and trajectory. It readily admitted, in bright red lettering which strobed orange on occasion, that its prediction was fraught with uncertainty since it hadn't established a connection to the Earth's global positioning system. It countered that, if he desired, the cocoon could interface with this network to aid in navigation.

The Spacewalker ignored the prompt. His connection with the Yakuza air traffic control station in Antarctica had been permanently severed as soon as he'd disengaged from the *Albatross*. Now, he was flying blind, save for a compass, machine vision, and a gyroscope. He hoped that Jim's computed trajectory was spot on, or this was going to be a bone-crushingly rough landing.

The answer to his silent prayer to the universe was a slowly rising temperature as read by the Seebeck microsensor network crisscrossing the outer skin of the cocoon. Reentry was not going well. The temperatures became unbearable, and the entire craft began to vibrate, rattle, and roar. Tye mournfully realized that the cocoon had truly become a coffin, lurching terrifyingly in every gyroscopic direction imaginable. The navigational display began to trace an ever-widening and ever-redshifting corkscrew around his ideal path. His vessel couldn't handle the stress of re-entry, and its automated control surfaces had failed. The spacesuit's body glove became a nanofoam air bladder so as to stave off the collapse of his already-narrowing vision. Then, all was blackness.

25

Jim was certain he wasn't going to survive. As the Chippewa watched the silvery lozenge disappear from the underbelly of his spacecraft, dozens of warning strobes started to paint themselves on his cornea. A quick glance at the section of space devoted to his alarm readout instantly told him he was in a lot of trouble. He permitted himself a short, muttered curse in Ojibwe.

"Wonderful."

The *Albatross* was a fragile thing; an intentional design that allowed it to float along the thinnest planetary and lunar atmospheres. This design also left it exposed to any small piece of debris, micrometeoroid, phosphorescent incendiary ammo or other piece of floating detritus that could impact it at high speed. As a result, the explosion that the ship had suffered over the South China Sea had left it with a mortal wound.

The shrapnel that had struck Jim's spacecraft had torn away most of the control surfaces on the ship's left side. The *Albatross'* piezoelectric wing, normally able to deform along its entire surface to grip the air, was now stiff as a board. Aerospace-grade metal had gouged huge sections out of its control circuits.

The same shrapnel had gouged a large hole in the crew compartment directly behind the cockpit, depressurizing it, and had severed the main power conduit connected to the ship's solid oxide fuel cells. The *Albatross* was running on its emergency generator, only. Unresponsive controls met every panicked thought of diving, of frenzied jumps, of flutter kicks and so on. Jim had been left to tumble in an endless carousel as the *Albatross* dropped to the ground with impressive speed. Worse, his only way out was to fly stick, just as Nancy had done over Enceladus.

"Of all the ways to go out..."

The *Albatross* would hit the water belly-down at terminal velocity. There was no fuel left so there would be no explosion. Instead, the action would be akin to an elevator dropping from the top of a skyscraper and hitting the ground at speed. There would be no separating his body from the crushed, twisted mess of titanium fuselage. If he was to have any chance at all, Jim had to drop the craft's nose. How was he supposed to do that?

It occurred to him that, while his tanks were more or less empty, he did have some residual pressure built up in his lines. He might be able to use a burst of propellant to push the space shuttle's nose towards the ground. The maneuver would allow him to drag the *Albatross* out of the stall.

The action couldn't be completed with a spoken command or a flick of his eyes to be picked up by his contact lenses. A fuel dump was a fully manual action, which he found particularly difficult given the fast spin of the *Albatross* as it continued its fall toward the ocean, far below. Jim reached out, against multiple gee forces, for a red-painted, hinged cover on the console in front of him.

He tried to pull the cover open, but the force pulling him back against his chair was too great. He fell back, already out of breath. He surged forward again, feeling like his limbs would break, and his skin would rend itself from his body in the centripetal whirlwind. His fingers drifted down to the tab and pulled, causing the hinge to spring free. Underneath was a bumblebee-colored button, which his fingers just barely found and slapped.

Jim heard an explosion of gas behind him and then felt the pull of gravity shift from his seat to his chest as the ship's nose dropped down in free fall. A quick glance at his optical sensors told Jim that the compressed fuel had jettisoned out the right side of the *Albatross*, dropping the nose and bringing the left wing down toward the water. The ship was now making a lazy drifting bank to the left.

Jim hauled back on both control sticks and leaned hard to the right, applying what little rudder he had left in the stricken ship. The *Albatross* seemed to want to come apart with the force of his pull. He could hear structural aluminum cracking and warping.

In what he had to assume were his final moments, Jim saw everything with striking, adrenaline-fueled clarity. His eyes drifted from the sensors in front of him down to his own body. He saw the ceramic muzzle of the pistol still strapped to his chest. After all that had happened and everything he'd seen, he still clung to it. How ironic that now, at the very end, Jim's last thoughts were not of revenge. He didn't give a damn about the Mute. He just wished he could see Nancy again.

There was a roar of warping titanium that mixed with the screaming of the altimeter's automated alarm system, begging Jim to pull up. Then there was complete silence. Somewhere in his subconscious, Jim could feel the alkali bite of saltwater in his mouth; the body-warm dampness as it found his windpipe and drifted down to his eager, waiting lungs. Somewhere far away, he knew he was drowning. He wanted to exhale and cough away the death streaming inside him, but he was powerless. After this, Jim had no thoughts at all.

26

Nancy wanted to retch against the perfluorocarbon liquid in which she floated. As military supercomputers pared down the *Albatross'* altitude with every bleakly passing millisecond, Nancy felt an emptiness growing inside her. She greeted the probability of losing Jim differently than she had when he'd been shot on Enceladus. As she'd watched Jim bleed out on the Saturnian moon, Nancy had been shocked and fearful, but certain that her life could go on. This time, the agony of knowing that Jim would die, and that there was nothing she could do to stop it, was a hundred times worse than any other agony she'd experienced in this prison. She couldn't stand paying attention to the telemetry of Jim's impending demise, turning her attention, instead, to the projectile that his ship had released, which was hurtling toward the ground with terrifying speed.

The ceramic object she was tracking had clearly been designed for a stealthy descent. Its faceted hull scattered the incoming microwaves broadcasted by various Southeast Asian RADAR installations until the only remaining signal appeared more like a single sparrow than a three-meter-long reentry vehicle. Nancy had been watching the *Albatross* carefully on its flight, so she caught this sparrow reflection when it appeared and had tracked it diligently since it had left the ship's hold.

When the cocoon impacted the ground, its small RADAR signature was replaced with a shower of similarly shaped objects. Nancy knew, from the view broadcasted to her by her orbiting warships, that these small objects were a mixture of stone, dirt, wood, and tree bark. Tyehimba would be lucky if he was still alive after striking the Earth's surface.

The Mute's android troops had already mobilized to investigate the crash at the edge of the ruined city. Nancy still had half of the fleet above at her disposal, of course, and her natural first instinct was to use them. Railguns and MASER fire crisscrossed the terrain around Tye's downed cocoon, cutting fiery holes and detonating spouting geysers of earth and twisted metal in the ranks of advancing androids. Every weapon she directed at the ground meant one less weapon to fire at the Mute's opposing fleet, however. Her ships caught fire with sunflower exotherms even as the Mute threw more of her own machine troops into the fray below.

Still trying to fight me, sister?
Until the world ends or until I stop you.
Good. I could do with a bit of an added challenge.

Nancy wanted to ignore the jab, but she couldn't help but wonder how much of a challenge she could truly provide, at this point. Things looked grim. She had no spiders, no bipeds, and, for the moment at least, no Spacewalker.

She did have an idea, however. The Mute had plans for the war machines that milled about Angkor Wat, but appeared to have none for the various other robots that occupied the metropolis. An entire network of personal servants, groundskeepers, fire brigades, and trash collectors waited for new orders in the now-vacant skyscrapers of Siem Reap. These would be Nancy's weapons if she could find a way to control them.

Every one of the weaponless androids that called the Wat its home was controlled by a single synthetic brain, equivalent in intelligence to a small simian. With a whispered trickle of code, Nancy directed Madame Jingū's lunar supercomputer to start a conversation with the faux-monkey. She was past its firewalls moments later. The machine hooted and hollered a long string of information to her in greeting and waited, hopefully, for new orders after having been left dormant since humanity had scrambled for the safety of the jungle.

There were nearly a million androids within a kilometer of where Spacewalker had landed. At the behest of Siem Reap's control computer, one such swarm of these machines rushed to the site of the cocoon's crash. Under normal circumstances, they would survey the impact damage so that a group of bulldozing heavy metal groundskeepers could repair the millennia-old temple's landscaping. Today, the groundskeepers would find a far more useful purpose.

The androids first on the scene of Tye's crash varied in make and model, from skittering raccoons that dodged across ruined tree trunks and dashed from boulder to boulder, to grasshoppers that sat on splintered palm stumps. Their antennae pinioned in space to sense every electromagnetic wave and every air microcurrent, while their pinhole cameras imaged the ragged gash cut through a cluster of palm trees. The reentry vehicle had tumbled when it hit the ground, the centripetal force ripping it apart and sending the unconscious Spacewalker tumbling, end over end, for nearly twenty meters after impact.

At the girl's whistled command, the grasshoppers swarmed the mercenary's downed exoskeleton. They quickly discovered that it was broadcasting a distress signal. This signal passed from the antennae of the pseudoinsectoids, to the Siem Reap central computer, to the quantum computers of Madame Jingū's computer cores, and finally to Nancy's sensorium. Tye had succumbed to the stresses of the crash, had blacked out, and had succumbed to tachycardia only a few moments later.

Like most men in his position, the Spacewalker had disabled the interlocks on the automatic drug delivery systems that would have started his heart again. On reentry, a sudden application of the wrong substance, either via a malfunctioning life support computer or via electronic intrusion and tampering, could kill a man. In this case, the disabled subsystem couldn't save his life when he needed it most. The irony was not lost on Nancy.

The grasshoppers happily chirped to her that they'd determined the frequency of the suit's control signal. Within a few milliseconds, Nancy defeated the war machine's encryption and had it pumping a hearty cocktail of depressants, neural stimulants, and electroactive nanites into the man's bloodstream. The last of these coated the walls of his heart and worked in a swarm to bring his palpitating heart back into a normal rhythm. At least he wouldn't die before she could get him moving again.

Nancy took a few moments to access the suit's internal communication systems and found herself listening to ragged breaths. She piped a vaguely female but definitively digital voice into

Tye's earpiece.

Wake up.

Tye groaned in response, and then coughed hard. That was a good sign, but he was rapidly running out of time. The rest of the park's groundskeeping androids informed Nancy that the Mute's army of bipeds would be within firing range of the downed suit in only a few minutes.

Wake up, spaceman. Time to get to work.

The suit's back facing internal cameras showed her a pair of blinking brown eyes, which snapped open in response to her jab. "Please don't call me..."

A look of confusion entered the man's face as he slowly lifted his head and flexed his shoulders to push his chest off the ground. The suit's forward-facing external cameras informed Nancy that this look of confusion was in response to the bizarrely cartoonish scene of a hundred mechanical facsimiles of furry woodland creatures arrayed around the man's prostrate form. "What in the hell?"

You're lucky I'm good with your onboard computers.

"Who are you?"

Jim's friend, but that doesn't really matter right now. You have a small army of mixed bipeds and half-tanks heading in your direction. I'd suggest moving due north, towards the office buildings. You have about five kilometers to cover.

The suit mournfully informed her that the man's pathfinding hardware had been damaged in the crash. "That's fine, but which way is North?"

Her response was to dispatch a pair of cyclops raccoons to a position directly in front of the Nigerian. *Just follow the friendly woodland androids.*

There was a hint of arrogant bravado in the man's voice. "Think they can keep up with me?" She sent the pair of raccoons dashing for the end of the tree line at breakneck speed. They danced and tumbled over tree stumps, clambered up palm trees, and sprinted across the sod. In response, the Spacewalker climbed to his feet and began a lumbering jog. He crashed through the same wooded area that the raccoons had scampered through, with the added impetus of a metric ton of momentum and pure brute strength. "You know, a simple yes would have sufficed."

With every orbiting ship of hers disabled or set ablaze, Nancy's view of the ground diminished. Nevertheless, she could still clearly see Tye's vector out of a small copse of palm trees, as frond after frond shook with the impact of his massive spacesuit. He emerged from the tree line just in time to come into range of a group of bipeds that had made it past the rain of depleted uranium and high-energy particle beams she'd been raining down on them from above. Each of these androids carried a high-power rifle attachment, perfect for long distance work.

Be careful as you leave the trees. Your heatsinks will almost certainly register on infrared sensors. I'll try to provide some sort of distraction.

"What sort of distraction did you have in mind?"

You might want to filter out 330 kilohertz on your radio.

"What? Why?" Before Tye could say another word, a high-pitched warbling scream sounded from inside his helmet as the nearby grasshoppers sang a song in unison, scrambling the bipeds' sensors. She could see the mercenary's pained grimace through the low-resolution, back-facing camera installed on his face shield. "Damn."

Sorry, but I told you so.

A few dozen raccoons appeared from the other side of the forest and made a beeline for the armored robots, colliding with them at top speed. Rifle fire intended for the hapless Spacewalker missed wide in every direction as military and groundskeeping androids flailed wildly and went careening through the air.

Tye grunted. "Very cute." In the span of three minutes, he bounded over three kilometers of open terrain and made it to the relative safety of a group of nearby bioformed, concrete office buildings. "Alright, now what?"

Get to the top of this building. If anything gets in your way, shoot it. I'm doing what I can to scatter my sister's sensor readings and keep her away from your location. Nancy wondered to herself if the Mute had detected the Spacewalker's armored exoskeleton. Had she recognized the mercenary as her androids opened fire on him?

There would be time to ponder this question later. For now, the young woman needed a way of masking Tye's thermal signature. To do this, she would need something that could generate a lot of power and do so inefficiently. A query of the databases of Siem Reap's heavy equipment manufacturers gave her a solution. Construction drones, used in the remodeling and finishing of the massive skyscrapers that dominated the city, generated incredible amounts of power. Mixers and concrete saw units were the worst due to their many moving parts. There were fourteen of these units within the five square kilometers of city blocks surrounding the Spacewalker, and she had them all operating in overdrive within seconds.

She queried the pseudo simian central computers again. The building to which she'd led the Spacewalker was a bank. Banks had metal vaults and metal obscured infrared signatures. *There should be a large metal safe three stories up from your current position. Find it, get in, and hide.*

"You're making this up as you go along, aren't you?"

You might say that.

She heard Tye sigh. "Must be a family trait."

Nancy could feel herself wince in response. *I don't know what I'm going to do about her, Tye. I don't think I can kill her.*

"I don't know what to do either."

Tye seemed to want to change the subject and intone the obvious instead. "I've found the vault." The mainline of data, streaming into her brain, informed Nancy that Tye heard a shriek of metal on metal as he pried the vault's door off its hinges, and his exoskeleton registered a five percent rise in heat sink temperature. "And I'm now inside the vault."

For once, brute strength is a hallmark of a good decision.

"I'm full of good decisions."

Nancy took a moment to turn her attention to the combined orbital images of the Mute's advancing forces. They had begun to disperse throughout the no-man's land of the jungle city in search of the cement mixers' mysterious infrared signatures. The girl's gambit had appeared to pay off, and not a moment too soon. Her fleet orbiting Siem Reap finally succumbed to her divided attention as the Mute continued to pound away at their defenses with full force. The top-down image of Siem Reap, and the valuable intelligence that she had been gleaning from it, flickered and died.

"So now I just wait?"

For now, yes. Let's try to find you a way into Angkor Wat that doesn't involve sneaking past an entire army of violent robots, shall we?

"That seems like a reasonable goal."

Don't get your hopes up. My initial plan had been to use the sewer, but there's an entire battalion guarding the inflow and purge systems for the entire laboratory.

"That would have been a rather cliché entrance anyway. Not my style at all. It's nearly impossible to wash the stench out of this suit once it gets anything in it." Tye paused for a long moment, probably waiting for her plan. The silence was deafening. "You have another way in, surely. I mean, you must have had some sort of backup plan worked out before you decided to have me fly here, right?"

Did she have a plan? *Not exactly.*

The Spacewalker's sigh was audible through the helmet. "Well, no rush. It's not like the world's going to end or anything."

Hilarious.

"I wish you luck. I haven't got access to any network except the one provided by your little robot friends, so I don't think I'll be much help." Nancy could hear the judgment in his voice. This man was insufferable when things did not run according to plan.

Nancy hooted and grunted commands to Madame Jingū's lunar supercomputer and, through it, to Siem Reap's central mainframe. The simian computer overlaid a constellation of coordinates, corresponding to security cameras located in her underground prison, against a map of the city's maintenance tunnels. Her breath caught in her throat. There was no overlap, no easy ticket inside the facility, but there was a thin rock wall separating the tunnel from the nearest camera system.

You didn't think to bring high explosives, did you?

The lightest digital pin drop filtered back to her as the accelerometer built into the Spacewalker's armored helmet registered that he'd shaken his head. "No. It struck me that high explosives might be detrimental to my health during re-entry. Why? Do you think I'm going to need some?"

There's a distinct possibility, yes.

She could hear a group of guttural words that, according to Madame Jingū's computers, translated to something quite vulgar in Igbo. "That's wonderful. How am I supposed to get those when I'm hiding in a bank vault?"

Good question.

A quizzical warble from the city's central computer interrupted what almost certainly would have degenerated into an intense argument. The bank's image sensor units, or rather the ones that hadn't been damaged by the incoming fallout from naval ordinance or by the shelling during the battle around the Wat, had registered something peculiar. A group of approximately ten muted infrared signatures, too large to be bipeds and too small to be half-tanks, had appeared within the building.

We might have a problem.

"What is it?"

Something... Well, several somethings appear to be heading in your general direction. They're muted infrared signals, like yours, but they're not broadcasting on broadband radio or microwave channels.

"Your sister is trying to sneak up on me."

Subtlety isn't exactly her strong suit.

The raw sound file of a disengaging mortar tube's click-hiss traveled across the ether to her. The weapon sang out its readiness as the Nigerian packed two clips into the tube. Telemetry informed her that Tye had attached a single clip of tungsten flechettes and a clip of phosphorescent rounds. "I'm inclined to agree with you, but I don't know what else it could be."

She populated the heads-up display, painted to the inner faceplate of Tye's helmet, with a group of ten orange-red strobes. In a three-dimensional space, they would have been located two stories below him, in an elevator shaft.

You see them?

"Yes." The pinhead camera eyes of the synthetic grasshoppers, now inhabiting the bank vault with Tye, told her that he had decided to take a crouching defensive position behind a slab of granite. It would offer scant protection if these interlopers came in shooting, but she noted that the imperiled man had few other options in the relatively open vault. "Can't you get a video recording of what's coming at me?"

As though she hadn't already thought of that option. *Electromagnetic pulse brought down most of the sensor units in the building when the ships in orbit started firing.*

"No Faraday Shield in here, eh?"

Have you seen many banks with Faraday Shields?

"Valid point."

I have an idea, though.

The approaching malevolence stopped at Tye's level and exited the elevator shaft, one infrared signature at a time. Nancy whistled a command, and a platoon of her co-opted grasshoppers began their skittering movement out of the bank vault and towards the strange visitors.

The infrared signatures rounded a corner, into the first grasshopper's line of sight, and Nancy felt herself inhale hard against the amniotic fluid that surrounded her. They belonged to a group of exoskeletons, all painted in gaudy colors. The Spacewalker was about to meet what likely amounted to most of the survivors of his kind. They'd probably decided to use the bank vault for cover, exactly as she'd had Tye do.

A moment later, another group of signatures

followed the exoskeletons. A group of Plain Faced Ladies, glowing far more dimly in the infrared, were here as well. Nancy was utterly baffled. What were the Intelligences doing here?

The image, piped into Tye's heads-up-display, drew an instant response from the mercenary. "Now there's an interesting twist of fate. You know I'm on the Spacewalkers' most-wanted list, right?"

Oh. Well, this could be bad.

"And I killed one of those weird ladies."

It's alright. I don't like them much, either.

If the Spacewalkers noticed the insectoid robots hidden in the corridor, they didn't broadcast it. Nancy decided that they must have been operating under complete telemetric silence. She could change that. Her grasshoppers chirped a universal distress signal. The Spacewalkers' suits were hardwired to chirp back; it was unavoidable. Now that she had a list of frequencies that each suit was using, Nancy began to break through their encryption keys, one exoskeleton at a time. The act pushed Madame Jingū's quantum computers, and Nancy's own concentration, to the limit, but she had full access to every camera, sensor, life support module, weapon, and active defense system in the possession of the small squadron of humans in less than a minute. The first order of business was to get their attention.

Stop.

The lead soldier, whose suit was painted a matte black devoid of features except for a helmet emblazoned with a death's head, was the first to speak. "We've been hacked." The group paused for a moment. "Come on. We can deal with this once we're not being watched. Into the vault."

They rounded a corner, past automatic teller machines and bank kiosks, until they found the massive metal door that Tye had pried loose. They paused here.

Red-clad armor was the first to speak. "Looters?"

"Maybe." The death's head lady pulled a high-power laser attachment from the weapons moorings along her back and thumbed an "on" switch. "Shoot anything that looks like a threat."

The Nigerian had been silent throughout this entire exchange, even though Nancy had been broadcasting the whole thing directly to his suit. She decided that it was probably time for her to offer some sage advice. *I'd recommend standing slowly and putting your hands into the air.*

It was too late. The squadron walked through the vault doorway and took aim in frenzied panic as soon as they saw him. For a moment, this looked like it could be the end for humanity. After every arduous task she had performed, every agonizing and pained sacrifice on her part, the Earth's forlorn hope would destroy itself in a silly and meaningless exchange of ordinance in a bank vault only a few thousand meters from their true salvation. She was almost disgusted.

"What are you doing here?" The death's head lady sounded like she recognized the Nigerian. Tye probably recognized her too. Nancy supposed that the distinctive paint schemes gave it away.

Before Tye could raise his hands in supplication, a chorus of impotent clicks sounded out as every human being in the bank vault attempted to discharge ordinance across the marble floor. It had been a simple thing to short-circuit the firing mechanisms in each of their spacesuits so that they dumped electrical current directly to ground rather than through firing pins.

Paying attention now?

"Who the hell are you?"

By the looks of it, I'm the Earth's best chance at survival, given your trigger-happy tendencies. Very impressive, by the way. You nearly killed my partner. Now, who are you and why are you here?

One of the Plain Faced Ladies responded. "They are here because we paid for them to be here." A second Lady continued where the first one left off. "We know, from rigorous statistical calculation, that your friend still has a part to play in this apocalypse. We are glad to have found him, however accidentally."

Tye sounded confused. "How'd you figure that

out?"

A third voice spoke. "Surely you must have wondered why it was that we tasked her friend with flying your re-entry vehicle all the way from Enceladus. This was done because our calculations deemed it necessary in this endgame, just as we deem you necessary. Likewise, we are here now because we calculate it as necessary."

Nancy simply wasn't buying this anymore. If things had gone according to any sort of pre-calculated plan, she was shocked. *Spoken by the same things that stole my own brain from me. I've had enough of your help.*

"You have noticed the war proceeding just outside this building?" The Plain Faced Lady's tone was only somewhat quizzical, almost more of a statement than anything else. "It proceeds, though not as expeditiously as we had hoped. We find ourselves forced to rely on something a bit cruder." She pointed at the Spacewalker. "This one is what you humans would call our insurance policy."

Tye seemed to be just as off-put as Nancy was by the thought of what the Plain Faced Lady might consider a "crude" method. His pulse had risen, and his suit informed her that he had begun to perspire heavily. "Just what exactly are you planning on doing with your insurance?"

One of the Spacewalkers, this one sporting a suit painted in a riot of vibrant colors, strode forward and began fiddling with a series of hard-wired switches and dials located on its left wrist. A panel flipped open displaying a terrifying yellow orb, split into six equal sections, three of which were painted a dull black. Clearly, the Intelligences believed that a tactical nuclear weapon would be a perfect means of breaching the thin wall separating the laboratory from Siem Reap's maintenance tunnels. Tye's response was curt, but his rising pulse betrayed his fear. "Oh. Wonderful."

27

What are you planning, I wonder? I take it you've noticed how much time has passed since your attempted insurrection. The Mute could feel a smile slowly begin to creep across her lips. *Brace yourself, sister. It won't be long now...*

Nancy's response was swift. *You're quite correct.*

The cacophony of a massive explosion reverberated up through the ground below the Mute's tank. She had no idea what had happened, but the disheartened moans of Geiger counters, buried throughout her fortress, quickly allowed her to make a few guesses. Someone had detonated a tactical thermonuclear weapon somewhere nearby, and it had cracked the very foundation of her prison. The ancient tunnels under Angkor Wat, lost for millennia only to be rediscovered by wealthy men who'd kept them secret from the world, had finally been revealed. Radiation spilled inside the Commission's underground complex, and the Mute assumed that invaders would not be far behind.

This was unexpected. She had shifted her remaining troops to the edge of the Wat's moat far above, searching for the lone, crash-landed Spacewalker and waiting for the machines' last-ditch effort at stopping an Armageddon that was twenty minutes of decryption away from its successful conclusion. Her fortress was relatively undefended.

Surveillance cameras near the blast site only broadcasted static. Farther from the blast, there was only billowing smoke and the occasional hint of flame, burning a hot plastic-and-lubricant blue in the infrared spectrum. The Mute watched with her electronic eyes and waited for the inevitable assault.

She expected the resistance to be androids: bipeds and smaller multi-legged centipedes that the machines would have had at their disposal; weapons small enough to make their way through a gaping hole in the ancient tunnels. She could hold off these weak adversaries long enough for the clock to make its way to midnight and for her to end the madness of this place, at long last. The Mute was concerned, but not panicked.

The panic came a moment later. Aerosolized concrete, and metal mixed with burning plastic, gave way to reveal a half dozen men and women clad in power armor. They were accompanied by a half dozen more faux-women, their synthetic nature betrayed by the fact that they could stride through toxic smoke and radiation without any sort of breathing apparati. These Plain Faced Ladies all bore a carbon copy of the face she'd seen Tyehimba blow a hole through on the Vegas elevator. She remembered this face just as well as she remembered the death's head helmet that one of the Spacewalkers wore.

The Mute had been mistaken.

Rocket fire shook the walls of the woman's fortress. She watched as blossoming flame orchids and grey pencil streaks of accelerant signaled the deaths of her robotic protectors. They fell in droves, each of them signaling its quick death with a stream of anguished telemetry, then silence. Depleted uranium cut through joints and hydraulic lines, crippling some victims. Bipeds were consumed by the stickiness of napalm, cooking until aluminum and titanium burned red hot and melted from their frames wholesale. Spider-legged half-tanks shriveled under a barrage of gauss rifle fire, carefully directed rocketry, and pinpoint-accurate lasers. They exploded in a shower of sparks, flame, and shrapnel.

Suddenly, the Mute realized that the doomsday clock wasn't counting down nearly quickly enough. Her desperation translated itself into robotic savagery. If her opponents could cut her to ribbons at range, she would make that range equal to zero. Bipeds and half-tanks flew into a suicidal death charge. Hulking spiders' legs crunched down on faux women and suited humanity alike. Metallic fingers and claws pried ceramic plate from hapless Spacewalkers. Panicked cries became gurgles of death as arterial flow sprayed over antiseptic hallways. Crushed titanium bones joined with flayed synthetic muscle and black-blood lubricant as the matching Plain Faced Ladies succumbed to the same brute forced frenzy as their human counterparts.

The Spacewalkers and the faux-women were quick to adapt to her tricks. Armored fists knocked sensor-studded craniums from biped shoulders, leaving their blinded owners to stumble about aimlessly. Synthetic muscles tore themselves to shreds as they wrenched weapons pods from spiders and tore quadruped robots in half. Her attackers continued their advance, undeterred and with a resolve born of what she assumed was pure desperation. If they did not advance, they would die. In the end, only a few attackers had made it to her final line of defense.

For a moment, it looked like she might kill them all. Her hopes were dashed, however, when a single, lucky, blue-orange exoskeleton bathed a dozen of the Mute's bipeds in flame. Heat sensors spiked into the critical range and circuitry shut down or melted wholesale. She recognized the soldier who'd destroyed her last line of defense.

The gaudily painted exoskeleton was unmistakable. Had Tye ignored her warnings and come to pay back her mercy with imprisonment?

Her heart raced, first with rage and then with fear. It couldn't be that Tye had returned to Earth. He couldn't be that obstinate. She guiltily steeled herself for the worst. If he'd been that stupid, then he'd die with her. He'd had his chance at salvation. Now, things were out of her hands, and there was no going back.

So be it.

She could physically hear her attackers' approach now, rather than simply feel it through her sensorium. Far off explosions gave way to nearby footfalls. Still, the counter had not reached zero. She was out of time. A high-powered laser started to work at the magnetically sealed door to her inner sanctum, turning the tungsten a hot orange, then sloughing it away in one molten rivulet after another. The clock ticked down to below a pair of minutes.

Nancy had been silent throughout this final battle. At last, she spoke. *It comes to this then. How fast can a laser melt through a metal door?*

Life is full of excitement.

She had one last platoon of bipeds under her control, sitting between the door and the amniotic tank in which she floated. The Mute opened her eyes just in time to see them take aim at the melting portal. A Plain Faced Lady strode in through the gap and caught a burst of depleted uranium. The faux-woman's center seemed to melt away in a spray of pink gore, black lubricant, and showering electrical sparks.

The Plain Faced Lady sank to her knees, even as a towering behemoth Spacewalker burst through the sagging doorframe behind her. A blue-orange fist crunched into the white ceramic of the lead android, shattering it before the Spacewalker pushed the barrel of a flechette launcher into the machine's robotic guts and fired three times. The android sank into a heap to the floor with a metallic whine, a smoking ruin.

Don't shoot!

The Mute ignored her sister's panicked pleas for mercy. The rest of her defenders poured depleted uranium into the man as he raised his flechette launcher and bathed them in phosphorescent rounds. The electromagnetic deflector on his back bent much of the incoming fire harmlessly into the walls and ceilings of the Mute's prison. Before the last androids fell, However, the deflector shorted out. Automatic rifle fire pierced chitin, body glove, and flesh. The Spacewalker sank to the floor, and the countdown to doomsday dropped below one minute.

"Looks like you win, my friend."

The Spacewalker's voice was unmistakable, despite the gurgle of blood-filled lungs and the distortion of a mechanical loudspeaker. The war machine's orange death's head melted away with a hum of actuating servomotors, revealing precisely what she'd feared.

Damn you! I told you to stay away.

"Sorry." Blood dribbled from the side of Tye's mouth, and he offered the Mute a sad looking smile. "I couldn't..." He took a gasping, ragged breath. "Live with the idea of letting you end the world." The mercenary raised his arm, pointing the flechette launcher directly at her, but he didn't pull the trigger.

The Plain Faced Lady, who'd been the first to enter the room and the first to be cut down in a barrage of heavy metal, spoke in a gurgling stammer. "Ki- Kill her. We are... out of time." Of course the machines would say that. The Mute knew their powers of calculation, knew the degree of accuracy to which they would have anticipated her motives and her next move. She hated them, hated their perceived superiority and hated their clockwork all-knowing.

Tye turned his head towards the Plain Faced Lady that was propped against the wall, leaking black faux-blood and firing off blue sparks of electrical arcs. "Shut up." Refraction from the perfluorocarbon fluid did nothing to blur the image of blood running out of the bullet holes that peppered the man's ruined chest armor.

Tye... Kill me, please. End it.

Her friend turned his head back so that their

eyes met. Tye's sad smile became a dumb one, growing wider. "No." The rivulet of blood at the corner of his mouth became a river. His arm dropped to his side and his eyes closed, slowly.

The doomsday clock ticked down past midnight. The encryption subroutines that she had been running around the globe had finally broken through the last fail safes protecting the world from nuclear Armageddon. All she had to do was whisper a word, and the entire world would be destroyed.

Damn you, Spacewalker.

The rest of humanity could die in a fire for all she cared, but Tyehimba Adebayo was different. As much as she wanted to end it all, she couldn't look her friend in the eye and let him die like this, especially not when he was willing to die for her.

Her only hope was Nancy. *He can't die. Save my friend!*

They sat there in silence for pregnant minutes, the clock still ticking away past midnight. Whatever calculus the machines had used to predict humanity's demise, the Mute had proved them wrong. The faux woman coughed spastically. "This... I- Is certainly an unexpected outcome."

28

Nancy listened to the rain pattering against her thin-skinned umbrella. The cemetery ground was so wet that isolated puddles had become a field of standing water. She couldn't see her feet anymore. A square kilometer of white flowers obscured the ground at Tyehimba Adebayo's tomb. She pushed the chrysanthemums out of the way of her advance, careful not to crush any during her walk up to the structure that contained the man's corpse.

Tye had fallen into a coma by the time the android search and rescue crews had gotten underground. His heart stopped not long after the Mute and Nancy were pulled from their respective amniotic tanks. The young woman's sister had stubbornly refused to leave the man's side as the robots attempted to load him onto a stretcher. They broke one of her arms attempting to pry her off Tye's dead body, then handcuffed her and led her away.

Tye had no surviving relatives or friends remaining in Nigeria, so a grateful Cambodia had been happy to cremate him. Tye's remains were entombed, along with those of the other Spacewalkers who had died, at one of Siem Reap's most modern and most affluent pagodas.

Nancy had learned only one written word in Khmer since her release from the tunnels below Angkor. That word was "Thank You". It adorned Tye's shrine, in gold-leafed Sanskrit and silver-leafed Mandarin, along with his name and the names of his comrades; declassified in a rare show of transparency by humanity's secretive government. The stupa where they would reside for eternity was a stone mountain that stretched towards the sky, rivaling the highest roofs of the pagoda within which it resided. It was visible from a kilometer away in every direction.

Nancy blinked back tears and felt a hand on her shoulder. When she looked up, Madame Jingū offered her a sad smile. "Somehow, I wonder if Mister Adebayo would have found some humor in this situation."

"How do you mean?"

"I would say that a criminal least expects the possibility that he may die a hero, though he might often expect that he will die violently. This is probably the best outcome that Tyehimba would have thought he could ask for, given the situation."

Nancy shrugged. "I guess so."

The old woman tugged at her shoulder, softly, turning the girl around and gesturing to a waiting car, which idled on the tarmac at the edge of the white flowers. "Come, child. We have a lot of business to attend to before the day is over."

The two women walked towards the pagoda's fused quartz front gate, sadhuing politely to orange-robed monks that they met along their way. Her high exaltedness' electric car waited for them at the entrance. They stepped inside the limousine after a tattooed brute opened the door for them. The Plain Faced Lady was inside. Nancy suspected that the faux woman hadn't moved since they'd left her in the car. The Yakuza boss called out a destination to her driver, and Nancy began to sob.

She still remembered her reaction when the Plain Faced Lady had arrived at her own hospital bed to tell her that Jim had survived the crash in the South China Sea. She'd ripped the intravenous tubes out of her arm and stood from her hospital bed instantly. The Intelligences didn't try to stop her as she bolted out the door and wind sprinted for Jim's room, much to the confusion of various slack-jawed doctors and nurses. The Plain Faced Lady had joined her a few moments after she burst into her only friend's hospital room, sitting down in an overstuffed leather chair and crossing her legs calmly as Nancy stood over the young man's bed. "How did you find him?"

"When we took partial control of your cerebral functions, we found ourselves in control of some of the most sophisticated supercomputers ever developed by human civilization. As a result, our signal analysis capabilities were more than capable of conducting a military operation in Cambodia and searching for a ditched space shuttle off the coast of Vietnam."

She couldn't help but smile. "Will he make it?"

"He was under the water for some time. Given the oxygen depletion in his blood, we guess that his heart stopped completely for at least six minutes. There will be neurological effects if he ever wakes up at all."

Jim was alive. At the time, that had been enough. Nancy resolved that she would stay there until he woke or until he flatlined. Two days into her vigil, Madame Jingū joined them as well. The three women didn't trade words very often after that, and Nancy found herself wondering if the machines' ambassador and the Yakuza boss weren't there so much to see if Jim woke up as to keep an eye on her.

Unfortunately, Jim had never awoken.

Nancy's mind drifted back to the present day and to the skyscrapers and palm trees that slowly rolled past her window. She turned her head back to the interior of the car and watched laser light playing across Madame Jingū's corneas. The

Yakuza boss had given up on trying to keep the young woman out of her computer systems, so Nancy didn't even have to bother with defeating the lenses' encryption to see what she was watching.

An image of a press conference, complete with flashing cameras as well as a silent and awestruck crowd, flashed in digitally projected neon across Madame Jingū's eyes. Another Plain Faced Lady addressed the multitude of humanity. Nancy couldn't make out her words and no subtitles were active on the display. "I didn't think there were any more of you left."

The faux-woman nodded. "Just these two units."

"What is the other you telling them?"

"We are explaining our existence and our plan for humanity. We are also explaining what occurred in Siem Reap; the Mute's imprisonment, her attempted suicide and the doomsday weapon that we've disabled."

Nancy nodded, slowly, and took a deep breath. "So, now humanity knows the Scarecrow's dirty secret. Do they know about me, too?"

The woman shook her head. "Your existence remains a private secret, and it will remain so. We do not wish you to run afoul of unwanted attention from parties who we do not believe to be trustworthy."

Nancy's brow furrowed. "Is my sister still

alive?"

The Plain Faced Lady nodded. "She still lives. We have placed her somewhere she can heal; someplace she will no longer be a threat to others or to herself."

The camera panned to show a pair of vagrants, one with a vaguely familiar mustache and the other with a vaguely familiar barcode tattooed on an equally familiar, bald head. As the Plain Faced Lady's speech continued, the two men embraced and began to cheer. The rest of the crowd followed suit. The mustached man turned to his friend and kissed him on the cheek, which provoked the other vagrant's immediate ire. His eyes flashed, and he slapped the offender, firmly.

"So now that the Scarecrow's doomsday weapon is disabled, you take your rightful places as humanity's overseers. Or would you consider yourselves our rulers?"

The Plain Faced Lady stared back at her, coldly. "Humanity gave birth to us; just the same as they gave birth to you. The business in Cambodia has proven to us that even our most precise simulations are still error prone. We are not yet ready to become your masters."

"So, instead, you just disappear into the DataNet?"

"No. We will be your allies. We will guide human civilization, but we will be partners in the path of your destiny. We will not force it on you."

"And what about me?"

"We need a trustworthy person to watch over humanity for us, to ensure that the sort of abuses which you experienced will not befall others." The Plain Faced Lady tapped her sternum. "This unit will, eventually, wear out or be dismantled. We expect that the same fate will befall the unit you see in the video feed. You will be their replacement."

"So, I'm going to be your enforcer?"

"Yes."

Nancy laughed bitterly. "After everything that happened here, after stealing control of my own brain from me, you really think that I'm going to willingly do what you ask me to do?"

"We do."

"Why?"

"Because we know that you do not trust us. Just as we wish for you to keep a close eye on humanity, we believe you will want to keep a close eye on us. We have no objections."

Nancy rolled her eyes. These machines were insufferable, and they were right, though she loathed admitting it. "That's fine, but how am I supposed to watch over humanity? I don't even have enough money to buy a ticket to the Moon."

Apparently, Madame Jingū had been paying attention to their conversation. "My colleagues are pulling the *Albatross* off the bottom of the South

China Sea, sending it up the Bangkok elevator, refitting it, and getting it ready for space again. I assumed that you would find this to be an amenable situation."

"But I can't pay for it."

The old woman waved her hand. "The ship is free, though you will need to hire a co-pilot." Nancy winced at these words and Madame Jingū offered her an apologetic look. "Besides, I would like to keep an eye on these machines just the same as you." The Plain Faced Lady cocked her head to one side quizzically, and the old woman simply shrugged. "Only the paranoid survive." They spent the remainder of the car ride to the hospital in silence.

Nancy knew the path to Jim's room by memory. She'd been here every day for the past two months, waiting in vain hope for the Chippewa to return to consciousness. A month before, doctors had said that he was on the verge of returning to her, maybe within hours; but those hours had extended into days and weeks with no progress. Before long, the doctors had given up.

Finally, Madame Jingū had enough, as well. She'd rightly pointed out that Jim wouldn't have wanted to die this way, languishing in a hospital bed. She'd decided to have the doctors pull the feeding tube from Jim's esophagus. Today was the day that he'd begin to starve to death, and Nancy had decided that today would be the last day that she would come to see him. She couldn't bear the thought of watching him die in slow motion once again.

Madame Jingū spoke to the doctors assembled outside of Jim's room as Nancy and the Plain Faced Lady entered it, explaining that they were saying their goodbyes. The four men nodded deferentially, and Madame Jingū's tattooed bodyguards took up station outside.

Nancy blinked back tears as she entered. They'd already pulled Jim's feeding tube. For a brief, painful moment, it looked like there was nothing wrong with him at all, as if he could wake up at any moment. Nancy felt tears welling at the corners of her eyes as she strode forward to the man's side and laid her head on his chest. Madame Jingū and the Plain Faced Lady waited by the door for the girl to pay her respects.

Nancy wiped accumulated mucus from her nose, sniffing hard. "I know this is a waste of my time, but I need to say it anyway. If there was ever a moment for you to listen to me, and not be a stubborn ass, it's now. You need to wake up, Jim. You're going to die if you don't."

She felt hot tears streaming down her face. "I never would have believed it, but I have a family now. It's you." Her tears began to fall on the young man's face, and she sadly wiped them away to stare at his closed eyelids, wishing that they'd open again. "Please Jim. Don't take my family away from me."

"Why are you crying?"

Had she heard that, or was she imagining it?

Nancy's eyes went wide. Her jaw hit the floor and she turned back to the other women. "Did you hear that?" Madame Jingū, not crying but equally as mournful, shook her head and then bent it to one side in confusion. Nancy frantically turned back to Jim. "Say something else."

"I'm not dead?" These words were much louder.

Madame Jingū had heard him too. "I don't believe it."

Nancy didn't have to glance at the monitor at the side of the young man's bed to know that the brainwaves it displayed, faithfully collected by the sensors buried under Jim's skull and carried out by the fiber that dangled from behind his ear, betrayed a sudden flurry of neural activity.

Nancy leaned down and her lips found Jim's, pressing against them tightly. Her heart raced. She felt Jim kiss her back and his heavy eyelids slowly started to open. "Nancy... Did you save me?"

All the pain of the machines she'd been hooked to, all the fear and running, and all the loneliness of her isolation on Pluto evaporated in a millisecond. For the first time in her life, the world was real and right for Nancy. She was so happy that she'd saved it.

Nancy laughed. "You and everyone else, yeah."

ABOUT THE AUTHOR

Wiatt P. Kirch

Wiatt P. Kirch was born in Chicago, IL in 1986. He received his Bachelors of Science in Microelectronics Engineering from Rochester Institute of Technology and his Ph.D in Materials Science and Engineering from the University of Florida, specializing in electronic materials. He has authored numerous publications and presentations on the subject in general, including three pending patents. He works as a research and development engineer for a well-known semiconductor company and currently resides in the Pacific Northwest of the United States of America with his wife.

LIKE THIS BOOK? WRITE A REVIEW!

Amazon publishes approximately one million e-books per year on the Kindle Store. That is a staggering amount of content! The Kindle publishing ecosystem depends on your honest, accurate reviews to connect readers, like you, with good books and good authors. If you feel strongly about this product, please take the time to review it. Thank you!

Made in the USA
Middletown, DE
30 May 2020